PROBABILITY
SPACE

NANCY KRESS

TOR®

A TOM DOHERTY ASSOCIATES BOOK
NEW YORK

This is a work of fiction. All the characters and events portrayed in this book are either products of the author's imagination or are used fictitiously.

PROBABILITY SPACE

Copyright © 2002 by Nancy Kress
All rights reserved, including the right to reproduce this book, or portions thereof, in any form.

Edited by James Minz

A Tor Book
Published by Tom Doherty Associates, LLC
175 Fifth Avenue
New York, NY 10010

www.tor.com

Tor® is a registered trademark of Tom Doherty Associates, LLC.

ISBN: 0-765-34514-5

First edition: September 2002
First mass market edition: January 2004

Printed in the United States of America

0   9   8   7   6   5   4   3   2   1

Praise for *PROBABILITY SPACE*

"Kress is so deft in supplying background information that I had no trouble in understanding the characters and the desperate situation they find themselves in."
—Gerald Jonas, *The New York Times Book Review*

"Kress proves her comprehensive mastery of the hard-science tale of interstellar war and intrigue. Kress sustains the pace and the suspense at the hightest levels, and if the body count mounts largely off-stage, its emotional impact on the well-drawn characters is nevertheless crystal-clear."
—*Booklist*

"This is the third book of a trilogy, but Kress provides all the information needed for it to stand on its own . . . it works perfectly as space opera."
—*The Denver Post*

"The action-filled final volume in Kress' Probability Trilogy spectacularly resolves the human-Faller stalemate . . . followers of the trilogy will find much to enjoy here."
—*Publishers Weekly*

"With a surprising and satisfying resolution, Kress offers an action-filled, thought-provoking story of space travel, political intrigue, and hard science that belongs in most sf collections."
—*Library Journal*

Praise for *PROBABILITY SUN*

*"Kress's always excellent characters wrestle with a splendid array of puzzles and problems, human, alien, and scientific: another resounding success for this talented sure-footed writer."
—*Kirkus Reviews* (starred review)

"The author grounds her morally complex plot in the physics of probability. As usual with Kress, her eccentric characters add depth. Readers will start this novel because of Kress's reputation, will read it for the adventure and will like it for the characters and the science."

—Publishers Weekly

"The immediate sequel to *Probability Moon* (2000). The questions that permeate the tightly paced story are whether scientists and the military can cooperate to learn the nature of the artifact—scientific storehouse or doomsday machine—and whether either of those parties will procure the cooperation of the captive Faller, whose perception of reality is unfathomably different from that of any of the humans. Displaying a typically strong synthesis of Kress' many gifts, the novel leaves the door wide open for at least one successor."

—Booklist

"Kress has blended such a nice set of surprises and inevitabilities that you should learn and read and enjoy them for yourself. You don't have to read *Probability Moon* to have a good time, but you'll probably search it out anyway."

—San Diego Union-Tribune

Praise for *PROBABILITY MOON*

"The author also weaves a fascinating tale exploring the norms of each society. The mystery slowly unravels as the two cultures interact. Each member of the large cast of characters has an individual struggle and quest, creating an intriguing plot. This book has something for everyone."

—VOYA

"Kress's *Sleepless* trilogy proved that she was a serious writer, worthy of considered attention. *Probability Moon* only emphasizes that."

—Locus

"Kress' characterizations are as sound as ever, but many will be agreeably surprised at her proficiency with military hardware and action scenes. Very impressive."

—*Booklist*

*"Twisty and compelling, brimful of ideas, with Kress's usual life-sized characters; top-notch work from a major talent."

—*Kirkus Reviews* (starred review)

". . . Naturally all of this is moving toward an explosive ending that Kress resolves handily in this volume while leaving plenty of intriguing questions for a future novel or two. Her characters and the planetary setting are well developed and the story moves at a brisk, suspenseful pace."

—*Portsmouth Herald*

BY NANCY KRESS

NOVELS

STORY COLLECTIONS

For Jamie

ACKNOWLEDGMENTS

I would like to thank both my editor at Tor, Jim Minz, and my husband, Charles Sheffield, for their many useful suggestions on revising this manuscript.

Heaven from all creatures hides the book of fate,
All but the page prescribed, their present state.

—ALEXANDER POPE, "AN ESSAY ON MAN"

PROLOGUE

MARS

July, 2168

Bellington Wace Arnold of Arnold Interplanetary, Inc., arrived late at his opulent office. Beyond the top-floor window and the piezoelectric dome of Lowell City, the sun was already well above the Martian horizon. Not much dust today. The sky was only faintly pink, and Arnold could see all the way to the hard clutter of the spaceport.

"System on. Messages."

"Yes, Mr. Arnold. Five messages." It meant five for-your-ears-only transmissions; Arnold's staff would have handled everything else. The wall screen brightened to visual. As he listened, Arnold settled into his desk chair and scanned the printouts his secretary had deemed important enough for his personal perusal. The chair, big enough to encase his impressive size, was made of imported Earth leather from calves genetically altered to produce hides in his favorite blue-gray.

The first four messages did not need his entire attention, even though two of them involved billion-credit transactions. There was a lot of money to be made in wartime, if you knew how. The longer the war with the Fallers went on, the better for Arnold Interplanetary.

The fifth transmission made him look up. There was nothing to see; this message was voice-only.

"Cockpit recording, personal flyer registration number 14387, transmission date July 3, 2168." Yesterday.

And then the voice of Arnold's son, Laslo Damroscher: *"Thass not 'sposed to be there."*

Slowly, pointlessly, Arnold rose from his expensive chair. Every line of his big body tightened.

The flyer had been a gift to Laslo on his eighteenth birthday. Arnold knew he did not love this son. Laslo, weak and whiny and easily led, was hard to love. A strange son for Bellington Wace Arnold to have, but then Laslo wasn't his son only. It still took two people.

Arnold had other, better, legitimate sons. Still, he had always provided well for Laslo, even though the idea that Laslo might ever need money was laughable. He was his mother's sole heir.

It had seemed a good idea to know where Laslo took his birthday-gift flyer, and what he did along the way. It might prevent danger, or embarrassment, or lawsuits. To that end, the flyer, unknown to Laslo, had been equipped with automatic continuous record-and-send equipment. A smart program flagged and relayed only those recordings that met certain parameters. None of the parameters meant anything good.

"Thass not 'sposed to be there." Laslo's voice, very drunk.

"What isn't supposed to be where?" Another young man, sounding marginally less drunk. *"Just an asteroid."*

"Isn't 'sposed to be there. Hand me 'nother fizzie."

"They're gone. You drunk the last one, you pig."

"No fizzies? Might as well go home."

"Just an asteroid. No . . . two asteroids."

"*Two!*" Laslo said, with pointless jubilation.

"*Where'd they come from? Isn't supposed to be there. Not on computer.*"

"*N-body problem. Gravity. Messes things up. Jupiter.*"

"*Let's shoot 'em!*"

"*Yeah!*" Laslo cried, and hiccuped.

"*What kinda guns you got on this thing? No guns, prob'ly. Fucking rich-boy pleasure craft.*"

"*Got . . . got guns put on it. Daddy-dad doesn't know. Illegals.*"

"*You're a bonus, Laslo.*"

"*Goddamn true. Mummy doesn't know either. 'Bout the guns.*"

"*You sure 'bout that? Isn't much your famous mother don't know. Or do. God, that body, I saw her in a old—*"

"*Shut up, Conner,*" Laslo said savagely. "*Computer, activate . . . can't remember the word . . .*"

"*Activate weapons. Jesus, Laslo. YOU gotta say it. Voice cued.*"

"*Activate weapons!*"

"*Hey, a message from th'asteroid! People! Maybe there's girls.*"

"*You are approaching a highly restricted area,*" a mechanical voice said. "*Leave this area immediately.*"

"*It don't want us,*" Conner said. "*Shoot it!*"

"*Wait . . . maybe . . .*"

"*You are approaching a highly restricted area. Leave this area immediately.*"

"*Fucking snakes,*" Conner said. "*Shoot it!*"

"*I . . .*"

"*Fucking coward!*"

"*THIS IS YOUR LAST WARNING! YOU HAVE INVADED A HIGHLY RESTRICTED AND HIGH-DANGER AREA. LEAVE IMMEDIATELY OR YOUR CRAFT WILL BE FIRED ON!*"

And then a fourth voice, speaking rapidly, "*Unknown craft . . . SOS . . . Help! I'm being held prisoner here—this is Tom Capelo—*"

A very brief, high-pitched whine.

"End flagged recording," said Arnold's system. "Transmission complete."

Arnold stood in the middle of his silent office. He tried to think factually, methodically, without haste.

The electromagnetic impulse carrying the flyer's last conversation would have sped at c toward the nearest far-orbit data satellite, of which Mars had thousands. There the information had been encrypted and relayed through closer satellites toward Mars. It had taken only a few minutes to arrive last night, when Arnold had been asleep. The transmission would have traveled ahead of the shock wave. The brief whine at the end of the transmission had been a proton vaporizer.

Laslo Damroscher was dead.

Arnold couldn't blame whoever had shot Laslo down. Laslo had been where he shouldn't have, had been adequately warned, had been old enough to understand that warning, had defied it anyway. Laslo, "Conner," and that boy in the other craft, "Tom," playing at war games when there was a real war on, pretending to be somebody famous to boost his own pathetic ego . . . irresponsible. All three of the boys. A corporation or a government had the right to protect its property. That was just reality. Most likely the restricted area had been government-controlled armaments, and in that case, Laslo's death would not even rate a trial. Not in wartime.

The irresponsible behavior that had gotten Laslo killed had not come from Arnold's genes. Arnold had made only one mistake in his entire life, and that mistake had produced Laslo. Whatever else Laslo's death might be, it was not Bellington Wace Arnold's fault. The responsibility lay elsewhere.

But . . .

To his own surprise, Arnold couldn't maintain his factual objectivity. Sudden memories flooded him: Laslo's birth, the beautiful baby in the arms of his preternaturally beautiful mother. Laslo toddling across the floor of this same office, holding out his small arms to be picked up. Laslo riding a toy red car, laughing and laughing. Laslo proudly printing his name for the first time, even though it was not his, LASLO D. ARNOLD . . .

Unexpected tears scalded Arnold's eyes. He stumbled back to his chair. It seemed he had loved his lost son, after all. Although never as much as the mother who had cosseted Laslo and spoiled him and ruined him.

At the thought of Magdalena, Arnold's tears vanished. He would have to call her, tell her. Send her the recording. For years Arnold had avoided any contact with the bitch. Well, it was going to be only minimal contact now: a prerecorded message. Her reaction to Laslo's death would undoubtedly be violent, irrational, vengeful. Dangerous.

He could at least spare himself Magdalena.

ONE

CAMBRIDGE, MASSACHUSETTS,
UNITED ATLANTIC FEDERATION,
EARTH

Three months earlier

Sometimes it seemed to Amanda Capelo that she had the best life of any of her friends at Sauler Academy. Her father loved her and her sister a lot more than her friends' fathers did. Everybody saw that. Plus, her father was famous. And her stepmother Carol was a nice person—she might have gotten somebody awful, like Thekla Carter had when Thekla's father remarried. But Carol was great. Plus, Amanda's grades were good, and her friends were the best, and even at fourteen she knew she was pretty and might even have a chance at being beautiful someday. She would go to college and become a scientist, like her father, although not a physicist because she didn't have the math sense. A biologist, maybe. Meanwhile she had a nice home and the right clothes and a vacation every year on Mars visiting Aunt Kristen and Uncle Martin. A good position on the spacetime continuum, Daddy said, and Amanda agreed.

Other times it seemed to her she had been afraid her whole life, ever since her mother died. Afraid that the war with the Fallers would come to the Solar System. Afraid that something would happen to Daddy or Sudie or her aunt and uncle. Afraid that somehow Daddy would lose his money and they'd have to live in the terrible parts of cities that she saw on TV. But then Amanda discovered that, until the night the men took her father way, she hadn't known what fear was at all. Not at all.

The evening had started badly, with another fight with her father. Before she turned thirteen, they'd never fought, but for the last year and a half it seemed they couldn't stop. She loved him more than anybody on Earth, but why couldn't he stop virusing her program? Other fathers weren't like him. Thekla's father let her go alone to the holos, and Juliana's father let her free-fall, and Yaeko's father would talk with her about absolutely anything that Yaeko wanted. There were so many things Tom Capelo would never talk about.

Amanda pondered all these things as she crept into her father's bedroom. She wasn't supposed to be there. But he was downstairs in his study doing physics, and when he did that he grew oblivious to everything else. Including her, Amanda thought with sudden resentment. No, that wasn't true. Her father loved her. But he either smothered her or ignored her. Why couldn't he just be *normal*?

Quietly she closed the bedroom door, and just as quietly pulled the box from under her father's bed. A meter square and fifteen centimeters high, it was made of a strong opaque plastic intended for long-term storage under adverse conditions. It had an e-lock, to which Amanda had figured out the code. It hadn't been hard; the code was the digits of her mother's birthday. You'd think a world-famous mathematician would have more imagination.

Or maybe not.

Amanda's throat tightened, the way it always did when she opened the box. Pushing several data cubes and two smaller boxes to the side, she lifted out the dress. Her heart started a slow thumping dance. This time, she wasn't going to just look at the dress. She was going to put it on.

On Coronus, brides marry in yellow, the color of the sun. Her father had told her that years ago, the one time he'd shown her the dress. Amanda suspected he'd been drunk, very unusual for him. Later she learned it was the anniversary of her mother's death. He never mentioned any of her mother's possessions again. Yet he had kept them, even after he married Carol.

Pushing the box back under the bed, Amanda stripped off her shoes, tunic, and shorts. She slipped the dress over her head and studied herself in Carol's full-length mirror.

During the last year, her body had bloomed into curves that still startled her, although secretly she was pleased by them. Yaeko still didn't have hardly any breasts at all, and Thekla's waist was getting too thick. Amanda wished she had Thekkie's eyes, though. Still, she looked nice in the dress and, thanks to being so tall, older than she really was. The yellow fabric that clung on top and flowed into a swirly skirt wasn't too big for her. Karen Capelo had been a small woman, like her husband and younger daughter Sudie. Amanda took after her aunt Kristen. Although with her long straight fair hair and gray eyes, she looked a lot like Mommy, too. Unlike Sudie, Amanda remembered her mother. She'd been almost eight when Karen Capelo was killed in an enemy raid on a peaceful planet.

Was she prettier than her mother? No, not really. Her mother's face had been really lovely. Amanda's nose was too long, and her forehead was sort of squinchy, and there was something wrong with her chin . . . If only her parents hadn't been such dinosaurs about having her and Sudie engineered! Not everybody was so archaic. Thekla had the most gorgeous green-blue eyes engineered for color and size and—

Her father was coming up the stairs!

Amanda's stomach clenched. She wasn't even supposed to be

home. She was supposed to be at swimming, but she'd skipped it and taken the bus home alone, which was forbidden. Her plan had been to avoid her father until the time when Yaeko's bodyguard was supposed to drop Amanda off at home, and then act like she'd just arrived. Her father would be furious. Swiftly she kicked the crumpled pile of her discarded clothes under the bed, opened the closet door, and slipped inside. She didn't dare click the door closed, her father was already coming into the bedroom, but she pulled it so that only a tiny crack remained.

It wasn't her father. For a frozen moment Amanda thought the man in her father's bedroom was Dieter Gruber: huge and blond and genemod. But Dieter had been left behind on World, at the other end of the galaxy, over two years ago, and anyway Dieter was always clumping and noisy. This man moved quietly as a cat.

He looked around the bedroom, closed the door again, and went down the hall.

Amanda squeezed her eyes shut tight. Who was he? What was happening? What should she do?

Softly she opened the closet, slid out, and pulled back one corner of the bedroom curtain. Another man stood outside beside a car. The rest of the street was quiet and dark in the April night, behind the lacy bare trees that were her father's reason for choosing this neighborhood in a quiet suburb three miles from Cambridge. "I may have to work with those dolts at Harvard," he'd said, "but I don't have to live with them."

Her father came out of the house with a third man. To Amanda's eyes, Daddy wasn't walking right. Too quiet, too calm, nothing jiggling or twitching. He never walked like that. She watched him get into the car with the two men, and then the man who'd been upstairs came out and got in, too. The car drove away.

Maybe it was a college meeting. Maybe her father left a note. Amanda tore downstairs to see. But even before she reached the kitchen table, where he always left her notes, she knew it hadn't been a college meeting. That big blond man had come upstairs in her house, and her father had walked like someone had done something to him. Drugs, maybe.

She should call the police.

"Bumbling incompetents with the intelligence of chairs, seventy percent of them," her father always said about cops, "and of the other thirty percent, half are in league with the criminals." What if she called the police and got one in league with whoever took her father? Or even one of the chair ones, who wouldn't know what to do? Her father would say that fifteen percent was a low probability of success.

Amanda stood very still. "Think," her father always said. "Reason it out. That's what you have a brain for." All right, she would reason what to do.

She couldn't call the police. They might be part of this thing. Even at school some girls talked in whispers about how the government was breaking down and an uncle or a cousin had disappeared. Of course, they were talking about the big government on Mars, not the little ones on Earth. On Mars everything about the war was worse than on Earth. But even so . . . government people couldn't be trusted. Who could?

Aunt Kristen, of course, in Lowell City. But if she called Mars, the men who took her father would know. Calls could be traced, especially ones to the capital of Mars, and even if the calls were encrypted, tracers could still tell if a call had been made, even if they didn't know what was said. Everybody knew that, from holo shows. Also, House would have recorded everything that happened by the front door and the first-story windows. The bad people would certainly pierce House's firewalls (Amanda herself could pierce them) and destroy the evidence of their kidnapping. When they did, they'd know that Amanda had come home early, had been in the house. Then they might come to get her, too.

Maybe they were already on the way!

She had to leave, now, right away. But she couldn't go to Carol's sister, where Carol and Sudie were visiting, because the bad people would surely know where Carol and Sudie were. Then they'd get Amanda. And she couldn't let that happen because she was the only one who had actually seen her father get taken away. She was an eyewitness. She had to get help for her father, and it had to be somebody she could absolutely trust, and it had to be somebody the bad people wouldn't suspect she'd go to, and it had to be somebody rich and powerful enough to help. Amanda knew that, too, from holo shows.

Marbet Grant. On Luna.

All the breath went out of Amanda and she almost cried with relief. Marbet was perfect. No one would think of looking for Amanda on Luna. And Marbet was the nicest, smartest, best person Amanda knew. Secretly Amanda had hoped her father would marry Marbet. Although Carol was nice, too, and maybe Carol was better for her father because Marbet was a Sensitive and her father was too ornery to want somebody guessing with such high probability what he was thinking all the time.

Now that the decision was made, Amanda turned efficient. She ran to her room, put on shoes, and crammed her dance bag with a few clean clothes and toiletries. All the time, she was thinking furiously. Her father had given her the code to the safe. She made House open it and pulled out her passport—but if she used it, couldn't she be traced? She took it anyway, plus all the money chips. Then she added the small blue plastic pouch with the stones from the vug.

The vug. A sparkling cave on the planet World, like Aladdin's cave in the story. Her father and Dieter Gruber had taken her and Sudie there, just once, when her father was making his important physics discoveries on World. Dieter had let Amanda and Sudie take double handfuls of the diamonds and gold nuggets on the cave floor and walls. Sudie had only wanted to play with them, but Amanda had been interested in how the gems got there. "Once this was the caldera of a volcano, right here," Dieter had said. "The gold precipitates out from circulating water heated by magma." It seemed so long ago. She'd been such a child.

Amanda put the bag of gems into her pocket, which was the first time she realized she was still wearing her mother's dress. Well, good. It would make her look older. Wait . . . yes! Quickly she ran back to her father's room, grabbed a handful of Carol's makeup from her drawer, and shoved it in the dance bag.

She turned off House's surveillance and left by the kitchen door. Quickly she disappeared into the dark woods behind the house. She and her friends played in these woods all the time; Amanda knew them well. "Manicured woods," her father always called them, "suburban Trianons with low probability of actual wildlife." Well, so what.

The woods smelled of spring earth, rich and fresh. It was cold under the trees, and Amanda shivered as she hurried, surefooted, along the moonlit paths. She'd forgotten her jacket.

Fifteen minutes later, she emerged on the other side of the woods, several blocks from home. She walked to the corner and caught a maglev to Cambridge. No one questioned her; the bus was full of kids just a little older than she was. (And her father said she was too young to ride the train alone at night!) Amanda sat in the last seat, propped Carol's hand mirror on her knees, and applied Carol's makeup, pursing her lips critically.

Now she looked much older. Maybe even sixteen.

What if the kidnappers killed her father?

They wouldn't kill him. Low probability! He was a famous physicist, and that was the only reason to kidnap him, so they probably wanted him alive to do physics for them. Yes. She had to stop thinking about what might happen to him and concentrate all her brain on how to help him. *"Think. Reason it out. That's what you have a brain for."*

At the Cambridge station, she studied all the signs until she figured out how to buy a ticket for the train to Walton Spaceport, halfway across the state. She used money chips at the ticket machine; they couldn't be traced. There were no kids on this train, but nobody bothered Amanda. She sat up straight in her seat, looking as old as she could, trying not to appear upset that her father had been kidnapped and she was afraid for her life and his life and nothing was the same as it had been two hours ago, when all she had wanted to do was find out that she looked pretty in her dead mother's yellow dress.

TWO

WALTON SPACEPORT, UNITED ATLANTIC FEDERATION, EARTH

At the spaceport, Amanda had her first big problem. She couldn't buy a ticket to Luna without showing her passport, which had her name on it, and maybe the people who'd taken her father could get the passport list. Also, a ticket to Luna cost more than she had in money chips. She'd have to cash in a gem, and how did you do that? She had no idea.

Amanda locked herself in a public bathroom. She took just one gem from the blue plastic bag. The bag with the rest of the gems she put in her underpants, shoving it down between her legs where it didn't show through the swirling yellow dress. Then she walked as confidently as she could to a public information terminal and put in her money.

"Ad search, diamond buyer, private, closest."

"Linked," the terminal said. "The advertiser closest to you that buys diamonds privately is Trevinno Brothers, Walton Spaceport, Building T, fifth level."

Right here! What luck! Although, it made sense. Probably a lot of people decided to leave Earth quickly and didn't want to be traced, and so they'd need a lot of money chips fast. But what kind of people would they be? Criminals, maybe. They might try to hurt her. Oh, God.

But what choice did she have?

She could call Marbet on Luna. Marbet might be able to arrange a ticket for Amanda from there. She could use a public phone.

No. If Marbet bought the ticket on Luna, she'd have to give Amanda's passport information, and it would be in the deebee from then until the next flight. The kidnappers might get the data and know where she was. But if Amanda bought the ticket at this end at the very last minute before the flight took off, there wouldn't be time for anyone bad to stop her until she was safe with Marbet. Marbet would know just how to protect Amanda. Marbet was rich and famous and had powerful friends (high probability). The important thing was for Amanda to get to Marbet.

For just a moment, she wondered if Marbet was really her best choice. A lot of people didn't like Sensitives. Marbet worked a lot of negotiations, criminal trials, dangerous government stuff. She got death threats. Maybe Amanda should go to somebody else.

There wasn't anybody else.

Lifting her chin, Amanda said to the terminal, "Search. Diamond prices, now, a diamond—" she hesitated, estimating, the diamond was big "—weighing ten grams."

"Price depends on diamond clarity, color, cut."

"Range."

"Ten thousand credits to one hundred thousand credits."

That much! And she had so many gems from the vug . . . too late, she remembered that half the gems were supposed to be Sudie's. Well, she'd bring that half back home.

She said, "Directions to Building T from here."

"Go down the corridor to your left, take the Number Sixteen train, get off at the third stop."

"Thank you," she said, even though her father always complained that it was stupid to thank machines. Her father . . .

"You're welcome," the machine said, which suddenly made her feel better. Her father didn't know everything. And he was the smartest man in the Solar System, so that meant the kidnappers didn't know everything either.

Train 16 was full of soldiers who whistled and called out to Amanda. Frightened, she let that train go by and waited for the next one. It was empty, and not very clean. Neither was Building T. The fifth level wasn't, as Amanda had supposed, the fifth story up, but the fifth story down. Traveling on the escalator, Amanda clutched her dance bag tighter. Too late, she realized the name of her school, SAU-LER ACADEMY, was emblazoned on the front. Anybody could have seen it. She turned the bag so the logo was against her body. Her heart was doing strange things, first beating fast, then in slow, painful thumps.

A woman looked at her as she got off the elevator, a bizarre woman with purple hair and flashing lights in her belly button and no top to her dress. Shocked, Amanda looked away. She should leave. This wasn't right. The woman abruptly laughed, a laugh that to Amanda sounded crazy, scary. She should just leave.

But the woman went away, and just down the dirty corridor Amanda could see an e-sign glowing: TREVINNO BROTHERS. BUY AND SELL. WITHOUT QUESTION. An animated question mark popped up and was instantly "killed," over and over. After six "deaths," more words appeared after WITHOUT QUESTION, so it now read WITHOUT QUESTION THE BEST.

Even I can tell that's not what they really mean, Amanda thought, and that gave her courage. She was smart enough to do this. This shop would buy her diamond without demanding her passport. It would only take a minute, and then she'd race back up the escalator to the train and return to the clean parts of the spaceport. It would only take a minute.

She walked up to the door and it opened for her. The inside was small and grubby, the foamcast walls badly discolored, but relief flooded through Amanda. It was a machine! No people, just a machine to buy things. No one to hurt her.

Almost cheerful, she stepped up to the terminal, which had slots and trays of various sizes barnacled onto its front. "I'd like to sell a diamond, please."

"Rest the gem on Tray A."

Amanda hesitated. What if the machine just swallowed the diamond without giving her any money? But if it did that, then Trevinno Brothers wouldn't stay in business very long, would they? Anyway, she had no choice. She laid her diamond on the tray.

It didn't get swallowed, but a clear dome settled over it and somewhere machinery hummed softly. The machine said, "Offer: five thousand credits."

That was a lot less than the library terminal had promised. Could this machine know she was only a kid? Maybe it was a near-AI. But near-AIs were very expensive, her father said.

Surprised at her own boldness, she said, "I want ten thousand credits. A library said my diamond is worth at least that much."

"Eight thousand credits."

"All right." It was enough for the ticket to Luna. And at least she'd gotten it up by three thousand.

Her diamond, still under the dome, disappeared. From another slot came a pile of money chips.

Amanda grabbed them without counting (machines were reliable, high probability), turned, and ran to the door. It was locked. The window, clear when she'd come in, was now opaque.

"Let me out! Let me out!"

"Not yet," a man's voice said behind her. Amanda whirled. "Why, you're just a little girl."

She was too terrified to say anything.

"A little girl whore, who suddenly has a huge uncut diamond. Who'd you take it off of, honey? Is he still alive to miss it?"

Amanda started screaming. It was almost as if the screams filled the air with powder as well as sound, because when she tried to remember later exactly what had happened, everything was clouded. But she recalled the man's hands on her, ripping her mother's yellow dress, fumbling first at her breasts and then at her underpants. And then there was the sound of ripping foamcast and the wall collapsed, and another machine was in the room. The man let her go and he started screaming. Something or someone picked her up, and she beat at it or him or her with her fists. A great rushing sounded in her ears, like a huge waterfall, and then nothing.

"Drink this," somebody said, and Amanda did. Immediately strength flowed into her body. She pushed the glass away, sat up, and looked around wildly. A shabby, tiny room with one bed and one chair and one picture on the wall and—

"It's all right," said a man standing beside the bed. "You're safe." He was short and skinny, with a scraggly little beard at the end of his chin. Dressed in dirty black jeans and shirt, he had the pasty, grayish skin of someone who seldom walked in sunlight.

"Who . . . who are you?"

"A more relevant question is, who are you? Amanda Susan Capelo, age fourteen, citizen of the United Atlantic Federation, daughter of Dr. Thomas Capelo and the late Karen Olsen Capelo."

He had her passport. Without thinking she thrust a hand between her legs, felt the blue plastic pouch still there, blushed furiously, and looked away. Something terrible stood in the corner. She gasped, "What's *that*?"

"That's my assistant. A very strong, very dumb robot who smashed through that fence's shop and carried you out of there. Don't thank it; it doesn't have sound sensors. It only does what I tell it to by handheld."

The thing in the corner was seven feet tall, a metal rectangle with three sets of flexible tentacles, built-in gun barrels, and three spray nozzles. Amanda looked at it hopelessly. Tears pricked at her eyes, hot and scalding, but she blinked them back. She wanted desperately, blindingly, to go home.

"Don't cry," the man said unsympathetically, "because—"

"I never cry!" Amanda snapped.

"—it won't help. If you're old enough to go traipsing around a quarter like Building T, you're old enough to control yourself."

"I didn't know it would be like this!"

"Of course not. Now tell me why you were there."

"You tell me first who you are!"

"You can call me Father Emil. I'm a Catholic priest."

"What's that?" Amanda said.

"Oh my dear God," he said, "you never heard of Catholicism? Not even *heard* of it?"

Amanda shook her head. She actually had a vague memory of the word coming up in history, her least favorite class, but she couldn't remember any details.

"Stop scowling, child. Do it. Catholicism is a very old religion, and the one true faith in a world that's forgotten faith. I run the St. Theresa the Little Flower Mission. I rescue lost souls who have fallen into thievery, drunkenness, addiction, or prostitution, which is what I thought you were. An underage prostitute in way over her head."

Amanda at least knew what a prostitute was. How dare he call her that! "I'm not a prostitute!"

"No, I see that. So what were you doing at a sleazy hot shop?"

She didn't answer, glaring at him instead.

"Come on, child," Father Emil said in that same dry, unsympathetic voice, "if you don't tell me what's wrong, I can't help you. What is the daughter of a world-famous physicist and war-pusher doing selling stolen goods?"

"They aren't stolen! And my father isn't a war-pusher!"

"Of course he is. The physicist Thomas Capelo, who gave the world the alien artifact that has the power to destroy not only an entire star system but the fabric of space itself. Thereby escalating the stakes in the war with the Fallers from mere destruction of humanity to destruction of the universe which a merciful God gave mankind, all so that egomaniac Stefanak can buy himself power."

Amanda was confused. Nobody she knew talked like that. The picture on the wall showed a man bleeding on a cross made of wood, in horrible pain. She said stubbornly, "My father only gave General Stefanak the artifact because the Fallers already have one. General Stefanak is using it to protect the Solar System!"

Father Emil snorted. "No use talking politics with a child, especially a child without faith. Just tell me why you were selling goods—stolen or not—at Trevinno Brothers."

"I need the money."

"Now we're getting somewhere. No, don't look away from the painting, child, that's our dear Lord who died for your sins. Why did you need money?"

"Why should I tell you?" Amanda demanded.

"Because I noticed you, a little girl painted like the Scarlet Whore of Babylon, and followed you to make sure you were all right. Because I smashed into Trevinno Brothers with the Wrath of God here to save you from a truly horrible and probably short life as a slave for the sex trade. Because I brought you here to safety in my mission and gave you some of my restorative drug, which I could ill-afford, when you seemed to be in shock. That's why."

Amanda pulled the eight thousand credits from her pocket and threw two thousand onto the cot beside Father Emil. "That's to pay for your drug!"

"I gave you too much of it, obviously. Manic grandiosity is setting in. But thank you, I'll take the money in a spirit of meekness, for the greater glory of God." He pocketed the chips. "Now tell me why you needed money."

Amanda studied Father Emil. He had given her a drug, he said so, and maybe it *was* making her braver. Maybe it made her not think so well, too. But she felt like she was thinking well again, and he *had* saved her from . . . that, and he wasn't trying to take her money. Maybe she could trust him. Besides, what was she going to do if she didn't trust him? The spaceport was a lot scarier place than she'd imagined.

"You are deciding to confide in me," Father Emil said. "That's good. The confessional is a sacred trust."

Amanda had no idea what he meant. He talked a little bit like her father, whose words sounded normal but sometimes had funny twists to them. "Ironic bitterness," she had overheard Aunt Kristen say once, but Amanda didn't know what her aunt meant and hadn't asked. Her father was just who he was. *Her father* . . .

"Don't start to cry now—"

"I told you I never cry!"

"—or the Wrath of God will return you to that hot shop. Now tell me why you need money."

She said sulkily, "I have to go to Luna."

"To Luna. Why?"

"To find someone who can help me. My father's been kidnapped."

His eyes widened. Amanda felt a mean satisfaction. For the first time, she'd had an effect on him. He said, "Dr. Capelo? Kidnapped? When?"

"Just a few hours ago."

"By whom? Do you know?"

"No. I just—"

"Tell me the whole story, Amanda. From the beginning. Don't leave anything out, even if you think it's not important."

She related the events, feeling a relief she didn't want to acknowledge. A grown-up was back in charge. Father Emil listened carefully. When she finished, he stood and walked to the picture on the wall. With his back to her, he said, "Who were you going to look for on Luna?"

"Marbet Grant."

"The Sensitive? Why?"

"She's a friend. I thought she could help find Daddy because she's rich and she knows a lot of people all over the Solar System."

He was quiet a long time. Then he turned away from the picture and touched his forehead, chest, left shoulder, right shoulder. Amanda wondered if he had a neurological disease, like Thekla's mother, who had uncontrollable tics.

"Amanda," he said, sitting beside her again, "I'm going to help you. You already know you can't show your passport for legitimate passage to Luna without entering the government deebees. If it *was* government people who took your father—"

"Do you think it was?"

A strange expression crossed Father Emil's face. He did the tic thing again, and closed his eyes. "I think God moves in mysterious ways, his wonders for to prove, and He tests our hearts in ways we cannot understand."

Amanda said impatiently, "What does that mean? Do you think the government took Daddy or not?"

"A tunnel-visioned rationalist. Your father's daughter. Thus are the sins visited on the children. Yes, Amanda, I think the government kidnapped your father. I also think they will blame it on the antiwar movement."

"*Why*? Why take Daddy?"

"Haven't a clue. I'm neither a politician nor a scientist, thank the Lord. Was your father working on some new big piece of science?"

"My father is always working on a big piece of science." Really, Father Emil didn't know much about scientists.

"Yes. Well. Maybe that was the impetus. Maybe not. The Lord provides."

"Provides what?" Amanda said, but Father Emil had turned away again. He went to the picture of the bloody man and knelt in front of it, his lips moving silently. On Father Emil's face was a look of such anguish that Amanda was afraid.

She had studied religion in history class, of course, although history was her least favorite subject and she hadn't paid much attention. Maybe there had been a religion called "Catholic." There had been so many. And all of them, her father said, were silly and irrational, which had further decreased Amanda's interest in them. But she nonetheless knew what Father Emil was doing. He was "praying," asking "God" for help. Help with what?

Amanda eyed the door. If she tried to leave, would the Wrath of God stop her? The huge metal robot looked as if it could stop an earthquake. And if she did get out the door, where would she find herself? Was she still even at Walton Spaceport?

Before she could decide what to do, Father Emil stood. "Amanda, I'm going to help you get to Luna."

She should have felt grateful, but something in his voice bothered her. She said cautiously, "Why?"

"Because the Lord does provide in mysterious ways, child. For both of us. I have friends, and they have ships, and you won't need to show your passport to any government deebee."

There was something wrong with this statement. Amanda thought, and found it. "But . . . even if you have ships, they have to be cleared and tracked by a spaceport, and that's the government."

"Not entirely. Or, rather, there are spaceport employees who are on our side, and who will enter data that records the takeoffs and landings of the ships accurately, but not who's aboard or why."

Amanda was bewildered. She said, "Why do they do that? What do you mean, 'employees who are on our side?' Our side of what?"

"Politics. Not everyone likes General Stefanak, you know."

Well, of course she knew *that*. Everybody knew that. Whole bunches of people thought General Stefanak was doing a terrible job of fighting the war with the Fallers. The news holos were full of demonstrations and editorials and stuff, all boring. Amanda lost interest. What did it matter what these people's politics were? "Science is above politics, and outlasts it," Daddy always said. The important thing was to get to Luna to find Marbet so she could help get Daddy back.

"All right," she said to Father Emil, "I'll go to Luna on your friends' ship. Thank you."

"Oh, child," Father Emil said, and again his lips moved in that pointless "prayer," until Amanda looked away. She wished he'd get on with it. She had to get to Luna as soon as possible.

THREE

LOWELL CITY, MARS

There are, Lyle Kaufman discovered, a thousand ways for a government to stop a citizen from doing something legal that the citizen wants to do. None of the ways involved violence, nor even threats. No deebees were penetrated, no information falsified, no lies told. No one ever actually said, "No."

Instead, files disappeared. Meetings were canceled due to "emergencies." People, whose retinal signature to electronic documents was vital, were temporarily out of reach, traveling beyond remote space tunnels on "war-related business." Information systems suffered breakdowns, viruses, input confusion, data bleeding, gate bubbles, and deebee atoll erosion. Kaufman had been trying for five months to obtain authorization to travel beyond the Solar System in a private ship, to the nonproscribed planet World, away from any known theater of war. He was still in Lowell City, as stuck as if he were welded to one of the huge struts holding up its piezoelectric dome.

"It was easier to move around when I was in the army," Kaufman complained to Marbet Grant. She had stayed on Luna until last week; both of them thought it would be easier for Kaufman to obtain initial travel authorizations if they didn't name the system's most famous Sensitive as a "staff member." But Kaufman missed Marbet. And the authorizations weren't coming through anyway. So last week she had flown from Luna City to join him.

"Of course it was easier to move around when you were in the army," Marbet said. "They want the army out beyond Space Tunnel Number One, fighting the war. They want citizens safely at home."

"I'm not so sure, Marbet. More and more of the army seems to be right here on Mars."

"I know," she said, and said no more. Both of them knew Kaufman's hotel was probably bugged.

It was a cheap hotel, the kind used by army dependents while they waited desperately for short-supply military housing. Small bare rooms, corridors swarming with children who had nowhere else to play except the narrow streets, drab foamcast walls without windows—for security reasons and because there was no view anyway. The war made everything on Mars more crowded and inconvenient. Kaufman, most of his life a soldier, barely noticed. Marbet did, and minded, and said nothing. Lyle had enough to contend with. She read his tension and his doubt and his unjustified guilt in every line of his body and every note of his voice.

Marbet Grant was a Sensitive, aggressively genemod in appearance. She was short and slim, with cheekbones that cut like knives above a wide, soft nose. Her skin was chocolate brown, her eyes emerald green, her short curly hair auburn. She looked wholly artificial, but the real genetic engineering had been of her mind.

Throughout history, there had always been people who were unusually sensitive to others, unusually adept at reading others' states of mind. Historians claimed it was a survival necessity of the underclasses: serfs, slaves, women, subject peoples. Life itself might depend on correctly reading the mood of the masters.

Evolutionary biologists pointed out that this fit well with Darwinian theory. Survival of the most accurately perceptive, those who could adapt to others because they perceived accurately what they must adapt to.

Social researchers documented the tiny, unconscious clues that signaled emotion and intent: minute facial changes, shifts in body distribution, voice intonations, rise in skin temperature. Cross-cultural anthropologists traced the existence of people good at perceiving these clues, almost always without knowing how they did it, in all societies.

But it was the genetic engineers who tied this perceptiveness to specific genetic patterns, subtle but identifiable combinations of otherwise disparate genes. And it was a single group of geneticists who engineered for it, starting with the most available research subjects— their own children. The geneticists had believed themselves to be giving their children a survival advantage, not much different than the augmented muscles, boosted intelligence, or enhanced beauty common to the rich. It hadn't quite worked out like that. Instinctively understanding your neighbor might aid you, but it disconcerted the neighbor. Many, many people do not wish to be understood. They would rather that their feelings and intentions remained hidden.

Still, Marbet worked continually. For corporations wanting an edge in negotiations. For law enforcement interviewing major crime figures. For the government seeking to know more about individuals than the individuals wished to give away. And, once, for the military seeking to understand the only Faller enemy ever captured alive. That Faller had died, but not before Dr. Thomas Capelo had learned from it the information that had changed the whole feel of the war.

All that had occurred on World, where Marbet had met Lyle Kaufman. Where together they had wrecked a civilization.

Marbet no longer tried to talk to Lyle about his guilt. Her talk had made no impression. Only going back to World might do that. If the authorities ever let them.

Those authorities had kept close watch on Kaufman for the last few years, just as they undoubtedly had on Marbet Grant and Thomas Capelo. All three knew too much about the dead Faller. So of course the room was bugged. General Stefanak's power depended on information as much as on the army presence steadily and inexorably increasing on Mars. It was an army fanatically loyal to Stefanak. The general had spent a decade building that fanaticism: promoting certain officers, transferring others to the colonies, manipulating all-important budget allocations. Some—many—said Stefanak was building to a dictatorship, under cover of martial law made "necessary" by the war. During the last year, fewer had dared say it too openly.

Marbet picked up the handheld—the hotel room didn't even possess a proper voice-activated house system—to flick on the news, and there he was, Sullivan Stefanak, Supreme Commander, Solar Defense Alliance Council. "—here tonight only because the danger to all Solar citizens is so great. A danger not from the enemy, but from our own people. The antiwar faction known as 'Life Now' represents—"

"Here we go again," Marbet said. Kaufman stayed expressionless, and knew that to Marbet he was not. His feelings about Stefanak were still confused. Kaufman was—had been—a soldier, and Stefanak was the greatest soldier of his generation. It was his leadership that had kept the Fallers, humanity's technological superior, from already winning the war. It was also Stefanak that was destroying the republican structure of the Solar System alliance, a structure inevitably fragile since Mars, not the more populous Earth, controlled the Council. Mars controlled the space tunnels. That was all it took. Mars—

"What did he just say?" Marbet said. Kaufman had not been listening. One look at her face and he began.

"—cowardly kidnapping of a civilian. Dr. Thomas Capelo, as you all know, is the Solar System's preeminent scientist, the man who deciphered for us the Protector Artifact that keeps our precious homeworlds safe from the enemy sworn to destroy every last vestige of human life. Life Now has finally gone too far! Dr. Capelo, father of two daughters, respected professor at UAF's venerable university of Harvard, was not even a combatant. Many regard him as a savior, and indeed—"

"When?" Kaufman said.

"Last night. SShhhh . . ."

"—grateful his family was not at home at the time—"

Kaufman thought rapidly. It could have been Life Now, yes. They were gaining strength. Their core of idealists was backed by some very powerful families and corporations with a lot to lose if Stefanak became dictator. But Life Now wasn't the only candidate for kidnapper. Kaufman had been stuck commanding a backwater space station for the last year of his military service. He was out of touch with Solar politics. But before that, he had been a military strategist in the Solar Alliance Defense Army. It wasn't inconceivable that some faction of the government itself, some faction bitterly opposed to Stefanak, had kidnapped Capelo. But why? Or . . .

He said to Marbet, "Do you know what Tom was working on now?"

She made a face. "Lyle, physics is so complicated now that I don't think even most of Tom's colleagues understood what he was working on. Maybe Tom himself didn't really know. It wouldn't be the first time." Her expression changed. She said, "I feel ill, Lyle. That food at lunch, I told you . . ."

Their signal. He followed her into the bathroom. She knelt over the toilet, he knelt beside her, and she whispered into his armpit, "You think Stefanak himself might have kidnapped Tom."

"How do you do that?" he blurted, before he caught himself. You'd think by now he'd have learned. She couldn't explain the minute changes in body language, facial tone, eyebrow movement—all of it—that she intuitively read, and when she did try to explain it, Kaufman couldn't follow. Her skill was wholly nonverbal.

He whispered, "Yes, I think it's possible that Stefanak himself might have had Tom kidnapped."

"Why?"

From the holoscreen in the hotel room Stefanak said "—my personal appeal for any information leading to the recovery of Dr. Capelo and—"

Kaufman said, "A way to discredit the antiwar movement, to use Life Now as an excuse to appropriate more power to himself. . . . I'm not sure. If so, it's a clumsy technique. More what amateurs would do."

"So you think Life Now abducted Tom?" And louder, "Oh, God, Lyle, I'm so dizzy . . ."

He said, "I don't know. If Stefanak wanted it to look like a Life Now operation, he might deliberately make a clumsy move . . . That's it, darling, just let it come . . ."

Marbet stuck her finger down her throat, retched violently, and sat up woozily. Lyle ran cold water on a cloth and handed it to her. Surveillance now had bona fide vomit to record.

When she rejoined him, he said, "Better now?"

"Yes, thank you. But let's not eat at Katouse again."

"Affirmative. Marbet, I'm going to call Carol."

"I doubt you'll get through."

He didn't. Kaufman left a message for Tom's second wife, offering whatever aid he could, whatever hope he could manage. Carol would have cops with her, UAF federal agents, family, and friends. Kaufman knew she and Amanda and Sudie would be safe; by now there would be enough soldiers ringing the Capelo household to form a company by themselves.

He took Marbet's hand. The two sat quietly, thinking about Tom

Capelo, that brilliant and difficult and complicated man. His two daughters adored him. They'd lost their mother in a Faller raid years ago, and if their father was also murdered . . .

The terminal sounded. Without a house system, it merely rang a bell. The screen flashed INCOMING RECORDED MESSAGE, and Marbet punched her handhold to bring it up. An unfamiliar woman, dressed in not-very-expensive business attire and with an unfortunate haircut, appeared on the screen.

"Colonel Kaufman, Ms. Grant, the Civilian Travel Section of the Martian Space Tunnel Administration, State Department, Solar Alliance Defense Council, is pleased to inform you that your application for a privately funded trip to the nonproscribed planet Osiris, Isis System, Space—"

"But we don't want to go to Osiris!" Marbet said. "Futile to interrupt," Kaufman could have said. It was a one-way recording.

"—Tunnel Number Eighty-nine has been approved. Flight plan, tunnel itinerary, and Tunnel Administration regulations follow. Be advised that the itinerary requires you to enter Space Tunnel number one between October sixteen and October nineteen of this year. Note also that this approval is not legally binding upon the Martian Space Tunnel Administration, may be withdrawn at any time without notice, and does not include any responsibility for the course or outcome of your expedition.

"The Administration wishes you a good trip."

Kaufman and Marbet looked at each other. Osiris was nowhere near World. It would take time to correct the bureaucratic "mistake"—weeks, months. Never.

Kaufman's clear brown eyes remained steady. *A steady man*, Marbet thought for the hundredth time. Calm. Not easily diverted. No one but she knew the calm, steady guilt, not easily diverted, that lay underneath. He gazed at her, and she read him clearly: He was done with official requests.

She said aloud, for the recording devices, "That's the wrong planet!"

"Nothing to do but start over," Kaufman said. "But, Marbet, it will take a while. We don't need to waste funds on a hotel, do we? Do you think we can still move in with your friend Amy?"

"Yes, she'll be glad to have us," Marbet said. "She told me just yesterday to come anytime. I'll start packing."

Let the State Department, or whoever, spend time looking for "Amy." Or looking for Lyle and Marbet, for that matter. They had wanted to do this legitimately, but had made contingency plans in case they couldn't. There was, as the government endlessly reminded everyone, a war on.

Every single war ever fought anywhere had spawned shadow battles between the warring governments and their own citizens. Black markets, war profiteering, blockade runners, quislings, conscientious objectors, organized crime and its less organized siblings. False government contracts, false traveling papers, false bills of lading, false passenger lists, and, for the really sophisticated, falsifying deebee programs. All it took were contacts and money.

Marbet had money. Kaufman, the career soldier, had not wanted to go underground for their expedition. Kaufman, the decent man, hadn't wanted to break the law. Kaufman, the ex-military attaché to the Solar Council in the war's hub at Lowell City, of course knew the people who knew the contacts.

There was no way Kaufman or Marbet could give practical help to Tom Capelo. They weren't even close friends; neither Kaufman nor Marbet had seen the physicist in nearly two years, although Marbet chatted occasionally via comlink with Capelo's daughter Amanda. She was a nice child, with a schoolgirl crush on Marbet. But Amanda had much closer ties, friends and family, in this awful crisis. When Kaufman thought of everything that had happened on World, it was no longer Thomas Capelo he thought of, but Dieter Gruber and Ann

Sikorski. Left behind on World by his, Kaufman's, decision, in the middle of a toppling civilization Kaufman had singlehandedly wrecked.

Marbet pulled out her case to start packing.

FOUR

LUNA CITY

Amanda couldn't believe it. Marbet was gone.

"Are you sure?" she said to Marbet's neighbor, the fat, kind woman who lived in the next apartment in Marbet's strange underground "building."

"I'm sure, honey," the woman said, wiping her hands on a kitchen towel. She had a strange accent. Somewhere behind her a baby wailed. "She gave me the code to her place, in case there's some sort of emergency. Went off to join her lover, she did."

Amanda folded her hands tightly together, a new habit. "Could I see inside her apartment?"

The woman hesitated.

"Please. I'm her niece. My stepfather and I weren't told she was going anyplace."

The woman glanced from Amanda to Father Emil, standing several paces back in the curving corridor. Father Emil wore black pants and shirt, although both were cleaner than they had been at his mission. The woman shook her head.

"I'm sorry, honey. Marbet didn't say I could let anyone in. You look all right, but she didn't say I could."

"But—"

The woman's kind eyes grew harder. Behind Amanda, Father Emil said, "That's enough, Jane. Come on, now. Thank you, ma'am."

The woman nodded, looking troubled. Amanda could see she wanted to help, but she also wanted to protect Marbet. That was nice; many people were too uncomfortable around Marbet to want to be friends. Amanda tried to smile at her before trudging back to Father Emil. Amanda had never thought beyond getting to Marbet. Now Marbet was on Mars, or so she'd told this neighbor, and what was Amanda going to do now?

"I'm sorry, honey," the woman called after her. "But I know you want your aunt to be happy. It wouldn't surprise me if she married that Colonel Kaufman on this romantic trip they're taking."

Amanda stopped walking. Marbet and Colonel Kaufman? He was all right, she guessed, but for Marbet . . . he wasn't good enough for Marbet! He hadn't even liked Amanda and Sudie much, and her father said Colonel Kaufman was one of those people that couldn't appreciate children . . .

Her father . . .

She clasped her hands more tightly together. The knuckles turned ashy. That was necessary, sometimes. Her father always said you couldn't accomplish anything worthwhile in tears.

"Who's Colonel Kaufman?" Father Emil said.

"He was the head of the expedition to World," Amanda said shortly. "The one where Daddy found the Protector Artifact and figured out what it did and how it worked. I *told* you."

"I didn't memorize every name you gave me, child. Not every detail of your life struck me as all-consuming, I'm afraid. Strive for a little humility."

Amanda ignored him. She hadn't realized, when Father Emil said he'd get her to Luna City with his secret friends, that he was going to go with her. Although at first she'd been glad he had come. It was scary getting on a ship with strangers, carrying a fake passport that said "Jane Verghese," listening to the news holo about her father's kidnapping, and then the news stories about her own.

The reporters had found out that Amanda wasn't with Carol and Sudie, or with any of her friends, and so they'd assumed she had been abducted along with her father. But the people who took her father must know that wasn't true. Maybe by now they also knew that Amanda was a witness to the kidnapping. They were probably looking for her. It was scary, and she'd been glad that Father Emil was with her, even though he was the most irritating person she'd ever met.

"God never wants humans to go to war, Amanda."

"So why are we at war? Why doesn't God stop it?"

"He's given us free will. We've chosen to go to war with the Fallers."

"I *know* that's not true," she said triumphantly. "The Fallers attacked us first. So they're the ones who chose the war."

"But the Fallers don't want war, either." When Father Emil got very intense, his scraggly little beard bobbed up and down as he spoke. "No intelligent species wants war. This war is kept going by human leaders, and perhaps by Faller leaders as well, who are using it as a way to gain, keep, or increase their own power."

That actually made sense; Amanda's father said the same thing. But then Father Emil spoiled his own point.

"If General Stefanak really wanted to end the war, he'd communicate that wish to the Fallers."

"But the Fallers won't communicate with us!" Amanda cried, exasperated. "They refuse to say anything at all! Everybody knows that!"

"I don't," Father Emil said. "It's just more government propaganda. The masses, such as for instance you, believe whatever political propaganda you're fed by your leaders."

"Well, then, priests, such as for instance you, believe whatever religious propaganda you're fed by your church!"

She saw immediately that she'd gone too far. Father Emil drew himself up to his full unimpressive height and said, "You cannot recognize false witness. Nor the Anti-Christ. Such are the signs of the Time of the End, and such is the sorrow of the slaughter of innocents."

Amanda decided he was crazy and tried to tune him out.

But that was scary, too. What was she doing with a crazy man as the only one to protect her? Father Emil had left the Wrath of God back at the Mission, with another person also called "Father." It was needed, he said, for "the work."

The ship that had brought them to Luna was small, designed for six people, but it was a real ship, not just a shuttle. It had bunks, a galley, storage areas, a tiny bridge. The three-man crew, two men and a woman, had not spoken to Amanda at all. They just watched her, wary and hard-eyed. It made Amanda nervous. If she'd gone around the house that sulky and rude, her father would have reprimanded her sharply. She asked Father Emil who they were, and he replied that God chose His own instruments to accomplish His glory, and it was not up to human beings, especially children, to question His choices.

Amanda decided that if these people were God's choice for instruments, then God was as crazy as Father Emil.

Now she trudged along beside him, in the long circular corridor that ringed H level of Luna City. A small tram rounded the curve, stopped beside them, and said cheerfully, "Hello! I make a circuit of this residential level every ten minutes, stopping whenever you instruct me to do so. Or, if you prefer, you can walk. All entrances to residential clusters are found on or just off this main circular corridor."

"We'll walk," Father Emil said, and the tram glided off.

"Father Emil—"

"Be quiet, Jane, I'm thinking," he said, with such an emphasis on the "Jane" that Amanda knew he was reminding her to not talk until they were back aboard ship. That was another thing. Father Emil was the most paranoid person alive, worse even than her father. Daddy always thought the universe was out to harm Amanda and Sudie. Father Emil always thought the government was out to listen to every little boring thing he said.

They reached the elevator, ascended, and came out under Luna City's dome, below the black sky set with glittering stars. It was a small dome, nothing like the domes on Mars. Father Emil said only eight thousand people lived here, all "Pharisees: scientists, technicians, military, and their rich dependents. No poor that can fit through the needle's eye." All the living and working places were below ground, safe from meteor bombardment. On the surface, under the dome, were only some foamcast buildings, a playground for little kids, and a garden with raked smooth sand set with boulders, benches, and some beds of what looked like genetically modified flowers developed from fungi.

The flowers were the first thing Amanda had seen since the kidnapping that stirred her interest, and she would have liked to kneel and examine them. They had broad, almost transparent green leaves and tiny blossoms in pale yellow. Probably they were genemod for low light. But Father Emil hurried her into her suit, out of the airlock, and onto the empty rocky plain between the dome and shuttle to the spaceport.

"Amanda," he said, and she realized he was on the private channel, so his words would reach only her, "I have a confession to make. I have sinned against you."

She looked at him sideways. If her father had said that, he would just have been being fizzy again, joking around like his usual ridiculous self. But Father Emil sounded as if he meant it.

"I lied. When I took you here to see Marbet Grant, I already knew she was on Mars."

"You did? How?"

"My friends found that out. It was easy, you know. Marbet Grant is a famous if disliked person, and certain trivial news channels report the movements of famous persons. Actors, Sensitives, celebrities like that woman Magdalena . . . I knew she left for Mars, alone, three weeks ago."

"That woman said Marbet wasn't alone! She was with Colonel Kaufman!"

"No," Father Emil said, "the woman said Marbet Grant went off to join her lover. Kaufman must have already been on Mars."

Amanda said hotly, "If you knew Marbet was on Mars, why did you take me to Luna City?"

"I wanted you to see for yourself that she was gone, hear it from someone unconnected to me or the organization. So you would believe it."

"All right, I believe it," Amanda said. She was angry, and upset, and confused. Grown-ups didn't talk to kids this way.

"But to obtain your belief, I lied," Father Emil said. "I ask your forgiveness."

"Aren't you supposed to ask God's forgiveness?" She had learned this from him.

"That, too."

Really, he was ridiculous. Her father would have made terrible fun of him. But Amanda could see that Father Emil was serious. It embarrassed her.

"I forgive you," she said awkwardly. "But where do we go now?"

"Back to the ship."

This wasn't what Amanda meant, but she trudged alongside him until they were through the airlock and unsuited. Then, to her surprise, Father Emil said, "Come into the galley, Amanda. The crew wants to talk to you."

The ship's living area consisted of a common room, ringed by closed bunks that were like sleeping in a dresser drawer, and a tiny galley into which was squeezed a table and six chairs. The three-man crew was waiting for her. She sat down awkwardly in one of the chairs, very aware of the light gravity. Father Emil remained standing.

"Amanda," said the captain, "the time has come to talk to you about your situation."

She nodded, a little scared. They looked so serious. She could only remember one of their names: Captain Lewis. He was a big man with a big nose.

He said, "We've done something for you, bringing you here to look for Marbet Grant. Now we need you to do something for us, something that will help you, too."

Again Amanda nodded. He was talking to her as if she were a grown-up, which both pleased and frightened her.

"You witnessed your father's kidnapping by government agents out to destroy the antiwar movement. We're members of that movement, as is Father Emil, who rescued you on Earth. We want you to make a broadcast, which will be beamed by satellite to the entire Solar System, telling exactly how the government agents took your father."

Now Amanda was confused. "But then the kidnappers will know where I am and come get me, too!"

"Not after your broadcast. The whole world will know where you are, and the whole world will be watching you. You'll be much safer than you are now. Safe with us."

"But . . . but I don't know who kidnapped my father. I don't know if they *were* government agents. My father does good physics work for the government. He decoded the Protector Artifact that keeps the Fallers from destroying the whole Solar System!"

"Great. That artifact makes it possible to destroy spacetime itstead," the woman said bitterly. Captain Lewis scowled at her.

"Your father was being used by General Stefanak," Captain Lewis said, "to help him carry on this terrible war. Dr. Capelo is a brilliant and good man, Amanda. Nobody doubts that. But he's a scientist, and science is not the same as politics."

Amanda nodded. That, at least, made sense: Her father always said "Science is above politics and outlasts it." But she didn't say that. It would be rude, since Captain Lewis was obviously more interested in politics than science. You didn't go around insulting other people's interests, unless you were Daddy.

Captain Lewis continued, "General Stefanak kidnapped your father in order to blame it on Life Now. You've heard him do it on the news holo. Life Now is full of people who want to end the war, who only want peace. Don't you want peace, Amanda? Don't you want the war to end?"

"Yes." Of course she did. Everybody did.

"The war killed your mother, didn't it?"

She could only nod. Father Emil said warningly, "Lewis . . ."

"Look at these pictures, Amanda." Captain Lewis opened an envelope and handed her pictures, one by one. Bodies all burnt up, lying on scorched grass, people screaming in pain . . . Amanda handed them back, feeling sick.

"Those are war victims, Amanda. Wouldn't you do anything you could to end the war so no more people get hurt like this? Wouldn't you?"

Again she nodded.

"Then General Stefanak has to lose his power. People have to see clearly the terrible things he's doing, like kidnapping your father just to make everyone think the antiwar movement did it. People think your father is a hero, Amanda. You know that."

"Yes . . ."

"And you want him back. Of course you do. Making the broadcast will help get him back because everyone will put pressure on the government to release him. He's a political prisoner, Amanda, and that's not right. You can tell the whole system that. Then the government will have to let him go."

There were too many words. Amanda couldn't think. Through her rising panic, she tried to sort through the words, understand what Captain Lewis was saying. Something about it wasn't right . . .

The woman—Amanda still couldn't remember her name— thought she was hesitating for a different reason. She said, in a new voice full of honey, "You don't have to worry about what to say in the broadcast, dear. We'll write it out for you so all you have to do is read it."

"I—"

"But not if you prefer to use your own words," Captain Lewis said, and now his scowl at the woman was ferocious. "All you have to do is tell the truth about how you saw the government agents kidnap your father."

Now Amanda saw the thing that wasn't right. "I don't know if it was government agents. I don't *know* who it was."

"It *was* government agents," Captain Lewis said. "It wasn't Life Now . . . that's us, and we didn't kidnap your father. Why would we? The result is that all the news holos are blaming us, and why would we do that? It just opposes people to our cause."

That made sense. Until Amanda thought about it. Then she said, "But . . . if I blame General Stefanak, then people will blame him. That would help your cause."

"Yes, it would. And yours, which is getting your father back. Everyone would know the government took him, and there would be enormous pressure to release him."

"Ye . . . eee . . . ssss, but . . . but *I* don't know if the government did take him."

"We just told you so," Captain Lewis said evenly.

"How do you know?" Amanda said. This was familiar ground; this was what her father did with her. *"What's your evidence, Amanda? Produce your reasoning. Why do you think that?"* This was how science worked.

"Because we didn't take him, and who else is there?"

Amanda was silent. She didn't know that Life Now hadn't kidnapped her father. Captain Lewis wasn't producing either evidence or reasoning. But if she said that, it would be like accusing him, which would be rude. After all, she didn't have any evidence, either.

So instead she repeated, "I don't know who kidnapped him."

"Oh, for Christ's sake," the woman said.

"I'm sorry, but I just don't know. I can't say, if I don't know for sure." That was a fact. That was what her father would want her to do: Stick to the facts.

"Are you saying, Amanda," Captain Lewis said, "that you won't make the broadcast?"

Amanda's stomach turned over. Captain Lewis's face had changed, and his voice. She was in terrible trouble. She clung to the one thing she knew for sure, the fact Daddy would want her to stick to because it was true. "I'm saying I don't know who kidnapped Daddy."

"Will you make the broadcast for us?"

It took all of Amanda's courage to say it. "I can't."

"No?" Captain Lewis was pushing hard.

"No," Amanda said in a small voice.

"After all we've done for you? All Father Emil has done? He saved your life!"

Amanda turned to look at Father Emil, still standing in the doorway to the small galley. His face had gone white. He said, "Dennis, this isn't what we agreed on."

"You told us she would make the broadcast."

"I can't! I don't know who kidnapped my father!" Amanda cried. Her head felt as if it might burst. She hated that. With as much dignity as she could gather, she got off her chair, went through the common room to her bunk, and pulled the curtain. She buried her face in her pillow.

I don't know who kidnapped him, she told herself fiercely, and clung to that, because it was what her father would have said and it was true and it was the only thing she was sure she understood.

She woke to fierce arguing and the dim sound of engines. They were in space, accelerating at one-gee. Her neck tickled and she groped for the patch and pulled it off. A sleeper, probably. Father Emil couldn't know that she didn't sleep long from somnambulizer patches. "A light drug responder," her father always said about her. Amanda lay still, a bit groggy, listening to the voices in the common room beyond the bunk curtain.

"—unconscionable!" Father Emil said, a word Amanda didn't know.

"And what would you have us do with her?" Captain Lewis said, and the anger in his voice brought Amanda out of the last of her sleep. "If she doesn't make that broadcast, the fact that *we* have her only reinforces the impression that we kidnapped them both. God, you smeared this with shit, Emil."

"I wanted to help. I thought she'd make the broadcast. And I wanted to get her somewhere safe."

"Oh, your motives were impeccable," Captain Lewis said sarcastically. "The road to hell and all that. We never should have listened to a Sunday revolutionary like you."

Father Emil said something Amanda didn't catch.

"The longer we have her," the woman said, "the worse the situation gets. No one will believe we didn't abduct her ourselves."

Father Emil said, "Amanda will tell them the truth about the hot shop and about me and about our bringing her to Luna. She's a truthful child."

"Then she'll also tell the world we tried to pressure her into making a broadcast. Unless she broadcasts voluntarily—which you said she would, Emil!—and does it soon, it looks to the eyes of the media like *we're* holding her."

"Aren't we?" Father Emil said.

"No, Goddamn it, we're doing what she wants! Now we're taking her to Mars in search of a genetic abomination and government stooge like Marbet Grant!"

The woman said, "Essentially, a fourteen-year-old kid is calling the shots for this spaceship. She has to make that broadcast. We can make her do it, Dennis."

"How?" Captain Lewis said. "Threats? Drugs? Don't you think she'll tell people about that, too, afterward?"

"Not if you terrify her enough."

"Lucy," Father Emil said, "stop right there. She's a *child*."

"A child in a position to hurt the entire Life Now organization, thanks to you," Lucy said bitterly.

Father Emil said, in a different voice, "Dennis . . . did Life Now kidnap Thomas Capelo?"

"Oh, God," Lucy said. "Amateurs."

"Yes, I am, Lucy," Father Emil said. "Amateur, Sunday revolutionary, as bottom of the organizational ladder as possible. Just a believer in its goals. Which is why I don't know the answer to my question and why I want to know. Did Life Now, or any of its affiliate antiwar organizations in the AWM, kidnap Thomas Capelo?"

Amanda clasped her hands tightly together. What would Captain Lewis say? But it was Father Emil who spoke.

"You don't know the answer, do you, Dennis? I'm in a bottom cell of Life Now, but you're not in a top cell. You don't know."

"We don't operate through kidnapping," Captain Lewis said, and even through the curtain Amanda heard that there was something wrong with his voice.

"You don't know that, either," Father Emil said.

Lucy said, "You're both losing sight of the main point. Amanda Capelo has to make that broadcast pinning the kidnapping on the government, and she has to do it now. *You* have to persuade her, Emil. You're the only one the little bitch trusts."

"She's not a little bitch, Lucy," Captain Lewis said. "But, Emil, Lucy's right. You have to persuade her, now, as soon as she wakes up."

"And if I can't?"

Captain Lewis said, "Then we've got a huge problem. We can't go on holding her, or we're kidnappers. And we can't release her to Marbet Grant, or Amanda tells the world how we pressured her to pin that kidnapping on Stefanak. Even if she doesn't tell anyone, the Grant woman will read that she's uneasy, that she's hiding something, that she's lying, and will get it out of her. Have you ever known a Sensitive, Emil?"

"No."

"I have. Go wake up Amanda, Emil, and get to work. Be persuasive. Be very persuasive."

Lucy said, "Wait . . . even if Emil does persuade Amanda, and she makes the broadcast, and then later Marbet Grant finds out Emil pressured Amanda . . . that's just as bad for us!"

"No," Captain Lewis said. "If she publicly recants her statement, she's just going to look like a confused kid. It's if she goes on stalwartly refusing to make one at all that she becomes a heroine insisting on 'truth.' "

"Which is what she is doing," Father Emil said. "She is an idealist, unwilling to lie. We should not consider that a sin."

"Oh, fuck sin," Lucy said. "This is practical politics, Emil, not airy-merry abstract religion. She's got to make that broadcast, almost as soon as we wake her up. And she's got to genuinely believe she's doing it voluntarily."

"And if—"

Another voice cut in, a very deep voice Amanda had not heard before. The third man. He had a thick accent. "If she does not, she is a grave liability to the movement. No one knows we have her. She must just disappear."

The other three started talking at once. The man with the deep voice silenced them all. "You are all dilettantes. The life of one child does not outweigh the lives of the thousands of children who will die if Stefanak is not stopped. Do not be so sentimental."

No one spoke until Captain Lewis said, "Salah—" at the same time that Father Emil said, "I will not allow that to happen."

"Nor I," said Captain Lewis. "We are not barbarians, Salah. It's the other side that are barbarians. Remember that!"

Salah said nothing.

Amanda lay rigid, waiting. After a long pause she heard Father Emil get up and leave the area. She knew it was Father Emil because she could hear the faint mutter as he prayed.

FIVE

EN ROUTE TO MARS

The curtain was pulled back. Amanda, pretending to be asleep, felt the wake-up patch laid on her neck and pretended to wake up. Father Emil stood beside her bunk. "Amanda . . ."

She nodded, too scared to say anything.

He looked at her hopelessly, a badly dressed little man with a scraggly beard and wrinkle-rimmed eyes. Then he climbed into the bunk, careful not to touch her, and sat with his back against the bulkhead and his knees pulled up to his chest. Amanda did the same and so they sat side by side, facing the heavy curtain, like bookends with nothing between them. And everything. Father Emil's lips moved soundlessly, and Amanda knew that once again he was praying.

"Amanda," he finally said, "I'm going to ask you once more. I don't want to hound you, or scare you, so this will be the last time you'll hear all this." After a moment he added, "From me, anyway."

She said nothing. Her hands were clasped together tightly. Father Emil was quiet so long she thought maybe he wasn't going to talk to her after all, only to God, but then he began and what he said was a surprise.

"The mission where I work is about saving souls. Getting the wretched to leave their sad and sinful lives and turn back to God. The mission is called the St. Theresa the Little Flower Mission after a saint, a holy woman, named Therese of Lisieux and nicknamed 'The Little Flower.' She wasn't really a woman, she was a little girl. Like you." He stopped.

"Oh," said Amanda, because she had to say something. Although she couldn't see what this Little Flower had to do with anything. And anyway Amanda wasn't a "little girl." She was fourteen.

"The Little Flower's mother died when she was very young, like your mother. When the Little Flower was still a girl, just a few years older than you, her father was taken away, too. At age fifteen she became a nun—"

"What's—"

"A woman who devotes her life to God and never marries. The Little Flower always tried to do the right thing, the thing that would most help others. She wrote a book about her life. I want to quote you two things in it, and I want you to think about both of them."

Father Emil didn't look at her. With his knees drawn up to his chest like that and his scraggly beard, he looked like a child grown horribly old before growing up. She turned her head to stare at the blue curtain.

He said, "The first thing the Little Flower said was, 'I tried very hard to never make excuses.'" He paused briefly, then continued. "The second is longer. It's a prayer that goes like this: 'My Lord and my God, I have realized that whoever undertakes anything for the sake of earthly things or to earn the praise of others deceives himself. Today one thing pleases the world, tomorrow another . . . but You are unchangeable for all eternity.' Do you understand, Amanda?"

"No."

"It means that today people want you to do one thing, tomorrow another thing, but that you should always do the right thing no matter who pressures you, without making any excuses. The right thing is eternal. It's always right."

Facts, Amanda thought. He meant "stick to facts." Father Emil was talking about what Daddy called "scientific integrity."

"I understand."

"Good. Then I'm going to ask you again. Remember that what is fashionable or widely believed today doesn't matter. The eternities matter, like kindness and helping people—the Little Flower devoted her life to helping people—and doing our small bit to stop evil in the world. Since all that is true, will you help stop the war by making this broadcast saying that government agents kidnapped your father?"

"No, Father Emil. I can't."

He said nothing. His lips moved in prayer. Then he drew aside the curtain and climbed down from her bunk.

Amanda waited for what would happen next. Nothing did. She heard no sounds. Finally, frightened, she peeked around the curtain. The common room was empty, and the door to the galley closed. So they were all in there, discussing her. Or else on the bridge, or in the storerooms.

She lay back and closed her eyes. When she opened them, she would be back home. She would be back in her own bedroom, waking up for school. Downstairs Sudie would be racketing around with the holotoons on, and her father would be in the kitchen cooking bacon and grumbling. Her bedroom would smell of bacon, and trees from the open window, and the sharp new smell of her book bag on the floor. She would get up and go to the bathroom and then go downstairs, and Carol would smile good morning, and Sudie would stick out her tongue at her, and Daddy—

She imagined it all, eyes closed, until she fell asleep.

• • •

When she woke, it was ship's night and all the lights were dimmed. Amanda looked at her watch: 0300 hours. She'd slept so much of the day that she woke up in the middle of the night.

No—something had awakened her. Sounds. Someone was in the common room. Someone pulled aside the curtain to her bunk. Salah, with something in his hand.

Amanda screamed. Frantically she scrabbled to the far side of the bunk. Salah cursed and reached for her. She kicked at his hand, and now she could see what was in it: a patch. He was trying to drug her.

"No! No!" She went on screaming, knowing it was hopeless. Her kick hadn't deterred him at all. He was too big and too strong and he'd said to the others, *She must just disappear . . . the life of one child does not outweigh the lives of the thousands . . .* But they had all yelled at him! Father Emil and Captain Lewis and Lucy, they'd all yelled at him and so Amanda had thought she was safe—"No! Get away!"

He grabbed her arm with one huge hand and effortlessly pulled her toward him. She hit him in the face, which seemed to have no effect at all. He was going to *kill her*—

Salah's head rolled off his body.

Blood gushed in a huge fountain from his neck, spattering on the ceiling and soaking Amanda. At the same time, alarms started to shriek and the ship system said loudly, "The hull has been breached. The hull has been breached. The hull—"

In a moment it stopped. The nanocoating extended itself to make a thin, temporary cover over the hole, which was so small Amanda couldn't see it.

"It won't hold!" Father Emil said. He stood there, incredibly, with a laser gun . . . you *never* permitted a laser gun to be used aboard ship! . . . in front of an open storage cabinet. "I don't know how to do a permanent patch—do you?"

Of course she did. Amanda scrambled down from the bunk and yanked open the bright red cupboard found in every chamber aboard every ship. She grabbed the permanent patch and ripped it from its bag, but then slipped on the blood covering the floor. Wildly she grabbed at something, anything. Father Emil caught her and pulled her to her feet. Gagging, she made herself climb back into the bunk. Then she couldn't find the hole.

"The hull has been breached," the ship began again, but not as loudly. "You are advised that a temporary patch must be replaced with permanent sealing. The hull—"

"The hole will be long and thin," Father Emil gasped. "I swung the gun to cut off his head, I didn't know how else to be sure . . ."

"The hull has been breached. You are advised that a temporary patch must be replaced with permanent sealing. The hull has been—"

Amanda found the gash. It now glowed bright red from the temporary nanos, a beacon. It was only the blood that had made it hard to see. She slapped on the patch and the expensive, highly engineered nanos began to fill in the minute breach. Ship stopped nattering.

In the silence, Amanda and Father Emil looked at each other.

"I was hiding in the storage closet," Father Emil said quietly. The violence seemed, strangely, to have steadied him. He had seen so much of it. His calm, in turn, steadied Amanda. "I guessed he would try to kill you and then put your body out the airlock. Once it was actually done, the others wouldn't have turned him in to the cops, because they couldn't have done that without admitting they'd had you. And the problem would be solved."

"Wh-where are the others?"

"Undoubtedly patched out. He would have patched me, too, but he couldn't find me. Salah wasn't a trained killer, just a fanatical believer in his cause. He probably decided I was praying in the cargo hold or something, and that by the time I got back, he'd be finished anyway."

"There's all this blood," Amanda said.

"Don't start crying, Amanda."

"I'm not crying! Do you see me crying? I'm—" What was she? "—disgusted!"

A small smile curved his mouth. "Oh. Then get a scrub brush."

She did, carrying herself on trembling legs into the galley. By the time she returned, Salah's head was gone. His body was wrapped in the heavy, dark blue bunk curtain torn free of its hooks.

Father Emil said, "This is nothing for a child to be doing, Amanda. Go get in the shower. Just don't empty the entire water tank."

In the shower she began to shake. That man had tried to *kill* her! If it weren't for Father Emil . . . oh, she wanted Daddy! She wanted to go home!

She clasped her hands in front of her, water streaming over them, until the shaking stopped.

When she finally left the shower, the common room was spotless. Not only from hand scrubbing but also from cleaner nanos, she guessed, which ate organic molecules and then swiftly died of them. The dead nanos had been sucked up as well. Salah's body was gone. Hidden? Out the airlock? She didn't ask.

Father Emil's eyes looked so tired; Amanda hadn't known eyes could look that tired. He motioned her toward an empty bunk, not the one she'd had before. "Go to bed, Amanda."

"I can't sleep."

"I know. Do it anyway. You're safe now."

Safe? Oddly, she believed him. "Where are we going?"

"Cleopatra Station."

Cleopatra Station orbited Earth, out beyond the Moon. It was a major solar transfer point, as well as a big city in its own right. "I want to go to Mars to find—"

"Go to bed, Amanda! Now!"

Lying in her new bunk, she waited, every muscle tense. She knew what Father Emil would do. She knew from the way he'd said "Go to bed! Now!" And she knew because Daddy would have done the same thing. Father Emil crept in just a few minutes later, and the sleep patch kissed her neck softly.

"Thank you," she whispered. It might not give her a very long sleep, but any sleep was better than none.

"Sleep well," Father Emil said. "You're a brave girl. The bravest and stubbornest and stupidest child I ever met."

She would have answered him, but she was already asleep.

SIX

SPACE TUNNEL #1

The ship *Cascade of Stars* left Mars in July, cleared as a merchant vessel to Titan and an emigration ship from Titan to the remote world of New Canaan. She was a huge ship, chartered to Liu Wang Interplanetary, New China Republic, Earth, although she had never been near Earth and probably never would be. Large enough to carry two flyers and two shuttles, her passenger manifest numbered eight thousand. Six thousand of these were Amish settlers bound for New Canaan, that quixotic attempt to create a non-technological civilization after first arriving on a high-tech starship. The crew was mostly Chinese. The cargo included plows and anvils for New Canaan and a near-AI for the government geological station on Titan.

The other two thousand passengers were a mixed group of business people, techs, scientists, government leaders, adventurers, and the unclassifiable group that travels around the Solar System displaying a polite detachment that never gives away their reasons for journeying. Some of these were crime leaders, some fugitives, some spies.

Ship etiquette demanded that you accept whatever identity a traveler chose to present. This etiquette did not, of course, apply to the government agents aboard who checked passports and itineraries.

Two of the unclassifiables were Lyle Kaufman and Marbet Grant. Lyle traveled under the name "Eric James Peltier," a retired army colonel turned physical-security consultant. Marbet traveled under no name at all, since none of the passengers or government agents knew she was there. Instantly recognizable as the Solar System's most famous Sensitive, she could not travel openly. However, she didn't have to.

The *Cascade of Stars* included two small cabins built off the flyer bay and unknown to most of the ship's officers, including the captain. The security chief had had them built, and rented them out at a fabulous profit shared only with such hand-picked crew as might discover it anyway. The profit provided plenty of funds for necessary operating expenses, such as bribes. No one at Liu Wang knew the vessel had been altered. There were advantages to being chartered in a different place from where you operated.

Marbet, confined to her cabin for the long, tedious journey from Mars to Space Tunnel #1, chose not to spend the time in drugged deep sleep. She had a freestanding terminal, books, some dumbbells, a music cube. Kaufman knew he couldn't have stood it, week after week of solitary living, seeing no one except the steward in the pay of the security chief, who brought her meals. Marbet said it wasn't a problem. She had all the data cubes from their previous expedition, and she was going to learn to speak World. "Last time, you know, I only went down to the planet once, and I had minimal contact with Worlders."

Lyle remembered.

He couldn't communicate with her during the voyage out; those were the rules. He played his part well, participating in shipboard conversation but never becoming personal. Probably most of the other passengers thought he was an important crime figure. Well, let them.

The key conversational pastime wasn't personal, anyway. In the first-class dining room, in the common rooms, in the gym, the game was "Guess Where General Stefanak has hidden the Protector Artifact." This game went on in several languages. It was a safe way to discuss General Stefanak even if there were government spies around; Stefanak himself proclaimed often that the Protector Artifact, activated at "setting prime eleven," was the savior of the Solar System. It protected "each and every one of our precious habitations from the kind of planet-destroying attack that the enemy used to fry the helpless planet of Viridian." The mixture of pompous rhetoric and street slang was pure Stefanak.

The artifact, discovered two years earlier, had been decoded by the brilliant, missing scientist Dr. Thomas Capelo. None of the gossipers aboard the *Cascade of Stars* understood the first thing about the physics that Capelo had worked out, or why the physics mattered. But everyone knew what the artifact's seven settings could do. Thanks to the media, even schoolchildren could recite the litany:

Setting prime one: a directed-beam destabilizer of all atoms with an atomic number higher than seventy-five. (Never mind that to human math "one" was not a prime; humans had not built the artifact.)

Setting prime two: a shield against settings one and three.

Setting prime three: a spherical destabilizing wave affecting all atoms with an atomic number higher than seventy-five.

Setting prime five: a shield to protect a whole planet against the artifact.

Setting prime seven: a wave to destroy a whole planet by destabilizing all atoms with an atomic number higher than fifty.

Setting prime eleven: a shield to protect an entire star system.

Setting prime thirteen: a wave to destroy an entire star system, turning civilizations into radioactive waste.

Now this Protector Artifact had been hidden somewhere in the Solar System by General Stefanak, its location known to no more than a dozen people.

"I'll bet it's in the Belt," said a woman, dazzlingly genemod beautiful, at the English-speaking dinner table. "Has to be. The largest number of floating bodies to hide it in."

"No," said a young man with a beard barbered into an amazing shape Kaufman had never seen before. Ah, the civilian young. "Too much traffic in the Belt. Settlements, trade, miners. No, it's hidden underground on a major planet. Maybe even Mars . . . that way Stefanak can keep a closer eye on it."

"What's to keep an eye on?" lazily said an older woman wearing huge antique emeralds. "It's automatic, isn't it? Set the thing at 'eleven' and it protects the whole Solar System. It isn't like you have to reset it, or get it serviced."

The young man said, "No, but you do have to keep it protected from those fucking antiwar groups. Those bastards would probably just as soon turn it over to the enemy."

"Oh, I don't believe that," said another man, not as well-dressed as the others, who looked at the young man disapprovingly.

The teenage girl traveling with the beautiful woman said, "Why keep it in the Solar System at all? As long as the Fallers believe it's here, the Protector Artifact is doing its job. They won't bring theirs here to attack. Meanwhile, we could take ours to their system and wipe them out."

Her mother said impatiently, "Alva, you don't know what you're talking about. If you bring our artifact to their system and set it off, and theirs is protecting *their* system, it will destroy the whole of spacetime. Dr. Thomas Capelo proved that. Honestly, I don't know what you learn in school!"

"Not that," the girl said hotly, "because it's not true. Both artifacts have to be set to destroy a whole system, at setting prime thirteen. Maybe *you* should study things more carefully."

The shabbily dressed man intervened to avoid war. "That will never happen—setting them both off at thirteen. If one side did, the other would be protected at setting eleven, so why would the second people ever go to thirteen?"

"I agree," said a man who'd been silent 'til now. "It's a nonviable scenario."

Spy, Kaufman thought, *or journalist*. Marbet would have known which from simply looking at the man. But after years attached to the Solar Alliance Defense Council, Kaufman recognized the technique: make a provocative statement, or agree with one, and see who reacts and how.

The young man with the fantastic beard scowled. "It could happen. How about this: We don't bring our artifact to their home system, but to one of their major military systems, and we set it off at thirteen to destroy the whole system. They see us bring the thing in, and try to beat us to the punch by setting *their* artifact off at thirteen to destroy our fleet. So both are broadcasting, or whatever they do, at thirteen, and bam! There goes spacetime."

"But," the young girl, Alva, said, and her whole manner was different debating him than debating her mother, "why would the Fallers have their artifact at a military system instead of protecting their home system, like we do?"

He smiled at her through the pieces of beard. "I don't know. Maybe they're afraid there might be side effects to their people."

The girl said, "Maybe we're afraid of side effects, too. Maybe our artifact isn't even in the Solar System."

"General Stefanak says it is, protecting us."

The spy-or-reporter gave a short bark of laughter. "There are no side effects, young woman."

Alva, flushing an unattractive maroon, turned to him. "How do you know?"

"General Stefanak says so."

"But have the physicists said so? Has Dr. Capelo?"

But this was getting too close to criticism of General Stefanak. The girl's mother said harshly, "Really, Alva, you don't know what you're talking about. Mr. Peltier, you've been in the army. I can tell from the way you carry yourself. Where do you think our general has hidden the Protector Artifact for maximum benefit to us all?"

Kaufman dabbed his lips with his napkin. He had no more idea than anyone else where Stefanak's artifact was. On the other hand, Kaufman had a good idea where the Faller artifact actually was, but that information was highly classified. None of it, however, was his concern any longer. He had retired from the army.

"I think," he said in his calm, authoritative voice, "that the most likely place for General Stefanak to have put the artifact is in the Belt." When challenged, always give the majority answer. It's the least conspicuous.

"I told you so!" the beautiful woman crowed. Her daughter looked close to tears. And why, Kaufman wondered, did such a conspicuously genemod beauty have such a plain daughter? Why hadn't the girl, too, been engineered? Maybe the mother had been afraid of competition. People were endlessly perverse.

"Wherever it is," the shabby man said, "it's Stefanak's trump card. As long as he has control of it, no one will dare remove him from power."

"Oh, I don't know," said the older woman, "there are a lot of crazies out there. What if some terrorist group, people even crazier than the antiwar people, found and seized the Protector Artifact? They could destroy the Fallers on their own say-so. In fact, they could destroy the Solar System, or threaten to do it, for ransom."

Alva, despite her sulky tearfulness, had been studying the woman.

Now she said abruptly, "I recognize you. You write holo thrillers! You're Ruth Pomeroy!"

The older woman smiled modestly, and the conversation swerved to holo thrillers, writing, and actors, none of whom Kaufman had ever heard until the bearded youngster said, "Do you know what I heard? Just last month, Magdalena was a passenger on this very ship."

"She was!" said Ruth Pomeroy. "Now there's a woman I'd like to write a thriller about."

"Well, if you wanted someone in your thriller to murder Magdalena," said the man who was either a journalist or a spy, "you wouldn't have any shortage of suspects. She has more enemies than General Stefanak."

"Whom," Ruth Pomeroy said daintily, "I understand she knows extremely well."

"Oh, surely not anymore," protested the beauty with the emeralds. "The woman must be at least sixty. And looks it."

"No, she doesn't," the bearded man said. "That body!"

"Who's Magdalena?" blurted Alva.

The journalist/spy laughed. " '*Sic transit gloria mundi.*' "

Alva's mother said primly, "Magdalena is no one you need to know about."

Deliberately the girl turned to the bearded man. "Who is she, please?"

He wasn't impressed by maternal dictates. "Magdalena started as a porn star, way before your time. They say she was born in a slum and clawed her way out. She was unbelievably sexy. But she stopped making holos a long time ago."

"And became even more notorious than in her holo days," said Journalist/Spy. "Not a model for a good life, young lady. Magdalena married into Stefanak's government, a man who was eventually executed for treason. But she never even stood trial. She inherited her husband's fortune and spent her time both investing the money and cozying up to whoever had power. When the war started, she got even richer off black-market military supplies. Maybe you know something about that, Colonel Peltier."

"Not my area, I'm afraid," Kaufman said, although he did indeed know something about it. He'd never actually seen Magdalena's porn holos, nor learned much about her earlier marriages and money deals. But in the current world of wartime government contracts, covert intelligence, corporate collusion, space-travel control, and military theft, Magdalena was a major force. No one knew how much of her reputation was truth and how much titillating exaggeration. The only verifiable truth was that Magdalena—the single name was all she used—constantly grew richer, more powerful, more dangerous.

Alva said wistfully, "Was she really so beautiful?"

"Yes," rhapsodized the bearded youth, who had obviously not yet learned to avoid dwelling on one woman's looks to another woman. "Black hair, huge blue eyes, the face of an angel. And that body—you've never seen such breasts or such a—"

"That will do," Ruth Pomeroy said coldly. "Genetic combinations can certainly bring strange results." Pointedly she turned the conversation back to General Stefanak and the artifact.

Kaufman sat eating his excellent dinner and considering what had been said. None of it was new to him, of course. Stefanak himself had told Kaufman, the only time they'd met, what he intended. Actually, he had told Tom Capelo.

"What are you going to do with my artifact?"

Stefanak had smiled at the pronoun, which Kaufman knew had been deliberate on Capelo's part, but hadn't commented on it. "We're going to take it to the Solar System, install it somewhere secure and classified, and activate setting prime eleven, thereby protecting all of the Solar System from Faller attack."

"I see. So you won't take it to the Faller system, activate it at setting prime thirteen, and fry their entire home system?"

"You've told us that's not possible without disastrously affecting the fabric of spacetime itself."

"What if I'm wrong?"

"We hope you'll continue to refine your theory, becoming more sure."

"What if I'm wrong about what setting prime eleven does?"

"Same answer," Stefanak had said.

Had Tom Capelo continued to "refine his theory"? Was that what had gotten him kidnapped: some new aspect of his revolutionary physics model that carried implications Stefanak hadn't liked? Stefanak had greeted Capelo by cheerfully saying he hadn't understood a single thing about Capelo's hypothetical probability force. But, then, there were only about a dozen people in the Solar System who did understand it.

"You look very thoughtful, Mr. Peltier," the genemod beauty said flirtatiously. "May the rest of us know your thoughts?"

"I'm thinking of what they might bring us for dessert," Kaufman said. "I hope it's better than that cream cake at lunch."

The *Cascade of Stars* was cleared without incident to go through Space Tunnel #1. Passports were checked, cargo inspected, data filed by the Martian Space Tunnel Administration. The administration had done all this during the stop at Titan, and now it did it all over again. The administration kept close control of the tunnels. They were the reason Mars now ruled the Solar System. Mars had gotten to them first.

The space tunnels had been discovered sixty years ago. A flexible, mappable network of wormholes, they made the galaxy into a giant instantaneous bus system. All you had to do was get your bus to the nearest tunnel, drive it through, and you emerged at another station at the edge of another star system. Double back through the same tunnel and you emerged at your place of origin—unless it was your craft's first time through a tunnel. Then you emerged in the same place as the directly previous craft. The bus system could reroute its vehicles.

Some systems had three or even four tunnels in orbit around them, although Sol had only one. Evidently whatever long-vanished race had constructed the tunnels had not considered Sol an important nexus.

The discovery of Space Tunnel #1 had rocked the struggling solar civilization. New disciplines sprang up: xenobiology, interstellar treasure hunting, holomovies shot under pink or yellow skies. Serious thinkers pointed out that humankind was scarcely ready to colonize the stars, having solved none of its problems at home. Nobody listened. The rich flourished on the new investments; the poor remained poor; Earth went on lurching from one ecological tragedy to another. Everything was the same, and nothing was.

The first years were filled with triumphs and disasters. Experimentation proved that a ship—or any other object—put through a space tunnel for the first time went to wherever the directly previous ship had gone. A ship that had gone through a tunnel and then went through it from the other side was automatically returned to its starting point, no matter how many other ships had used the tunnel in the meantime. Somehow—that most operative word in human understanding of tunnel technology—the tunnel "remembered" where each individual ship had entered tunnel space. It was an interstellar "Chutes and Ladders" composed of all chutes.

After fifty-six years, science still knew almost nothing about how space tunnels actually worked. Not even the work of Dr. Thomas Capelo had helped much. The physical objects, panels floating in space in the general shape of a doughnut, were completely impenetrable. The science was too alien. The best guess was that the panels created a field of macro-level object entanglement, analogous to the quantum entanglement that permitted one particle to affect its paired counterpart regardless of distance, thus eliminating any spatial dimension to the universe by treating it as a single point. But this was merely a guess. Achieving entanglement for an object the size of a warship—let alone *controlling* the phenomenon—seemed unthinkable. Yet there the tunnels were.

The *Cascade of Stars* waited until the Space Tunnel #1 configuration was changed to open on Herndon System, which was accomplished by sending a flyer back from Herndon toward Sol. Several other ships waited in line as well. When it was her turn, the *Cascade of Stars* maneuvered into the tunnel. First-time tunnelers gathered on the observation deck, but there was nothing to feel, and not much to see. The stars of the Solar System, the odd floating panels of the tunnel on all sides, and then the stars of Herndon System. Disappointment was audible: hmmnnnnnn.

A few hours were enough to traverse Herndon System space from Tunnel #1 to Tunnel #32. Again, Mars Administration checked passports and cargo, but much more cursorily. Four systems later, in orbit around Tunnel #389, administration was still checking, even though no one but Amish colonists was going down to New Canaan, and no one at all was coming back up.

It would take the *Cascade of Stars's* shuttles several days to land six thousand Amish. Nearly all the other passengers had disembarked in earlier systems. Kaufman passed only anxious, black-clad people laden with bundles on his way to the vehicle bay.

The security chief had arranged the timing. Only his people were present. Marbet was packed. She and Kaufman climbed into one of the two flyers, which would be reported to Berrington Corporation as lost due to mechanical failure. The craft had been extensively, expensively rebuilt. Somewhere between a flyer and a shuttle, it performed as well as neither one. But it could go, more slowly than a flyer, through space, and it could land, more roughly than a shuttle, on the surface of a planet. It had cost Marbet a price that made even her blink.

"You sure you can fly this thing?" she said lightly to Kaufman.

"Since cadet training. Are you glad to be freed from solitary confinement?"

"Yes and no. It was very peaceful, Lyle. Although I missed you."

"Can you speak fluent World yet?"

"We'll find out." She smiled, and he pushed down his misgivings and flew away from the *Cascade of Stars*.

New Canaan System had two tunnels. Kaufman flew through the other one, which gave onto Caligula System. This was a remote military base, one tunnel away from World. Kaufman's flyer was hailed as soon as it emerged from the tunnel.

"Identification," the patrol ship said. Kaufman noted its prominent weapons.

"Flight #6754B, civilian, from Mars via posted tunnel route. Aboard: Colonel Eric James Peltier, SADA, retired, and Ms. Ellen Fineman, citizen. Husband and wife. Citizen numbers to follow." Eric James Peltier and his wife Ellen Fineman were very recently dead in the South American Hegemony, which had the faultiest reporting of any member of the Solar Alliance Defense Council. Especially now. General Stefanak was not popular in the Hegemony. Kaufman had no passport for Ellen/Marbet, but this far out from Sol, military usually relied more on verified forwarded flight approvals than on individual civilian passports. Kaufman held his breath.

Silence. Then a voice said on the comlink, "Your flight is filed, Colonel Peltier. However, orders are no flights to World System. I don't know how you got approved this far."

Money. "I don't understand! We have approvals!"

"Please wait, Colonel, while I check this. What is the purpose of your mission?"

"Personal. My wife is a cousin to Dr. Ann Sikorski, left on the planet World during the last approved scientific mission." Effective lies stay as close to the truth as possible.

"Checking . . ."

"Soldier, is the World System proscribed?" Kaufman said.

"No."

"And are all approvals in order?"

"Yes, sir," the voice said, in automatic response to the authority in Kaufman's voice.

"Then I don't see the difficulty."

"My orders are to let no ship through this tunnel."

He wasn't going to budge. Kaufman went to his second tactic. "Please refer my request to your commanding officer."

"Yes, sir."

Kaufman turned off the comlink. "Get comfortable, Marbet. We're going to be here for some time."

"I don't understand. Why don't they want anyone in the World System? There's nothing left there. We took it all."

"I don't know. But I'm hoping they would rather let us go through than turn us back and have us start asking inconvenient questions on Mars."

It didn't take as long as Kaufman expected. In less than an hour, a tiny flyer left the patrol ship and zoomed into the tunnel.

"What is it, Lyle? Why are you so surprised?"

He still wasn't totally used to her ability to read his thoughts from the body language he didn't know he was using. He said, "They're checking with someone on the other side of the tunnel. I didn't know anybody was there . . . oh, Christ. I hope they're not going to comlink down to World to raise Ann in order to check our story. Ellen Fineman was most certainly not her cousin."

They waited, Kaufman rehearsing contingency plans if they were identified. God, it would be a mess. . . . But then the flyer returned through the tunnel in a half hour and he relaxed. "They weren't talking to Ann, the time lag from the tunnel to World is fifty-four minutes. But, then, who were they talking to on the other side?"

"Colonel Peltier, you are cleared for tunnel passage."

Marbet reached for his hand. He squeezed it, then turned on the flyer's engine.

To Kaufman's surprise, the *Murasaki* orbited on the other side of the tunnel. That was same warship that had been there nearly three years ago. But then it had been guarding the system that held the alien artifact and Dr. Thomas Capelo's attempts to decode it. What was the *Murasaki* guarding now? There was nothing here. To keep a warship off duty for three years during a war which humans were losing . . . it didn't make sense.

"What's the *Murasaki* doing here?" Marbet asked.

"I don't know. But if McChesney's still in charge, he'll recognize us. Oh, hell . . ."

"This is the *Murasaki*," said the comlink. "You are cleared to proceed directly to the planet World. Verify your destination."

"The planet World," Kaufman said, trying to disguise his voice. He wasn't very good at this. But the *Murasaki* said, "Proceed. Good luck."

"Thanks," Kaufman said, and kicked the flyer into acceleration. They were going to World.

SEVEN

LOWELL CITY, MARS

When Amanda Capelo finally woke up, it wasn't at the place she expected to waken, Cleopatra Station. Someone had kept her in deep sleep — *not* the sleeper-patch kind! — for the whole long trip to Mars. The ship, a different and larger one, had just landed at Lowell Spaceport.

"You can't do that without telling me! It isn't fair!" she cried to Father Emil, who stood beside her bunk.

"They did it. Get up, Amanda, you have two hours to get your legs back. The drugs are already in your system. Get up."

"Two hours 'til what?" She sat up too quickly, unused to the lighter gravity. She'd experienced deep sleep before, for part of the long trip from Mars to Space Tunnel #1 with Daddy. When you woke up, you needed to do physical therapy, and you still didn't feel right for about a week. Amanda hated it. They had no *right* —

Her hair didn't touch her shoulders.

When she sat up, it didn't swing forward, but it wasn't tied back or up. She groped with one trembling hand at her head, pulled forward a tress. Short! And black, not blonde!

"What did you do to my hair?"

"Cut and dyed. Don't waste time on trifles. Get—"

"My hair!" she wailed. "My hair! My hair!" Father Emil stared at her, dumbfounded. Finally he spoke.

"You can be almost murdered—*twice*—can assist at a murder, can hold out against an entire adult organization . . . and you break down over a haircut?"

"My h-h-hair!"

"Get up! Now!"

She did, to peer into a shiny bulkhead. A poor enough mirror, it still showed an alien: a girl with short black hair and bangs. Dressed in some dark blue coverall.

"Amanda," Father Emil said, with great forced patience, "stop that. Now. We're on Mars. Get up and follow the phys-therapy holo instructions before I put you under again."

Actually, she looked older with her hair cut. Alien, but older. And a little bit exotic, like Yaeko. And they had brought her to Mars, where Marbet Grant was. Soon she would see Marbet. She put up a hand to smooth the black bob.

The holovid turned itself on. Painfully Amanda grasped the bar beside her deep-sleep bunk and began the first muscle-restoring exercise. Father Emil left before she could ask him any more questions.

He came back when she'd finished the holovid and sat panting on the edge of her bunk. Everything in her body hurt. Father Emil carried a tray of food. Famished, Amanda fell on it. She'd probably lost weight, that was a good thing. In deep sleep, fed through tubes, you always lost weight. Amanda wanted to become as slender as Marbet.

On the other hand, Father Emil had also lost weight, which was not a good thing. His wrist bones stuck out. His cheeks looked like chisels. He looked sick.

The exercise and food restored her thinking. "Has anyone found my father?" She held her breath; he might say they'd found Daddy's body, or that Daddy was free again, or —

"No, child. He's still missing, and the government is still blaming Life Now. There have been riots, protests. Most of the membership has gone underground."

She refused to answer this. "Were you in deep sleep, too, Father Emil?"

"No."

So he looked like that even without tube feeding. "Are you taking me to Marbet as soon as I get my legs back?"

"Amanda, Marbet Grant isn't on Mars."

She stopped with fork suspended in the air. "She has to be!"

"Because you want her to be? Doesn't work like that, child."

"But you said she was here! Where is she?"

"She disappeared. No, not kidnapped. She and Lyle Kaufman left Mars together months ago, just after we left Earth. Apparently they'd spent months making application to the State Department for permission to travel to World. All the applications were denied because of wartime travel restrictions. The best guess is that they found a way to get there illegally."

"How could —"

"Oh, don't be naive, child. We did it. Do you suppose anybody but Life Now knows you're on Mars? You're an illegal now."

Amanda pushed back the tray. Suddenly she wasn't hungry anymore.

"An illegal, and the same problem you were before. Amanda, if anyone knows you're here now, Life Now will get the blame for kidnapping you. Just like we told you three months ago."

Three months ago? She'd been en route to Mars for three months. It was —

In a small voice she said, "What date is it, Father Emil?"

"July third. The month of Our Lady."

It meant nothing to her.

"If Life Now is accused of kidnapping you with the solid proof that you've been with us, as opposed to merely speculative accusations, people will die. I want you to remember that."

"Where am I going?" she asked. Her stomach felt sick. "Oh, please, can I go to Aunt Kristen? She lives in Tharsis, right here on Mars, I could—"

"I don't know where the organization is going to put you. It's out of my hands. Our instructions, Dennis's and Lucy's and mine, were simply to bring you to Mars and turn you over to the Life Now top cell. They'll know what's best for everyone concerned."

Amanda stared. "You're . . . you're not going to take care of me anymore?" *Protect me?*

"I'm going to take you to a place where you'll be met by the Life Now leaders. They'll know what's best for everyone concerned," he repeated, and didn't meet her eyes.

Something was wrong. Father Emil didn't sound like himself. Fear rippled through Amanda.

"Come on, child. The car is here."

She followed him through the ship, because she couldn't think what else to do. They didn't see a single other person. *I can run*, she thought desperately. Ships had exit ramps, and cars had to wait at the bottom of them, and there would be a few seconds in the open air when she could scream and run and shout out her name . . . Lowell Spaceport was a busy and crowded place. She'd been there, on visits to Aunt Kristen. Someone would hear her, maybe even recognize her despite the short black hair . . . She must have been in all the news holo, like Daddy was. Someone would see . . .

The "car" was a closed nuclear-energy transport that waited in the ship's sealed cargo bay.

"No," Amanda said. "I'm not getting in it."

"Then we—I—will drug you," Father Emil said.

Then why hadn't they done that already? Carried her still asleep from her bunk to the car . . . If they were going to kill her, they'd have done it already. So they weren't going to kill her. It must be all right. Father Emil wouldn't kill her. He'd stopped Salah from doing that!

Father Emil wouldn't kill her. But after he'd given her to these "leaders," they might. And Father Emil would never know, not for sure. That would be his excuse to himself.

"They're going to kill me!" she cried. "To 'solve the problem!' After you leave me there with them!"

"Nonsense, Amanda. They wouldn't do that."

"You and Lucy and Captain Lewis wouldn't. But Salah would, and what if the leaders are more like him than like you?" *"She must just disappear . . . the life of one child does not outweigh the lives of the thousands . . ."*

"Nonsense," Father Emil repeated, and didn't meet her eyes, and it was all very, very wrong.

She bolted, running toward a pile of strapped-in crates at the far end of the cargo bay. He caught her easily. She struggled, but even though Father Emil looked sick he was *strong*, and within a minute, straps bound her. She threw herself on the ground and kicked at him, and he fought to get straps around her ankles, too. His face was gray and purple veins stood out around his nose.

"No, no, help!" she screamed, but there was no one inside the cargo bay. He got her into the lead-shielded car.

"Vehicle, go. Cargo bay doors, open," he gasped.

Prerouted programming. Open comlinks with the outside. Amanda started screaming. Maybe the comlinks were two-way and somebody, anybody, would hear her on the other end.

No one responded. The car glided forward. Amanda screamed until she was hoarse.

She lay on the floor, Father Emil facing her on a small metal seat.

His lips moved continuously in prayer. She jerked violently to try to kick him, and he leaned forward as if to move her. He slipped a piece of paper into her coverall pocket. His eyes said, *Don't say anything, don't say anything, don't say anything.*

She stopped screaming, panted hard, and watched him. He went on soundlessly praying.

She felt the car stop and guessed they were at one of Lowell City's airlocks. Usually all passengers' identities were checked at this point—wouldn't someone come to open the car? Amanda wasn't even sure whether she still had her "Jane Verghese" passport. Surely someone would check the car . . .

No one did. Life Now must have found a way to cheat. The car started again and rolled on. That at least told Amanda something: Cars were only permitted in one of Lowell City's three great domes, the one filled with factories and warehouses. East Sector. That's where she must be.

Every few seconds Father Emil glanced at his watch. Finally he said, "Vehicle, stop. Override programming. Password 'Ghandi.'" The car stopped. "Vehicle, open door." It did.

In one swift moment he had freed her from the straps. "Amanda, run! Go with God, child—" He pushed her out the door.

She didn't completely have her legs back yet. She stumbled, fell. Father Emil watched her from the vehicle, which had erupted into sound from the comlink: "—*traitor*, afraid you couldn't be trusted—" They had been monitored.

She was in a temporarily deserted street between two windowless buildings. No street on Mars was ever deserted for long. Amanda staggered to her feet and tried to run, but her legs would only lurch forward in an uneven gait that made her afraid of falling. Father Emil stepped out of the car, finally meeting her eyes. He said, "Run! You've got a little time before they can get here, but I don't know how much—" His eyes widened.

Amanda turned to follow his gaze. A woman strode out of the building beside them, walking purposefully forward. She carried a gun.

Instantly, it later seemed to Amanda, Father Emil was standing between her and the advancing woman. He held something in his hand. The woman fired. There was no sound, but Father Emil toppled over. The woman did, too. Someone else, a passerby who had just rounded the corner, screamed.

The scream brought other people. Suddenly the narrow street was jammed with people. Someone pulled Amanda back, to what he must have imagined was safety. He jabbered at her in a language she couldn't understand. More people came running. A cop suddenly appeared, and then two soldiers in the uniforms of the Solar Alliance Defense Army. There were shouts and questions. From nowhere a robocam from Martian Transglobal News buzzed in.

Amanda slipped to the edge of the crowd, then down another street. No one noticed her. She tried to walk naturally, despite her space legs, despite her panic. Father Emil was dead. Father Emil was dead. Father Emil was dead.

He'd died helping her get away.

She'd seen the thing in his hand. Would the soldiers recognize it? She didn't know. But she recognized it. She'd seen it before, and she'd been terrified then, too. Maybe terror made you remember things. What had been in Father Emil's hand was a weapon, one of the many that had studded the sides of the Wrath of God, protector of the St. Theresa the Little Flower Mission.

She walked until she couldn't stand up anymore. By moving always in the direction with most people, she eventually reached the clear walk-tunnel to Lowell City's huge main dome. The tunnel, too, was made of clear piezoelectric plastic, broad enough to be open to trucks as far as the Main Sector. Amanda sank to the floor to rest.

She pulled out the paper Father Emil had put in her coverall pocket. It was folded around something hard. The paper was hand-written:

> *Go to the Ares Abbey at Rho Street 8451. Ask for Brother Meissel. Give him this letter. Take a sled, ten percies anywhere under the main dome. 'My Lord and my God, I have realized that whoever undertakes anything for the sake of earthly things or to earn the praise of others deceives himself . . . but You are unchangeable for all eternity.'*

Inside were a ten-percy coin and another letter.

Amanda folded it back up. *My Lord and my God* . . . She still thought Father Emil was a lunatic. But he had gotten himself killed for her. And despite his note, he belonged to an organization that undertook "earthly things." It was all very confusing. She was tired of being confused, and afraid, and hunted. She was tired.

Nonetheless, she made herself stand and trudge through the tunnel. Above the roof, the Martian sky shimmered with pink dust. On many walls were large holoposters of General Stefanak, and soldiers thronged the main streets. Flatbed trucks carrying goods from the industrial East Sector to the main dome passed her, but only very gradually. Everything in Lowell City moved slowly.

The city consisted of three domes, each anchored to a circling concrete wall one and a half meters high that anchored the struts shaping the domes. The main dome enclosed about twenty square miles; each of the other two were about half that. In Main Sector a slender tower soared along the high central strut. Called "the Summit," it housed the Solar Alliance Defense Council. General Stefanak's office occupied the top floor, commanding Mars.

Where the tunnel met the main dome, the trucks stopped. Robots transferred goods to the much smaller sleds, the only transport permitted in Main Sector except for military vehicles. The sleds came in two varieties: flat or with four open seats. Amanda called one of the latter by the number printed on its side, and it rolled up to her on the flat, computer-controlled tracks that squiggled over the entire city.

"Rho Street Eight-four-five-one," she told it, depositing her ten-percy in the slot. Most people used credit, of course, but the percies remained in circulation. They were untraceable.

"Rho Street Eight-four-five-one," the sled repeated and rolled off. It had no sides or top, and Amanda sat with her newly short hair falling forward to hide her face as much as possible. But no one paid her any attention.

The sled had a small audio terminal mounted on the front with a limited selection of channels. Amanda touched NEWS.

"—latest unprovoked attack by subversive organizations trying to bring down the government. Killed was a Catholic priest identified as Emil Fulden and a Martian citizen identified as Maria Greta Silverstein. Government sources speculate that the killing was occasioned by General Stefanak's planned rally at Kepler Park this evening, and that—" Amanda stopped listening.

They had it all wrong. Everybody had everything all wrong. All her life, she'd thought that adults knew what they were doing, knew how things really were. All her life.

She wouldn't cry. Amanda Capelo did not cry.

It took all her remaining strength to get off the sled at Rho Street 8451. It was a windowless building made of foamcast, like most of Lowell City, with a red door. A metal plaque said in small letters: ARES ABBEY OF THE BENEDICTINE BROTHERS.

Amanda spoke to the door. "I'm here to see Brother Meissel, please. Father Emil told me to come here."

No house system answered.

She repeated her message, adding, "My name is Jane Verghese." She'd found the fake passport in an inner pocket of her coverall. Father Emil must have put it there.

Father Emil, lying in his own blood in the Martian street . . .

"Let me in!" Amanda told the door. Still no response. People pushed by her. Lowell City, like all Martian domes, crowded everything and everybody close together.

Now she spied a second, smaller plaque to the right of the door. It read PLEASE KNOCK in several languages. This place, whatever it was, didn't even have a *house system*. What had Father Emil sent her to?

Wearily Amanda banged her knuckles on the door. She had to do it twice before anyone opened.

"Brother Meissel, please, I—"

"Why do you wish to see Brother Meisel?" the man said. Amanda looked closer. It was a boy, not a man, just a few years older than she. He wore a weird, long robe of rough brown cloth. Silently Amanda handed him the letter. Then, not caring that it was rude, she pushed past him into a small stone-floored anteroom where she'd glimpsed a stone bench carved of red Martian rock. Gratefully Amanda sank down on it. The boy closed the heavy abbey door and disappeared.

After a while—she couldn't tell how long, time seemed strangely distorted—a man appeared, holding the letter. He wore the same brown thing as the boy. His voice was deep and calm.

"Hello, Amanda. I'm Brother Meissel. You're safe here with us, just as Emil said."

"He's dead," Amanda said.

"He's gone to join our Lord Christ," Brother Meissel said quietly. "God rest his valiant soul. Now come with me, Amanda. You are safe, you know. No one will find you here."

Amanda didn't believe it. But she rose and staggered after Brother Meissel, because she didn't know what else to do. Uncle Martin and Aunt Kristen were on Mars, but in Tharsis, half a planet away. Amanda had no way to get to Tharsis. Anyway, Father Emil had told her to stay at the abbey because she would be safe there. Maybe this time someone was telling her the truth.

EIGHT

WORLD

From the sky, the planet looked just the same.

Hurtling down through the atmosphere, Kaufman watched the single, equator-spanning continent grow larger and larger. Now he saw its lush foliage, sparkling lakes and seas, occasional mountains. Closer, and the amazing kaleidoscope of colors appeared: World was alive with flowers, cultivated and wild, growing in huge fields and tiny plots, crimson and cobalt and rose and lemon and colors Kaufman couldn't name but Worlders all could. Closer still and the pattern of scattered villages, neat fields, white-dust roads appeared. All unchanged. Then they were down, in the old landing place between the Neury Mountains and the village of Gofkit Jemloe.

Kaufman said into the silence, "I never thought I'd see this place again."

"Nor I," Marbet said.

"Shared reality," Kaufman said, and the joke was so sad, so sour, that Marbet didn't reply.

He added, "Do you think there's anything left?"

"Of course there's something left. Just not what there was before. Human beings are very resilient, Lyle."

"These weren't human beings."

"Close enough," Marbet said, but she didn't really know. She'd met only a few Worlders, very briefly. Kaufman hadn't met a lot of them, either, and he was not as intuitive as Marbet (no one was), but he had seen "shared reality" in action. He'd witnessed the blithe assumption that two Worlders' conception of a situation was the same. The sharp head pain when it wasn't, a head pain that Ann Sikorski had demonstrated was hard-wired into Worlders' brains, the result of millennia of evolution in the presence of the buried alien artifact in the Neury Mountains.

That same artifact that Kaufman had removed, giving it to General Stefanak. With it had gone the culture of World: the shared assumptions physiologically enforced, the impossibility of any premeditated violence, the elaborate social structures for working and mating and sharing, all based on not being able to feel differently from everyone else around you. All gone, because of him.

He could have recited by rote Ann Sikorski's last known message:

This is the final report of the World anthropological team. Not that I think my report makes any difference to you. The natives of World are surviving, although not without tremendous strain and uncounted casualties. The infrastructure of communication and trade and centralized governance is all gone. There is some looting and rioting, probably not as much as if they were human. They're starting to defend themselves by turning the villages into small forts, with stockades and local justice. The planet-wide civilization is gone along with the biological basis that gave rise to it, thanks to you. What's taking its place is frontier isolation, eco-

nomically possible without starvation only because this is such a fertile planet. In that isolation most non-practical art will disappear. So will much of the manufacturing that depended on wide trade to sustain it, and the easy exchange of ideas. Religion is bound to fragment. Within a generation, World will be made up of very small pre-Renaissance enclaves, and their own version of the Dark Ages will begin. But don't worry your conscience, Lyle— they're surviving. End of report by the Planet World team, Ann Pek Sikorski, biologist, and Dieter Pek Gruber, geologist."

"Stop it, Lyle," Marbet said. "It was not your fault. And I'm getting tired of saying that to you. See if you can raise Ann."

He opened the link. All the human comsats still orbited World; they would orbit it for hundreds of years. The natives had been given nine comlinks, in trade. But only Ann Sikorski or Dieter Gruber would answer this frequency. Kaufman let the comlink shrill for a full minute. No one answered.

He recorded a message: "Ann, Dieter, if you can hear me, please answer. This is Lyle Kaufman. This is a real-time link; Marbet Grant and I are on World. Please answer."

Marbet said gently, "Let's start toward the village, Lyle. They may know where Ann and Dieter are."

They hadn't even armed themselves when Kaufman's comlink shrilled. He answered it, "Hello? Ann?"

"It is Dieter!" a joyous voice called.

Two years fell away and Kaufman was back in the Neury Mountains, listening to Dieter Gruber and Tom Capelo argue about mental effects of the buried artifact. Dieter Gruber, cheerful, insensitive, a huge blond hulk engineered according to somebody's ludicrously exaggerated idea of a Teutonic prince. Dieter, without whom the Protector Artifact would have stayed buried in the submontane cavern where it had lain for fifty thousand years.

"Ach, Lyle, is that really you? You are back? Ann, Ann, come quick, it is Lyle!"

So Ann Sikorski was still alive, too. Thanksgiving flooded Kaufman. One more death off his conscience.

"Lyle?" Ann's voice, quieter than her husband's, and infinitely more steely. Ann the idealist, who had stayed behind in the civilization humans had ruined.

"Yes, it's me. And Marbet, too. We're at the old landing site near Gofkit Jemloe. Are you in the village? Or at Hadjil Voratur's?"

"No," Ann said quickly. "Don't go either place. We're in a different village, half a day's walk from you. But you can't . . . Do you have a surface craft?"

"No. Only a misbegotten cross between a flyer and a shuttle. It won't make surface hops."

"Then don't move. Dieter will come to you."

"Come to me? But why—"

"I said *don't move*." The link went dead.

Marbet studied his face. She said, "They think it's too dangerous for us to be out there by ourselves."

He didn't answer. Travel on World had always been open, easy, safe. In a monolithic culture in which any act of violence would hurt the perpetuator almost as much as the victim, violence had been rare. Before.

They went back inside the flyer/shuttle, Kaufman feeling something between ridiculous and scornful. He had been a soldier, with combat experience. Marbet and he had the latest personal weapons available to civilians. And Ann Sikorski wanted him to wait before facing a hypothetical mob of short aliens with no history of warfare and a technology level stuck at hand-forged bicycle wheels. His mood, usually calm, blackened. Marbet left him alone.

They left the door open, sat, and waited. Eventually a smear appeared on the horizon, moving very fast. It grew into Dieter Gruber on a motorized bicycle. He raced up to them and threw himself off the bike, enveloping each of them in a huge bearish hug. "*Lieber Gott!* You are really here!"

"Yes," Kaufman said, disentangling himself from Gruber. Kaufman was not a hugger. "And more to the point, so are you. You are well? And Ann?"

"I am very well. Marbet, beautiful as ever! But why do you come? Is there another scientific expedition?"

"No," Kaufman said, "no expedition."

"We came to rescue you," Marbet said mischievously. She had received Gruber's hug with pleasure, and her glance at Kaufman said that the exuberant Gruber, bursting with health, obviously did not need rescuing. "But why wouldn't you let us come to Gofkit Jemloe?"

Gruber instantly sobered. "We are not in Gofkit Jemloe. Hadjil Voratur . . . it is not good."

"Tell me," Kaufman said. Here it came: What he had done to this planet.

"Hadjil Voratur and his son Shosaf are dead. Killed by marauders, during the time after shared reality went away. They would not believe when we told them not to try . . . anyway. Gofkit Jemloe is an armed camp, under a cousin of Voratur's, a very dangerous person. Febin Frillandif. He has recruited an army . . . Worlders were peaceful, you remember."

As if Kaufman could forget.

"Peaceful, yes, but they are human. Well, no. But when everything changed, those scum who had been controlled by shared reality were controlled no longer. Frillandif is subduing all the villages around, one by one. He is building an 'empire.' "

Like Stefanak. Kaufman said, "And you and Ann and Enli?"

"We are in Enli's village, Gofkit Shamloe. They have tried to attack, but Ann and I brought with us some weapons they of course had never seen . . . and you have brought more."

"Yes," Kaufman said. Two years . . . Gruber's weapons must have been either extensive or well hoarded. Or else the local warlord had only tried attacking once. "Couldn't you just take him out?"

"Yes. But Ann will not let me." After a moment Gruber added, "Although you, Lyle, could do it with the ship."

Kaufman could. Fly over, hit Gofkit Jemloe with a proton beam . . . No, he could not. The village, if not the household, must be full of civilians, children. Ann was right. These people would have to work out their own means of dealing with the despots they had never had before. If there was one warlord, there would be others.

Marbet, watching Kaufman, said to Gruber, "You didn't want us to travel to you because of these marauders."

Gruber looked surprised. "No. I know Lyle can take care of himself. It was for another reason. I wanted to warn you, give you time to prepare yourself."

"For what?" Marbet said.

"There is another Terran here," Gruber said, and even through his surprise Kaufman noted that Gruber used the Worlder word for humans. "She is . . . *Scheisse*, here they come! There is no escaping the woman!"

Another vehicle raced toward them, so fast that Kaufman barely identified it before it was on them. A skimmer, jet-powered, flying an even two feet above the terrain. A huge skimmer, heavily armored, not quite military but the closest civilian analogue that Lyle had ever seen. It jerked to a halt and the door flung open. Out stepped a woman, furious.

Marbet made a small sound, but Kaufman didn't even hear her. *Not possible.* But there was no mistaking her, not that body nor that incredible, ruined face . . .

"Marbet Grant," Magdalena said, "at last. A long way to go to track you down. So tell me, since you seem to be the only one who knows . . .

"Where the hell is Amanda Capelo?"

• • •

Kaufman looked from Marbet to Magdalena, and back again. Marbet looked like nothing so much as a riled cat; if she had had fur, it would all be standing up. Magdalena repeated her outrageous question. "Ms. Grant, what have you done with Amanda Capelo?"

"I haven't done anything with Amanda Capelo!" Marbet spat. Kaufman had never seen her this way: agitated, unsure. "I don't even know what you're talking about!"

Kaufman said swiftly, "I didn't get a chance to tell you, Marbet. Amanda was kidnapped along with Tom. The press didn't discover that until twenty-four hours later, and you were already sequestered aboard ship, so I . . ." At the look she threw him, Kaufman trailed off.

"And you've had no chance to tell me since, Lyle?"

He said nothing. Tom Capelo's children had never greatly interested Kaufman; he didn't much like children. During the weeks aboard the *Cascade of Stars*, he had genuinely forgotten about Amanda. Marbet would not have wanted to hear that.

"I see," she said coldly; no point in not telling Marbet something. His minute shifts of body language gave him away. Marbet turned to Magdalena. "Tell me what happened."

Magdalena actually seemed amused at whatever she thought was happening between Kaufman and Marbet. The presence of a Sensitive, which made nearly every other human in the galaxy at least mildly nervous, didn't seem to affect Magdalena at all. All she said was, "The press reported that Amanda was kidnapped also, as 'Lyle' here tells you. But she wasn't. I have contacts in various places who easily discovered that. However, I haven't been able to discover where she is. She came to your apartment in Luna City, looking for you, in the company of an unidentified man. After that, she traveled to Lowell City as an illegal aboard a Life Now ship. On Mars, however, she vanished. She was looking for you, but by that date you'd already left."

Kaufman wondered, *how much else does she know about Marbet and me? Probably everything*. This was Magdalena, after all, shadowy star of countless stories in the intelligence community. Most of the stories were undoubtedly false, but not all. Magdalena found out whatever she wanted to find out.

Kaufman shifted uncomfortably. For the first time, he noticed that three more people had gotten out of Magdalena's skimmer. Two augmented, genemod men who could be nothing but bodyguards, and a native child. A child? What was Magdalena doing with a native child? And why hadn't he, Kaufman, noticed the three before this minute? He was trained to notice things.

He knew the answer. Magdalena. She was probably in her fifties, her face had wrinkled a bit, her eyes were colder than almost any soldier Kaufman had dealt with. Yet her body was still spectacular and, more important, she still had the magnet, whatever that powerful thing was that surged sexual vibrations around one woman and not another. Magdalena in person had more of it than any other woman Kaufman had ever met. He was ashamed of himself for feeling what he was feeling. Also, there was no chance that Marbet would not know it.

He said, to say something rational, "Why are you looking for Amanda?"

She turned those extraordinary eyes on him, and again he felt her amusement. She knew.

"I need her in order to find my son."

Whatever Kaufman had expected, that wasn't it. He repeated stupidly, "Your son?"

"Yes. Whoever kidnapped Dr. Capelo is also holding my son, Laslo Damroscher."

To Kaufman's ear, Magdalena said this in the same level, husky voice (ignore the undertone of that huskiness!) in which she'd said everything else. But evidently Marbet heard a difference. Her invisible cat's fur relaxed, and she looked at Magdalena with no more than her usual keen alertness.

Kaufman said, "This doesn't really seem the place to discuss it. Shall we go with Dieter to this village he named?"

Gruber, forgotten until this moment, made a gesture Kaufman couldn't decode. Magdalena said pleasantly, "Couldn't wait to come dashing out here to warn them about me, could you, Dieter? Fortunately, Essa here overheard Ann on the comlink. She told me what was going on."

The native child, who looked just pubescent, darted forward and threw her arms around Gruber's knees. He backed off and tried to dislodge her, an act Kaufman instinctively sympathized with. But the child, a skinny girl with bright black eyes and brown neckfur, hung on, babbling in World. Her skull ridges crinkled with emotion. Kaufman looked at Marbet.

"Essa is begging Dieter's pardon," Marbet translated. "I'm not really fluent yet, but I think she's saying Pek Magdalena offered her something wonderful to tell Magdalena things . . . I'm not sure . . . to tell her everything . . . she offered . . . *you didn't.*"

This last was addressed, flatly, to Magdalena, who merely shrugged. Marbet and Gruber looked appalled. Kaufman, the only non-speaker of World, said irritably, "What? What did she offer the girl?"

Marbet said in English, "A ride in her spaceship to other worlds. Magdalena, you know that's not possible."

"More things are possible to me than you think. And why not? She's an enterprising kid."

"You lied to her."

"Maybe not."

Kaufman could see that Magdalena was enjoying this fencing and

Marbet was not. Gruber had succeeded in peeling the child off himself. She now stood beside Magdalena, and Kaufman had the uneasy feeling they were alike in some way he couldn't name. He tried to get things back on track.

"Marbet and I are going to the village. Gruber, can you lead us there?"

"No need," Magdalena said. "There's room in my skimmer for you both. Gruber can follow on his bike."

"I'll ride with Dieter," Marbet said, and Magdalena grinned.

Kaufman had been left with no choice. He didn't know the territory. He climbed into Magdalena's skimmer, followed by the silent, robot-like bodyguards. What exactly were they genemod for?

No matter. His business was not with them, nor even with Magdalena, whom he sat as far away from as possible. His business was with World, and what he had done to it.

NINE

GOFKIT SHAMLOE

There was a stockade around the village, a hand-built thing of rough-hewn tree trunks. There were fields, and small groups of people evidently working them. There were flowers, as many flowers as before. But, Kaufman realized, he couldn't tell in what ways the village was different from before he'd removed the artifact, and in what ways it was the same. He had never, in his brief previous visit to World, been in an alien village. All he had seen was the lavish compound of the trader Hadjil Voratur, the grassy plain where the shuttle had landed, and the Neury Mountains landscape that had housed the buried artifact.

He could easily tell that Ann Sikorski had changed.

He remembered her as gentle, no match for his decision to remove the artifact from World no matter what happened to the natives. She'd been thin, with long fair hair, a soft-spoken and cerebral person, a superior xenobiologist. The woman striding toward him with marked hostility was muscled, strong, obviously a farmer. Her face was browned from sun and her hair cut very short. "Lyle."

"Hello, Ann."

"So you're back. Where's Marbet?"

"Riding with Dieter. They'll be here in a minute. Ann, you look well. We were afraid—"

"That I was dead? Almost, more than once. But the society is surviving, Lyle, despite you. We're surviving."

"Pek Kaufman!" a native cried.

He recognized her—the translator Voratur had used, the woman Ann had befriended. Enli Pek Something. She was much bigger than most of these aliens, and clumsy. She came toward him, smiling, a small child in her arms. On her way she plucked a yellow flower from a bush and presented it to him. "May your garden bloom forever!"

He remembered the ritual words, all he had learned of the language. "May your blossoms rejoice your ancestors."

Ann said caustically in English, "You're supposed to offer her a visitor's flower."

"I'm surprised all these rituals persisted."

"Don't take it as evidence that you caused no serious change, Lyle. Everything's changed. It's just that Worlders hold onto all the old flower-related forma because now they're the only shared reality they have left."

Enli, Kaufman knew, understood English. Ann was dressing him down in front of a native. She had indeed changed.

Dieter's bicycle roared up. Ann and Marbet and Enli hugged and chattered in World. Left out, Kaufman surveyed the village.

Low round houses—Worlders thought straight lines were ugly—made of wood, roofs thatched, set around communal cookfires. World was fertile, resources abundant, the climate benign, without seasons. The houses were painted deep red or purple, evidently favorite colors, with high arched windows. Everywhere flowerbeds rioted in glories of color, making the settlement look much richer than it actually was. The stockade circled three sides; the fourth sloped down to a river. A complicated system of buckets and pulleys brought water uphill.

Natives began to seep out of the houses, mostly very old or very young, the latter tended by the former. The rest must be at work in the fields. The ones Kaufman could see looked healthy, well nourished, dressed in simple roughly spun tunics (what had they worn before? He couldn't remember.)

Enli said, in English, "Come into my house, Pek Kaufman and Pek Grant and drink—" she hesitated, the word probably didn't exist in English "—something to drink."

"Thank you," Kaufman said.

Magdalena said in his ear, "A half-hour, Colonel. Then I talk to you and Marbet Grant. There are lives at stake."

He didn't reply. She walked toward another hut and Kaufman, Marbet, Ann, Dieter, and Enli went into Enli's house, which was a single large room. There was no glass, Kaufman saw, in three of the four windows, and air circulated freely. Blankets, pillows, and small low tables furnished the room. Two of the neatly folded blankets were woven of rich, embroidered cloth looking worn; the other two were new, rough homespun. The pillows showed the same division, and the wood of the tables.

Ann looked at him. "Before and after, Lyle. People spending time on self-defense and subsistence farming have neither the time nor the division of labor for comfort, let alone art."

"Ann," Marbet said gently, "enough."

"Not nearly enough. You haven't seen the graveyard."

Enli said loudly, "Berrydrink?" On the walk into the house she had invented a word in English.

It was better than just berry juice, Kaufman found. Richly flavored, a blend of different tastes. The "bread" Enli offered was also good.

Gruber said something in World to Enli, who laughed and held out a piece of bread to her child. Clearly Ann and Dieter were accepted here, welcome. No, more than that—they were part of this alien community.

"Enli," Kaufman said in English, "I have come from Terra to see how World lives without shared reality. Can you tell me this?"

She turned on her pillow to look at him. Her skull ridges wrinkled, but Kaufman had not had enough exposure to Worlders to know what emotion was being expressed. Enli's eyes, the deep soft black of ash, met his steadily.

"We do not share reality now," she told him in slow English, "so we create our own realities. Some places, like Gofkit Shamloe, create good realities between people. Not all people, but most. We talk, and work, and teach our children, and honor our ancestors in the world of spirits. It is difficult sometimes, to look at someone and think, What does she think? It is very strange."

"Go on," Kaufman said when she paused.

"Other places create bad reality. They steal, which is all right, but they kill the owners to steal." Her skull ridges contorted. "Sometimes they just kill. They think . . . they think maybe they should be rich traders, or . . . I don't know what they think. It is difficult. I teach Confit—" she indicated the child "—to not hurt people. But if killers come, he must hurt them. It is difficult."

This speech seemed to have exhausted and disturbed Enli. She picked up the baby, who wiggled to get back down and then began to fret.

Ann said, "We've established trade relations with two of the closest villages. Not because anyone has anything to trade, but because it creates an alliance. Maintains contact. Also a larger gene pool, and a potentially more powerful defense against places like the Voratur compound, which is enslaving serfs to support them. They're amassing an army to extend their power."

Marbet said, to spare Kaufman, "Do you want to know what's happening in the Solar System? You've had no news for what, two or three years?"

"*Ja*," Gruber said eagerly. "What happens with the war? With the artifact? What is this about Tom being *kidnapped*?"

Marbet began to tell them about Stefanak, Life Now, the Fallers, the Protector Artifact, Capelo. Enli tended her child. Kaufman got up and walked outside, his guts too roiled to let him sit still.

A mistake. Magdalena awaited him. Once more he looked at those brilliant eyes, aging face, still lush body, and felt the unmistakable and involuntary stirring in his loins. This time she didn't mock him for it. She had other things on her mind. "Come with me, Lyle. There's something you must hear."

When he didn't answer, she grabbed his hand. He shook himself free but followed her to another house, virtually identical to Enli's on the outside. But not inside, where it held a bed and other human furnishings. She had a ship somewhere. The girl Essa sat cross-legged on a pillow, polishing a bowl. She grinned at him.

"Listen," Magdalena said, and switched on a data cube.

"*Thass not 'sposed to be there.*" Laslo's voice, very drunk.

"*What isn't supposed to be where?*" Another young man, sounding marginally less drunk. "*Just an asteroid.*"

"*Isn't 'sposed to be there. Hand me 'nother fizzie.*"

"*They're gone. You drunk the last one, you pig.*"

"*No fizzies? Might as well go home.*"

"*Just an asteroid. No . . . two asteroids.*"

"*Two!*" Laslo said, with pointless jubilation.

"*Where'd they come from? Isn't supposed to be there. Not on computer.*"

"*N-body problem. Gravity. Messes things up. Jupiter.*"

"*Let's shoot 'em!*"

"*Yeah!*" Laslo cried, and hiccuped.

"What kinda guns you got on this thing? No guns, prob'ly. Fucking rich-boy pleasure craft."

"Got . . . got guns put on it. Daddy-dad doesn't know. Illegals."

"You're a bonus, Laslo."

"Goddamn true. Mummy doesn't know either. 'Bout the guns."

"You sure 'bout that? Isn't much your famous mother don't know. Or do. God, that body, I saw her in an old—"

"Shut up, Conner," Laslo said savagely. *"Computer, activate . . . can't remember the word . . ."*

"Activate weapons. Jesus, Laslo. YOU gotta say it. Voice cued."

"Activate weapons!"

"Hey, a message from th'asteroid! People! Maybe there's girls."

"You are approaching a highly restricted area," a mechanical voice said. *"Leave this area immediately."*

"It don't want us," Conner said. *"Shoot it!"*

"Wait . . . maybe . . . ?"

"You are approaching a highly restricted area. Leave this area immediately."

"Fucking snakes," Conner said. *"Shoot it!"*

"I . . ."

"Fucking coward!"

"THIS IS YOUR LAST WARNING! YOU HAVE INVADED A HIGHLY RESTRICTED AND HIGH-DANGER AREA. LEAVE IMMEDIATELY OR YOUR CRAFT WILL BE FIRED ON!"

And then a fourth voice, speaking rapidly, *"Unknown craft . . . SOS . . . Help! I'm being held prisoner here—this is Tom Capelo—"*

A very brief, high-pitched whine.

"Tom!" Kaufman said.

"So it is Dr. Capelo? You recognize the voice?"

"Yes," Kaufman said. "But I don't understand how—where and when was this made?"

"July third, coordinates in the Belt," Magdalena said. "I checked the location. There is nothing there now, and this recorder had a pick-up range of less than a hundred clicks. The recorder indicated that the two separate voices came from separate loci. But after that, the captors turned off the recording equipment."

Kaufman's mind raced. Tom had been held in the Belt, probably in a hollow asteroid habitat, and from the warning and prompt firing, something important had been housed nearby, although not with him. The Protector Artifact? Stash it there with maximum defenses, and stash Tom nearby to . . . do what? Work on it? Maybe, but only if you had the kind of mind that didn't realize that there was a huge gap between experimental and theoretical physics, that Tom Capelo practiced the latter, and that theoretical physicists did not need to be in the presence of the phenomena they invented equations to explain. Kaufman could easily imagine military officers who did not realize any of this. Tom had been brought to World originally to make sense of the artifact, and he had. What had they wanted him to do now?

And Magdalena said neither Tom nor the artifact housing was there now. They'd been moved. She'd also said—

"What do you mean, 'After that, the captors turned off the recording equipment'?"

"Laslo was doing what he always does," Magdalena said, pushing a strand of her black hair off her face. In her deep blue pants and silver-embroidered tunic she looked completely out of place in the native hut. "Laslo wants to do without my guidance, which he can't. So periodically he plays these idiotic games, disappearing for weeks or months. My son is very immature for his age, I'm afraid. Still, I don't think he anticipated that this flight would end with him and his friend being captured alongside the great Dr. Capelo."

Kaufman stared at her. Yes, she believed it. But he'd heard the warning, the characteristic weapon whine . . . Laslo's ship had been vaporized.

He said carefully, "Do you have any further indication that Laslo is still alive?"

"Of course he's still alive. You don't think Stefanak is going to murder Thomas Capelo, savior of the Solar System, do you?"

"No, but—"

"Where Capelo is, so is Laslo," Magdalena said.

Kaufman looked into those blue eyes, bluer than sapphires, and saw absolute conviction. She believed her son was alive and with Capelo. She had to believe it; nothing else was bearable. Kaufman was looking at self-delusion in a character strong enough to elevate it to madness.

He said carefully, "Could your contacts gain any indication of where Dr. Capelo might have been moved?"

"No. And believe me, I tried. Security is tighter than a virgin's ass. My only lead was Amanda Capelo. She wasn't taken along with her father, so maybe she saw something at some point that would give me a clue. She might not recognize it as a clue, but I might."

He said, still very careful, "World seems a long way to come yourself to hunt for Amanda on that slight evidence."

She smiled. "You're right. I'd have sent somebody, except I was warned in advance."

"Warned of what?"

"Then you don't know. You'd already gone through the tunnel. By now, there's been a revolution. Stefanak declared martial law and the anti-Stefanak forces have tried to overthrow him."

Kaufman's stomach tightened. "Tried? Did they succeed?"

Magdalena shrugged. "I don't know. I was warned. A friend sent me word. 'Leave the Solar System. Pierce has decided to move on the eighteenth. The navy will lead it off.' I got out."

Pierce. Solar Alliance Defense Navy Chief Admiral Nikolai Pierce, a bitter rival to Stefanak. And if Magdalena had the connections that Kaufman had always heard attributed to her, she was right to get out. Pierce would have had her killed instantly. Her vast, shadowy, quasi-political empire backed Stefanak.

She said, "I have a flyer bringing me news. He's due to arrive at this tunnel in a few days. Meanwhile, this Godawful backwater is as good a place as any to hide until things are decided."

"Until things are decided"—she spoke about political and military control of the entire Solar System as though it didn't matter who won. Perhaps to her, it didn't. Her only concern was her son. Kaufman found such misplaced single-mindedness unnerving, grotesque.

He said, "And if Pierce does win? You plan on hiding on World forever?"

She smiled at him. "Of course not. But you should know that the days immediately following a coup is the time when all sorts of people disappear. 'Casualty of the fighting.' I have a lot of enemies, Lyle. If Pierce wins, he'll move to restore at least the semblance of order, and then I'd be a lot harder to kill without considerable publicity. No matter who wins, I'll go back. Your primitive little planet here is just a convenient temporary storm shelter. And of course I hoped you had Amanda Capelo with you. You might have, you know. But you haven't heard from or about her?"

"No," Kaufman managed. He had been a soldier under General Sullivan Stefanak, Supreme Commander Solar Alliance Defense Council. He had, despite everything, admired the man. And now Stefanak might be deposed, or imprisoned, or murdered. Revolution . . .

"Yes, I could see that from your first reaction. And your pretty Sensitive's. I'll find him, you know. Laslo."

She had his attention again. He looked at her closely. She believed it. She would find Tom Capelo, and with him would be her Laslo. Pity flooded Kaufman.

She saved him from speaking by adding, "Meanwhile, of course, if your little girl Amanda is still in Lowell City, it isn't going to go very well for her. Or the whole rest of the population. Essa, what is it now?"

Humbly the native girl handed Magdalena the bowl, polished to a blinding shine. She said something in World, which neither Kaufman nor Magdalena could follow. "What?" Magdalena said irritably.

"She asks," said Marbet's voice behind him, "how long it's going to be until you take her in the flying metal boat to other worlds. She says you promised, through Enli."

"Oh, soon," Magdalena said.

Kaufman turned to look at Marbet, standing in the doorway. Marbet said, "Lyle, Ann wants you," and walked out. Kaufman followed. She led him not to Ann's hut but to another one, empty except for a small table, two plain floor pillows, and a rolled-up sleeping mat.

"This is where you and I will stay. Lyle, you shouldn't trust anything Magdalena tells you."

"How long were you standing there? Did you hear that data cube?"

"Yes." Marbet motioned for him to sit on one of the pillows; she took the other. "That part is real, I think. She's looking for her son, and she genuinely believes he's alive and with Tom."

"He's not alive."

"I know."

"Have you ever met her before?"

"No."

"What else could you see about her now?"

Marbet was silent for a long moment. Finally she said, "I already knew something about her. You can't do Sensitive work in negotiations without sooner or later coming across one of Magdalena's corporations. As part of my preparation for dealing with her people, I've been shown holos of her, and I was briefed on what's known of her history. Do you know it?"

"No."

"She was born in Atlanta, on Earth. Her mother was most likely a whore. What's definitely known is that the mother, or somebody, left the baby in a box in front of a government clinic in the Plumbob, Atlanta's worst section. Not even cops will go in there."

"Go on," Kaufman said.

"The baby was adopted by a nurse at the clinic, Catalune Damroscher, who was or became a peen addict. She named the child 'May.' Maybe Catalune Damroscher started out wanting to be a good mother, but she abused little May horribly. There are records in ten different free clinics of the child being beaten, burned, kicked. May didn't talk until she was four years old.

"When she was six, she disappeared off any records, anywhere. The next year Catalune overdosed on peen and died. Nobody knows where May went or how she lived between six and sixteen."

"I see," said Kaufman, who didn't. How could a six-year-old survive in the Plumbob?

"May turned up in two-one-two-five on the pleasure beaches of North Carolina. Those places are very heavily guarded, but somehow she got in, and became the mistress of a rich man named Amerigo Dalton for three or four years. She's mentioned in old deebees of gossip columns, things like that. She went from Dalton to Evan Kilhane, the porn producer, or maybe there were men in between. Kilhane gave her the name 'Magdalena' and launched her porn career. You probably know at least the outline of the rest."

"Yes," Kaufman said. Magdalena's sorry childhood had stirred him. "But I didn't know she had a son."

"By Bellington Wace Arnold. Illegitimate. Lyle, if you go on looking like that I'm going to slap you."

"Looking like what?" A mistake, he shouldn't have asked.

"Like a man about to weep over an injured kitten. Listen to me. Magdalena is dangerous. She didn't have her son genetically engineered because she's so arrogant she believed that any child of hers would be wonderful without any artificial help. At the same time, she's furious inside at the perversion of genes that brought her the beauty which ruined her life."

He said skeptically, "Was all *that* in the official records?"

"Of course not," Marbet snapped. "I saw it in every line of her when she stood listening to that data cube. Magdalena is furious at what Laslo is. She also has focused on him every thwarted desire of her entire life, every single denied impulse. I'll bet she's never had one genuine orgasm."

That was too much. Kaufman stood and stretched, feigning nonchalance.

"Don't pretend with me, Lyle. You're about as indifferent to her as a bear to honey. She destroyed any potential that son of hers might have had through controlling him, excusing him, smothering him. He hated her and worshipped her and they probably fought constantly."

Kaufman said, "Don't you think that's a lot to get out of one short exposure? Even for you?"

Marbet stared at him. The longer she gazed, the more uncomfortable Kaufman became. She could see so damn much!

Finally she turned away, saying over her shoulder, "We need to have our things brought here from the flyer. Don't let May Damroscher fool you, Lyle. She's a person consumed, and you are no match for her at all."

TEN

LOWELL CITY, MARS

The Ares Abbey of the Benedictine Brothers was the strangest place to live that Amanda could imagine. Everyone was kind, but no one made any sense.

The first few days she had stayed in bed, terrified and exhausted. Brother Meissel had brought her food and sat on the edge of her bed, which embarrassed Amanda because all she had on was somebody's old tunic that she was using as a nightshirt, and anyway she hadn't bathed and might smell bad. Brother Meissel talked about faith and prayer and the testing of the spirit until Amanda pretended to be asleep, and then the "priest" would go away. Often she fell asleep, but she always woke to nightmares about her father or about Father Emil.

Once she interrupted Brother Meissel to say abruptly, "Why do people have to die?"

"You mean Father Emil," Brother Meissel said.

"Yes. He . . . he . . ."

"He died to save your life, is what you think."

"Didn't he?" Amanda said, confused.

"No," Brother Meissel said. "He died for the greater glory of God."

This made no sense to Amanda, who had clearly seen Father Emil shot down as he tried to protect Amanda. Daddy said people died because their telomeres gave out, plus Nature no longer needed them after they passed breeding age. That wasn't exactly comforting, but at least it made sense.

"Father Emil's soul is with God," Brother Meissel said. Amanda couldn't think of anything polite to say to this, so she said nothing. She had no answer. Father Emil had been a good person. It wasn't right that he should die like that, shot down in the street to lie in his own blood.

After a few days, her natural resilience asserted itself, and she got out of bed, looking for a holovee. She didn't find one. In fact, to her incredulity, there was no terminal anywhere in the abbey. No terminal! She had never before been in a place without any terminal. "The things of this world are not our concern," Brother Meissel told her, twitching his long brown dress. "A terminal would only distract us from our sacred work. However, there is a flat-screen TV to receive news in an emergency. I will have that set up for you in the refectory."

Amanda said skeptically, "If you don't have a terminal, how would you even learn there *was* an emergency to turn on your flat-screen for?"

"In the refectory, Amanda. And only there."

She explored the abbey, with its many "chambers." Every room was called a chamber, although most of them also had other names, words Amanda had never heard before: refectory, chapel, stillroom, choir stalls, cellarer's office. Each chamber had a purpose, and everyone in them was engaged in that purpose whenever they were there, which they were at the same time every single day. There was no "living room," no lounging around, no spontaneity. And yet no one seemed unhappy.

Not that there were very many people to be either unhappy or happy. Seventeen "brothers" in the entire place, and fourteen never left, ever, under any circumstances. Amanda was appalled to hear that. Only Brother Meissel and Brother Wu were allowed to leave the abbey to buy things or go to the bank or do normal living. The abbey was a "cloistered order," she was told. More strange words. The boy who had first let her in was a "postulant."

What everybody did, mostly, was sing and feed people. Three times each day Brother Meissel and Brother Wu carried the huge vats of food the others cooked to "outside the grille." The grille was a real thing, a thick elaborate grid of steel made to look like intertwined trees and leaves. The fourteen "cloistered brothers" stayed in that part of the building between the grille and a wall that backed right up to the descending piezoelectric arc of the city's main dome.

There was a small space between the abbey wall and the dome wall, no more than a foot wide. In this space nondegradable rubbish was stored: a broken bedspring, some plastic crates not needed at the moment, a wheel that Amanda could not imagine ending up there. Exploring, she poked around in the various piles of rubbish, then stood to gaze out over the wall. Beyond the thick, multilayered plastic spread the red rocky ground of Mars.

People came to the crowded room beyond the grille to eat for free. Brother Meissel and Brother Wu served them, squeezing between the packed, tiny tables. Space was expensive in Lowell City. After the meal, some of the people stayed to hear the brothers sing.

That, Amanda thought, was why they really came.

The brothers sat hidden behind the grille, in their individual "choir stalls," and sang music such as Amanda had never heard before. Beautiful, haunting music, with no recorded instruments or synth music to accompany them. "Plainchant," Brother Meissel called it. They sang with an intensity that Amanda didn't really understand, as if the music were not just music but something else. "We are praying," Brother Meissel said. "Singing the Holy Office. Your ignorance is appalling, Amanda."

Six times a day they sang, although outside people only came to three of them. The times had more strange names: Lauds, Prime, Terce, Sext, Vespers, and Matins. Some of these were in the middle of the night and Brother Meissel wouldn't let her go to them. Amanda needed her sleep, Brother said. She liked to go to the other singings, however, even though the words were in Latin. She wasn't interested in the words but in the sound.

Amanda stayed, always, behind the grille. The brothers knew she was there, but no one else on Mars knew. Nor would anyone come in to find her, Brother Meissel said. No one ever came behind the grille.

"How do you get money to buy food and things?" practical Amanda said, having observed that nobody paid for the meals or the singing. ("It's not a performance, Amanda.") Brother Meissel said the abbey received donations from Earth.

"Why?"

"For the greater glory of God."

Apparently the flat-screen TV was a donation, too. It sat on a rough table at one end of the refectory. ("Oh! It's a dining room!" Amanda said.) She was allowed the TV only because of her father, and she was permitted to turn it on only when the refectory was empty. She sat at the end of a hard, backless foamcast bench meant for four people, her arms hugging her knees in the pants Brother Meissel had sewn for her, and watched newscasters and avatars and important people, even General Stefanak, talk about her father's kidnapping months ago. It was still news.

"No trace of eminent physicist Dr. Thomas Capelo, decoder of the Protector Artifact, who vanished last—"

"Gone into thin air, bonus? No clue who. No—"

"Citizens of the Solar System, until each and every one of us is safe in our own homes, atrocities like the disappearance of—"

"—terrorist groups like Life Now! They seek to betray us to the enemy! They will do anything, even kidnap a man of science like Dr. Capelo, in order to discredit—"

"War traitors—"

"Collaborators in—"

"Never rest until Dr. Capelo is restored to—"

"Dr. Capelo and his young daughter Amanda, fourteen years old—"

"Reward for any information leading to—"

Amanda went over and over that night in her mind. She could see the big blond man in her father's bedroom, the man waiting beside the dark car, her father walking unnaturally stiffly between two other men. Nothing she could remember told her who they were, or why they had come.

Once Amanda caught a brief interview with her stepmother, looking shaken and pale. Carol merely said she had been at her parents' with Sudie, and then asked anyone on Earth, or anywhere else, with any knowledge at all of what had happened to her husband and stepdaughter to comlink the system number on the screen.

"Amanda, that's enough," Brother Meissel finally said. "You've watched enough. Brother Killian needs your help in the kitchen." Brother Meissel believed in keeping "idle hands" busy. Amanda went to pound Martian-grown herbs to flavor soysynth.

Food at the abbey was plentiful but boring. Sometimes her mouth watered for an orange, or a candy drop. Once she dreamed of lemons.

After she'd been at the abbey for two weeks, the newscasts changed. There were no more mentions of Amanda's father, or of anything else except General Stefanak.

Amanda ran to Brother Meissel's office and knocked on the door.

"*Deo Gratias* . . . what is it, child? Why do you look like that?"

"The TV says there's a revolution in Lowell City! Right here! Now!"

Brother Meissel went still. After a moment he said, "I will come." He followed her to the refectory and listened for a while. Amanda watched his lips move in prayer.

"Brother Meissel . . . what's happening? What does it mean?"

"I can't be sure, Amanda. The reports are very confused."

"It says there's fighting outside!"

"Yes."

"What are we going to do?"

"At this moment," Brother Meissel said calmly, "we are going to sing Terce. Turn off the screen, Amanda."

"But—"

"Turn it off. It is time for Terce."

However, when the singing, which Amanda had learned to call "the Holy Office," was over, Brother Meissel permitted the TV to be turned back on and everyone to watch it. Even ancient, half-deaf Brother Killian left his kitchen to cluster around the ancient TV. They were all there when the announcement came.

"A grave occurrence has just been reported," said the elderly, human newscaster the abbey preferred to watch. Amanda preferred a jazzy avatar named Stix, but had never said this. "The enemy, the so-called 'Fallers,' have attempted to penetrate Space Tunnel number one and enter the Solar System. Due to the treasonous betrayal of humanity by high-ranking officials in the Tunnel Administration, three Faller ships actually passed through the tunnel, where they were destroyed by alert ships of the Solar Alliance Defense Navy loyal to General Stefanak."

"Oh my dear Lord God," Brother Wu said, and made the sign of the cross.

"As a result of this action, General Stefanak has declared temporary martial law until those leaders of the military, who have inexcusably betrayed humanity, can be identified and removed. All citizens of Lowell City are now under curfew. No one may be on the streets between twenty hundred hours and oh six hundred hours each day. For the general safety, army soldiers will be checking buildings for enemies of the Solar Alliance. Your cooperation is urged in this endeavor to protect our homes and families. General Stefanak made this statement a few moments ago:"

The newscaster disappeared and General Stefanak filled the screen, bald and fleshy, powerful shoulders straining against the shoulders of his uniform. Whenever Sudie had seen him on holo she'd hidden her face, saying he was too scary. Amanda had always mocked her sister for that, but Sudie was right. General Stefanak looked scary.

"Citizens of Lowell City, the corruption in our government runs deep. I have begun to root out and—"

A dull boom shook the room. The priests looked at each other. "What is it?" Amanda cried.

Brother Meissel said calmly, "Just a warning about curfew, I imagine. Brother Wu, please check outside."

Old Brother Killian said to Brother Meissel, "The child . . ."

"I know," Brother Meissel answered. "Not yet."

Brother Wu returned. "It's all quiet out there. But a lot of soldiers have suddenly appeared on the streets."

"Martial law," Brother Meissel said. "The searches will be next."

"What will we do?" cried Brother Kawambe, excitable and not very bright.

"We will sing Vespers. It is almost time."

"But if the Fallers return with their artifact . . . what that physicist said about destroying the fabric of space . . . if the Fallers come through the tunnel again into the Solar System . . ."

"There were no Fallers at the tunnel," Brother Meissel said patiently. "That was an excuse for Stefanak to declare martial law and attack his enemies in the council. Calm yourself, Brother Kawambe. Amanda, a word with you, please."

The others filed to their stalls to sing Vespers. Amanda, her chest tight, wrenched her attention away from the TV.

"In the next few weeks," Brother Meissel said, "the abbey may be searched, perhaps more than once. Soldiers will probably come behind the grille, although I will try to dissuade them from invading sanctified space. When they come, you must hide. I'm going to show you where. Do you know what a priest hole was in the seventeenth century?"

"No," Amanda said.

"I can't imagine what content fills your history software. Follow me, please."

The "priest hole" was a secret place reached through a hidden panel in an unused cell, which was what the brothers called their tiny bedrooms. Brother Meissel showed Amanda how to press the places that opened and closed it. The hole was big enough for two people, three if they squeezed, but half the small space was taken up by a surface suit, complete with boots, helmet, and oversized airtank.

"What's that there for?"

"Just in case. Here is how you operate the second door. It leads outside, to the rubbish heap." He showed her.

"In case of what?"

"In case God calls upon someone to need it."

That was the sort of thing Brother Meissel always said, and that was the tone he said it in. The tone allowed no argument. Amanda said resentfully, "My father always says you shouldn't make a statement you can't express clearly in either words or numbers."

"I'm sure he does," Brother Meissel said imperturbably. "One more thing, Amanda. If you come in here, and if time permits you to do it safely, I want you to bring the chalice with you."

The chalice was the gold cup kept behind the altar, which Brother Meissel used when he "said Mass." It was very pretty, Amanda thought. It was also supposed to be very holy. She said uncertainly, "But . . . won't the soldiers see that it's missing? And know you must have a hiding place somewhere?"

"Soldiers? Recognize the absence of a chalice? You must be joking," Brother Meissel said. "Just remember, please."

"I will," Amanda said. She would like to have said more—to tell him how scared she was, to ask him what the soldiers would do to the abbey—but she knew better. Instead she returned to the TV, leaving the brothers to sing Vespers with no audience whatsoever.

ELEVEN

LOWELL CITY

Brother Meissel was wrong; no soldiers came to search the abbey. Amanda could see why. They were too busy fighting to take over essential city services.

The holo station was first. Privately run, its employees filmed their own shock as Admiral Pierce's soldiers entered the station that broadcast to all of Mars and most of the Belt, as well as sending data packets to Earth, Titan, and the Space Tunnel. The soldiers were polite. They ordered the employees to leave, and they did. Then uniformed, armed soldiers began operating the equipment.

"Now we see only what they want us to see," Brother Wu said. But he, too, was wrong. The next morning Amanda crept out of her cell at 0500 hundred, only to find all the brothers already clustered around the TV. It displayed a single static message, without audio:

THIS STATION HAS BEEN RETURNED TO THE PEOPLE, UNDER THE PROTECTORSHIP OF THE NEW MARS PROVISIONAL DEMOCRATIC GOVERNMENT. BROADCASTING WILL RESUME SHORTLY.

"Our Father, who art in heaven . . ." Brother Meissel prayed aloud.

Amanda, astonished, looked from Brother Meissel to the screen. "What does it mean?" she asked, but no one answered her until the prayer, in which all had joined, was complete.

"It means that Admiral Pierce's faction has taken the station," Brother Meissel finally said. "They claim that General Stefanak can't win the war with the Fallers. That's their justification for the insurrection. There must be fighting all over the city."

"Fighting? But we're at war with the Fallers, not with Admiral Pierce!"

"Out of the mouths of babes," someone said.

"But Daddy . . . my father always says you can't fight in a Martian dome! You might breach the dome!"

"Depends on what weapons you use. Brother Wu, where do you think you're going?"

"I'm going outside to see what is happening."

"You are not. The affairs of Caesar are not our affairs. We must perform the Holy Office. Lauds begins in ten minutes."

Brother Wu pointed soundlessly at Amanda.

"All right, then," Brother Meissel said. "Be careful, Shing."

"I will."

While the other brothers sang Lauds, Amanda stayed with the TV, waiting for it to do something. Before it could, Brother Wu returned. His full round face was rigid. "I only went as far as the end of Sigma Street," he told Amanda, the only one in the refectory. "They're fighting over the life-support facility. I saw Pierce's soldiers use laser guns on Stefanak's troops that—there!" He pointed to the TV.

". . . intensely to keep the oppressing forces from cutting off water or air to the city. Victory resulted at oh six hundred hours, and this station is thankful to report that the life-support facility is safe in the hands of the rescuing forces. Our commander, Admiral Pierce—"

Amanda didn't listen anymore. She stared at the screen, which showed a young SADC soldier being sliced in half by a laser gun. The picture immediately and ineptly swung to a different shot, but Amanda had seen it.

Her mother, bending over the fish pool, and the Faller ship suddenly swooping down from the sky . . . screaming and screaming but not from her mother who already lay sliced shoulder to hip, a surprised expression on her beautiful face and her father running and shouting, her mother's blood on the stone by the pool dripping into the pool and the fish—

Salah, falling back from her bunk, his head toppling off his shoulders within a fountain of spurting blood—

Father Emil, lying in the street—

"Amanda," a voice said calmly, "go into the priest hole."

The blood dripping into—

"Amanda. Go now to the hole." It was Brother Meissel, returned without her hearing him.

"Yes," she gasped. "All right. But you—"

"There are no but's. Go to the hole and put on the s-suit."

That brought her fully back. "The s-suit? Why?"

"Because I told you to." Then he relented. "In case the fighting breaches the dome."

"They'd have to be crazy to do that!" Amanda said, and realized immediately that the sentence was her father's.

"I believe they are. But if General Stefanak is killed—"

"They're trying to kill *General Stefanak*?" Amanda said. It was like trying to kill the sun. General Stefanak had been the center of the Solar System for her whole life. He was as much a fact as light, or air.

The TV picture, still ineptly jumping around and changing focus, showed soldiers guarding the Summit. Amanda recognized the building immediately; the entire Solar System recognized the building.

General Stefanak's headquarters, built under the highest part of Lowell City's central dome, the towering central support for the dome struts rising hundreds of feet from inside the building itself. As she watched, soldiers outside the Summit began to crumple. No one was firing at them, no one was using tanglefoam, the soldiers were in full battle armor. And they crumpled.

"What . . . what . . ." Brother Kawambe. When had the brothers finished Lauds and crowded into the room? Amanda hadn't even noticed.

Brother Meissel said, "They're using genemod viruses to stop breathing."

Amanda gasped; she couldn't help it. Genemod viruses were completely illegal. They could wipe out everybody. Daddy said you could engineer them to stop replicating after a set number of generations and then die, but were these viruses made like that? And even if they were, who would breathe them before the terminator gene kicked in? Who already had? Brother Meissel? Brother Wu? Herself?

The soldiers at the Summit had breathed them in.

"Amanda, go," Brother Meissel said.

She hugged each of them first, wasting precious time, not caring. Outside the abbey a huge noise started, people running and screaming. Panic.

Amanda ran to the priest hole, pressed the catches with trembling fingers, and pulled out the s-suit. Easier to put it on outside the hole. She could still hear the panic outside in the streets. And then, over it, another sound, inside: singing. The brothers were singing the Holy Office.

But it's not one of the times! Amanda thought, crazily. No matter. They were singing anyway. And then she realized it wasn't the Holy Office but some other chant, one she'd never heard before. *"Dies irae, Dies illa . . ."*

She snapped on her helmet and the chanting, along with all other noises, ceased.

Amanda started to crawl into the hole. But then she realized that once in there, with the helmet on to protect against viruses, she wouldn't be able to hear or see anything at all. She'd have no idea what was happening. If soldiers searched the abbey, she wouldn't even hear them coming.

They wouldn't care if they found her. General Stefanak and Admiral Pierce were fighting a war inside Lowell City. They were not going to be looking for Amanda Capelo.

She clumped in her heavy boots back into the heart of the abbey. In the choir stalls the brothers all knelt and sang. Amanda had a sudden flash of how it would look on TV — a short adult or tall child in an s-suit complete with helmet, thumping along between rows of singing priests. Crazy.

At Brother Meissel, she stopped, wondering how to say it without removing her helmet. She didn't have to say it. He made his way to the altar, came back with the chalice, and handed it to her. Amanda clumped back to the hole.

Inside, she opened the second door and emerged at the rubbish pile, beside the concrete wall that anchored the dome struts. Nearly every building used this space, where the dome slanted down too close to even stand erect, for discards or storage. Awkwardly pushing the chalice ahead of her, Amanda crawled behind building after building, circling the dome by staying beside the concrete wall. When she finally reached a building suspicious enough to wall off its rubbish area, she had also reached a narrow service alley between buildings. She walked along it to the street, less than a block from one of the dome's eight airlocked gates.

She was just in time to see the dome come down.

A military flyer passed high overhead. Had it fired a proton beam, the entire city would have been vaporized. But it merely fired a fo-cused laser, sweeping the beam across the piezoelectric dome. It sliced a half-kilometer-long surgical cut through plastic, through metal struts, through the buildings and objects and people below.

The struts buckled and began to fall.

Amanda raced toward the gate. She couldn't hear the falling dome, nor the sirens that must be screeching as the atmosphere es-caped. Everything happened silently. Windows blew outward from buildings. People opened their mouths and screamed silently. Those who, like Amanda, wore s-suits struggled toward the gate, crowded through, and began to run. Amanda pushed herself until her lungs throbbed with pain and her legs gave way. Then she dropped to the red ground and twisted to look back at Lowell City.

It looked like half a clear beach ball stoved in on one side. She was too far away now to see details. Only the sagging plastic and the sharp edges of broken struts poking the morning sky. All the people she knew must be dead or dying inside.

Could Brother Meissel and the others have made it to one of the two smaller domes? Those looked intact. No, the brothers wouldn't have even tried. They'd have stayed in their choir stalls, behind the grille that was supposed to keep out the world, singing. *Dies irae, Dies illa . . .*

Amanda choked back sobs. She would not cry—she would not. Instead she began again to walk, staring straight ahead, her panting loud inside her helmet. It was ten minutes more before she realized she still carried the golden chalice, relict from the Ares Abbey of the Benedictine Brothers on Mars.

The Martian plain, which looked so even from inside the dome, was covered with regolith, large rocks, and enormous boulders. Between them hurried figures in s-suits, shuttle buses, private land cars, skimmers. They all moved in the same direction. Amanda did, too, because everybody else was. The vehicles raced past her. Eventually she saw the ships on the horizon and realized everybody was heading toward the spaceport. As she walked, she saw a ship lift off from the ground.

Although she didn't know it, Amanda had fled Lowell City from the gate closest to the spaceport. She had a head start on the hundreds trying to reach the port. Forty thousand people had lived in the central dome of Lowell City. Most of them were now dead, suffocated by lack of air and frozen by the intense cold. Some had been able to reach the gateways to the other two smaller domes. Everyone who could get their hands on an s-suit had left the city by vehicle or foot for the spaceport, before their air tanks gave out.

Amanda walked, numb, because she couldn't think what else to do. She was young and fit. She reached the spaceport before all the civilian ships had gone, the ships in turn fleeing the desperate people who scrambled and fought to get aboard one of them, any of them.

The scene was so eerie that her numb mind shivered. In complete silence, suited figures with bubble heads jumped out of vehicles and ran toward shuttles and hoppers and flyers. The military ships, in a separate part of the field, were surrounded by armed 'bots who killed anyone without the proper codes. Those civilians with legitimate codes unlocked their private ships. Others swarmed over to them, pushing and shoving to get aboard. Some owners were armed; people went down in tanglefoam or with their suits pierced. Other people stood quietly apart from the fighting, apparently knowing they had no hope, waiting for the inevitable. Amanda saw two figures carrying an s-cot between them. A baby.

She gasped and turned away. But there was nowhere to go. She didn't have a ship. She couldn't fight to get on one, and she wouldn't have fought if she could. She was going to die. So many other people had died . . . Father Emil and Brother Meissel and Brother Wu and excitable, dim Brother Kawambe . . . and Amanda's father. He was probably dead, too.

She sat down. Even through her suit the rocky ground felt cold. She sat on it and waited to die, and her only thought was that she hoped it wouldn't hurt.

Later, she never knew how long she'd sat there. Maybe just a few minutes; the scene at the ships had not changed. Her backside felt frozen. Someone loomed into her field of vision. Amanda looked up, but she could see nothing behind the tinted face plate of the other person's helmet.

The suited figure touched the chalice in her arms.

Then it peered closely at Amanda. Her own face plate was clear. The other person started, grabbed Amanda's hand, and pulled her upward. She stumbled, and all at once she was running, towed along by whoever this was toward a far section of the field. As they approached the land hopper standing there, another figure gestured wildly. The crowd around the craft was small, maybe because it was only a land hopper, incapable of leaving Mars. But it was a crowd, and as Amanda ran, gasping, she saw the second figure stop gesturing and fire a laser pistol at someone trying to charge up the hopper's ramp. The interloper crumpled to the ground.

Amanda was pulled past the guard, who aimed its pistol at her. But the person towing her kept on pulling, and the other figure didn't fire, and then she was up the ramp and the door closed and Amanda collapsed onto the deck, gasping, yanking off the helmet that she suddenly felt was suffocating her, just before she felt the hopper lift off the surface of Mars.

She looked up. Two teenagers stood looking down at her, a small swarthy girl and a taller boy. A second boy, in an s-suit but without a helmet, piloted the hopper. The first boy panted as badly as Amanda; he was the one who had been towing her. He didn't seem able to catch his breath. But even bent double and wheezing, he was beautiful.

The girl said something in a language Amanda didn't know. The girl's tone, however, was all too clear: She was furious. The pilot laughed and said something. He made a quick chopping motion with his arm.

The first boy, panting less now, straightened. This made the girl start an even more furious tirade. The boy ignored her. He stared at Amanda.

"*Christos . . . is* you! Ah-man-dah Capelo!"

The girl stopped scolding and looked dumbfounded. The pilot turned to stare. Amanda didn't know what to do. Fear turned her cold body colder.

Then the tall boy said in heavily accented English, "Welcome aboard, Ah-man-dah Capelo. Glad are I you are not dead!"

She shook her head helplessly.

"I by Mars to look at your father! Welcome aboard!"

They were Greek, Konstantin told her. Greek Orthodox, which meant nothing to Amanda. Konstantin Ouranis was the tall boy who had saved her life, stopping at first for no other reason than she had been carrying a chalice for a religion she neither shared nor understood. When he'd seen her face, he recognized her from the newscasts. He was eighteen years old, had been born in Thessalonika, and knew her father's work. He wanted to be a physicist. He had come to Mars to ask Martin and Kristen Blumberg if they had any more of Dr. Capelo's work that hadn't yet been published.

All this came out slowly, painfully, as Amanda and Konstantin wrestled with language. The pilot had set the hopper down on a smooth stretch of plain in sight of absolutely nothing but red regolith.

He and the girl listened intently, as if listening hard could somehow make Amanda's words intelligible to them. "They have not English," Konstantin explained. "I have English one year on school."

"You still do better than I do in Greek," Amanda said shyly. Konstantin beamed.

The girl was his sister Demetria. The older boy, twenty, was Nikos Papandrea, Demetria's boyfriend. Both sat hunched intently forward, eyes flicking back and forth on the speakers' faces.

Konstantin said, "You to come by where?" His face looked concerned, interested. He had dark brown eyes and curly black hair: gorgeous eyes, gorgeous hair. His skin was a golden brown, the color of honey.

"I was in Lowell City," she said shyly. "At an abbey."

"Pardon me?" Konstantin said.

Amanda searched for simple words. "I was with priests. Mass. The Holy Office." Inspiration seized her. "At a house of God."

"Splendid!" Konstantin said. Maybe his English software had been British. "You are at house of God, you are . . ." he searched for a word ". . . to hide?"

"Yes, I was hiding. From the men who kidnapped . . . who took away my father."

"Yes, yes," Konstantin said and translated for Demetria and Nikos, who made the sign of the cross just as Brother Meissel had done. Brother Meissel . . .

"They're dead, aren't they? All the priests in the house of God?"

"Dead. Yes," Konstantin said, and took her hand. At his touch Amanda felt a strange sharp shock travel up her spine. "Sorry, I are."

"Thank you. They were good to me."

"Splendid," Konstantin said softly. "Good peoples. You to hide at house of God. And your father, Dr. Thomas Capelo, he to hide at house of God also?"

"No. I don't know where he is. We weren't kidnapped . . . weren't taken together. I saw him taken."

"You see your father take? Who?"

"I don't know!"

Nikos said something sharply and Konstantin stopped to translate. Nikos made a long voluble reply.

"Nikos say bad people to take your father. Dead now, maybe. Maybe no."

"He's not dead," Amanda said stoutly. "I know he's not dead. They probably need him. He's the galaxy's best physicist! There's no other reason to kidnap him!"

"I beg your pardon?"

Amanda tried again. "My father is not dead. Bad men took him, they need him. To do science."

"Ah, yes, science," Konstantin said reverently. "Dr. Thomas Capelo!"

Amanda nodded. They seemed to have reached an impasse. Suddenly Amanda realized she'd been hogging the whole conversation. She blushed. "You and Demetria and Nikos . . . you live at Lowell City?"

"Demetria and me live at Greece. By Earth. We to visit Mars. Nikos live at Lowell City with father of he."

Nikos suddenly snorted and made a very rude gesture with his hand, one that Amanda's father would never have permitted.

"Nikos not to like father of he," Konstantin explained.

Amanda was shocked. "But . . . was his father in Lowell City? When the dome collapsed?"

"Father of he by little dome. Maybe okay, maybe not okay. Nikos not to care."

"But . . ." She was silent, trying to take it in. Nikos didn't care if his father was dead or not. "But, can you radio him, or something?"

Konstantin spoke in Greek to Nikos, who repeated the rude gesture while answering. Amanda blushed. Konstantin said, "Father of Nikos to radio for Nikos sometime, maybe. This . . ." he pointed at the hopper bulkheads, evidently lacking the word, "you say how?"

"Hopper."

"Yes. Splendid. This hopper are of father of Nikos. He to want this hopper again."

Nikos's father would want the ship back, but wasn't that interested in his son. No, Konstantin must be wrong. Or he was just exaggerating, the way Yaeko did at home when she said she hated her mother. Yaeko argued a lot with her mother but she didn't really hate her, and Nikos and his father weren't really indifferent about each other's deaths. They couldn't be. Awkwardly, Amanda changed the subject.

"Where are you going now?"

Konstantin translated and a long discussion followed in Greek. Demetria tried to say something and Konstantin, to Amanda's surprise, turned on her with a sharp order, completely different from the gentle way he spoke to Amanda. Demetria stopped talking immediately and cast her eyes down. Even Nikos seemed to defer to Konstantin . . . but that couldn't be right, could it? Nikos was older, and it was his ship. Or at least his father's.

Finally Konstantin turned back to Amanda. "We go where you are to want go. You to hide. Yes?"

Amanda thought. Where did she want to go? Marbet Grant wasn't even on Mars . . . but did Amanda need Marbet anymore? General Stefanak might have kidnapped her father, or Life Now might have, but maybe neither one was in power now. If Admiral Pierce had won the fighting, then Amanda was safe. Admiral Pierce had no reason to follow Amanda, or to keep a guard on Aunt Kristen's house in Tharsis. Admiral Pierce wasn't part of whoever had taken her father. But had Admiral Pierce won the fighting, or General Stefanak?

"Konstantin, can you turn on the radio? To see if Admiral Pierce or General Stefanak won?"

He seemed to understand, if only the names and the word "radio." He gave an order to Nikos, who turned on the news. It was in English; there must not be enough Greeks on Mars to broadcast in Greek.

"—triumphant victory for freedom from military control as exemplified by martial law. Admiral Pierce has ordered the end of the curfew, effective immediately, so that survivors can begin the rebuilding of Lowell City's central dome. Now that Sullivan Stefanak is dead, Admiral Pierce will assume the role of Supreme Command of the Solar Alliance Defense Council, and—"

Amanda stopped listening. So he was dead, General Stefanak. It felt very strange. He had always been in charge, always been powerful, as long as Amanda could remember. She felt peculiar, as if gravity had suddenly failed.

"What it to say?"

She spoke slowly and clearly. "Admiral Pierce won. He's the leader now of the Solar Alliance Defense Council."

"Admiral Pierce!" Nikos suddenly said, and broke into a huge smile. Amanda didn't know why.

"Admiral Pierce good by business of my father," Konstantin explained.

"What business is your father in?"

"Many business. One, shipping from Earth at Mars. Big big shipping. Ouranis Corporation," Konstantin said proudly.

Amanda had never heard of them, which wasn't surprising. Her father always dismissed business as dull and unimportant compared to science.

Konstantin added, "My father not to like Nikos for Demetria. Demetria not to listen."

"Oh," Amanda said. She was out of her depth. Still, would her father someday . . . if she liked a boy, somebody like, say, Konstantin . . . but Konstantin wanted to be a scientist. It would probably be all right.

She blushed again at her own thoughts.

"So where you to want go, Ah-man-dah Capelo?" Konstantin said.

"To Tharsis. Is that all right? My aunt and uncle live there. I can stay with them."

"I beg your pardon?"

"My aunt. Sister of my father. In Tharsis."

"Sister of Dr. Thomas Capelo, yes," Konstantin said, "at Tharsis. I to go there anyways, to ask from Dr. Capelo's work. Splendid."

Nikos said something. Konstantin answered; Amanda heard the words "Tharsis" and "Dr. Capelo." Nikos shrugged and started the hopper's engine.

"Why does he do what you say?" Amanda asked Konstantin shyly. Really, it wasn't any of her business. But he didn't seem offended.

"Nikos have no money. Demetria are girl. I have all money of my father sometime," Konstantin said, cheerfully and brutally.

Amanda couldn't think of anything to answer. After her first grateful reaction, she was starting to feel uncomfortable. Had Konstantin really come to Mars to talk to Aunt Kristen about her father's work? Or was that just something he'd made up after he recognized her at the spaceport? He knew a lot about her father. Did that mean he knew even more, which he wasn't telling her?

She never used to think this way, questioning everybody's motives.

But then Konstantin held out his hand to pull her up off the floor and into a hopper seat, and at the touch of his fingers, warm and golden, she forgot that she had any doubts at all.

TWELVE

GOFKIT SHAMLOE

Kaufman, to his own surprise, did not see the angry side of Ann Sikorski again. Nor was the Ann he saw the gentle xenobiologist he had known on the *Alan B. Shepard*. This Ann was brisk, competent, more concerned with the material and the needful than with the intellectual. She spoke briskly of wagon axles, infant ailments, zeli gardens, jiks whose milk supply flagged. She never mentioned physiological cascades or quantum effects in the brain.

"I don't understand it," Kaufman said to Marbet, "she used to be so interested in cerebral functions. She had an entire theory of shared reality, which neurotransmitters were involved, how they affected Worlders' brains . . . all of it."

"She's not going back, Lyle," Marbet said.

"Did she tell you that?"

"She didn't have to."

"Not going back to the Solar System? Ever?"

"No. This is her life now."

So he had come all this way, hoping to expiate at least some of his guilt by rescuing a person who turned out not to want rescuing. And if Ann stayed, so would Dieter. Kaufman's mission to World with regard to them was pointless.

It seemed pointless with regard to World, too. Day after day, Kaufman saw neither the broken, savage, reverted-to-barbarism culture he had expected, nor an intact culture unaffected by what he had taken from it. Instead he witnessed a functional, matter-of-fact people adjusting to the daily tasks of survival (wagon axles, jik herds), combined with an undiminished spiritual life centering on flowers.

"You weed that allabenirib bed," Marbet said to him, "and I'll take the pajalib."

Kaufman had spent all his savings plus most of Marbet's, had broken the law to travel illegally, risked jail if his journey here were discovered . . . and his presence was totally superfluous. World was neither flourishing nor destructing—it just *was*. There was nothing Kaufman could do to help, except for weeding the flower bed of allabenirib. He knelt and began pulling.

"They want masses of these on the altar for tomorrow's ceremony," Marbet said, energetically pulling at the ground around the pajalib bushes. "Hospitality flowers, you know."

This was not how he'd imagined atoning for his guilt toward World.

"No, don't pull that, Lyle—that's a plant."

"Oh, sorry."

Not at all what he'd imagined.

He said, "I'm surprised Enli lets us work on the flower beds at all. The vegetables, yes . . . but not the all-sacred flowers."

Marbet said quietly, "Try not to be bitter, dearest."

She knew. She always knew. Kaufman tried. It was just that, since leaving the army, he wasn't sure what he was anymore. Not a soldier, as he'd been his whole life. Not a rescuer, which was plainly unnecessary. Not an instructor or a diplomat on World, which needed neither. Such thoughts were foreign to him, who had mostly lived his life by simply doing the task in front of him as well as he could, without thinking too much about how or why it got there. Now, it seemed, he was going to have to think about who he was and what he was going to do.

He didn't like it.

The Worlders were quite clear on what their own activities meant. Enli's child was undergoing some sort of ceremony, and the entire village was frenzied with preparing for it. Kaufman had gathered that the ceremony had once had something to do with being declared "real," but now that shared reality had gone, the ceremony wasn't that. Maybe just a naming ceremony. Kaufman had forgotten Enli's child's name. Or maybe it wouldn't have one until tomorrow. Was the kid a girl or a boy?

What was he going to occupy himself with for the rest of his life?

"Good," Marbet said. "Now let's do the trifalitib."

"Tell me again when this thing takes place."

"Tomorrow. It's exciting, isn't it? Confit will be three, in World years."

Confit. That was the child's name. Kaufman still couldn't remember its sex.

Ann walked toward them from inside the stockade. She looked cross. "Marbet, Lyle, have either of you seen Essa?"

"No," Marbet said. "Has she disappeared again?"

"That girl is better at getting out of work than anyone I've ever seen. Enli told her to pound all that cari to bake the bread for tomorrow, and she hasn't done any of it."

Marbet straightened from her weeding and flexed her back. "How did Enli become responsible for Essa, anyway?"

"It's a long story. The short version is that Essa was a servant in

Hadjil Voratur's household, and when the Change came, she ended up with us because she had no one else. She drives Enli to distraction."

Marbet said lightly, "And now Essa wants to visit other worlds."

"Magdalena will never take her," Ann said shortly. "She just promised Essa that in order to stir up trouble."

At the mention of Magdalena, Kaufman weeded harder.

Ann added, "Magdalena's activities are inexplicable enough without taking an alien child into space. Why does she stay here, now that she knows you can't help her find Amanda Capelo? And she disappears nearly every day in her skimmer, long trips. Where does she go? She's shown no interest in World for its own sake, that's for sure."

"No," Marbet said. "She's just using World as a place to wait."

"To wait?" Ann said. "For what?"

Marbet looked at Kaufman. He said, "There may be a revolution on Mars. Stefanak could be toppled, since many people think he's not waging the war against the Fallers aggressively enough. Magdalena has close ties to Stefanak, personal and business, and she needs a safe place to hide while the solar situation is settled and she can use her intelligence information to decide on her best scenario. A flyer will send her news from the tunnel as soon as there is any."

Marbet added quietly, "And the waiting is costing her every ounce of restraint she has."

Ann said, "Even I can feel that when I'm around her. It's like she's a volcano, set to blow. I can't imagine what it must feel like to a Sensitive, Marbet."

Marbet changed the subject. "How are the preparations for tomorrow coming?"

"Very well. Although that's why I was looking for you two. Lyle, I want to ask your help."

His help? Kaufman stood.

Ann looked graver than usual. "The two closest villages are coming to Confit's flower ceremony. That's really important, because as you know, since the Change each village has become pretty much isolated. They're afraid of each other, because naturally they don't know how to deal with strangers without shared reality. But Dieter and Calin and I have been trying hard to reestablish at least trading ties with Gofkit Mersoe and Gofkit Tramloe. Worlders have always been great traders, you know. And tomorrow they're each sending visitors to Confit's ceremony."

Ann stopped; she seemed embarrassed. Kaufman waited. He didn't see how he could help with this. He didn't even speak World.

"This could be a real breakthrough, Lyle. But only if the visitors get here and back safely. The marauders at the old Voratur compound have gotten more organized in their attacks. Two groups of people traveling between villages, carrying food and presents, are natural targets. They enslave captives, you know, to work the Voratur fields to feed the warlords. They're . . . never mind. Anyway, Dieter will go to Gofkit Mersoe on his bike early tomorrow and escort the visitors here. He's got tanglefoam, laser guns . . . he can get them here safely."

Kaufman said, "What have the warlords got?"

"Knives, spears, and clubs. They haven't even invented the bow and arrow yet, thank God. But Dieter can't be in two places at once. You're armed, Lyle, you have to be. Will you go to Gofkit Tramloe and escort the visitors from there to here?"

He was ashamed at how glad he was to be useful again. "Of course."

"Thank you. Do you need to get arms from your ship?"

"No." Dieter had assured him the locked, untended ship was safe behind an electrobarrier. "But, Ann . . ."

"What? Look, there's that worthless girl over there behind those bushes . . . Essa! You come here, Essa!"

"Ann," Lyle said, "the ship has real weapons. I could do a flyover Voratur's compound and solve your warlord problem once and for all."

He had her full attention again. The angry Ann, eyes diamond hard. "No, thank you, Lyle, we're not trying to teach these people more violence than we've already brought on them. Magdalena offered to do the same thing. We refused her, too."

Kaufman said, "Why haven't you already asked her to escort the visitors? She's been here much longer than we have, and you've been planning this ceremony for weeks."

"I'm not going to ask Magdalena for anything," Ann said, and Kaufman wondered if Dieter reacted to Magdalena the same way he did. Marbet, of course, would know, but Kaufman wasn't about to ask her.

Ann continued, "She pays Gofkit Shamloe well for food and water. That's all we want from her."

So that's where the beautiful embroidered pillow in Enli's house had come from. Kaufman said, "I'll need a villager to guide me to Gofkit Tramloe tomorrow and—" But Ann had stopped listening to him. She spoke heatedly in World to Essa, who had bounded up to them with something in her folded fist. Kaufman caught the words "Enli" and "cari."

Essa, looking totally unrepentant, unfolded her fist. On it sat a tiny data cube and an even tinier nano housing. Kaufman said, "Where did she get that?"

Essa jabbered back at Ann. Marbet translated for Kaufman. "She figured out how to take apart the casing of her comlink. Apparently it's mostly casing. Those are the working insides, still working."

Kaufman didn't look at Ann. It was he who had traded nine comlinks with the natives in the first place, on the previous expedition, over Ann's vigorous protests. The comlinks' range was limited to the planet, unlike Ann's, Kaufman's, and, presumably, Magdalena's. Theirs could reach anything in orbit around the tunnel, with a fifty-four-minute lag.

He asked, "Who has the other eight comlinks? Who does Essa talk to on hers?"

"Nobody," Ann said shortly. "The others belong to the marauders, they were all in Voratur's household. If they still even have them. But even Essa knows better than to try to raise anyone with hers."

Kaufman would have taken it away from her. An irresponsible child . . . Worlders had strange ideas about personal property. They tolerated stealing, but not confiscation. Maybe because it would have once violated shared reality? Apparently Ann now participated in these ideas.

Marbet said reasonably, "If she doesn't raise anybody with the comlink, how does she know it still works?"

"She doesn't, really," Ann said. Kaufman, ex-army, looked at the intact data cube and nano housing and thought, *It still works*.

Ann took Essa off to pound cari bread. Marbet, done with her weeding, went with them. Before Kaufman could return to his own weeding, he saw Magdalena walking toward him.

"Lyle?"

"Yes?" She looked older by sunlight than by starlight. But she still walked with the spring of a young girl.

"I just wanted to tell you that I haven't had any news yet from the tunnel. My informant on Mars had said the move against Stefanak was set for yesterday—" as if Kaufman could forget! "—but I still have no idea if it succeeded, or on what scale, or with what outcome. I thought you'd want to know."

To know that she had nothing to report? Kaufman knew a subterfuge when he saw one. He said gravely, "Thank you."

"Are you going to this native do-ha tomorrow?"

So that was it. Magdalena hadn't been invited. No, that wasn't possible; villagers did things en masse, a relic of shared reality. Everyone in the village was automatically assumed to be part of the ceremony. Magdalena was in the village. Ergo.

"Yes," he said. "I'm escorting the visitors from Gofkit Tramloe here early tomorrow morning."

"Guard duty, um?" she said, making it sound menial. "I suppose it's necessary. But maybe you can answer me a question. Is one supposed to give this child a present at the ceremony? I certainly don't want to commit a social gaffe."

Kaufman studied her. Sarcasm, and under it . . . more sarcasm? Or did she actually want to know? He couldn't read her, not even after a lifetime of dealing with politicians and military and corporations with hidden agendas. No wonder she was such a formidable force. She was far more complicated than the average general. Deviousness and brains and beauty.

Beauty?

Yes. Still. Despite.

He played it straight. "I believe a gift is in order, yes. Marbet and I are giving the child something."

"What?" she said, and Kaufman saw that she knew he didn't have the faintest idea what Marbet planned as a present. Magdalena tossed him a knowing smile and sauntered off. Against his better judgment, Kaufman watched her until she was out of sight.

I could have him, Magdalena thought. However, it would be a lot of trouble. Decent men so frequently balked at first. Or maybe she couldn't have Kaufman, maybe he'd remain faithful to that genemod mind reader of his. Once, the mere uncertainty and challenge would have excited her. Now, it just didn't seem worth the effort.

No one understood, not really. They thought her predatory, cold. And she worked to maintain that illusion, to keep hidden and safe her real self. Only hidden things were safe.

She wanted—had wanted all her life—to feel safe.

That's what the money was for, what the men had been for, what the endless covert deals were for. Why couldn't the fools understand this basic fact of life? Only power kept you safe. If you had enough of it, you could control any situation that threatened you, and then you were safe.

Growing up, she had never felt safe, not for a minute. She didn't remember her mother except as a cloud of sickening fear, a giant who hurt her over and over. Her mother's name could still make the back of her neck go cold. *Catalune*.

May Damroscher hadn't even felt safe with Sualeen Harris, although Sualeen had been the only person she'd ever loved, until Laslo. Sualeen had lived down the block from May and Catalune. She noticed that six-year-old May was often in pain, and she examined the bruises and burns and cuts. She didn't call any authorities; these people never did. She merely informed Catalune Damroscher that May lived with her now and if Catalune set foot anywhere near the kid, she was dead. Catalune knew Sualeen Harris meant it. She turned May over to her and never saw her adopted daughter again.

Sualeen Harris had a huge sprawling family of ill-defined kin of no namable ethnicity. They were walking examples of genetic warfare: black, white, Hispanic, Vietnamese, Punjab. Some were criminal and some were not, some were marginally less impoverished than others, some were literate and some were not. They were all, under Sualeen's energetic bullying, kind to May. When she turned twelve, Sualeen lined up all the males in her family from eleven to seventy and told them that if any of them laid a hand on May, they were dead men walking. Like Catalune six years before, they believed her, and the men who had been eyeing May's developing breasts averted their eyes.

Sualeen's great regret in a life filled with hunger and cold and death was that she could not afford carved, real-granite headstones for her family's graves. She tried to save for these, but always the money was needed for something: a new baby, bail money, payoffs to cops, something. Often Sualeen visited the great sprawling public cemetery a four hours' train ride from the city and mourned that her loved ones' graves were marked only by anonymous numbers on cheap foamcast. When the tumors finally got her, unchecked by any medicine, she knew that foamcast was all she would get, too.

Two days before she died, lying in a fetid sweltering room in great pain, she called May to her. "Go . . . May, go . . ."

"Where, Sualeen?" May said.

"Go . . . where the rich men are. It gonna come to you, honey . . . however. Get what you can out . . . out of it."

May didn't ask what "it" meant. She knew.

"Money . . . backyard . . . buried under tree . . ."

"I love you," May said, for the first and last time in her life.

"Go . . ."

May didn't go. She stayed for the coma, holding Sualeen's hand, and the death, and the funeral. At the graveyard there was only a foamcast marker with an anonymous number. Two days later, alone in Sualeen's house, a Harris uncle raped her.

May lay quietly, not struggling, knowing it would be futile. Penetration hurt her, and blood stained the floor. Afterward the uncle, caught somewhere between defiance and shame, didn't look at her as he pulled up his pants and swaggered out the door. She was sixteen years old.

May pulled up her own pants. Her body shrieked, from vagina to the base of her spine. Leaving the blood unwiped on the floor, she stumbled out to the backyard tree—there was only one, dying of some blight—and dug with a fork until she found the box with the pathetically small number of money chips. But it was enough for a train ticket to North Carolina and a monokini when she got there.

She walked up to a guard outside the elite enclave she had seen simulated in holomovies. The guard's eyes widened, then narrowed. May smiled. Despite her vaginal pain, she let him do what he wanted in exchange for entrance to the beach. She noted, with detachment, that afterward he wore the same look of mingled defiance and shame as the Harris uncle.

May went onto the beach and slowly walked up and down the water's edge, looking for shells. That was how she met Amerigo Dalton, who became the third man to penetrate her in twenty-four hours. May bit her lip and endured it. She needed Amerigo Dalton, and even then she'd known that he was going to be only the first of many.

But not, she decided, Lyle Kaufman. At least, not right now.

Walking into her pathetic primitive hut, Magdalena batted at a flying insect. The two bodyguards, whom she noticed less than she noticed air, trailed her and took up their posts at the door. She sat down on one of the laughable native cushions and tried, yet again, to fight off the daily despair.

Laslo. Where was he? Who had taken him? What effect would the coup d'etat on Mars—assuming that fuckhole Pierce actually brought it off—have on the capture of Laslo and Capelo?

She knew very well that Laslo was her . . . what had that professor called it, so many years ago? Somebody's heel. Some Greek. The place she could be hurt.

So many sweet memories. Laslo clambering onto her lap with a toy: "See, Mommy!" Laslo laughing at a puppy. Laslo saying, with a four-year-old's artless pleasure, "What a pretty day today!"

Laslo, in later years . . . No. Not those memories. All adolescents were difficult, look at that alien terror Essa. Laslo was just going through a normal rocky phase, he'd grow out of it. This was no more than another of Laslo's maddening, cruel "escapes" from his mother. But maybe this time he'd learn a real lesson from his misadventure, kidnapped and cooped up with a famous physicist for months. Laslo hated being cooped up and he wasn't much good at science.

When his captors came to move both him and Thomas Capelo to a more secure location—exactly what Magdalena would have done in their place—Laslo must have thought they were letting him go. Time he learned better. Only his mother could release him, and maybe after she had, he'd have a greater appreciation of the life she worked so hard to give him. Yes, this whole thing might have a beneficial effect on Laslo.

Cheered, Magdalena rose gracefully from her pillow. She had to find some sort of suitable gift for that alien brat of Enli's. What did you give a primitive native child? It wasn't like she could just order a toy from F.A.O. Schwartz-Mars. Well, there had to be something suitable in her ship. Time to check it out anyway.

She snapped her fingers to summon the bodyguards to her skimmer.

THIRTEEN

GOFKIT SHAMLOE

The next morning, Kaufman bicycled to Gofkit Tramloe in the company of Enli's mate, Calin, to escort the visitors back to Gofkit Shamloe for the flower ceremony.

"Are you sure you can still ride a bicycle?" Marbet had asked him the night before, lying wrapped in each other's arms in their hut.

"Isn't it supposed to be something you don't forget?"

"That's what they say."

He'd chuckled. "You can't ride a bike, can you? You never learned."

"No. I never did. God, it's dark here. I'm used to Luna City; we never go completely black. And Earth. I've only lived where there's city lighting."

Kaufman had seen darkness this deep, in combat situations. He preferred not to talk to Marbet about those. And he welcomed the impenetrable blackness for another reason. Sometimes it seemed that Marbet actually read his mind, so good was she at interpreting his tiniest body gesture or tone of voice. In the blackness, silently making love, she could detect neither. Try as he would—and he had tried hard—Kaufman had been unable to keep Magdalena out of his mind while he caressed Marbet.

Now he checked his arms and mounted his bicycle. Calin, too, was armed, with tanglefoam and a high-powered laser gun. Ann didn't know about the latter; she wouldn't have approved. But Kaufman was not going into combat—if you could dignify spear-throwing with that word—with a lieutenant armed only with tanglefoam. Tanglefoam range was far less than spear range. And Calin was the steadiest and calmest native he'd met on this planet. Despite Calin's speaking no English and Kaufman no World, Calin had easily mastered the laser settings during the secret training session Kaufman had given him yesterday. Kaufman, an experienced judge of soldiers, trusted him.

Calin held Enli's hands against his stomach for a long moment, then released her and got onto his own bicycle. Kaufman kissed Marbet and they set off for Gofkit Tramloe, leaving behind them a predawn village already frenzied with preparation for the flower ceremony. Food smells drifted after them on the air. People shouted; above the general noise Kaufman could hear Essa's excited, irritating laugh. Dieter had already left for Gofkit Mersoe, farther away.

It was obvious that the road between villages was little used. Unpaved, it had apparently once been so traveled that the dirt became hard-packed. Now weeds poked through the ground, in places so thick that he and Calin had to dismount and walk their bicycles. The encroaching underbrush would make good cover for attackers. Kaufman stayed alert, glancing every few seconds at his heat sensors, but the only thing they registered, or that Kaufman saw, were the ubiquitous rabbit-analogues called frebs.

What he mostly saw were flowers. All over again Kaufman was astonished at the floral life of World. No one tended these roadside beds anymore, yet they burst with the color and scent of hundreds of species of spectacular flowers. Beyond the roadside beds, wildflowers bloomed in almost equal profusion. If the marauders at Voratur's old compound did indeed succeed in introducing war to this part of the planet, it would be a war fought among endless gardens. Blood on the allebenirib.

It would be so easy to take out the entire compound. One burst of proton beam. And, Kaufman admitted to himself, it would make him feel less guilty. But he would abide by Ann's wishes. She was going to live here; he was not. Thank God.

They reached Gofkit Tramloe without incident. There Calin exchanged long, fulsome speeches, accompanied by flowers, with the seven natives journeying to Gofkit Shamloe. Kaufman hung back, knowing that these people were not used to humans; even Calin seemed foreign to them since the cessation of shared reality. Children darted peeping glances at the strangers from behind bushes and walls. This town, too, had a stockade.

The journey back was much slower, and on foot. By prearrangement, Kaufman and Calin left their bicycles at Gofkit Tramloe. Two of the visitors were old. One, in fact, was a shriveled crone with bright black eyes who looked older than rocks, apparently a very honored state. ("They are bringing a grandmother's mother!" Enli had exclaimed excitedly, which meant nothing to Kaufman.) She rode in a crude cart pulled by two strong young men, serene and majestic among the flowers, food, bottles, and presents being sent by the village. Kaufman hoped she wouldn't die of old age on the way.

He put Calin at the front of the procession and himself at the rear. If bandits were going to attack, it would be on the way back: more loot, more slaves. The natives all sang, making more noise than Kaufman would have liked (rule out detecting an enemy by sound). But no one attacked. They saw no one until they were in sight of Gofkit Shamloe, when the official delegation paraded out to meet the visitors.

Instantly Kaufman knew that something was wrong.

Ann was among the greeters. Kaufman could not read alien expressions very well, but Ann's was clearly disturbed. Dieter? Kaufman ran over his options for a hostage situation within the Voratur compound. Although it was difficult to see how Dieter's group could have been captured. Dieter was as well armed as Kaufman.

"It's Essa," Ann whispered to him when the procession had wound into the village. "She's missing!"

"Doesn't she do that periodically?" Kaufman asked.

"She wouldn't have done it this morning. She wouldn't have missed this for anything, it's the most excitement we've had in a year."

"What do you want me to do?" Kaufman said, hiding his irritation.

"I don't know. Enli's very upset. She—"

"Has anybody looked for Magdalena? Essa seems fascinated by her. Maybe she's with Magdalena."

"Lyle, Magdalena's at the ceremony. Everybody is, except Essa. Look, here comes Dieter."

A dust cloud floated on the horizon in the direction of Gofkit Mersoe. Ann and Kaufman brought up the rear of the first procession, which was supposed to have entered the village green and have completed all its speeches before the second procession arrived. It wasn't dissimilar, Kaufman thought, to an admiral's inspection.

Inside the stockade, the impression was even stronger. The communal green had been transformed. Pillows and low tables were scattered thickly over the ground. Every hut was hung with flowers. Plates mounded with food almost hid a long trestle table built while Kaufman had been gone. The Gofkit Shamloe villagers, dressed in carefully preserved festival clothing from before the Change, sat in rows on fallen logs at the edge of the green, the children preternaturally quiet and stiff. Gofkit Shamloe's old piper, Solor Pek Ramul, played softly.

Kaufman caught sight of both Marbet and Magdalena, standing together near the back of the seated villagers. Marbet, very short, wore a gown Kaufman had seen before, a modest drift of pale green fabric so light that the whole thing rolled up smaller than his fist and weighed a mere three ounces. She looked beautiful. Magdalena looked . . . Why the hell would a woman in exile, or whatever she was supposed to be, travel with a dress like that? And did she wear it at Enli's child's ceremony out of respect or mockery?

The dress was at least part holo, part heavy fabric in fantastic streaks of color that kept subtly changing as the holo played over the cloth. It was studded with jewels that may or may not have been real, or holo, or something else. The bodice, cut very low, clung to Magdalena's breasts and waist before flaring into a stiff long skirt. She had pulled her hair into shining loops on the top of her head, strung with more jewels. Her lips and eyelids were gold. She held herself proudly, and next to her Marbet, a foot shorter, suddenly looked insignificant. Kaufman looked away.

Enli and Calin, parents of the honored child, were making long speeches to the grandmother's mother, still in her overladen cart. Kaufman resigned himself to several hours of singing, flowers, and talk in a language he didn't understand. Ann's comlink shrilled, startling them both.

"What . . . Dieter knows better than to call now, unless something's wrong," Ann said. She moved behind Kaufman's bulk, pulled out her comlink, and switched the message from stored to live. It wasn't Dieter.

"—have me oh come quick they'll hurt me again come—" The link went dead. Essa.

Kaufman glanced around. Incredibly, no one else had heard. He clamped a hand on Ann's wrist and drew her back between two huts until he could pull her behind a wall.

"Is there a location indicator on Essa's comlink?"

"Yes. She's in Voratur's compound. Oh, Lyle!"

Kaufman thought rapidly. "I need Dieter, and two Worlders. Young, calm men who can take orders. Calin can protect Gofkit Shamloe, I'll give him more arms. But post lookouts, because Essa will have told them what's going on here today. She won't have been able to help herself. And I want Magdalena's skimmer. You get Dieter aside as soon as he gets here and tell him to unobtrusively meet me at the skimmer. I'm going to circle around the back of the huts and talk to Magdalena."

"Lyle, you and Dieter can't go now! It's the start of the ceremony!"

He took her hands. "Ann, the marauders want information about the villages. They may torture Essa. I think I can get in and trade for her without anyone of ours dying. But I have to go now."

She nodded. Kaufman trusted her to find two steady young alien males and to inform Dieter. Kaufman slipped around the back of the huts, along the slope to the river bank. He wasn't really surprised when Magdalena met him halfway; she would have seen Ann reach for her comlink and then Ann and Kaufman withdraw. There wasn't much Magdalena missed.

She looked wildly incongruous beside the crude wooden huts, on the rough grass-analogue, in her magnificent jeweled dress, her full breasts on display. Kaufman told her briefly what had happened. "I need your skimmer, please."

"Only if I go with you."

"No. This is a military action, however tiny. I don't want to have to look out for you."

"It's probably going to be a trading action, after an initial scare to the natives, and you know it. I drive the skimmer or you don't have it."

Kaufman bit back his retort. He didn't have time to argue. "All right. Wait at the skimmer."

He circled back. Ann stood just beyond the stockade with two men, one young and large, one middle-aged, small, and potbellied. "This is Solin Pek Harbutin and Camifol Pek Narfitatin. Camifol is a good negotiator."

"All right. Send Dieter to the skimmer as soon as he arrives. And you've got to extract Calin from the ceremony and bring him here right away."

Ann looked appalled, but she went back into the stockade. Kaufman pulled out his laser gun and began showing the two natives how to use it. Ann had chosen well. They both looked frightened but determined, and they followed his wordless instruction closely.

When Ann reappeared with Calin, Kaufman told him how to post lookouts and repel an attack on the village, if he had to. Ann translated. From the length of her speech Kaufman suspected she was adding edits of her own, but he didn't have time to investigate.

Magdalena had moved the skimmer closer to the village. She had changed from her gown into a gray coverall, but her hair was still in its elaborate jeweled upsweep. The two natives stayed as far away from her as the skimmer would allow. Since the skimmer sat only six, and one seat was needed to bring back Essa, Magdalena had left her two bodyguards behind. Probably she thought that Kaufman and Dieter would serve as sufficient protection. After what seemed a long wait but wasn't, Dieter arrived.

"Lyle! What do you plan, how do we get her back? *Scheisse*, those bastards . . ."

Kaufman shut him up and explained. Magdalena lifted the skimmer and set off at top speed; evidently she already knew where the Voratur compound was. The two natives clutched the arms of their seats but said nothing. Brave men, Kaufman admitted. By any standard. What if he had to cooperate with totally alien allies: Fallers, for instance? He couldn't imagine it.

"We're here," Magdalena said, decelerating hard. Kaufman suspected she was enjoying herself. She released the door and the four men stepped out.

Kaufman had seen action on two planets and a moon. He had served under that master strategist, Colonel Syree Johnson. He had participated in the negotiations that kept the Belt from seceding from the Solar Alliance in 2159. He had persuaded a SADA general to send the expedition to World that had dug up and decoded the Protector Artifact. Next to all that, negotiations with the marauders barely deserved the name. It took two minutes, and he could have done it alone. Kaufman was a little ashamed of his contingent preparations.

Dieter called out in World to send out the child Essa. There was no response. Kaufman used his laser full strength, wide sweep, to take off the top of the compound's ornamental gate. Noise from inside, but no one emerged. He fired again, lower, and wood and stone came crashing down. More noise. A minute later the ruined gate was shoved open thirty centimeters and Essa was pushed through it.

She stumbled, got up, and ran wobbling toward the skimmer. Kaufman expected wounds; she had cried over the comlink *"oh come quick they'll hurt me again come—"* It was a good sign that she could walk at all. Dieter ran forward and scooped her up, Kaufman covering him with the gun. They all climbed back into the skimmer.

Essa's arm hung at a strange angle. Broken. Three burns blistered the skin on the same arm. Her face was swollen from crying and contorted with pain. Dieter reached into his pocket and slapped a patch on Essa's neck. "Ann gave me painkillers. And I think I can splint this arm until we get to Ann . . . hold still, Essa!"

The girl had started to laugh and babble. The patch had cut in. Kaufman had seen this on the battlefield: sudden euphoria at the abrupt cessation of pain and danger. But soldiers were supposed to contain the euphoria. Essa never contained anything.

Dieter said, "She says they grabbed her before dawn, pretty close to Gofkit Shamloe, in the cari field, and—hold still, *verdammt!*"

Kaufman said dryly, "Ask her what she was doing alone in the cari field before dawn."

Dieter translated Essa's reply. The tiresome girl still bounced in her seat, ignoring her broken arm now that it didn't hurt her. "She says she wanted to try out the comlink, to see if the other eight we gave Worlders still worked. She put out an all-frequency call—you know, Lyle, that only means the frequencies we gave them originally, the comlinks were preset. Next thing she knew, she was being grabbed and carried to Voratur's. They searched her, but she'd already—be still, Essa!"

"Knock her out," Lyle said. "Here." He handed another patch to Dieter, who hesitated. But Essa began jabbering again at the top of her lungs, and Dieter applied the patch. Instantly Essa slumped in her chair.

Kaufman said, into the welcome silence, "What else did she say?"

"Only that they searched her, but she'd hidden the comlink insides back in her neckfur, and they didn't find them. They asked her many questions about Gofkit Shamloe, what supplies we have there, what weapons I have, and when she wouldn't answer, they hurt her. I don't know what she finally told them."

"Everything they asked," Kaufman said. But it didn't really matter. He turned to Magdalena to tell her to lift off.

She stood frozen, staring at Essa's arm. The break, the burns . . . Kaufman looked again, but that's all there was. Marbet had said that Magdalena had endured much worse. If the rumors about her were true, she had caused much worse. Then why . . .

It took a moment until Kaufman understood. This was a child. Essa looked very small slumped in the chair, her smooth flesh blistered in ugly painful burns, her young bone brutally cracked. A captured child. Like Laslo. Who, his mother was using every ounce of her inner energy to believe, was still alive and unhurt by his own capture.

"Magdalena . . ." Kaufman said gently. "Magdalena, take the skimmer back to Gofkit Shamloe."

He thought he might have to repeat the instruction, but Magdalena turned instantly and started the engine. Everyone sat. Kaufman turned his head back to Dieter.

Dieter said, "Magdalena, *bitte* . . . you are going the wrong way."

Kaufman lunged out of his seat. He was too late. Magdalena had circled the skimmer, soared above the Voratur compound, and fired. A proton beam—how the hell had she gotten a civilian skimmer fitted with a proton beamer! The compound vaporized. Gone.

"*Lieber Gott!*" Dieter cried. The two natives looked at each other fearfully. Kaufman seized Magdalena by the shoulders and turned her around.

"You had no orders to do that!"

"I don't take orders." Her frozen look had vanished, replaced by a coldness as complete as Kaufman had ever seen. "Now those pathetic little villages won't have to be afraid anymore. They're safe." She turned back to her controls and sent the skimmer down to normal altitude.

Kaufman sat down again. Well, she was right. Gofkit Shamloe and its fledgling trading partners were safe now. All Kaufman had to do was convince Ann that he'd had nothing to do with it. Ann, and the rest of three villages.

If shared reality had still existed, Kaufman realized, all humans would now be declared unreal. Shared reality was gone, thanks to him. Worlders would not get excruciating head pain because of this massacre. But Kaufman couldn't believe it was going to endear humans to Worlders, either. Ann had tried to show them that humans weren't all violent. Now Enli and Calin and the rest would think that even the humans on their side were dangerous, treacherous, untrustworthy, unpredictable.

And they would be right.

A comlink shrilled, and for a moment Kaufman thought it was Essa's, possibly still stored in her dense, dirty, matted neckfur. But the comlink was Magdalena's. She put a privacy link in her ear and listened. By the time the message—probably stored since she answered nothing into the link—was finished, they'd reached Gofkit Shamloe. Magdalena set the skimmer down.

"That was my informant at the tunnel," she said quietly to Kaufman and Dieter. "He just came through from Caligula space. The coup d'etat succeeded. General Stefanak is dead, half of Lowell City is destroyed, and Admiral Pierce controls the Solar Alliance Defense Council."

"What do—" Kaufman began, but Magdalena cut him off.

"Things should have settled down a bit by now. I'm leaving immediately for the tunnel. You can come, or not, to get Capelo at the same time. This skimmer is returning to my shuttle in ten minutes.

"So decide if you're coming with me."

FOURTEEN

THARSIS, MARS

tavros Ouranis's land hopper was designed for short jumps around Mars, not for traveling the ten thousand kilometers from Lowell City to Tharsis. The hopper looked, to Amanda's eyes, like a deformed plane. Made of ultralight plastics, it had huge wings, necessary for flight in the thin air, and a small fuselage, much of which was taken up by stored fuel and air-conversion equipment. Both breathable air and the jet engine depended on a judicious mixture of liquid oxygen in the tank and CO_2 from the Martian atmosphere. Even so, they would need to stop every place possible for refueling. The hopper carried a maximum of four not-too-heavy people.

"To go need two days," Konstantin told Amanda, "because . . ." His English failed him and he made motions with his hands.

"We have to zig-zag," Amanda said, and Konstantin nodded.

"For to fuel, you know. Splendid."

The first day, Amanda listened to the news in English. It was difficult to sort out. Admiral Pierce was now in command of the Solar Alliance Defense Council; that much was clear. But some places seemed to be fighting back. At least according to the newscasts that abruptly started, ended, and reappeared at a different frequency. Other newscasts said the entire population of Sol System was relieved to have Stefanak gone and someone in power "with the people's best interests at heart and the will to win this terrible war." There may or may not have been a resistance movement to Pierce on Earth. The Belt was definitely in resistance, but the Belt stations and outposts had always been among Stefanak's biggest supporters. Except that another newscast said the "dissident elements" in the Belt had been identified and arrested and now "freely elected representatives fully support Admiral Pierce's efforts to focus the Solar System on winning the war with the Fallers."

It was very confusing. Amanda listened for hours, while Nikos flew to another of Mars's small domed cities, landed, and went through the airlock to arrange for refueling. She would have gone on listening indefinitely, except that Konstantin had other ideas.

"Not news now, Ah-man-dah," he said in his wonderful accent. They were alone in the hopper; Nikos and Demetria had gone out to get fuel and food. "Now to talk at me." He turned off the radio.

Amanda thought that was pretty rude—he hadn't asked her, after all—but he was smiling at her and she found herself smiling back. His teeth were white and even against his red lips and honey-brown skin.

"We to find your father," Konstantin said, and when he stated it, Amanda could believe they would. "I think very much at your father. At his work. Look!"

He flipped open a handheld and brought up a directory. Amanda saw title after title of her father's papers, listed in both English and what she presumed to be Greek. Konstantin selected and brought up one on the tiny screen. "Look . . . your father at Protector Artifact. Setting prime one, directed-beam destabilizer, inverse-square law, short range, destabilize atomic numbers above seventy-five."

"Your English is much better when you talk about physics, Konstantin."

"Is physics. Is *your father*. Setting prime two, shield against setting one and setting three. Setting prime three, destabilize, wave, inverse-square law, short range. Setting prime five, shield one planet. Is Protector Artifact. Setting prime seven, destabilize one planet, atomic numbers above fifty. Setting prime eleven, shields one star system. Setting prime thirteen, destabilize one star system. Like Viridian."

"I know this," Amanda said. Konstantin ignored her, rushing on.

"Two Protector Artifacts at one star system . . . fabric of space to destroy. Look!" He pointed dramatically at the Greek on the notepad screen, pure gibberish to Amanda. At least half of the paper seemed to be equations.

"Konstantin, are you saying you can understand my father's papers on the Protector Artifact? Really?"

"I do physics. Not like Dr. Capelo. Little physics. I to try . . . look!"

He brought up another screen, as incomprehensible to Amanda as the first. But she could read the look on his face. "This is your work? You're working on the same thing as my father?"

"Little physics," Konstantin said solemnly, "very little. Calabi-Yau spaces. Flop transitions."

Amanda couldn't tell if "little physics" meant his physics was minor or if he meant that he was working at quantum level. Nor did she have any way of reading the mixture of Greek and mathematics he pointed to so proudly. She did know that her father had worked out what happened to proton beams when they hit a Faller ship equipped with the beam-disrupter shield.

As Amanda understood it, the beam had its probability of path altered, so it disappeared into a Calabi-Yau space, where its energy was used to effect a flop-transition to the shape of that tiny dimension. She knew, too, that if both Protector Artifacts, the human and the Faller, were brought together in the same star system and set off at setting thirteen, the large three-dimensional universe would also undergo a flop transition. The wave would spread outward at the speed of light, changing all the fundamental particles, and everyone would die. Amanda knew her father had proved the math of all this. But that was all she knew.

Konstantin must be the smartest boy she'd ever met.

She said shyly, "Are you at a special school for physics?"

"I go at university to physics."

A college student! "Are you in your first year?"

"Yes. First year by English, history, all that. But I go at university graduate student to physics. I go at Dr. Claude Dupuis."

"I've heard my father say that name. He's famous."

"Your father, yes," Konstantin said. "We to find your father. At you. At I, too. I to meet Dr. Capelo."

"Yes, of course you can meet him. I'd like that." To her great embarrassment, Amanda felt herself blush.

"You very pretty, Ah-man-dah," Konstantin said gravely. "I can to kiss you?"

"No!"

"Okay. Sometime, maybe. I like you very lots."

"Well, I like you, too," Amanda mumbled, intensely uncomfortable. To her relief, Nikos and Demetria returned, squeezing into the tiny space with a heated canister of food and making a great deal of noise.

It came accompanied by singing, as always. Somehow, in Amanda's dreams, the brothers chanting the Holy Office on Mars had gotten mixed up with her father's kidnapping on Earth, so that when General Stefanak grabbed Daddy and threw him into the black car, the air was filled with the plainchant of Matins: *Benedicte, Deo gratias* . . . "Don't worry," Father Emil said to her as she stood frozen at her father's bedroom window, "God will provide, or else Admiral Pierce will," and she turned to him in indignation to see that blood gushed from him and had spattered all down the front of her mother's yellow dress.

"Ah-man-dah," Konstantin said gently. "Ah-man-dah, stop to sleep now. Stop to sleep."

She woke clutching his arm. Nikos and Demetria snored in their chairs. Outside the hopper, the sky was just lightening to the deep rose of dawn. The hopper smelled foul; no one had been out of their s-suits for two days. "Wh-where are we?"

Konstantin grinned. "We to Tharsis. At evening we come. You to sleep. Look!"

He pointed to the horizon. Amanda saw a high gleam of metal: the struts of a dome. They were parked at the Tharsis spaceport. Aunt Kristin was here, and Uncle Martin, and they would know what she should do next. Adults would be back in charge.

"Not to cry, Ah-man-dah."

"I never cry!"

"Womans to cry," Konstantin said with great authority. "Mans not."

She scowled at him and stood up in the tiny space. "Can we go now? Will you wake up Nikos and Demetria?"

"Nikos not to go by you and I. They here. Father of Nikos want hopper. Very angry. He to come at Tharsis."

"And Demetria?"

"Demetria to come by me," Konstantin said, sounding shocked. "She not to stay by Nikos here alone!"

Amanda reached for her helmet. If Nikos's father was coming to the hopper, she would just as soon not be here. Konstantin had radioed his own father two days ago to assure him of his and his sister's safety. Although Amanda hadn't understood the Greek conversation, Konstantin's tone had been affectionate.

Still, it was odd to her that Konstantin's father would just let Konstantin go roaming around Mars, even if he was eighteen, in charge of his sister. Daddy never in a billion years would permit that. And there was Nikos's father, angry about the hopper, but Konstantin hadn't said he was concerned at all about his son. It was very weird. There were more weird people in the world than she had ever suspected before all this terrible stuff started happening to her.

Konstantin woke Demetria, who protested angrily. Konstantin silenced her with a sharp word. Why should he be in charge when Demetria was only a little younger, just because he was a boy? Amanda decided not to ask this, even if she could have found English that Konstantin could understand.

The three of them went through the airlock onto the dawn plain. The sun was just breaking above the horizon, hard-edged in the thin air. They caught a shuttle bus to Tharsis, where soldiers demanded their passports. Amanda had already shown Konstantin the forged passport the Life Now people had given her . . . when? Only a few months ago, but it seemed like years. Salah and Lucy and the others never appeared in her dreams, only Father Emil and the good Benedictine brothers. Brother Meissel . . . No, don't think about it. Think about Aunt Kristin, and a hot bath.

"We to find your aunt?" Konstantin asked, inside the dome. "Where?"

Tharsis was much smaller than even the auxiliary domes of Lowell City. There were no sleds. Streets radiated from the four gates toward the central square. Aunt Kristin and Uncle Martin's apartment was at the edge, on the third floor of one of the city's oldest building. It had a spectacular view. The building wasn't near this gate, however, but the gate on the opposite side of the dome. Even at this early hour, there were people hurrying through the narrow streets. Amanda didn't want to be recognized.

"Come this way," she said to Konstantin and took his hand. She led him and Demetria through the circular back streets to the apartment building. The tiny elevator—stairs took up too much space—carried them to the third floor. Amanda knocked.

For a brief disoriented second, she expected to hear Brother Meissel's "*Deo gratias.*" But she would never hear that again.

Konstantin said, "Your uncle not to have house system?"

Of course they did. She was disoriented, after the weeks without a system in the abbey. Amanda said, "System, open the door. This is Amanda Capelo. Check voice pattern."

"Hello, Amanda," the system said, and opened the door.

Uncle Martin, a light sleeper, must have heard the knock. He came hurrying out of the bedroom, knotting a robe at his waist, and stopped cold. "Oh, my God!"

"Martin? What is it?" Aunt Kristen, rushing out, and then, "Amanda! Oh, Amanda!" She grabbed Amanda, hugged her hard, held her away to see if it really was true, and hugged her again. "Amanda!" Aunt Kristen started to cry.

She looked so much like Daddy. The same thin dark face. Amanda felt her chest tighten.

Uncle Martin said urgently, "Amanda, is Tom with you? What happened? Where did you come from?"

Konstantin answered. "Dr. Capelo are not by here, no. I to bring Amanda."

Uncle Martin stared at him. "Who are you?"

"Konstantin Ouranis."

"Ouranis? Wait . . . you're the kid who kept trying to contact Tom about physics. And then you sent a message you were coming to see Kris here on Mars."

"Physics, yes," Konstantin said. "Splendid. My sister, Demetria." Demetria nodded graciously.

"Amanda," Uncle Martin said in his quiet way, "please tell us what happened."

Amanda had finished hugging them. Now she worried that she probably smelled bad. She hadn't had a shower in three days! Of course Aunt Kristen and Uncle Martin were too polite to say anything, but still . . . She tried to forget about smells and focus on what had happened. There was so much.

"Start with what happened the night of the kidnapping," Uncle Martin suggested.

"Let me at least get them some coffee first, Martin," Aunt Kristen said.

Demetria, for the first and last time in Amanda's hearing, recognized an English word. "Coffee!" she cried, so ecstatically that Konstantin frowned and Amanda, against all reason, laughed out loud.

Coffee, and cake, and explanations. Amanda was hoarse by the time she'd finished telling her aunt and uncle everything that had happened. Aunt Kristen held her hand tightly. Oh, it was good to be here.

Uncle Martin said, "So you thought that since General Stefanak is no longer in power, and he may have taken your father—*may*, mind you—it was safe to come out of hiding and come here."

"Yes," Amanda said, but at something in his tone, she was suddenly uneasy. "Isn't it?"

"I don't know. Things are very unpredictable these days. Certainly Admiral Pierce's coming to power hasn't resulted in your father's being freed yet. Amanda, there are some friends of ours I think you had better stay with until—"

"Visitors," the house system announced. "Solar Alliance Defense Council soldiers. They ask immediate admittance."

"Oh, God," Aunt Kristen said. "Martin, tell them she's not here!"

"I don't think it will make any difference," Uncle Martin said quietly.

It didn't. The door opened to three soldiers. Two moved quickly through the apartment, taking up posts on either side of Amanda. The third, an officer, said to Uncle Martin, "Dr. Blumberg, I am Major Harper, SADC. Your niece Amanda Capelo entered this residence fifteen minutes ago."

"Yes," Uncle Martin said.

"I assume her arrival was unexpected."

"Yes. What is this about, Major?"

"Is this the first time you've seen Miss Capelo since her disappearance the night of April second on Earth?"

"I think you know it is," Uncle Martin said quietly. "What is your business with my niece, Major?"

"Admiral Pierce wishes to convey his congratulations that Miss Capelo is unharmed. Have you knowledge of her father's whereabouts, Dr. Thomas Capelo?"

"No. And neither does Amanda."

"Admiral Pierce wishes to talk to her. My instructions are to convey Miss Capelo to Lowell City."

"But I just came from there!" Amanda cried. She'd come out from the kitchen when she heard her name.

"Hello, Miss Capelo," Major Harper said courteously. "You must come with us."

"No! I won't! Where's my father?"

"We hope you'll be able to help us determine that," he said, and even Uncle Martin looked surprised.

"You mean," Amanda cried, "you don't *know* where Daddy is?"

"Miss Capelo," Major Harper said patiently, "the situation is complicated, and I'm not at liberty to discuss it with you here."

Amanda set her chin. "I want my aunt and uncle to go with me."

"Certainly, if you prefer."

That was a surprise, too. Amanda decided to push. "And Konstantin. He's . . . he's a physicist."

Major Harper looked skeptical. Konstantin stepped forward. "Konstantin Ouranis. My father is Stavros Ouranis. I am by Ah-man-dah."

"Stavros Ouranis?" Something passed behind the major's eyes. "Does he know where you are?"

"Yes, yes. All okay at him."

"But . . . Mr. Ouranis, I'm sorry, but my orders do not include you."

Konstantin scowled. Amanda saw that he was not used to being told "no." Major Harper took Amanda's elbow; she was being led forward before she knew what was happening. "But . . . but I need a bath first!"

"I'm sorry, that's not possible," Major Harper said, but he did allow Uncle Martin and Aunt Kristen to change hurriedly from their nightclothes to coveralls. Amanda said to Konstantin, "Stay here, Konstantin. I'm sure my uncle and aunt won't mind. I'll be back as quick as . . . how long will I be in Lowell City, Major?"

Major Harper only smiled.

"Well, stay here with Demetria, okay?"

"Splendid," Konstantin said, flashed his white smile, and touched her arm. Once again Amanda worried how she smelled. Oh, she wanted a bath!

Major Harper and his soldiers led her toward the elevator, and back to Lowell City.

FIFTEEN

WORLD

S o decide now," Magdalena had said to Kaufman, although
Kaufman could see no reason for her sudden haste. She had
hung around World for a while now. So her demand for an
immediate decision was no more than a show of power: *Jump
when I say so.*

He didn't let his irritation dictate his decision. He said, "I'm
coming with you. Just let me get Marbet." He started for the skimmer
door. Magdalena nodded and raised her comlink again, presumably
to tell her two bodyguards to gather necessary items from her hut
and report to the skimmer. Before she could link with them, Kaufman
had her pinned against the bulkhead.

"I'm sorry," he said, "but I need more time than I think you'll
be willing to give me. Not too much more, Magdalena, but enough
to talk to Ann."

She had too much sense to scream or fight; neither would have
been useful. He tied her hands behind her back and then to the leg
of a skimmer seat. Dieter said, "Lyle . . . you have thought this
through?"

"I just don't want her to leave without us. Tell the two natives to return to the ceremony, without disrupting it, and send Ann and Marbet to the east side of the stockade."

Dieter translated. The two Worlders scuttled out of the skimmer, their skull ridges deeply crinkled. Kaufman left Magdalena with the unconscious Essa, and he and Dieter strode to the stockade's east wall.

"Lyle, what . . . they're right in the crucial part of the flower rites!"

"Where are Magdalena's bodyguards? It's important."

"In her hut, I think. She told them to stay there until she com-linked them. They're not exactly interested in the flower ceremony."

"Good. Marbet, the revolution on Mars succeeded. Stefanak is dead, Pierce is in power, and Magdalena is leaving for the tunnel immediately. I think she may be our best chance to find Tom. She has connections that you and I don't. But we need to decide now."

Marbet gazed at him. She said slowly, "When did our mission change from rescuing Ann and Dieter and possibly helping World, to rescuing Tom?"

"We can't help World," Kaufman said. "There's nothing for us to do here. Or—don't you think so?"

"I always thought so," Marbet said. "But I wasn't sure *you'd* come to that realization. The other reason we came, to rescue Dieter and Ann . . ." She turned to them quizzically.

Ann said, "We're staying. Nothing has changed for us because you two came here. This is our home now."

"Dieter?" Kaufman said.

"*Ja*, we stay." He put his arm around his wife.

Marbet said, "But you can't leave those two bodyguards here, Lyle! It would be profoundly unfair. No matter how much use they'd be against the Voratur-house marauders!"

Kaufman and Dieter exchanged looks. Kaufman thought, *Let Dieter tell Ann what Magdalena did to the marauders*. Dieter's return look said sarcastically, *Thanks a lot*. But Dieter didn't protest.

Aloud Kaufman said, "If you and Dieter are really staying, then there's room in the skimmer and shuttle for the bodyguards. Magdalena's shuttle, not ours—that holds only two. I'll let her call them from the skimmer. So, Dieter—"

"'Let her'?" Ann said suspiciously. "What do you mean, 'let her'?"

"No time. Dieter will explain. Good-bye, Ann. You're doing wonderful work here, undoing what I did."

Her long, plain face softened. But all she said was, "Take care of yourself, Lyle. You, too, Marbet."

Dieter threw his arms around them both in a bear hug. Kaufman endured it; Dieter was what he was. Kaufman turned to Marbet. "Five minutes in our hut, Marbet. Just grab some clothing and equipment. I don't want Magdalena's bodyguards to get to her skimmer before we do. Don't let the natives see you, if possible, and—"

"Not possible," Ann said. "I'll explain all this later to Enli. Now I have to get back to the ceremony." She was gone, and from her decisive stride, her long, embroidered native tunic might as well have been combat boots and full battle armor.

Ann Sikorski was, Kaufman realized irrelevantly, a happy woman.

Dieter followed his wife. Marbet had already left for her and Kaufman's hut. Kaufman returned to Magdalena.

"We leave in just a few minutes," he said placatingly. "Marbet is coming, Ann and Dieter are staying. If I untie you and let you summon your thugs, are you going to tell them to take me apart?"

Magdalena studied him. "And if I say 'yes'?"

"Then they stay here and you stay tied."

"All right, Kaufman, I won't instruct them to mash you into paste. But why should you believe that?"

"Well, not because I trust your word," Kaufman said. "But I

don't think you really want me either dead or left behind on this planet. I might be useful to you, at some point."

"I don't see how."

"Nor do I, yet. But we know different people, have different allies, can call in different favors. Is it really worth it to you to lose that potential advantage just for the satisfaction of punishing me? I've only delayed you about fifteen minutes, you know. And of course, you always have the options of setting your thugs on me later. When your dance card isn't quite so filled."

Magdalena laughed. "You really were a good military negotiator, weren't you?"

"Still could be," Kaufman said pointedly.

"You and your tame Sensitive could return to the tunnel in your own flyer."

"You are where the action's going to be. Tom and Laslo." Kaufman felt a twinge, evoking her son's name. But it was her one vulnerable spot. Use whatever you can. He was going to need Magdalena's contacts to reach Tom, and if Kaufman took his own flyer, she could easily escape him.

"All right, Lyle," Magdalena said, saying his name with Marbet's intonations, a delicate mockery. "I'll summon my 'thugs' without telling them you tied me up. Untie me."

He did, first glancing out the door to make sure Marbet was approaching. Magdalena was quite capable of leaving without her. Marbet rounded the edge of the stockade, still in her long drifting gown, her arms full. Kaufman released Magdalena.

Curtly she comlinked her bodyguards. Kaufman reached to unstrap the sleeping Essa. He would leave her on the ground; Ann would come for her as soon as she could.

"Leave the kid there," Magdalena said. "No, don't look at me like that, Lyle—this isn't your call. She goes with us. I promised, didn't I?"

"You can't, she's native to this planet . . . don't bring her just to get back at me!"

"You flatter yourself. Leave her."

"No."

"Oh, yes, Lyle. Come on, Rory. We're leaving."

Her bodyguards arrived at the skimmer at the same time as Marbet. The senior one climbed in, looking hard at Kaufman. Kaufman had no chance against him. Augmented, almost certainly, and possibly engineered as well. Magdalena smiled.

Both the junior thug and Marbet carried loads of belongings. "Dump those in the corner and sit down, we're going," Magdalena said.

"But . . . Essa! Lyle—" Marbet began, and was thrown to the floor as Magdalena slammed the skimmer into high speed.

Her shuttle was parked ten kilometers away, in the middle of an empty field. In plain sight, it was nonetheless protected by an e-barrier, and evidently Magdalena didn't care who saw it. Kaufman blinked at first sight of the shuttle. It was as big as the military shuttle he and Dieter had had on their previous expedition, when they'd dug up the artifact. That expedition had arrived on an SADN warship. What the hell was Magdalena's ship like?

"Take off immediately," Magdalena said. "Rory, stow the skimmer. Lockers inside for all that loose stuff, we'll sort it out later. Kendai, bring that alien girl and strap her in."

If the junior bodyguard was surprised at this command, he didn't show it. Marbet said again, "Magdalena, you *can't*. Lyle—"

"Lyle has nothing to do with it," Magdalena said, clearly enjoying herself. "Nor do you. Essa goes with us."

The two women faced each other. Marbet said, "Essa can't survive off-planet. This is all she's known. Why are you doing this?"

"Look at the Sensitive being," Magdalena jeered. "How do you know Essa can't adapt off-planet? She wants to go. Are you saying the engineered superwoman should make decisions for the poor inferior backward alien? Very colonialist of you, I must say."

"You're only taking her to make Lyle and me uncomfortable," Marbet said. "It's in every line of you."

"Why don't you ask Essa?" Magdalena said sweetly. "When she wakes up, of course . . . places, Rory. Let's blow. Better strap in, Sensitive."

"*Lyle —*"

"There's nothing I can do," Kaufman said, knowing that if Marbet hadn't been so upset, she would never have made him admit it aloud. He didn't look at Marbet as he strapped himself in.

Magdalena piloted. During the lift through the atmosphere, no one spoke. Essa slept through the entire flight. Kaufman watched World fall away beneath him. Green, lush, and . . . what? Doomed, he would have said a week ago, and writhed now at his hubris. He was not the destroyer of worlds. Not even the rescuer of fellow human castaways. Ann, Dieter, and World all managed their existences very well without him.

And yet he had changed the directions of those existences. So he was neither destroyer nor savior nor neutral force, but something more elusive. More ambiguous, less clear. He, Lyle Kaufman, who had prized the unambiguous clarity of following military orders, while remaining emotionally untouched by those orders.

Not now. Any of it.

Lyle Kaufman gazed down, and watched the beautiful planet dwindle, and hoped to God to never see or set foot on World again.

Magdalena's ship was as big as a *Thor*-class vessel. Crew of thirty, Lyle decided professionally. Suspicious attachments fore and aft; this ship was armed with a lot more weapons than any civilian liner should be. Her name, Kaufman noted wryly, was the *Sans Merci.*

" 'Palely loitering,' indeed," Marbet muttered sourly. Kaufman didn't know what she meant, and didn't ask.

As soon as the shuttle had docked, Magdalena disappeared. To call the *Murasaki*, Kaufman guessed. As far as he knew, the warship was still in orbit around the tunnel, still inexplicably. Magdalena must have gotten ship permission to enter the star system. Otherwise, she wouldn't be here.

Two years ago, Colonel Ethan McChesney, SADC Intelligence, had been in charge of the *Murasaki*. McChesney, who had reported directly to Stefanak, had headed the Special Projects group that brought a live Faller to a SADN warship. The only live Faller humans had ever captured, which Marbet had slowly, painfully, learned to communicate with, until it was killed.

Was McChesney still aboard the *Murasaki*? Why was the warship still here? And who did Magdalena know to enable her to come and go with impunity—it was exactly the right word—past the *Murasaki*?

Whoever it was, the shift in power in Lowell City must have affected his or her standing. Not to mention the standing of Magdalena herself, well-known "friend" to the late Sullivan Stefanak. No wonder Magdalena looked concerned.

However, she looked much less concerned when she reappeared on the observation deck two-and-a-half hours later. Kaufman and a very silent Marbet had been given tiny quarters with four bunks. Kaufman had dumped Essa in one of them . . . better the alien girl stayed with Marbet, who could at least talk to her, than at the mercy of Magdalena, self-proclaimedly *"Sans Merci."* The room opened off a corridor leading to Magdalena's stateroom, her bodyguards' flanking rooms, a galley separate from the crew's mess or officers' wardroom, and, at the end of the corridor, the observation deck, filled with comfortable furniture and with a spectacular view of stars. Magdalena's personal domain.

She entered the observation deck briskly. Kaufman and Marbet had been talking in low voices, and even Kaufman knew that nothing they said mattered as much as what they didn't say. Marbet was disappointed in him: for allowing Magdalena to bring Essa, for leaving World on Magdalena's ship instead of their own, for his confused sense of what he was doing now. Look for Tom? Where? How? Three months ago, he had said there was no point in looking for Tom.

Ah, but that was when I thought I had a purpose for being on World, Kaufman didn't say. What was his purpose in looking for Tom Capelo?

What was his purpose if he didn't look for Tom?

"You're all right," Magdalena said, with her mocking smile. The blue of her coverall darkened her eyes to sapphire. "McChesney will pass us through the tunnel without boarding. He'll never know you two are my highly illegal passengers."

"And then what?" Marbet said evenly.

To Kaufman's surprise, Magdalena answered her. "McChesney won't know anything about the political situation, not this far out at the rat's ass end of the galaxy. We go through the tunnel to Caligula space. It's military, I know people there. Pierce hasn't had time to change the commands at remote outposts, at least I hope not. But everybody will be very stirred up. A few people I know may be in considerable danger. It may be possible to arrange . . . deals."

Her smile was intended for Kaufman, he knew, the ex-soldier. He put deliberate amusement into his voice. "Magdalena, I hope you're not implying that I don't know there is corruption in Stefanak's military. That assumption would be beneath you."

"And you, Lyle. But you may not know how much corruption. Always clean, weren't you? Like McChesney. And always loyal to Sullivan, too."

It was the first time Kaufman had ever heard anyone use General

Stefanak's first name. He didn't ask why McChesney, if he was so clean, was dealing with Magdalena at all. He didn't really want to know the answer.

Marbet said, "The war with the Fallers doesn't concern you at all, does it? Except as a source of profit."

"It's a dirty universe, Sensitive."

Light footsteps ran down the corridor. The next moment, Essa, still in her gaudy celebration tunic, burst onto the observation deck. She saw the clear wall of stars against black space, with World a blue-green dwindling orb in one corner. The alien girl stopped dead.

Marbet rose swiftly. "Essa, don't be frightened. We—"

Essa said something in rapid World. Kaufman remembered that she had been in space once before, among the nine aliens Ann had brought up to the *Alan B. Shepard*.

Marbet answered soothingly in World, reassuring.

"Space!" Essa said in English. She threw herself at Magdalena's feet, looking up adoringly, her black eyes bright as stars and her skull ridges so crinkled that her head looked like a prune.

It appeared that Kaufman had been wrong again. Essa did not look frightened or displaced.

"Space! Essa!" she said, and Magdalena looked mockingly at Marbet and laughed.

SIXTEEN

AT SPACE TUNNEL #438

I t took Magdalena's ship four days to reach the tunnel. That was at an acceleration of nearly two gees, which made everyone uncomfortable. People stayed still in their chairs a lot, except for Essa.

She was all over the spacious ship. An irate officer dragged her onto the observation deck by one skinny arm. "This alien was in the engine room!" Kaufman refused to say he was sorry. Essa wasn't his responsibility.

Somehow, she was Marbet's. Marbet spent hours with Essa every day, teaching her English. "She's very intelligent, Lyle, but one of the least fearful people I've ever seen. She isn't scared of anything unless it's physically threatening her life at that very moment. She's terribly vulnerable. What are we going to do with her?"

"I didn't think we were going to do anything with her. Magdalena is."

Marbet said quietly, "You know that's not true. It would be criminal to leave a child like that with Magdalena."

"Marbet, when we return to Sol I won't know if my false passport had been discovered. I don't know if I'm subject to criminal charges. I don't know where we're going to live, or how I'm going to earn a living. Do you really think it's fair to saddle me with an alien child?"

"No, I don't. But as Magdalena so helpfully pointed out, it's a dirty universe. We've got her." Marbet paused. "Or at least, *I* do."

Kaufman didn't like the implications of that. "Are you saying that when we get back to Mars, or Luna, or wherever, we're not going to be together?"

"I'm not saying that, no. I *am* saying that you need to make some decisions, and you're not making them. You're just drifting, and it's turning you jumpy and unpleasant. At least find something to do with yourself on ship, Lyle." She turned and left. Kaufman could hear Essa calling for her from the observation deck.

Kaufman knocked on Magdalena's stateroom door. Rory, the older bodyguard, lounged in a chair outside. Kaufman ignored him.

"Yes?"

"It's Lyle Kaufman. May I come in?"

The door's e-lock clicked.

Her cabin was large and lavish. Rory followed him in. Magdalena lay on the enormous bed, listening to a music cube. She wore a coverall the intense blue of her eyes, and her black hair was loose on the pillow. Damn it, she was older than he by at least ten years, maybe fifteen, she should not have this effect on him. Nor know it. Marbet was right; he wasn't balanced.

He said testily, "I want to ask if I can have unrestricted access to your ship's library, and if you regularly download scientific journals into it."

She studied him. "Why?"

"I want to read the physics journals for the last six months, if you have them."

"Can you understand physics journals, Lyle?" She smiled.

He kept his voice even. At least, unlike Marbet, she couldn't deduce his thoughts from minute changes in body language. "Not most of the math. But there are abstracts and conclusions, and there are journals that translate breaking events for the educated laymen."

"What events do you think are breaking?"

"I don't know. That's the point. But if you want me to help you find Tom—and Laslo—I need to know as much about who took him as possible, and why. Maybe it's connected to something he was working on."

She frowned. "I'm sure the police and the reporters thought of that already."

"Probably. But I'd like to look anyway." *For something to occupy myself with*, he didn't say aloud.

"All right. I'll instruct the system to let you in. It's retina-keyed. But, Lyle . . . just so you know. There's nothing personal in the ship's library. In case you thought you'd break some firewalls."

"I'm not interested in your personal files," he snapped, and regretted snapping. It gave her a small victory. He made himself say, "Thank you," and was disturbed all over again by the mocking smile she gave him in return.

Damn her.

Kaufman couldn't use the terminal in his room; Marbet spent too much time there, teaching Essa English while lying on her bunk (which, because of Essa, was pointedly not "their" bunk). The acceleration was harder on Marbet than anyone else. She'd lived for years on Luna; she'd spent six months on Mars; World had point-nine Earth's gravity. She spent much of her time lying down. Kaufman, energetic by temperament, was irritated by her constant horizontal position. It seemed lazy. He knew this was unfair.

The only other terminal available to Kaufman was on the observation deck. Magdalena had purchased the most comprehensive commercial packet available, automatically fed to her system as soon as the packet arrived in whatever area of space she happened to be occupying. The *Sans Merci* had apparently passed through Space Tunnel #438 in August, so the library included journals and commentary through then. Kaufman sat in a comfortable chair, heavy hands on the armrests, and talked to the computer for the next three days, trying to follow Tom Capelo's thoughts through his published papers.

Kaufman was not trained in physics. But he had always been fascinated by it. And because he had been there when Tom formulated his great breakthrough about probability, Kaufman had followed the evolution of that theory ever since. The theory's evolution, the resistance it met, the confirmations made by other scientists, the objections and loopholes—all the give and take of scientific discourse.

Actually, the entire Solar System had been fascinated by Dr. Thomas Capelo's theory, even those who didn't know a proton from a protein. The theory, people knew, somehow had produced the disrupter beams that let Faller ships shrug off human particle-beam weapons. Even more important, it somehow had produced the Protector Artifact that kept the enemy from frying the Solar System.

That last, Kaufman knew, wasn't accurate. The artifact worked whether humans understood the science behind it or not. Capelo had explained why it worked, but that fact had been far less interesting to the Solar Alliance Defense Council than the fact that it did work. Soldiers were neither physicists nor engineers. They had wanted Capelo to discover what each setting on the artifact did. He had done that. But he had also discovered why.

As Kaufman understood it, Capelo had justified, both in a model and mathematically, the existence of a particle he'd named a "probon." Each probon, like all fundamental particles, was made of tiny vibrating threads, and each was a smear of probabilities. It existed at the quantum level, in the seething roiling frenzy that is the quantum world, in which particles are constantly deflected, constantly breaking apart and reforming, constantly erupting from the energy of the vacuum and disappearing again.

The probon was a messenger particle, just as gravitons were messenger particles for gravity and gluons for the strong force. The message the probon carried, the force it transmitted, was probability. In the universe as human physics knew it, probability decreed that the path an object took *was* the average of all paths, the path resulting from wave function amplitudes squared, the path that gravity-warped-by-mass made into the path of least resistance. Mass told space how to curve; space told mass how to move.

But actually, as physicists had known for two hundred years, a particle took all possible paths. A proton beam fired from a warship traveled directly to its target, traveled obliquely to its target, reached its target by detouring first to the Andromeda Galaxy. All possible paths. Including through the six curled-up dimensions of spacetime, the tiny Calabi-Yau spaces. The proton beam traveled through the Calabi-Yau dimensions countless times because the dimensions were so tiny, returning each time to its starting place. But, ultimately, the average of all these circuitous journeys was the least-resistance sum-over-paths integral, because that's the force probons carried and it operated everywhere, just as gravitons made gravity operate everywhere.

Large masses could warp gravity, sometimes to extremes, which was why black holes existed. The Protector Artifact, that strange leftover from an unimaginable race, warped probability.

The artifact focused probons, shot a huge number of them at an incoming particle stream, just as a laser focused and shot photons. The artifact thus warped probability, in the same way huge mass warped gravity. The energy to do that was certainly available; the strength of the force transmitted by a messenger particle was inversely proportional to the tension on its threads, and Capelo had calculated fairly low tension for the probon, let alone the energy in the protons. All the energy of these tiny vibrating threads brought about a different path, one of low but not zero probability under "normal" circumstances, and now of 100 percent probability. So the proton beam went not into its target but into one of the six Calabi-Yau spaces, the curled-up dimensions of the universe.

Once it was there, it couldn't just lose all that energy; the law of conservation of energy didn't allow it. So the energy brought into the Calabi-Yau dimension, energy which hadn't been there before, did something else. It effected a space-changing flop transition, changing the shape of that tiny, curled-up dimension into a different shape. *Without* affecting our larger, three-extended-dimension universe at all. The energy started by making a tiny tear, and to repair the tear, the Calabi-Yau shape evolved into a different shape, which mathematicians had known was possible almost as long as they had known of Calabi-Yau shapes. The process was called a flop transition.

The enormous energy needed to alter the beam's probable path, to change the vibration of its threads, exactly equaled the net energy of the heavier probons minus the energy lost to quantum agitation. The new vibrational energy exactly equaled the energy needed to effect a space-changing flop transition in a Calabi-Yau dimension of a certain probable configuration. A piece of the dimension was unfolded, and then refolded into a subtly different shape, like refolding a part of a complex origami. All the equations balanced, led into one another with natural rightness.

But there was a price.

As the Calabi-Yau space evolved through the tear, that affected the precise values of the masses of the individual particles—the energies in their threads. The tiny vibrating threads that made up, say, a proton beam, always smears of probability, now vibrated at a different resonance. It had, in fact, ceased to be a proton at all, and had become a different, unknown particle. This was possible because matter itself, at the deepest level, was itself a manifestation of probabilities. The probabilities had been changed.

When you applied the equations to the large, three-extended-dimensions universe, the price became terrible.

The probability energy focused by *two* artifacts was huge. It was enough to do to the three-dimensional universe what smaller amounts did, over and over, to a small, curled-up dimension of the universe: effect a space-changing flop-transition into a different shape. It did that the same way it did it in the tiny dimensions, by first tearing the fabric of spacetime.

But in the tiny dimensions, it was a tiny tear, easily repaired with the energy pouring in at the same time from the entire probability-altering event. In the large extended three dimensions, there wasn't enough energy. The "tear" would spread, and the total dimensional shape of the universe—now a benign hypersphere extending fifteen billion light-years before curling back on itself—would undergo a topology-changing flop transition.

But the vibrational patterns of the threads that make up spacetime were intimately dependent on the shape of the dimensions in which they vibrated. Not the size, but the shape. If the three extended dimensions of the universe underwent a flop transition, its threads would vibrate in different patterns, *giving rise to different fundamental particles*. Extended spacetime itself would be different, the disturbance to its fabric traveling outward at light speed.

And every living thing in the universe—humans and Fallers, bacteria and viruses and genetically recreated elephants, would die.

This much Kaufman understood, at least superficially. Now he tried to follow the work that had been done, by Capelo and others, on the probability equations and their implications. He was looking for something, anything, that might have led someone to kidnap Dr.

Thomas Capelo. To keep Capelo working on some specific idea, or keep him from publishing some specific idea, or something. Anything.

Kaufman didn't find it.

All he could discern from the masses of equations and heavy prose in the journals, or from the breathless, sensationalized speculation in the popular press, was that there was one huge hole in Capelo's theory. It didn't account for macro-level quantum entanglement. That was the most accepted idea about how the space tunnels worked, and Capelo had not tied together probability, as a fifth universal force, with quantum entanglement. Some physicists saw this as a flaw so fundamental that it invalidated Capelo's whole theory. Others saw it merely as a blank to be filled in as the theory was refined and added to. Capelo himself, in the one interview with him in Magdalena's library, seemed to see it as neither.

It gave Kaufman a little start, seeing that thin dark face with its inevitable irritable expression, come up on the terminal. Capelo had never suffered fools gladly. He said that yes, quantum entanglement had not yet been accounted for. No, he didn't think that invalidated his theory. No, he didn't think he'd published prematurely, given that General Stefanak had ordered him to do so and everyone in the scientific world knew how profound was the military understanding of physics.

Despite himself, Kaufman smiled. Same old Tom.

But Kaufman was no nearer to any idea of why Capelo had been kidnapped. Perhaps it had, as Stefanak had claimed, been Life Now, seeking something major and emotional to blame on the Stefanak regime.

Perhaps it had been the Stefanak regime, seeking something major and emotional to blame on Life Now.

Perhaps it had been some third party, a ransom attempt aborted midway.

Perhaps Tom was already dead, as Stefanak was.

Kaufman had gotten nowhere, and had wasted three days doing it. But, then, what else did he have to do?

"Lyle!" a voice screamed down the corridor. Marbet. "Lyle, come quick!"

Marbet never screamed. Kaufman hurled himself out of his chair, despite the gravity, and ran clumsily to their cabin.

She'd spent too much time just lying on her bed, Magdalena thought, and that was bad. It wasn't the gravity. She could handle gravity, handle her ridiculous passengers, handle McChesney and, in Caligula system, that bastard Hofsetter. What Magdalena was having trouble handling was the fear.

What if she couldn't find Laslo? Two people might keep her from him: Admiral Pierce and Laslo himself.

She hadn't really expected Stefanak's assassination. Her mistake: She'd overestimated his hold on his power. Somehow Sullivan Stefanak had slipped up, or a brute like Pierce would not have been able to pull off his coup. She, Magdalena, should have foreseen that possibility, should have guarded against it. Definitely her mistake. And Pierce was capable of simply sequestering Laslo somewhere for a very long time, just to make Magdalena crawl and caper and cede territory she otherwise would never surrender to an asshole like Pierce. Well, if she had to crawl, she would. Just don't let Pierce keep her at it for years.

The other fear was Laslo. Magdalena could easily visualize a scenario in which Stefanak's most trusted aides, immediately after the assassination, might panic. They'd jettison everything nonessential, including Laslo. And Laslo might then put himself in hiding, away from his mother's control that he so desperately needed but was too weak to accept. It could take her years to find him, if he'd had time to pull major funds from her account or his father's and prepare a hiding place. While she was stuck traveling back to Sol System from the backside of the galaxy.

But that had been necessary, too. The first rush of a new tyrant's power was always the most confused, dangerous time. Pierce could easily have made her disappear. Now, when he must be discovering the limits of his reach, and when her contacts had a firmer sense of the situation, she had a far better chance of playing that situation so that he could not kill her without public notice.

But Laslo . . .

She had to stop this. Brooding never solved anything. Magdalena despised brooders; they were weak. Action was the only thing that forced the universe into submission. Too few people understood that—although, oddly enough, among them was that otherwise misdirected straight player, Kaufman.

Magdalena swung her long legs against the gravity and off the bed. She sat up, and heard someone screaming.

Instantly Rory, in the corridor, had flung open her door and drawn his gun. "No, I'm fine, Rory. It's Marbet Grant. Come with me!"

As quickly as her leaden legs allowed, Magdalena moved down the corridor. The bunkroom door was open and Lyle Kaufman was already darting through it in response to the Grant woman's shout: "Lyle, come quick!"

Magdalena crowded into the room behind Rory, who shielded her. But there was nothing to shield anyone from, only the alien child lying on the floor, clutching her head.

"What is this? What's wrong with her?" Magdalena demanded. Everyone ignored her.

"It started about a half hour ago," Marbet said rapidly to Kaufman. "How close are we to the tunnel?"

"About an hour out. Marbet, how can you be sure?"

"Easily," Marbet snapped. She knelt on the floor beside Essa, scooping her up into her arms and murmuring to her in her native language. "Watch. I just told her that she's Essa, she's aboard a flying metal boat in space, that I am Marbet . . . watch."

As Marbet murmured, the alien's face stopped contorting. The ugly wrinkles on her bald head smoothed. She clutched at Marbet, listening, but she no longer looked hurt.

"Now," Marbet said, "watch this . . . oh, God, I hate to do it but you need to see!"

She began talking again in World. The child looked at Marbet in consternation, and her skull started to crinkle. Within thirty seconds she was clutching at her head, clearly in pain.

"I told her," Marbet said rapidly to Kaufman, "that we're headed back to World, that you and I hate each other, that flowers are not important during a trade. And look."

"Look at what?" Magdalena demanded but the two of them went on ignoring her. She felt her face harden. How dare they pretend she wasn't here?

Kaufman said in a strange voice, "I still don't see how that can be happening. Shared reality only existed in the presence of the artifact. In the field it generated around World."

"Yes," Marbet said. "*Yes.*"

Kaufman stood very still. "McChesney."

"Hand-picked for the original Faller project by Stefanak," Marbet said. "How trusted do you have to be for that? And still there."

"The *Alan B. Shepard* docked with the *Murasaki* to take on supplies," Kaufman said. "I was in brig, but an ensign told me. Docked on this side of the tunnel."

"And McChesney's still there!"

The two of them stared at each other until Essa whimpered. Marbet bent her head over the child and spoke comfortingly.

Magdalena said tightly, "Kaufman, what are you gibbering about, both of you? What's wrong with that kid?"

"She's experiencing shared reality. Again."

"So? What does that mean?"

For the first time, Kaufman looked at Magdalena. She recognized the calculation in his eyes. When he spoke, it was with great deliberation: a sum totaled and reached.

"It means, Magdalena, that Essa is once again in the presence of the probability field she spent her life in. It means Dieter Gruber's insane theory of brain evolution was right. It means that the Protector Artifact isn't hidden somewhere in the Solar System, under Stefanak's or Pierce's control.

"The artifact is right here, aboard the *Murasaki*."

SEVENTEEN

AT SPACE TUNNEL #438

Automatically Magdalena said, "It can't be."

"Why not?"

"Because it makes no sense, Kaufman. Stefanak had the artifact in the Solar System, set at eleven, to protect the entire system from Fallers."

Kaufman said, "You don't know that. Not for sure. The thing was supposedly hidden."

"But why would Stefanak have done anything else with it? There's no point!"

"Yes, there is. I'm going to sit down, Magdalena. This gravity." He eased his tall body onto a bunk. After a moment's hesitation, Magdalena did the same. Rory remained standing beside her, but she hardly noticed. A bodyguard was not a person. On the floor, the Grant woman cradled the alien, who seemed to have recovered but whose silly neck-furred face looked as if she enjoyed Marbet's attention.

Kaufman said, "Stefanak didn't have to actually have the artifact in the Solar System to stop the Fallers from bringing in theirs and frying us. All he had to do was make the enemy *think* the artifact was in the Solar System. We know they monitor our outpost electromagnetic broadcasts, and that they know a hell of a lot more about us than we do about them. For two years the human media's stated, discussed, shouted that the Protector Artifact is somewhere around Sol. Just as theirs is around their home star."

"Still no good," Magdalena said. "Think, Kaufman. Stefanak had no reason to mislead Fallers—and humans—like that. No reason to keep the artifact in this remote backwater, instead of in the Solar System."

"Yes, he did," Kaufman said. "The artifact expedition didn't only include physicists, you know. Ann is a xenobiologist. She has documented exactly how the Worlder brain adapted over fifty thousand years to the strong probability field the artifact generated when it was buried on World—and was permanently turned on at setting prime eleven. They evolved shared reality."

"So?"

"So there was another part of the first and second expeditions' reports on World. It wasn't published because there's no hard evidence. But I experienced it myself, and I told Stefanak about it myself."

Magdalena snorted. "*You* told Stefanak?"

"The one time I met him. He was at the board of investigation to determine if I'd be court-martialed. I wasn't, so there's no public record of that, either. Surprised?"

"Don't play games with me, Kaufman. What did you experience for yourself about the artifact?"

His face changed. Magdalena recognized the look of a man remembering something he'd rather not. Marbet was watching Kaufman closely. Usually Magdalena managed to put Marbet's abilities out of her mind, but now she wondered what the Sensitive saw that Magdalena did not.

Kaufman said, "I experienced the effect of the artifact on the human brain. Personally, when it was still buried. I went with Tom Capelo and Dieter Gruber into the caves, and my mind just blanked. Emptied completely. If I hadn't been pulled out of there on a rope, I'd have just stayed standing blankly in the same spot until I starved to death."

"That's crap," Magdalena snapped. "McChesney's aboard the *Murasaki* with an entire crew and, supposedly, your artifact, and his mind's not empty. I spoke to him this morning. And you said Essa was just now affected by this 'field,' but we obviously weren't."

"No. The field isn't uniform. It's toroid . . . shaped like a doughnut. Only at the thickest section Gruber and Capelo and I blanked. And the alien guide with us never did. She evolved in the field. Her brain can handle it."

"You've no real proof that—"

"I *felt* it," Kaufman said, and in his quiet conviction Magdalena heard truth. He'd experienced what he said he had.

He continued. "Stefanak knows all about the toroid field. Gruber had it in his report, and I told him in person. When the artifact is turned on at setting prime eleven, the setting that protects an entire star system from any sort of quantum-weapon attack, you also get the mind-blanking toroid. My guess is that Stefanak didn't like that. An unknown mind-altering field brought through space tunnels, which we also don't understand, and installed in the Solar System itself? You probably don't know this, but an earlier, larger artifact exploded when a warship tried to take it through the tunnel, killing everybody aboard and obliterating the artifact." He was silent a moment. Remembering Syree Johnson? Soldiers could be such sentimentalists.

"So," Kaufman continued, "why take the risk if you don't have to? And Stefanak didn't have to. He got the same political effect if everyone only *thought* he'd installed it in the Solar System as if he actually did."

Marbet said abruptly, "It would fit easily in the *Murasaki* cargo bay. It's only twenty-five meters in diameter."

Kaufman said, "And soldiers don't come any more loyal than Ethan McChesney. He's SADC Intelligence."

Magdalena thought rapidly. It was possible Kaufman was right. She'd known Sullivan Stefanak; his vanity was his brain. He never did fizzies, not even during sex, not wanting to muddy his thinking. He might very well have been reluctant to bring into the Solar System something that could empty human minds. Even if it only affected people within a certain "toroid" range. Maybe especially then, if the range was unclear. Nor would he want to risk the artifact blowing up, like this other artifact Magdalena was hearing about for the first time.

Was Kaufman telling the truth? Yes, he was. She might not be a Sensitive, but she trusted her own judgment.

So if Stefanak had indeed stowed the Protector Artifact aboard the *Murasaki* . . . but Stefanak was dead. So—

She said rapidly, "Pierce doesn't know where the artifact is. If he did, he'd be here already, to kill McChesney and take control. His coup was days ago. There's been time to get a flyer here, so there would have been more than enough time to order military from Caligula System to capture the artifact."

Kaufman said, "I add it up that way, too."

Marbet spoke. "How do you know Admiral Pierce hasn't done that? Left McChesney in charge and the artifact here, for the same reasons Stefanak did?"

Magdalena laughed derisively. "You don't know Ethan McChesney. Or Nikolai Pierce. No, Pierce doesn't know where the thing is."

"Not yet, anyway," Kaufman said. "But our question is—what do we do with the knowledge?"

Magdalena said instantly, "Talk to McChesney. The artifact is the most powerful bargaining chip in the galaxy."

Laslo.

Marbet stood, leaving Essa on the floor. "But what are you trying to bargain for, Magdalena? Or you, Lyle? I don't understand what either of you is trying to accomplish."

Magdalena's eyes rolled. Well, that's what you'd expect of a dim-witted Sensitive, all feeling and no ability to plan. People like Marbet Grant never understood that you held chips long before you needed a specific bargain. Although Magdalena knew what hers was going to be.

Laslo. Soon. She'd be with him again.

Apparently Kaufman had something different in mind. "It's not what we want to accomplish, Marbet," he said slowly. "We want to find Tom, but it's possible Pierce doesn't know where Tom is, any more than he knows where the artifact is. What I'm thinking is—"

Magdalena cut in. "If Pierce doesn't know where Capelo and Laslo are, he'll damn well be motivated to find out if we tell him we've got the Protector Artifact!"

Marbet said acidly, "You don't have it. McChesney does."

Magdalena laughed. "Same thing, Sensitive. Ethan's no fool. He's got to be shitting his pants wondering what to do now that his boss is dead and Pierce is getting slowly around to having Stefanak's Intelligence Corps neutralized."

Marbet said, "I don't think—"

"Be quiet," Kaufman said, so harshly that Magdalena turned to him in surprise. "Let me finish my sentence."

"Finish it, then," Magdalena said. She had never before heard him rebuke the Grant woman; it was pleasurable.

"What I'm thinking," Kaufman said, "is that the key point is not what we want to accomplish with the Protector Artifact. It's what Pierce will want to accomplish. Magdalena, you've obviously had civilian dealings with him. I've had military ones, when I was attached to the SADC. He's not like Stefanak. Stefanak, despite all his faults, was basically reasonable. He could balance risk with conservation of advantage. But—"

"Sure he could," Magdalena said scathingly. "That's why humans are losing the war."

Kaufman ignored her. "But Pierce is a much different organism. As a commander, he goes way beyond daring. He's not only a risk taker, he's an insane gambler. There are those who say he's just insane. I think it's entirely possible . . ." He stopped.

Both women had already seen it. Magdalena spoke first. "You think he's capable of taking the Protector Artifact to the Faller home system and turning it on at setting thirteen. To destroy their entire system. Betting that their artifact is also somewhere else in some other system. Or that they don't understand the consequences of two artifacts trying to fry each other in the same system. Or maybe that they do understand but, once we've set off ours, won't do the same so that at least the fabric of space will survive."

"Yes," Kaufman said. "I think Pierce is capable of all that. Do you?"

Magdalena closed her eyes. Truth tore at them anyway. *Laslo* . . . "Yes," she finally said. "I think Pierce is capable of all that."

There was a silence. Into it Essa said suddenly in her fledgling English, "We go now? Go in tunnel? Go more stars?"

Marbet pulled the child close. No one answered her.

"We go now? Go in tunnel? Go more stars? Essa go more stars!"

"I think," Kaufman said, "we should talk to Ethan McChesney."

EIGHTEEN

LOWELL CITY, MARS

Lowell City crawled with soldiers wearing green bars on their caps.

Amanda shrunk closer to Uncle Martin. She hadn't had any private conversation with her aunt and uncle at all; Major Harper and his men had stayed close beside her on the flight to Lowell City and in the shuttle bus from the spaceport. The dome had been repaired, but some of the buildings were still rubble. Others stood but still had their windows blown out. And everywhere swarmed these soldiers with green bars.

"The emblem of the Freedom Army," Major Harper said. He must have caught her staring. Amanda blushed. "Soon we will have Lowell City completely functional again, and cleansed of all its enemies."

Amanda had thought the Fallers were the enemies.

Guards at the gate passed them through into the main dome, where a car waited. Military cars, the only kind permitted in Main Sector, were narrow enough to fit through the streets and so never carried more than four. Amanda was afraid that Major Harper would eave Aunt Kristen and Uncle Martin behind, but he didn't. Instead he left his soldiers, and the car drove him, Amanda, and her aunt and uncle to the Summit.

More soldiers with green bars.

"Major Harper . . ."

"Yes, Amanda?"

"Could I please have a shower before I see Admiral Pierce? Please?"

Major Harper turned his head to look at her, and it seemed to Amanda that something softened behind his eyes. "Yes, I think that can be arranged, if you can do it in fifteen minutes."

"I can! Thank you!"

But at Tharsis, she remembered, he'd said there wasn't fifteen minutes to spare.

She thought she'd be allowed to keep Aunt Kristen with her, but instead she was steered gently but firmly to a door on the third floor and sent in alone. It turned out to be a sort of guest room, small but comfortable, with an attached bathroom. Amanda hesitated. Her father always said every square inch of the Summit was under constant surveillance—did that mean that someone would be watching her if she took off her clothes? The thought turned her hot and uncomfortable.

She settled for showering in her underpants, trying to keep her breasts shielded as much as possible with her arms. Then she took off her wet underpants under cover of a big fluffy towel and pulled on her trousers, without underwear, the same way. Trousers, tunic, and bra were also dirty, but at least she felt a little cleaner. She couldn't stomach the smell of her socks, however, so she put on her boots without them. They chafed against her bare feet.

On the dresser in the bedroom were a comb and a brush. Amanda untangled her hair and, for the first time in weeks, saw herself in a mirror. She gasped. The black dye had half grown out of her fair hair, with the choppy short haircut Father Emil had given her back aboard ship—how long ago? Months. It seemed like years. Now she looked like a freak, a total idiot.

And Konstantin had seen her looking like this.

A knock sounded on the door. Amanda dropped the brush and opened the door to Major Harper.

"Ready, Miss Capelo? Come with me, please."

"Where are my aunt and uncle?"

"Comfortable in guest quarters. You'll see them soon."

Amanda said, "Can't they come with me to see Admiral Pierce?"

Major Harper didn't even answer, just led her briskly by her elbow to an elevator to the top of the building. Amanda felt her heart begin a slow, hard hammering that made it difficult to catch her breath.

They passed more soldiers, finally entering a room at the very top of the Summit. "This is Miss Capelo, sir."

"Fine. Leave us, please, Major."

Major Harper saluted, and Amanda was left alone with the new supreme commander of the Solar Alliance Defense Council.

After the years of holos of General Stefanak's imposing bulk, Admiral Pierce looked small, although he was of average height. He was lean, with thin, long-fingered hands. Amanda especially noticed the hands. She was too nervous to register much about the office except that it had a huge desk, a row of wall terminals, and a wonderful view of Lowell City at Admiral Pierce's feet, with the red Martian plain beyond.

He said courteously, "Thank you for coming, Miss Capelo."

As if she'd had a choice!

His voice was low and musical, which surprised her. She'd have thought an admiral would sound rougher, somehow. Or maybe that was just Stefanak again.

"Miss Capelo, I know you have been through a great deal in the past month. And the hardest of all, I'm sure, has been worry over your father."

She nodded, her throat suddenly too tight to speak.

"I completely understand your worry. Dr. Capelo, from everything I've been told, is not only a great physicist but a wonderful father. I'm in regular contact with your stepmother and sister, you know, and I want you to know we're taking good care of both of them."

Amanda nodded again.

"You've been very brave on your father's behalf, Miss Capelo. Now I'm going to ask you to be brave for his sake one more time. We have very good reason to believe that General Stefanak had your father kidnapped. We don't know the reason, but we think it was probably so that his corrupt regime could blame it on Life Now. Which, of course, they did. Believe me, Miss Capelo, I'm as anxious as you are to get your father back. Science should remain above politics, if it's to do its job."

"That's what my father always said," Amanda blurted. She felt herself relax a little. Admiral Pierce seemed really nice, like he understood.

"Your father's a wise man. Now, our problem is this: We don't know where your father was hidden by Stefanak. No, don't look like that—the situation is far from hopeless. I have my very best intelligence operatives locating secret military records, questioning the traitors we've captured, doing every single thing we can to find your father."

He had moved closer to her. The fine, long-fingered hands folded in front of his chest. "Miss Capelo, we need your help. We think only a very few people in Stefanak's regime knew where your father was being kept. So far, we haven't been able to identify those people. It's crucial that we do so. They're the ones who will lead us to your father. Do you understand?"

"Yes, but . . . how can I help?" The folded hands had begun to twitch a little. She watched them, mesmerized.

"Oh, you can indeed help. You can do something very important to help your father. If you're willing to do so. Are you?"

"I'll do anything!" Long, thin fingers, twitching while folded together.

"It's possible you remember something about what you witnessed the night of April second. You were watching from an upstairs window—"

How did he know that? Amanda wondered, startled.

"—and you might have seen some identifying mark, something very small, in how the kidnappers looked or talked or behaved. So small that you probably don't even know you know it. Amanda, do you know what a Pandya Dose is?"

Now she was even more startled. "I've seen it in the holomovies. But I didn't know it was real!"

He smiled. His fingers still twitched. Amanda made herself look away. "Oh, a Pandya Dose is real enough, although it's not as dramatic as in the holos. It's an injection into the brain, past the blood/brain barrier, of a selective-cell activator. That means—"

"I know what a selective-cell activator is," Amanda said, offended. After all, she was going to be a biologist!

"Wonderful. You're a very intelligent young lady. Then you know that the dose contains a chemical that intensifies the chemical cascade in the brain connected with memory."

"Cyclic-AMP response elements, plus LTP proteins."

Now Admiral Pierce looked startled, but Amanda felt a little ashamed. Her father always said only mediocre minds showed off.

"You *are* intelligent. So I'm sure you understand that the Pandya Dose works by shutting down most of the cortex except for long-term memory, and by sharpening that until you recall every single detail your senses registered for a given occasion. Details that your conscious brain doesn't usually have access to because it would become too overloaded with trivia. Are you willing to take a Pandya Dose so we can learn anything about the kidnapping that might help us find your father?"

He really was nice. Concerned, caring . . . Amanda didn't look at the fingers. She nodded vigorously. "I'll do anything!"

"You're a wonderful daughter and a great patriot," Admiral Pierce said, which made Amanda pause because her father always said patriotism was a front for power games. But the admiral was summoning another man, who led Amanda away, and suddenly she was in a room with a couch and lab bench and doctors.

"Now?" she said. "We're doing it now?"

"Just lie still," a woman said, smiling warmly.

"Will it hurt? What are those tubes for?"

"Nothing will hurt," the woman said, and it didn't. Amanda felt a patch on her neck, and her scalp went sort of numb. *I'm helping find my father,* she thought fuzzily, and all at once she was certain everything would be all right. Of course it was! In fact, she felt happier than she ever had in her life . . . Then she slid into sleep.

"Amanda."

"Five more minutes . . ." But the alarm was ringing and she would be late for school and today was Yaeko's birthday party. Amanda had bought Yaeko a great present, she'd be so surprised . . .

"Amanda. Wake up now, honey."

She came to with a start and tried to sit up. Something was wrong with her bones. They wouldn't support her, and she sank back on the bed.

"Stay still, honey. Your muscles have weakened temporarily. Just stay still." It was Aunt Kristen's voice.

Amanda turned her head and was surprised at how hard it was

to do. Other things were wrong, too. Her lips were dry. She licked them and tasted blood.

Aunt Kristen wiped her lips, raised Amanda's head on her arm, and held a glass of water for her. Amanda sipped. It took all her strength.

"Damn them!" Aunt Kristen said. "No, I don't care who hears me, Martin. They could have at least kept her properly hydrated!"

"A Pandya Dose is not supposed to go on that long, Kris," Uncle Martin said, and Amanda had the impression he, too, didn't care who heard.

Amanda croaked, "What . . . happened?"

"You were out for twenty-four hours, dear. You'll be fine, but right now your throat is raw from talking for so long."

She had talked for twenty-four hours? What had she said for that long? Amanda tried to concentrate, and slowly the experience drifted back into her mind. That was in the holomovies, too. A Pandya Dose didn't make you forget what you had said under its influence. The villain was always horrified at how much he'd told the good guys.

"They asked . . . about . . ."

"I said don't talk, dear," Aunt Kristen repeated, in that voice that said, *I mean it.* Amanda shut up.

But she could think without hurting her throat. The doctors had asked her about much more than the kidnapping. They'd made her describe every single last thing she'd done, every single person she'd talked to, between her flight to Walton Spaceport on Earth and the arrival of Major Harper. All of it: Father Emil and looking for Marbet on Luna and Salah's attempt to kill her and the brothers at the abbey and Konstantin. Amanda felt her face go hot. What had she said about Konstantin?

"What is it, Mandy?" Aunt Kristen said. "What did you just think of?"

"Did . . . did they find out where . . . Daddy is?"

"They wouldn't tell us that," Aunt Kristen said. "They just said you'd been very helpful and we can take you home now."

"Home?"

"To Tharsis, not Earth. They want you to stay on Mars for now."

Uncle Martin said darkly, "Potential press value."

"SShhhhh, don't talk," Aunt Kristen said, and it wasn't clear to Amanda if she was speaking to Amanda or to Uncle Martin.

Amanda tried to remember more. Herself talking and talking and talking . . . she had told them about Konstantin! . . . and the doctors leaning over her and asking questions, asking a lot of questions, especially about Marbet Grant . . .

Amanda had told them Marbet wanted to go back to World.

That was supposed to be a secret. Marbet had told her in confidence, months ago, when Amanda had asked to come visit Luna during winter vacation from school. *"I'd love it, but I might not be here, Amanda."*

"Where are you going?"

"I'm not sure yet."

"I'll bet you're going back to World. To see Dr. Sikorski and Dr. Gruber and Enli."

"You should be a Sensitive yourself, Amanda. But let's not say anything to anyone, all right? Travel outside the Solar System is so . . . difficult."

"You can trust me, Marbet!"

She had felt so grown-up that Marbet would confide in her like that. And now she'd told a friend's secret, one of the worst things you can do. When Juliana had told Yaeko a secret of Thekla's, that Thekla liked Misha Chuprikov, it had almost ruined the whole friendship.

Then the doctors had asked her a lot of questions about her trip to World, and her father's work there, even though that was *years* ago. And—this was weird—even more questions about the trip back from World to the space tunnel, with the Protector Artifact aboard. How long had it taken, what had people said, how long had they docked with the *Murasaki*. Until this moment, Amanda hadn't remembered that they'd docked with the *Murasaki* at all. But the doctors had asked a whole lot of questions about it. It was baffling.

The whole thing was baffling. Most of all, she didn't understand why Admiral Pierce wouldn't say if he now knew where Daddy was. That was the point of the whole Pandya Dose! And he'd seemed so nice!

"I don't . . . understand," she rasped, and Uncle Martin gave a short hard laugh.

"No one does, Mandy. But now we do the only thing we can. We take you home, and wait to be told more."

Home, to Tharsis. Was Konstantin still there? Had he waited for her? She turned to look at Aunt Kristen. Her neck felt stronger now; she was feeling better every minute. She noticed more patches stuck on her arms.

"Aunt Kristen?"

"Yes, honey?"

"Before we go, can . . . can I see a hairdresser?"

Admiral Pierce did not fly them back to Tharsis. They never saw Admiral Pierce again. Major Harper thanked them, said they were free to leave, and had them escorted to the door. "It's a good thing I have credit here," Uncle Martin muttered.

He checked them into the Lowell Hilton overnight. Soldiers with green bars on their caps checked their retinas, smiling courteously. Everyone was so polite, Amanda thought. At least that was better than General Stefanak.

Uncle Martin caught her smiling back at one of the soldiers. " 'A man may smile and smile and be a villain,' " he said, which sounded like a quotation. Amanda didn't ask. Uncle Martin had once taught literature; it gave rise to quoting disease, her father always said.

Her father! She would see him just as soon as Admiral Pierce found him!

She felt freer and lighter than she had in months. Uncle Martin sat at the hotel room terminal to arrange transportation back to Tharsis the next day, and Amanda and Aunt Kristen went shopping. At last she could get out of her sweaty, stinking clothes! She bought trousers and a tunic in light blue, plus some additional things for her stay in Tharsis. Aunt Kristen took her to a hairdresser, who trimmed her hair and stripped out the patchy black dye. Then he made it a soft gold, brighter than her natural pale wheat color. Amanda looked in the mirror and smiled. She looked pretty again.

"Thank you, Aunt Kristen!"

"You look so much like your mother, honey. More and more."

"Daddy won't ever talk about her."

"No, that doesn't surprise me. Tom only allows himself a very limited range of emotions."

That surprised Amanda. She'd never heard anyone criticize her father before . . . if it even was a criticism. Aunt Kristen was talking to her as if Amanda were grown up. Amanda said shyly, "Am I like my mother in other ways?"

Aunt Kristen smiled. "You're a mixture, honey. You have some of Karen's calm and optimism, and some of your father's rationality and daring. You're you."

"I love you, Aunt Kristen."

Her aunt hugged her. "Can we talk about this boy you've installed in our house?"

Amanda felt herself blush. "He saved me after the dome was breached in Lowell City—I told you." Involuntarily she glanced up at the dome, intact again. But how could anyone trust it to stay that way? She would be glad to get back to Earth, where you could count on the air . . . and Konstantin, too, was only visiting on Mars.

Aunt Kristen was watching Amanda. "I see," she said wryly. "Well, he seems like a nice boy."

"He is! And guess what—he wants to be a physicist, like Daddy! He's really smart."

"Smart is good," Aunt Kristen said neutrally.

"Do you think Daddy will like him? When Admiral Pierce finds Daddy?"

Aunt Kristen stopped walking. They stood in the middle of the shopping-district square, surrounded by the plenty Mars mostly imported from elsewhere. Aunt Kristen looked around to make sure no one was near enough to hear. She said, "Honey, I know how badly you want your father back. We all do. But I want you to be prepared for the fact that Admiral Pierce may not return him to us."

The bright air seemed to darken. "You mean . . . Daddy might be dead."

"He might. But he might also be alive and Admiral Pierce will not release him, for the admiral's own reasons."

"But he *said*—"

"I know what he said, honey. And I know you liked him, and you like all the politeness his men have been ordered to show. But under all that courtesy, Piece is a very dangerous man, much more dangerous than General Stefanak. I wanted to tell you this before they took you away for questioning, but that major stuck so close that Martin and I didn't get a chance. You're old enough to know how things stand on Mars, honey. Especially after all you've been through already."

Amanda's knees trembled. But she kept her voice steady. "Tell me."

Again Aunt Kristen checked that they weren't overheard. "People who oppose Pierce just disappear. Stefanak balanced a hunger for power with a sense of fairness, although he'd sacrifice the fairness to the power if it came to a choice. Pierce seems to have only the power sense. We've heard from Tom's colleagues ever since he disappeared, you know. All of them have been questioned about what Tom might have been working on, and what it might be applied to in terms of either the Protector Artifact or any weapons. One scientist, Dr. Ewing, never returned from questioning."

Amanda vaguely remembered Dr. Ewing. She said uncertainly, "A tall man with a reddish beard?"

"Yes. He was an obscure scientist and a Martian citizen, so it was easier for him to disappear than some of the others. We don't know why."

"Maybe he's with Daddy!"

"He might be. Or it may be that questioning Dr. Ewing went . . . wrong. Some people are fatally allergic to Pandya Doses, you know. I just want you to be very, very careful. Konstantin Ouranis's father is a big supporter of Admiral Pierce. Business interests that—yes, the color's nice, but it's a rather big change, isn't it?" She touched Amanda's hair. A soldier had walked close to them.

When the soldier had passed, Aunt Kristen didn't resume the discussion. She merely took Amanda's hand and held it, whispering, "Be careful, honey. Don't ever criticize Pierce to your new friends. Remember that."

Amanda kept a tight hold on her aunt's hand as they walked back to the hotel. In five minutes, Aunt Kristen had made everything look different. Yet Amanda could see why Aunt Kristen had done it. "Face facts squarely," her father always said. Amanda needed the facts.

Oh, why couldn't facts ever be *good*?

Aunt Kristen had said that Amanda had her mother's calm and optimism, with her father's rationality and daring. It was the nicest thing anybody had ever said to her. So she would try to live up to that. To stay calm, to stay optimistic, to look at everything rationally. That was what she had to do.

She'd done it before.

Carefully, Amanda began to think. She went over everything she and Konstantin had said to each other, everything she could remember saying under the Pandya Dose, everything Aunt Kristen had said. She would face all the facts, sort through them, try to make sense of them. "Science is organized data," her father always said.

A half hour later, during which her aunt respected her silence, Amanda felt she had all the facts straight, at least as well as she could. There was only one thing that still puzzled her. She still didn't understand why so many of the questions the doctor had asked her concerned the trip to World three years ago. Especially the trip back, from World to the space tunnel, when they'd been bringing the Protector Artifact to the Solar System. It was old history. Why were Admiral Pierce and his soldiers so interested?

She couldn't think of any answer.

"I got train tickets for oh six hundred hours tomorrow," Uncle Martin said. "Amanda, you look fantastic."

"Thank you," Amanda said absently. It still didn't make any sense.

NINETEEN

ABOARD THE *MURASAKI*

Kaufman and Marbet stood in the conference room aboard the Solar Alliance Defense Navy warship *Murasaki*, having the first shouting argument of Kaufman's life.

Initially they had faced the torrent calmly if tensely, each determined to row upstream until the other was convinced. Right after docking, a sullen MP, heavily armed, had shown them to this room. Another MP conducted Magdalena elsewhere. Kaufman, expecting to be met by the ship's commander if not by Ethan Mc-Chesney himself, had protested this, but the somber MP had ignored him.

Now Kaufman said, "If it weren't for Magdalena, we wouldn't have ever gotten aboard this ship. McChesney trusts her, not us."

"Then he's as big a fool as you are, Lyle. She's not trustworthy. It's in every line of her, every movement. She doesn't care about the artifact being aboard, or what it might be used for. She doesn't even care that Stefanak is dead and Pierce is in power except as it affects her private plans and business interests. And Stefanak was a former lover!"

For some reason, this angered Kaufman more than the rest. "You don't know that."

"Yes, I do," Marbet said coldly. "Much as you'd like to be in Stefanak's former place. God, she's *old*, and all too used, and you're still sniffing around her like some dog around a bitch in heat."

"If that's the level your much-vaunted 'sensitivity' shows you, I'm glad I don't share it."

"No chance that you ever will. You see about as much as any man blinkered by lust. She's using you, and using McChesney, too. But at least he isn't frothing with testosterone. I hope."

"Which, in your opinion, I am."

"Yes!"

"Are you sure what you're experiencing isn't insight, but jealousy?" Kaufman said, and immediately regretted it. He'd crossed some emotional line, and he knew it, and he'd also left himself open to the retort he knew she'd make. The torrent was swirling them both downriver.

"Jealousy, Lyle? You really flatter yourself. Since we first landed on World, you've been far less sexually appealing than you apparently think you are. You've been self-pitying, and self-absorbed, and making a fool of yourself around that woman. I haven't been in the least tempted to jealousy, since that implies desire. You're about as desirable to me as a tomcat licking both its wounds and its swollen prick."

Now Marbet looked as if she'd said too much. Which she had. There were words, Kaufman knew, which could not be unsaid, and not be forgotten. They lingered forever, like subtle poison. There were good reasons he'd never married.

She knew she'd gone too far. Hand to her lips, she said, "I'm sorry, Lyle. That was a terrible thing to say."

But she didn't say it was untrue.

He said stiffly, "We should get back to the practical decisions here. McChesney is going to walk through that door in a few minutes, and he's going to listen to Magdalena and to me and to you, and then he's going to decide what to do. It would be better if we'd already decided what we think should be done."

"Take the artifact to the Solar System, where it should have been all this time, protecting humanity with setting prime eleven. Radio everybody at every star system we pass through that we're doing that. With so much public attention, Pierce will have to let it go on to Mars, and have to leave us alone as heroes who discovered and corrected Stefanak's lies."

"That's one possibility," Kaufman said.

"We're being overheard, aren't we?" Marbet said suddenly. "That's why you look like that!"

Kaufman didn't know how he looked, and didn't care. He said irritably, "Of course we're being overheard—don't be naive."

"Then why bother to—"

"You wouldn't understand," Kaufman said, thereby settling the pointless, stupid, destructive score. He should have told her instead about the official surveillance record, about the necessary military games to get your point of view on it. For later, just in case. By not telling her, he'd also thrown away a valuable aid to rebuilding a working relationship between them. But she'd goaded him into it. Women.

He wasn't supposed to be able to be goaded like that. His career had been built on that negative capability.

The door to the conference room opened and Magdalena and McChesney came in, Magdalena saying, "Well, since the game's up anyway . . ." She smiled pointedly at Kaufman. Oh God, Magdalena had been listening, as well as McChesney. She'd heard what Marbet had said about lust.

McChesney said hoarsely, "I turned on the Faraday cage. Let's talk."

Colonel Ethan McChesney had been in SADC Intelligence his entire military life. He'd masterminded the capture of the Faller whom Marbet had learned to communicate with, the only human to ever succeed in capturing a Faller alive. McChesney had been in charge of several Special Projects for Sullivan Stefanak, and as far as Kaufman knew, had carried out all of them with competence, thoroughness, discretion, and as much morality as was possible in Intelligence. That had made him invaluable to Stefanak, whose own morality was more intermittent. If you're going to ride political winds, it's good to have an anchored pole somewhere in case you need it.

The same qualities, however, now made him dangerous to Nikolai Pierce. McChesney was a loyal, much-too-knowledgeable operative of a deposed enemy. The most expedient thing for Pierce was to empty McChesney of his considerable covert knowledge with a Pandya Dose, and then dispose of him. The only reason Pierce had not already done this was that he probably didn't know yet where McChesney, in his Special Compartmented Information project known only to a few people, physically was located. It was only a matter of time before Pierce found out. Somebody among those few people would be forced to tell.

McChesney knew all this as well as Kaufman, probably better. McChesney looked terrible. When Kaufman had seen him last, two years ago, Ethan McChesney had been a sleek, quick man with the comfortably padded body and shiny dark hair of an otter. Now he was too thin, his hair dull, his movements clumsy. McChesney had given his life and loyalty to an organization that was now trying to kill him. For some men, betrayal was worse than death.

The four of them sat at one end of the big foamcast conference table. Kaufman shoved the quarrel with Marbet out of his mind and concentrated. "Let's start by going over the facts, all right? The Protector Artifact is aboard this ship, Ethan. We know that beyond a doubt." *Knowledge pinned on the behavior of an hysterical alien child*, he didn't say.

McChesney didn't try to deny it. "Yes. The artifact's been here since you brought it up on the *Alan B. Shepard* three years ago. It was stowed on the *Murasaki* when you docked with us for supplies, on General Stefanak's direct orders. Only two people were told at this end: me and Commander Chand."

Kaufman changed tactics. He wasn't going to have to bargain information out of McChesney. On the contrary, McChesney looked like a man glad to finally be able to share a crushing burden. Kaufman said, with sympathy but not too much sympathy, "And you've been responsible for it ever since."

"Yes. The crew hasn't even been rotated, and of course they all wonder about that, but there's nothing anyone can do. Until Magdalena's ship came through the tunnel, we'd had only one previous contact for two years."

Completely out of touch. Only physical objects, not message-carrying waves, passed through a space tunnel. McChesney had orders not to send anything through to Caligula space, the military outpost on the other side, and nothing had come through for him. The entire crew of the *Murasaki* might as well have been missing in action, which was probably what their relatives had been told. No wonder the MPs in the docking bay had looked unhappy.

Kaufman encouraged him. "So you had no idea of the growing power of Pierce's faction, or that General Stefanak was threatened."

"None."

"And you learned of the coup . . . when?"

"When Magdalena's ship came through. We're old friends," McChesney said, and Kaufman was careful not to look at Marbet. "I couldn't let her aboard, but she'd recorded recent newscasts and beamed them aboard for me."

In exchange for letting her down to the planet, Kaufman thought. No, there was more to it than that. He waited to hear what.

Magdalena obliged. "Come on, Ethan, you might as well tell them all of it. When I gave you the news that Stefanak might go under, you asked me to find a place on that backwater planet to hide the artifact from Pierce, if it came to that."

Kaufman was startled. He hadn't expected that. But it made sense. McChesney knew what Pierce was—knew that Pierce, unlike Stefanak, was crazy enough to actually use the artifact at setting thirteen. Take it to the Faller home system and try to fry the enemy, despite the risks to spacetime.

McChesney said, "I know Pierce from way back. Stefanak was different. He was a good soldier. Pierce doesn't listen to anyone he doesn't want to hear. He'd do it, Lyle."

"I know he would," Kaufman said somberly.

"And anyway, Ethan," Magdalena said, "if you had to run, it'd be a hell of a lot easier to run without that artifact. Which the entire military is looking for."

McChesney was too schooled to look irritated at the charge of self-interest. Or maybe too honest. No one wanted to end up dead. Nor did McChesney pretend that the *Murasaki* could mount a convincing defense, warship though she was, against the kind of force Pierce could send through the tunnel. No way.

Magdalena added, "And as I already told Ethan, I found a place on World to hide the thing. Not in the Neury Mountains where you dug it up, that'll be the first place they look. An underwater cave on a remote island, big enough and isolated enough. Marbet can bribe the local natives into silence."

"She goes off on long trips in that skimmer, I don't know where," Ann had said of Magdalena's stay in Gofkit Shamloe.

"Good," McChesney said. "There are two problems. First, I couldn't take it down before now because if Pierce's forces come through and the *Murasaki* isn't in orbit around the tunnel, they'll forcibly board her and I don't know how they'll deal with the crew. I'm responsible for these men. It seemed better to take the chance that Pierce wouldn't be able to locate me right away and wait for the *Sans Merci* to get back from World. She can take the artifact down. With luck, they'll never know she was here. Her passage shows up nowhere on the *Murasaki* records. They'll search the ship, they won't find the artifact, none of my men will know anything, even under drugs, except me and the commander. Chand will show up on the records as having died of cardiac arrest four months ago."

"Chand will go with me in my flyer through the tunnel," Magdalena said. "You didn't think I was going to accompany the artifact on its trip back down to the planet, did you, Lyle?"

Kaufman ignored her. "And you?"

McChesney said evenly, "Pierce knows I have other reasons to avoid his questioning besides the artifact."

Suicide. The two soldiers gazed at each other. For some men, yes, betrayal was worse than death.

Kaufman said only, "It sounds like the best plan to me, Ethan. But you mentioned a second obstacle."

"Yes." McChesney glanced at Magdalena, and something furtive in the look alerted Kaufman. Beside him, Marbet suddenly sat up straighter.

McChesney said slowly, "The second obstacle is Dr. Thomas Capelo. He's aboard."

Nothing had ever surprised Kaufman so much in his life. But . . . it made sense, sort of. Put Tom where the artifact was so that—

"Laslo! Where is he?"

"Who?" McChesney said. Magdalena rose to her feet, knocking over her chair. Kaufman found it hard to look at her face.

"Laslo Damroscher! My son! He was with Capelo!"

"There isn't anyone with Dr. Capelo, Magdalena," McChesney said.

"You're lying! Laslo's here!"

McChesney looked both apprehensive and bewildered. "No, only Dr. Capelo was brought aboard. Much later than the artifact—just a few months ago. He—"

"Give me my son!" Magdalena said, and her voice rang of splintering glass.

Kaufman rose. "Magdalena, if Colonel McChesney says he's not here, then he's not. Stefanak's men—"

"If you're lying to me, Ethan, I'll have your liver, you know I will. I want to search every square inch of this ship for myself."

Kaufman made a gesture to McChesney that Magdalena couldn't see: *Let her*. After a long moment, McChesney nodded. Kaufman said, "You can search the ship, Magdalena. But first you have to remove your flyer from your ship and let the artifact be loaded onto it. The artifact has to start down to World. After that, the colonel and I will go over the ship with you. Not before."

"Still negotiating, Lyle?" she said with a flash of her old mockery. But she couldn't sustain it. The strain was too great. "All right . . . load the fucking thing."

McChesney said patiently, "You'll have to give the orders to your crew. Bring the ship into cargo-exchange configuration with the *Murasaki*."

She didn't move. Kaufman took her arm and gently pulled her toward the door. She shook him off but followed McChesney out, leaving Kaufman and Marbet alone.

Marbet said, "When she shatters, she'll rip up the galaxy if she can."

"I know."

"Are you sure her son is dead?"

"As sure as I can be without having been an eyewitness. I told you about the recording. That was Tom's voice. I think Stefanak had a decoy artifact location set up in the Belt, something for his enemies to find if they looked hard enough. I think he had Tom housed there, too, for whatever reason. Then, after Laslo accidentally stumbled across the site, Stefanak decided to move Tom. I don't know why, or why he put Tom here. Maybe Tom knows."

Marbet said, "We didn't even ask to see him!"

It was true. Chagrined, Kaufman said, "Magdalena was so . . ."

"I know. Lyle, she's not completely sane. You can't rely on her, no matter how much you think you need her. In fact, why do you need her, now that we've found Tom?"

"I don't know yet. Let me think. Don't lecture me, Marbet."

Her green eyes darkened. "I didn't realize I wasn't allowed to comment. Tell me what else I'm supposed to do or not do. Am I going down to the planet with the artifact as Magdalena said, to— what was it?—'bribe the local natives into silence'?"

"Of course not. You and I and Magdalena and the commander have to all be out of the World system before Pierce's force arrives, if it does arrive. And Tom, too. A good thing Magdalena's flyer will seat six. Our flyer is still on World. The *Sans Merci* will have to vaporize it, in case Pierce does land a detail on the planet. Come on, let's get McChesney to take us to Tom."

She didn't get out of her chair. "Aren't you forgetting something?"

"What?"

"Essa."

Oh, God, he had forgotten her. The alien kid had been nothing but trouble since the beginning.

"Don't look so put-upon, Lyle," Marbet said acidly. "If it weren't for Essa, you wouldn't know the damn artifact was here in the first place."

He said evenly, "Essa can go back down to the planet in Magdalena's ship. That's where she belongs. Are you coming to talk to Tom?"

She rose silently and followed him.

McChesney's ship came alongside. With the two cargo bays sealed to each other, no one could see what was transferred. This was how the artifact had been moved from the *Alan B. Shepard* to the *Murasaki* three years ago. Kaufman had been aboard. Supposedly he had been in charge of the entire expedition to dig up, investigate, and transport home the artifact—but he had never been told that the artifact was being left on the *Murasaki*. Suddenly, he wanted to see the thing for himself.

McChesney and Magdalena stood inside the joined cargo bays. Her crew trundled the artifact, resting in a metal ring mounted on a wheeled platform, from one ship to the other. The artifact looked exactly as Kaufman remembered. A sphere of dull gray that looked like metal but was actually an allotropic form of carbon that resembled, but wasn't, a known class of fullerenes. Spaced evenly around its circumference were seven protuberances, each a small raised crater. Inside each crater were two nipples, spaced apart. The craters were marked in primes, although apparently the unknown makers had also considered "one" a prime: one, two, three, five, seven, eleven, thirteen, each indicated by raised dots outside the crater.

To activate a given setting, you had to depress both nipples. Kaufman's team, under the leadership of Tom Capelo, had tested settings prime one, prime two, prime three. Prime five had, sometime during fifty thousand years of burial on World, acquired two small rocks wedging its nipples inward, which meant that setting prime five had been permanently depressed. Causing, according to Syree Johnson, the protection of World against the weapon that had fried the entire rest of the World star system. Also causing, according to Ann Sikorski and Dieter Gruber, the quantum-effect probability field that had led Essa and her people to evolve shared reality.

Settings prime seven, eleven, and thirteen had only been worked out mathematically, by Tom Capelo. They had not been tested. Unless you counted the "test" by the Fallers, presumably at setting prime seven, that had irradiated the entire human-colony star system of Viridian. Millions of people had died.

Kaufman reached out and touched the artifact.

"A kick in the head, right?" Magdalena said. "All this time all the good citizens of the Solar System thought this thing was there, protecting them at setting eleven. And Stefanak had it here, instead. Why was that, Lyle? You're the fellow soldier."

"I don't know," Kaufman said. Magdalena's mocking tone was back to normal, but her eyes glittered like broken glass, and her body was so taut that every muscle would ache by evening. "Ethan, I'd like to see Tom Capelo."

McChesney glanced at him bleakly. "As soon as we're done here and the *Sans Merci* takes off."

Kaufman didn't argue. Hiding the artifact from Pierce was priority one. He didn't ask what McChesney had told, was going to tell, the *Sans Merci* crew. Kaufman knew. They were going to have to stay on World until it was safe to send for them, maybe years. They wouldn't be told this until they had all been ferried down and scattered into hiding among the tiny villages or in the Neury Mountains. It would be hard for Pierce's soldiers to find thirty men on an entire planet, especially when they didn't know they were supposed to be looking. As for the *Sans Merci*, she would be sent to burn up in World's atmosphere.

Probably only the captain and exec knew all this now. Whatever deal Magdalena was cutting with them would undoubtedly make it worth their enforced exile.

Marbet said to McChesney, "There's an alien girl aboard the *Sans*

Merci. She has to be dropped off by shuttle at coordinates I'll give you."

"An alien girl?"

"It's a complicated story," Kaufman said, and McChesney clearly had no interest in hearing it.

Nor did he pay attention to Marbet, who said clearly, "Do you realize you're restoring shared reality to this planet?"

Restoring shared reality. Kaufman hadn't realized, either, hadn't stopped to think about it. Oh, Ann . . . after all the work you've done to create a society without it! Enli, Calin, the village with its barely weathered stockade . . . Not priority one. Ann would cope. World would cope. Kaufman's concern was the entire galaxy.

Setting prime thirteen, according to Tom Capelo, could destroy it by altering the fabric of spacetime itself.

Kaufman waited for McChesney to take him to Capelo.

TWENTY

ABOARD THE *MURASAKI*

My God, it's the cavalry. Or are you the savages, Lyle?"

"Hello, Tom," Kaufman said, surprised at how glad he was to see Capelo. After months of seeing Tom's face, and then his daughter's, on the news holo, months of speculation about whether the physicist was dead or alive . . . and here he was. Thin, but Tom had always been thin. Intense. Furious.

"What the fuck are you doing here? What the fuck am *I* doing here? Are you here to give me more military orders from El Generalissimo Stefanak?"

"No, I'm here as a civilian," Kaufman said, because he had to start somewhere.

"My family?"

Kaufman hesitated. But truth had always been the only way to deal with Capelo; everything else cost too much later on. "Your wife and younger daughter are fine. Amanda seems to have disappeared. We hoped she was with you."

Capelo went ashen. "She . . . she wasn't even home when I was abducted."

"Apparently she was. The news holos said she left her swimming class early. Her friends said she told them she was going home. Tom, there's no evidence that whoever took her took you, and in fact if that were the case, she'd probably be here with you. There's been no political demands, no ransom requests. If they didn't take her along with you, my guess is that she hid in the house and then later went into hiding somewhere." Kaufman hoped this was true.

A little of the color returned to Capelo's face. "She's an unusually resourceful kid."

"I believe it," Kaufman said. He'd decided on a strategy: Hit Capelo hard with everything at once. "Tom, we need to talk to you quickly. A lot has happened, and we think the artifact might be used at setting prime thirteen in the same star system as the Fallers' artifact."

"No one would be stupid enough to do that, not even Stefanak."

"Stefanak's dead. Nikolai Pierce brought off a military coup."

"Pierce? He's crazy as a syphilitic shark!"

Kaufman had never heard a more apt description. "Yes. He didn't know the artifact was actually here, aboard the *Murasaki* . . . did you?"

"Of course I did, what do you suppose Stefanak's thugs brought me here for? Soldiers know nothing about science. They were stupid enough to think that a theoretical physicist has to actually be in the presence of a phenomenon to do its math. Good thing they weren't trying to force Sarinsen to extend his work on black holes."

Marbet said, "What were they trying to get you to do?"

"Figure out why the artifact affected brain functioning. Stefanak refused to put it in the Solar System until he knew it wasn't going to turn his soldier's brains into pulp. Although I don't know how he'd tell the difference. Hello, Marbet. Hello, McChesney. The jailer himself—I'm honored."

So that was the reason the artifact—and Tom—were here. Not

that it mattered now. Kaufman said, "The artifact is on its way back down to World. Pierce didn't know where it was; evidently Stefanak kept that information highly restricted. But he'll learn eventually, and he'll come after it, and we think he'll use it to try to fry the Fallers' home system. We're trying to prevent that."

Capelo stared. "Well, aren't you three the reverse Prometheuses. Promethei. And when Pierce's army gets here and finds our merry little band?"

"That's why we're leaving. Now. Get together anything that identifies you and—"

"There isn't a whole lot. The kidnappers didn't let me gather up the family photo album."

"—wipe the ship system of any work you did while you were here. Now."

"I'm moving, don't turn all authoritarian on me, Lyle. And just how are we leaving? Is Colonel McChesney graciously loaning us a flyer plus free passage? He shouldn't—who the hell is *that*?"

Magdalena burst in, shoving Marbet out of the way. McChesney must have escaped her briefly, but here she was again, and even Kaufman stepped out of her way. She looked as if any contact with her would burn. He had never seen such eyes: desperate, frightening, pathetic.

"Is my son with you? Laslo Damroscher? My son?"

Something in her question, half demand and half plea, quelled Capelo's usual sarcasm. Kaufman remembered that he, too, had a daughter missing.

Capelo said gently, "No, ma'am, I don't have your son here, or anyone's son. I've been imprisoned here alone for months, and transported around the galaxy alone for months before that. I'm sorry."

"He was with you! You spoke to him!"

Too late, Kaufman saw the tsunami coming. He tried to head it off. "Magdalena, it—"

"Listen!" She pulled the data cube from her pocket, the same cube Kaufman had heard on World. The two drunken, young, stupid voices filled the room.

"Thass not 'sposed to be there." Laslo's voice, very drunk.

"What isn't supposed to be where?" Another young man, sounding marginally less drunk. *"Just an asteroid."*

"Isn't 'sposed to be there. Hand me 'nother fizzie."

"They're gone. You drunk the last one, you pig."

"No fizzies? Might as well go home."

"Just an asteroid. No . . . two asteroids."

"Two!" Laslo said, with pointless jubilation.

"Where'd they come from? Isn't supposed to be there. Not on computer."

"N-body problem. Gravity. Messes things up. Jupiter."

"Let's shoot 'em!"

"Yeah!" Laslo cried, and hiccuped.

"What kinda guns you got on this thing? No guns, prob'ly. Fucking rich-boy pleasure craft."

"Got . . . got guns put on it. Daddy-dad doesn't know. Illegals."

"You're a bonus, Laslo."

"Goddamn true. Mummy doesn't know either. 'Bout the guns."

"You sure 'bout that? Isn't much your famous mother don't know. Or do. God, that body, I saw her in an old—"

"Shut up, Conner," Laslo said savagely. *"Computer, activate . . . can't remember the word . . ."*

"Activate weapons. Jesus, Laslo. YOU gotta say it. Voice cued."

"Activate weapons!"

"Hey, a message from th'asteroid! People! Maybe there's girls."

"You are approaching a highly restricted area," a mechanical voice said. *"Leave this area immediately."*

"It don't want us," Conner said. *"Shoot it!"*

"Wait . . . maybe . . ."

"You are approaching a highly restricted area. Leave this area immediately."

"Fucking snakes," Conner said. "Shoot it!"

"I . . ."

"Fucking coward!"

"THIS IS YOUR LAST WARNING! YOU HAVE INVADED A HIGHLY RESTRICTED AND HIGH-DANGER AREA. LEAVE IMMEDIATELY OR YOUR CRAFT WILL BE FIRED ON!"

And then a fourth voice, speaking rapidly, *"Unknown Craft . . . SOS . . . Help! I'm being held prisoner here—This is Tom Capelo—"*

The very brief, high-pitched whine.

"Oh my God," Capelo said. "That was me, before they moved me. I had rigged a short-range transmitter—stupid keepers had no idea what I needed for my work, I wish I'd asked for a proton beamer. They might have given me one. The flyer turned up on the asteroid's screen, I could break that firewall easily enough, and I sent a message—"

"A message that caused the other craft to be captured, right? We know that much," Kaufman said loudly. He stood behind Magdalena, nodding at Capelo. He didn't really expect this crude ruse to work: Capelo was too insensitive and Magdalena too sharp. But Kaufman was wrong. Something—maybe empathy over a missing child—boosted Capelo's sensitivity. And unwillingness to know dulled Magdalena's. It was a clear indicator of her delusions.

"Yes," Capelo said, "my message caused the other craft to be captured. But they didn't put the occupants here with me. They must have taken them . . . somewhere else."

Magdalena's body sagged in disappointment. "Do you have any idea where? Any idea at all?"

"No." Capelo's eyes were miserable with sympathy.

"Then we have to leave instantly. I need to reach my contacts in Caligula space, before Pierce replaces them all. Come with me to the shuttle, Ethan. Dr. Capelo, thanks for nothing." She swept out.

Capelo said to Kaufman, "What the hell—"

"Tell you later. But she's right, we have to leave instantly, and we need her contacts. Do you know who she is?"

"No."

"Magdalena."

"I still don't know who she is," Capelo said, and Kaufman realized yet again how far removed the mental stores of physicists were from those of everybody else.

"Never mind. Come on, Tom."

Capelo said flatly, "Her son's dead."

"I know. Let's *go*."

"I'm coming. Although if you've really sent the artifact back down, and if Pierce has no idea where it is, there's probably less hurry than you think. How long ago was this coup?"

"About a week."

"Well, think, Lyle. If any of Stefanak's men who knew the artifact's location, and mine, were still alive, they'd probably have been here by now to do something. If Pierce is just looking at random, it could be months before he catches a clue. I mean, how could he know where Stefanak was likely to stash the thing, given the entire tunnel system?"

"I don't know. But I don't have your faith in randomness, either."

"Not randomness, Lyle. Probability. That's my field, remember? My touchstone, my livelihood, my curse, my—"

Alarms sounded all over the ship.

"What is it?" Marbet said. "Lyle?"

Kaufman had already run to Capelo's terminal, keyed in the standard codes connecting officers to bridge information from anywhere on the ship.

"*Lyle?*"

"We're under attack," Kaufman said. "Human ships. Four of them, coming through from Caligula space.

"Pierce's force is here."

Magdalena heard the alarms. They pulled her out of despair, and she was obliquely grateful.

Laslo hadn't been with Capelo. Not ever. She had wasted weeks tracing him and his princess daughter, all for nothing. She was no closer to finding where that bastard Stefanak had actually imprisoned Laslo. She'd have to start all over again.

The important thing was to use her Caligula System contacts as soon as possible. Major Hofsetter, in charge of space tunnel traffic, had passed her through the Tunnel #438 to World in the first place; his commander hadn't even known about it. Of course, Hofsetter, that fat ugly profiteer, had hated doing it. But Magdalena had known exactly how Nate Hofsetter was making millions off the war on the black market—was, in fact, making them with the cooperation of one of Magdalena's dummy corporations—and so he hadn't had much choice.

Hofsetter wasn't among the navy that Pierce would have replaced. Neither Pierce nor Hofsetter knew she knew it, but a percentage of Hofsetter's profiteering gains went back to Pierce. Hofsetter was safe. The Caligula commander, on the other hand, General Donnor, was probably already dead. A loyal Stefanak soldier. Well, good riddance to her. Magdalena had always found it a pain in the ass to work around the bitch.

Hofsetter wouldn't know where Laslo was, but if she pressured hard enough, he might know someone somewhere with access to Special Project information. She'd have to press pretty hard. It would cost her.

Damn Laslo! Children never understood the trouble they caused their parents. Laslo was no different from the rest. When she found him, they'd have a major reckoning. When she found him . . . when she found him . . . Capelo had said . . .

For just a moment, her certainty almost cracked. Then the alarms sounded.

Alarms! They were under attack. Pierce's forces from Caligula, oh, God. Well, it just meant she had to start negotiations earlier. Hofsetter might be with them. If not, she'd be able to get to him.

The others, however, Kaufman and Grant and Capelo and McChesney, were dead men walking.

Magdalena ran along the corridor to the conference room, alarms sounding in her ears. Rory and Kendai ran beside her. She burst in, and Kaufman was still there. Capelo had gone, probably, with McChesney. Now that she thought about it, Magdalena could see that Capelo would be all right. Pierce would want to exhibit him, the great physicist abducted by Stefanak but rescued by Pierce's heroic troops as they restored order to the galaxy.

She said rapidly to Kaufman, "Get up on the bridge with Capelo, you idiot. That's your only chance. If he protects you, if he threatens to tell the press how you were murdered by Pierce's troops, then they won't kill you. They can't. Get up there!"

"I was coming to look for you," Kaufman said. "We're not going to play it that way, Magdalena. Tom and Marbet are in hiding. I don't want you to tell anyone they were ever aboard. Please."

"Not tell—"

"You don't have anything to gain from telling them that Tom and Marbet are here. Nothing. And they won't give you any truth drugs, will they? Not yet. They already know why you're here."

She suddenly remembered that the Faraday cage was still up in this room. Nothing was being recorded or detected.

"Kaufman, you're a moron. They'll give you a Pandya Dose, not to mention McChesney and Chand."

"Not if they think I'm just another sailor on this ship."

"They'll check the ship's roster."

"Maybe. In that case, they'll uncover me. But I think they're mostly interested in the artifact. Once they have it, they may just leave with it. I don't think Pierce is planning on warehousing it here the way Stefanak did."

Of course he wasn't. Magdalena said, "McChesney and Chand—"

"Can't tell them anything." His face didn't change; he was a soldier. But Magdalena understood what he meant. Chand assumed she would be leaving too publicly to take him with her. Ethan McChesney and Prabir Chand were already dead.

She said harshly, "Ethan wasn't alive anymore anyway."

"No," Kaufman agreed. "The moral center of his universe collapsed."

"Some people hinge their entire universe on one thing, and when that goes, they crumple," Magdalena said with scorn. "Weaklings."

Kaufman was watching her very closely. Something moved behind his eyes. Magdalena didn't like it.

"All right, Lyle. I'll go along with your desperate scheme. As you point out, I don't have anything to gain by turning you in. So I never saw you or Capelo or our famous redheaded Sensitive. Good luck."

She turned and strode out, toward the bridge. That's where the takeover would be. She had work to do. She had to explain why the artifact was now streaking toward the planet in her ship. ("McChesney commandeered it.") She had to explain why she was in the World system in the first place ("Business interests"—embarrassing details furnished if pressed). She had, most of all, to start a second search for Laslo.

Despite herself, Magdalena felt a rush throughout her entire body. Maneuvering, plotting, trumping the opposition. This was what she did best. She was back in the game.

TWENTY-ONE

ABOARD THE *MURASAKI*

After Kaufman had secured Magdalena's cooperation—to the extent anything connected with her could be "secure"—he moved swiftly to ship's laundry. McChesney had given him the access code. Inside, 'bots busily cleaned clothing and bedding, unaware and uncaring that the ship was under attack. If the *Murasaki* were blown up, it would be with clean uniforms for all hands.

Kaufman put on the uniform of a seaman first class. This crew had been cooped up together for two years and knew each other all too well. But Commander Chand had apprised his officers of the situation, and they would order the crew to say nothing. It had been Chand's last order.

Don't think about Chand or McChesney. Concentrate. Kaufman knew he didn't look like crew, didn't carry himself like crew. This would require careful and constant effort.

He ran to the lower deck battle station. The four crew looked at him distrustfully, but they reconfigured for him and no one said anything. They'd been told he was coming. Kaufman grabbed battle armor from station stowage and pulled it on. It had been a long time since he had supervised battle stations. He thought he remembered what to do, which was good because the crew was just waiting for him to make a mistake. He needed them on his side.

"Call me 'Armbruster' if you have to call me anything at all. And I'll remember this afterward. Remember it for all of you."

Their faces cleared. One of them, bolder than the others, said, "Sir, are we—"

" 'Armbruster!' Seaman first class!"

"Sorry, sir . . . Armbruster. Are we going to surrender?"

"Yes. Battle stations are just a precaution."

"But these are SADN ships coming through," another said. "I don't get it!"

Of course they didn't. They'd been out of contact for two years, and they never knew the artifact had even been aboard. Kaufman was willing to trade chain-of-command for survival.

"There's been a revolution in the Solar System," he said, rapid and low. "General Stefanak is dead, and—"

Someone gasped.

"—and Admiral Pierce is in power. These are Pierce's troops, securing the *Murasaki* by whatever means necessary. However, I don't think they're going to fire on us." *I hope.* "Battle stations are just precautions. Now, please, no more talking."

"Just one more question, s . . . Armbruster. After the surrender, are we going home?"

"Probably." Crew were crew. To most of them, it didn't matter who was supreme commander, not as much as it mattered whether they got leave. Kaufman understood. The Fallers should be the enemy anyway, not other humans.

The alarms suddenly ceased.

"All crew on parade deck," the system said loudly. "No exceptions. Stow battle gear first."

"Even the engine-room guys," a seaman said. "Jesus Planetary Christ."

The "parade deck," standard on all war ships, was a bare open room used for anything that required full assembly of crew and officers. For its intended use, it was cramped. Between such assemblies it was used for receiving dignitaries, showing holomovies, anything else that happened to come up. Kaufman squeezed in among the crewmen in proper formation, stooping his shoulders a little and keeping his head slightly down. From the way the crew glanced at the MPs, Kaufman guessed the MPs were off whatever warship was now docked against the *Murasaki*. The MPs were conspicuously armed.

When everyone was assembled, the screen on one wall brightened to show the bridge. A commander stood there, in full dress uniform, flanked by strange officers. Kaufman saw no sign of Magdalena.

"Crew of the *Murasaki*, this is Commander Blauman. I am now in command of the *Murasaki*, by order of the Solar Alliance Defense Navy. Commander Chand and Colonel McChesney have been relieved of command, having been discovered to be traitors to the war effort. They are now on their way to the Solar System for court martial."

Kaufman felt the crew stir around him in surprise.

"I know this will be a shock to you, having spent two years aboard this ship with no communication from beyond the tunnel. Since that time, humanity was fortunate in having undergone a revival of the war effort. The traitors who have not been willing to advance that effort have been eliminated, including the traitor and coward General Stefanak. Under Admiral Pierce's Freedom Army, the war against the Fallers will be fought with all the concentration and effort the SADC is capable of, so that we can have as speedy a victory as possible, and our home system and colonies will once more be safe."

Someone cheered and a few seaman took it up, raggedly. Most looked dazed.

"You crew have done fine duty without leave for a long time, making a valuable contribution to the war effort. In view of that, the crew of the *Murasaki* will be placed in rapid leave rotation, replaced by crew from Caligula Station, and reposted to Solar System defense. I expect all of you to be back home within two weeks."

This time the cheer was hearty and genuine. Seamen glanced jubilantly at each other. Kaufman saw the woman in front of him do a little clogging dance with her feet, her body still at attention.

"For now, I ask each of you to resume normal duty. The *Murasaki* officers are also on leave rotation, and some of them will be relieved of duty today. Your new section officers will assemble each section to discuss the rotation. Dismissed." The screen blanked.

The seamen broke into capers and cheers and horseplay. Only a few looked thoughtful or frowning, pondering the larger implications of this hasty change of command. Most were simply thrilled to be going home. Kaufman left inconspicuously with a chattering group. In the corridor, he faded back until he was alone, then used the codes McChesney had given him to enter the life-support housing.

It was the best place for concealment. Fully automated, its operations were usually checked only by external monitors, unless those revealed a problem. Kaufman was about to take the most important action of his entire life. Life support. Yes. Nice joke. Please let it not be black humor.

He slipped through the door and quietly e-locked it behind him.

TWENTY-TWO

ABOARD THE *MURASAKI*

The life-support housing was a jumble of machines, ducts, storage crates, sealed vats, and damaged 'bots. Here air and water were cleansed for most of the ship. Kaufman ducked under huge low pipes, maneuvered around whirring sealed machinery. In a back corner Capelo and Marbet sat on the deck with their backs against the bulkhead, Marbet hugging her knees.

"Everything go all right?" she said.

"So far," Kaufman answered. He sat on the other side of Capelo from Marbet. Their quarrel, unimportant next to everything else, nonetheless lay over them like soot.

Capelo said, "So now what? Here we are, rats who can't even leave the sinking ship by the traditional mooring lines. Have you considered what comes next, Lyle?"

Kaufman said, "Are you any closer to solving the problem of macro-level quantum entanglement?"

Capelo stared incredulously. "What? You want to talk physics *now?*"

"I read a few weeks ago that your current work was trying to figure how macro-level entanglement fit into the probability-force theory. Entanglement like that of the space tunnels. Is that what you've been working on?"

"In simplistic terms, yes. But why bring it up now?"

"I was wondering," Kaufman said, "if you weren't kidnapped because of what you're currently working on."

Capelo made a rude noise. "Not a chance, Lyle. What I'm working on is so theoretical and esoteric that no one in the military would care. It has no practical applications, no engineering possibilities, no use in blowing things up or killing people or bringing off coups d'etat. I told you, Stefanak's thugs abducted me and brought me to the artifact because Stefanak was nervous about bringing something that affects brains into the Solar System, not unless he could obtain additional brilliant insights from me."

Marbet said, "Do you have any?"

"Nary an insight. Now, Lyle, how do we get out of here? I defer to your military strategy."

"We wait for Magdalena," Kaufman said.

"Some strategy."

Capelo was right, of course, but Magdalena was necessary. In the hurried minutes before Blauman had boarded, Kaufman had put together a plan with more soft spots than a rotten apple. But he couldn't see any alternative.

Marbet said, "What's happening out there?"

"The crew's been mustered and apprised of the changes. The new commander, Blauman, is rotating them out as fast as possible. Dispersed and happy to be on leave, they're much less likely to question anything. Junior officers, the same. The *Murasaki* will probably be pulled out of here as soon as the artifact is retrieved, which is what Blauman is undoubtedly doing now. Magdalena will recall her ship, she doesn't have any choice. They could easily overtake and capture it."

Marbet said, "What if you somehow blew up the *Sans Merci*? And the artifact with it?"

Capelo said, "I don't think it's possible to destroy the artifact. It self-protects, remember, against any proton beam or nuclear blast we threw at it. What would you use?"

She said, "But you know what Pierce is going to do! He'll take it to the Faller home system and set it off at prime thirteen, to destroy their home star!"

Capelo said slowly, with no trace of his usual sarcasm, "That's why we're speeding secretly back to the Solar System, isn't it? To alert the press so that Pierce can't do that. With press outcry, he wouldn't dare risk the Fallers' setting off their artifact at prime thirteen in the same star system."

"No," Kaufman said. "That's not what we're doing."

Both of them stared. Kaufman said, "I've been thinking. I don't think we can get there in Magdalena's flyer before Pierce's troops get to the Faller system with the artifact."

Capelo argued, "We'll have a head start if we can get out of this tin can by today. The navy first has to retrieve the artifact from Magdalena's ship, and then it has to go through all the confirmation of orders and passage-through-tunnels mumbo-jumbo between here and the Fallers' system. How many tunnels is it?"

"Five."

"How many to the Solar System?"

"Eight. And Magdalena has only got clearances from Blauman for the first three, as far as Artemis System. He wants her out of here, but he doesn't want her getting all the way home before Pierce brings off his heroic action."

"Well," Capelo said, "we'll still have a head start, and—"

"Listen, both of you," Kaufman said. "I've had time to think it through. It isn't going to work. Tom, there'll be no 'confirmation of orders and passage-through-tunnels mumbo-jumbo.' Not this time. Pierce will have this set up beforehand, ready to go as soon as he finds the artifact. It's a surprise attack, don't you see? Surprise attacks depend on speed and precision planning, that's basic military tactics. Pierce wants to present the Solar System with a *fait accompli* — 'Look! The war is over! The Faller system is destroyed!'

"We, on the other hand, would have to depend on Magdalena's negotiating to get us through a minimum of five tunnels without being identified and maybe killed. And then on the Sol side of Space Tunnel number one, we'd still have to summon the press, convince them we're not crackpots, and wait for the news datapackets to reach Mars and Earth. It won't work. We don't have time."

Marbet said, "Then we're helpless. We can't take the artifact away from the navy, and we can't get public opinion to intervene. But . . . won't the Fallers have their artifact set at prime eleven? That would protect their whole system anyway, and it's a stalemate."

"Except," Capelo said, "we know the bastards move their artifact around. They fried the entire Viridian System, didn't they? Maybe they've taken their artifact somewhere else for an attack, and then Pierce goes to their home system and destroys it." His voice turned bitter. "Well, would that be so bad? They are the enemy, you know. They've killed millions of us."

Marbet laid a sympathetic hand on Capelo's arm.

Kaufman pushed down impatience. They didn't see the situation whole. But he was going to need both of them on his side. Plus the unpredictable Magdalena, at least for a while. "Tom, if it were just frying the Faller system, none of us would be so upset. But you, more than anybody, know what happens to spacetime if we set off the artifact at prime thirteen in their system and they do the same thing."

"But perhaps they won't," Marbet argued. "After all, *they* know what will happen to the fabric of space . . . they told *us*, remember? Maybe they won't retaliate."

Capelo snorted. "And let us win? Think, woman. The Fallers never communicate, not even to tell us why they're at fucking war with us. They never take prisoners. They never allow themselves to be taken prisoner. They'll set it off so they can take us with them. Albeit slowly . . . remember, the wave that reconfigures the fabric of three-dimensional space is going to travel at c."

She said somberly, "Then we better hope that the Fallers have their artifact in their home system and turned on to prime eleven. That way we get a stalemate."

Kaufman said, "No. You don't understand."

"Oh?" Capelo said skeptically. "What don't we understand? Irresistible force meets immovable defense, and everybody goes home. Which is maybe what we should do, if the errant Magdalena doesn't dump us out into deep space somewhere."

Kaufman thought of all that could go wrong . . . which was everything. "Surprise and precision planning," he'd told Tom Capelo. This idea was the exact reverse. Haste, desperation, enormous risk, and then the universe's largest Pyrrhic victory ever. But there was no choice, and no time.

"I have a different plan. There's military information you don't know. We don't have a lot of time before Magdalena comes for us, so listen carefully. Some of this is classified, for higher clearances than you two have."

"My, my," Capelo said, "I'm honored."

"You know that one of the other tunnels out of Caligula system, Tunnel Number Four-three-seven, goes to the Allenby System. We came that way; there isn't any other route to World. The Allenby System is barren. Three gas giants, no humans, no Fallers. It has a second tunnel orbiting pretty far away from the first one, abnormally far away, which is why it took so long for Tunnel Four-three-seven to be discovered. That's Tunnel Number Two-one-zero, the Allenby-Artemis Tunnel, and we came through that, too."

"Is this a personal-history lesson?" Capelo said, and again Kaufman ignored the sarcasm. Tom couldn't help it. It was his only defense against fear.

"Artemis System is big. A colonized planet, a colonized moon, a space station, major SADC presence. We refueled there. Artemis System has five tunnels, which is why it's such a crossroads for humans. One of those tunnels is the one we would take toward Sol. Artemis System would be a prime target for Faller attack, which is why, everybody figures, there's so much military there. And everybody is right, but only partly right. One of the tunnels, Number Two-one-eight, is never reconfigured and never used. It's probably the best fortified spot in the galaxy, after Space Tunnel number One at Sol."

Marbet said quietly, "Two-one-eight leads to the Fallers' home system."

"No, not directly," Kaufman said. "That would be a bit too close to them. Tunnel Number Two-one-eight leads to an unnamed system with the military designation 'Q.' It's barren, and it has two tunnels. One is Number Two-one-eight, the other is Number Three-zero-one. Three-zero-one leads to the Fallers' system. Look, I'll draw you a picture."

Kaufman traced a line with his finger on the deck, but there was no dust. Damned efficient air-siphon cleaning. Silently Marbet pulled a handheld from the pocket of her coverall and handed it to him. Kaufman sketched clumsily:

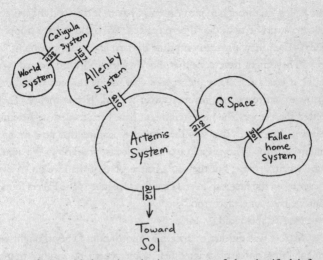

Kaufman said, knowing the importance of the classified information he was revealing, "We have an agreement with the Fallers that we stay out of Q System."

Capelo sat up straighter against the bulkhead. "An agreement? What are you talking about? They never communicate with us!"

"No. It's a tacit agreement. We've fought four separate battles there. The idea was to bottle them up in their home system. It didn't work; they appeared in Viridian System and wiped it out, which means their home system has two or more tunnels, not just Number Three-zero-one. We lost all four battles in Q System. Worse, we lost them to a single warship. It had the artifact aboard, set to prime two."

"The beam-disrupter shield. So none of our ships could hit it."

"Yes. It just picked off ours one by one. Four times." Kaufman was silent a moment. The SADC had lost good men in those battles. He'd known some of them. "After that, we stopped going through Tunnel Number Two-one-eight into Q System."

Capelo said, looking at the sketch on the handheld, "Why didn't the Fallers go through it, into Artemis System? If they had the artifact aboard at prime two, they'd be protected. We couldn't have stopped them. Then they just turn on prime thirteen and destroy Artemis."

"They might have done that. But they fried Viridian instead. We think it was a test. They didn't *know* that setting thirteen would destroy an entire system, no more than we did. It was theory. They tested the theory. The next step might have been to destroy Artemis System. Except . . . that was the time they learned that now *we* had an artifact, too. They monitor our broadcasts, you know. We aren't sure where or how, but they do a better job of it than we do. We've never taken the first step in cracking their language. The Fallers found out we have an artifact, too."

"So?" Capelo said.

Marbet was quicker at discerning motivation. "They thought we might bring our artifact into their home system by another tunnel route. They thought we might have figured out alternate routes in —"

"They're wrong," Kaufman said. "But they don't know that."

" — and so they moved their artifact to their home world and set it at prime eleven. To protect themselves. We're back to a stalemate."

"They might have done that," Kaufman said. "But there's an alternate speculation."

"Seems to me a lot of this is just speculation," Capelo said.

Marbet snapped, "You're an odd one to make that charge, Tom. Your profession consists of turning speculation into theory into fact."

Capelo laughed, unwillingly. Kaufman smiled at Marbet, his first genuine smile since their quarrel. He went on, "The other tunnel or tunnels out of their home world must lead to Faller colonies, or at least to military outposts. Humans have never appeared at any of them. So as time goes on, the Fallers deduce that we know only one way into their home system: through Q space. And they think we can't even be sure of that route, since no human has returned alive with the information.

"Also, both sides seem to have reached a kind of tacit agreement: Humans will not go through Tunnel Number Two-one-eight into Q System, because it's too heavily fortified. And Fallers don't go through Tunnel Number Two-one-eight in the other direction, into Artemis space, because our side of the tunnel is just as heavily fortified. No one can win. We both carry on the war elsewhere."

Marbet said, "But, Lyle, I still don't see how this means Pierce won't have a stalemate if he takes our artifact into their system. He sets it off at thirteen, they defend at eleven, nothing happens."

"No. There's more. We know that when the artifact is used as a weapon at settings one and three, there's a zone around it that is not affected. That doesn't destabilize. We've known that ever since Syree Johnson did her first test. She was close to the other artifact and she wasn't affected, but her shuttle, farther away, was. The shuttle pilot died. Every atom above atomic number seventy-five destabilized briefly, sending out improbably high numbers of alpha particles. At settings seven and thirteen, atoms destabilize above atomic number fifty. But there may still be a 'safe zone' immediately around the artifact. Which is why the Faller ship carrying the thing to Viridian wasn't destroyed as well."

"Not necessarily," Capelo argued. "They could have sent the artifact through the tunnel with a pre-set detonator for setting thirteen. It blows, Viridian is fried, they wait for the wave to pass, and then they go back into the system and retrieve their artifact. After all, we went in later and took high-resolution photos from space of the Viridian colony."

Kaufman had seen those photos. He pushed away the memory. "Yes, it might have happened that way, Tom. Or there might be a safe zone around the artifact, before the wave effect begins. We don't know. But here's the speculation: The Fallers know more about all this than we do, because they've fried a star system at setting thirteen and we haven't."

"No," Capelo said, "because *our* artifact has been sitting aboard the *Murasaki* while I supposedly probe it with my mental scalpel. Morons."

Kaufman knew he had to let Capelo make these interjections; it was the only way to get Capelo to go along with Kaufman's plan. He knew this from past experience with the physicist. But the interruptions were taking precious time. Kaufman talked faster.

"The Fallers know more about the artifact's working than we do. They know that we only know one way into their home system. We tried and tried to find a second access tunnel, and we didn't. So if they guard the Q-space–Faller-home-system tunnel from us, they're absolutely safe. *Unless* we bring our artifact aboard a ship turned to setting two, the way they did, and barrel our shielded way through the tunnel.

"Yes, they could keep the artifact at setting eleven to protect the home system, but they'd still have humans in their home system. Everything we know about the Fallers says they can't stand that. They're the most xenophobic life form anyone has ever seen. They'll do anything, the speculation goes, to keep us out of their star system. Marbet, you're the only human being to ever have actually communicated with a Faller, and he would tell you absolutely nothing until you told him that we had an artifact, too. Then he tried to say, 'Don't ever bring the two artifacts together and set them off in the same system!' "

"Get to the point," Capelo said impatiently. "This floor is hard."

"The point, Tom, is this: Faller military strategy and Faller psychology both say the same thing. Their artifact is not in their home system set at prime eleven. It's in Q System, their 'front yard,' set at prime two to protect the ship or station it's on, so that if we show up again in their yard they can blow us away with conventional weapons or atomic bombs, while remaining protected themselves. And if by chance we should bring our artifact into Q System, they'd know it because their weapons won't work against our ship. So they'll set their artifact off at prime thirteen and fry the entire Q System, except themselves, in the safe zone. When the wave is passed, they'll pick up our artifact, if it still exists, and then they've got two. If it doesn't exist, then the Fallers now have the only artifact in existence and they come to fry Sol."

"My God," Marbet said. "Did Stefanak know this theory?"

"Of course. It's the reason he never tried to use his artifact to attack the Faller System. Stefanak was ambitious and ruthless, but he wasn't stupid."

Marbet said, "Pierce isn't stupid, either."

"No," Kaufman said. "But unlike Stefanak, neither science nor engineering interest him. Tom, I don't think Pierce *believes* your probability theory. To him it's just garbled blue-sky intellectualizing. He believes in the artifact destroying material objects such as planets, because he's seen the physical results. Destroying spacetime is an abstract to him.

"But even if it's true, he thinks the Fallers will never set off their artifact at prime thirteen in the same system as our artifact, because we might do the same, and the Fallers definitely do believe this gobbly-gook about destroying the fabric of space. They believed it enough so that they told you about it, through Marbet, in order to prevent it happening inadvertently. So Pierce believes they'd never set off their artifact at prime thirteen in Q System, and anyway, probably nothing will happen if they and we both do."

"Madman!" Capelo said.

"Yes. But I think that's what he's about to do. Take the artifact to Q System and set it off at prime thirteen there to wipe out the Faller units. Maybe pick up their artifact afterward, maybe not. Either way, Pierce's ship waits until the wave has sufficiently passed, travels unimpeded through Tunnel Number Three-zero-one, and fries the Faller system without defense."

Marbet said, "Then Pierce is wrong. The Fallers will detect that our ship has set off the prime thirteen wave . . . can they? Before it reaches them? I thought it traveled at c."

"It does. No, they won't know it's coming until it hits them. But remember how it works, Marbet. It causes all atoms with an atomic number above fifty to destabilize, but not instantly. The atoms emit more alpha radiation than usual, then more, then more. There's time to activate their artifact at prime thirteen, especially if it's rigged to do that automatically, with a device made of atoms with atomic numbers lower than fifty. Not hard."

"So they see we're coming to wipe out their home star system, and they prefer instead to destroy spacetime itself."

"Why not?" Kaufman said. "That way they take us with them."

She burst out, "But Pierce must know all that!"

"I told you . . . *he doesn't believe it*. He's counting on one of three scenarios. One, their artifact is set at prime eleven in their home system, protecting it — that way he gets a stalemate and has lost nothing. Or, two, their artifact is in Q System, there's no safe zone, he destroys their ships and his own but he's fried Q System and in a little while he can go scoop up one or even two artifacts, before the Fallers beyond Tunnel Number Three-zero-one even know what happened. Or, three, their artifact is in Q System and the enemy is too much in thrall to their own physicists to risk destroying spacetime. So they can't stop Pierce and he goes through, protected by setting two, and fries the Faller home planet."

Capelo said somberly, "You can't know all this, Lyle. You and Stefanak and Pierce and everybody else really are just spinning speculative scenarios."

"Yes," Kaufman said, "but only one of the scenarios is acceptable. The third one won't happen; the Fallers will destroy spacetime rather than let the humans win. Stefanak knew that. Pierce is too blinded by egomania to see it. He wants to consolidate his power by being the greatest war hero in the history of humanity.

"The second scenario, both artifacts at prime thirteen in the same star system, results in a flop-transition that changes spacetime so much no one, human or Faller or bacteria, survives. Not acceptable.

"The only scenario that *is* acceptable is the stalemate. I don't think that the Fallers' artifact is currently in their home system, set at prime eleven, protecting them. I think, and the military advisors in Stefanak's more rational regime apparently agreed, that the Faller artifact is in Q System. So someone has to convince the Fallers to move their artifact and change its setting."

Capelo and Marbet stared at Kaufman. In the cramped space between the bulkhead and machinery, they looked like scrunched-up dolls, limbs momentarily frozen and mouths agape. Finally Capelo said, "And who's going to convince them of this?"

"We are," Kaufman said, and explained his insane plan.

TWENTY-THREE

THARSIS, MARS

When the house system let Amanda, Aunt Kristen, and Uncle Martin into the apartment in Tharsis, every room was full of flowers. Huge bouquets everywhere: genemod roses, pink and striped; gardenations, with the fullness of carnations and the intense fragrance of gardenias; humble dahlias; masses of the fast-growing, low-light blooms Martians called "rockflowers." All the flowers in Tharsis, Amanda thought dazedly. All gathered here in one place.

"Ah-man-dah!" Konstantin cried, bounding forward. "You are by home now!"

"Oh, my God," Aunt Kristen said under her breath.

"Hello, Dr. Blumberg, Mrs. Blumberg," Konstantin said politely. "I get flowers at Ah-man-dah. Because she to come by *home*."

"They're beautiful," Amanda breathed. Wait until the girls at school heard about this!

"You are beautiful more," Konstantin said admiringly, gazing at Amanda with her newly blonde hair and pretty clothes. "Very beautiful! Splendid!"

"It smells like a funeral parlor," Aunt Kristen said, and Uncle Martin shot her a warning look.

"And your father? You to find him? He to come also?"

"We didn't find him yet," Amanda said, and her whole last conversation with Aunt Kristen came crashing back down on her. Aunt Kristen said that Admiral Pierce, who was not the nice person he'd seemed, might not return her father. That Daddy might be dead, killed like the people who'd opposed Pierce and had just disappeared, including her father's friend Dr. Ewing. That Konstantin's father was a big supporter of Admiral Pierce, and Amanda was therefore to be very careful to never ever criticize the admiral in front of Konstantin or Demetria.

"Admiral Pierce will to find your father," Konstantin said confidently. "Will to carry him at you."

"Do you really think so?" Amanda said.

"Oh, yes," Konstantin said.

Maybe he was right! After all, even Aunt Kristen had said that Konstantin's father was big buddies with Admiral Pierce, whereas Aunt Kristen had never met the admiral at all, not even on this last trip to Lowell City with Amanda. So shouldn't Konstantin know more about Admiral Pierce than her aunt did? It was a cheering thought. Amanda smiled gratefully at Konstantin.

"What smells like food?" Uncle Martin said, pointedly changing the subject.

"Demetria to cook. Come!"

"Thanks for the invitation to my home," Aunt Kristen muttered.

The small dining room table groaned with Greek food, or as close to Greek as Demetria could get with ingredients available on Mars. Amanda's mouth filled with sweet water. Even Aunt Kristen looked happier. Everyone ate, Demetria beaming wordlessly at her success.

"Tell at me what to happen by Lowell City, Ah-man-dah."

Amanda swallowed a sticky mouthful of Martian baklava and said carefully, "They asked me questions. I told them all I could, and Admiral Pierce said they would look for Daddy."

"Splendid. My father to look also."

Aunt Kristen stopped chewing. "What?"

"I call at my father, by Greece. He to know very many important peoples. I ask by him to help to look to Dr. Capelo because I to stay at the house of the daughter, beautiful Ah-man-dah. I say Ah-man-dah by Lowell City, at Admiral Pierce, for questions. My father is of very much interest. He says yes, he to help."

Aunt Kristen closed her eyes.

Uncle Martin said, with noticeable constraint, "Thank you, Konstantin. I know . . . I know you meant well. We all hope Dr. Capelo will come home soon."

"Very great physicist," Konstantin said seriously. "Much respect by physicists. Dr. Stajevic call from Earth by you, Mrs. Blumberg."

"And did you view the message, Konstantin?" Aunt Kristen said evenly.

Amanda held her breath. Her aunt and uncle were strict about personal privacy.

"Oh, no," Konstantin said. "House system to say message are come. Is at you, not me."

Amanda breathed again. Aunt Kristen said, "Excuse me," and left the room, closing the bedroom door.

Uncle Martin said, "Konstantin, won't your parents be missing you and Demetria? Won't they want you back on Earth?"

"Oh, no. We go by Earth at school. Not at summer. To tourist by Mars now. Very interesting, splendid. I to care at Demetria."

Demetria, hearing her name, looked sulkily at her brother. Was that because of Nikos, Amanda wondered? This family operated nothing like the ones she was used to.

Aunt Kristen returned. "Dr. Stajevic wanted to know if we have any private papers of Tom's related to what he was working on. Apparently Stajevic is working in the same area, and until Tom disappeared, they'd been exchanging ideas. Stajevic has what he called 'a new line of attack,' and if we have anything of Tom's, he was going to post it on the Net so that he, and anybody else involved in the same problem, could have access to it."

Uncle Martin said, with a quick glance at Amanda, "But Tom may be coming back to post it himself."

"That's what I told him," Aunt Kristen said, attacking her gyro with unnecessary force.

There was a long silence, so long it grew painful. Finally, to break it, Amanda said, "What . . . what was Daddy working on?"

"Macro-entanglement. To fit into the theory of probability. He has promising initial equations," Konstantin said, with the sudden increase in English proficiency he managed whenever he spoke of physics. He must, Amanda thought, memorize whole sections of scientific papers.

Aunt Kristen looked startled. "How do you know that?"

"I read physics by the Net. Always. Dr. Capelo to post always. Parts of theories, also, not finished. Dr. Capelo to ask at other physicists by help. To find physics answers. Great, great man."

Uncle Martin said, "Kris, if that's so . . . maybe we should ask the Boston police for any papers they confiscated from Tom's house, and let this Dr. Stajevic post them."

"I'll think about it," Aunt Kristen said.

When they'd finished eating, everyone went into the living room. Uncle Martin brought up a news channel on the terminal. Konstantin sat at one end of a sofa, Aunt Kristen at the other end. Demetria and Uncle Martin had taken chairs; the center of the sofa was the only place left to sit. Amanda settled awkwardly beside Konstantin. This close, his scent came to her, and something in her chest tightened. She felt herself blush. Good thing he wasn't looking at her!

"—surprise departure from Lowell City to Space Tunnel Number

One aboard the navy flagship *Vladivistok*. A spokeswoman for Admiral Pierce told the press that an undisclosed 'military emergency' at the tunnel required the admiral's presence. She further announced that the *Vladivistok* was traveling with all possible speed to minimize the time Admiral Pierce will be away from Mars. Speculation has run high about the nature of the military emergency, but no additional information has been forthcoming from the Summit. It is unclear at this time whether Admiral Pierce intends to actually leave the Solar System through Space Tunnel Number One.

"In Admiral Pierce's absence, he has appointed General Yang Lee as acting commander of the SADC. However, Admiral Pierce has assured the Solar Alliance that he will be in constant radio contact with the acting commander. Meanwhile, in the Belt—"

"My father is by Space Tunnel Number One," Konstantin said casually.

Aunt Kristen looked at him. "I thought you said your father was in Greece."

"Oh, yes. In Greece. And by Tunnel Number One. And by the Belt. And by Mars. My father to own many many ships, many flyers. My father are many places always."

"I see," Aunt Kristen said, and Amanda knew that Aunt Kristen thought Konstantin was bragging. Well, he wasn't! Those were just facts! Amanda's father always said to put facts first, and that's what Konstantin was doing, and there wasn't anything wrong with that.

Konstantin said, "Tomorrow is Sunday."

"Yes?" Amanda said, when no one else spoke.

"You to come to church by me, Ah-man-dah? To hear Mass. Church must to be by Tharsis."

He meant a Catholic church, Amanda realized. Konstantin thought she was religious. Well, he'd first seen her outside the spaceport holding Brother Meissel's gold chalice, which stood now in the master bedroom.

An unexpected tide of emotion swept her. Brother Meissel, Ares Abbey. The deep voices chanting plainsong: Lauds, Prime, Terce, Sext, Vespers, Matins. " 'When you have become God's in the measure He wants, He Himself will bestow you on others.' That's St. Basil, Amanda, remember . . ."

"Ah-man-dah?"

Her father always said religion was stupid superstition for people who didn't want to think. But Brother Meissel thought, and he wasn't stupid, even though nothing he said actually made any sense . . . It was very confusing. Why did everything have to be so confusing?

"Ah-man-dah?"

"Yes, Konstantin. I'll go to Mass with you tomorrow. Uncle Martin, is there a Catholic church in Tharsis?"

"I don't know." Uncle Martin was looking at her in astonishment, Aunt Kristen with apprehension. Well, let them! Was it such a crime to go to church with a boy you liked? A guest in your home?

"Splendid," Konstantin said. Amanda's aunt and uncle were still looking at her, making Amanda feel very uncomfortable, when Demetria suddenly jumped up. "Coffee!" she said loudly, and Amanda was grateful to her even though she didn't really know why.

On the way back to the dining room, Amanda was struck by another thought. Konstantin, from the peek she'd had at the spare room, was sleeping in there. Demetria's little bag was stowed beside the sofa, so probably she'd slept there. Where would Amanda sleep? To her intense annoyance, she felt a hot blush sweep up her neck and face. Everybody would notice!

But, in fact, no one did. Konstantin was telling Demetria something in Greek. And Amanda heard Aunt Kristen, behind her, say to Uncle Martin in a very low voice, "Why do you think Pierce is going to the tunnel so fast?"

"I don't know," Uncle Martin responded, and Amanda breathed more easily. They hadn't seen her blush after all. It was all right.

It was all going to be all right.

TWENTY-FOUR

CALIGULA SPACE

Tom Capelo and Marbet Grant stared at Kaufman as if he were a lunatic. In the cramped hiding space at the back of the life-support room, crowded by overhead ducts and whirring machinery and dusty crates, Kaufman silently agreed with them. Everything was in shadow. The machines threw a lot of heat. Kaufman felt the sweat form on his neck, under the unfamiliar seaman's tunic.

"It can't work," Capelo said slowly, with no trace of his usual sarcasm. "Lyle . . . *think*. It can't possibly work."

Marbet said, "It depends on too many improbabilities. Magdalena, the navy guard ships at five different tunnels . . . *five*. And then, at the end—"

"Aren't I the one who's supposed to be thinking in probabilities?" Capelo said acidly, and Kaufman saw that at least one person had returned to normal. Whatever "normal" could be in this situation. He let Capelo vent. It was the only way to handle him.

"If I were going to draw up sum-over-paths probability for this insane idea," Capelo continued, "it would lead right into the toilet. Lyle, we can't do it."

"What else do you suggest?" Kaufman said mildly.

"Anything else!"

"All right, I'm waiting. Maybe you'll have a better idea, Tom— I'm certainly not disputing that you're much smarter than I am. But you need to have it soon, because Magdalena's going to come for us and we won't have another chance to talk alone."

"I won't do it, Lyle. I want to see my daughters again in this lifetime."

"All right. Go home, see your daughters. And when the fabric of spacetime is destroyed because two artifacts get set off at prime thirteen in the same system, calculate how much time you'll have to ever see them again."

"I have," Capelo retorted. "The flop-transition wave travels at c, so it will be centuries before it reaches the Solar System. The Faller home world is over a thousand light-years away from Earth!"

"Are you sure it travels at c, Tom? Dieter said that when the first artifact was destroyed right here at this very tunnel by Syree Johnson, there was an instantaneous effect on World, a billion clicks away. Are you positive there isn't some sort of macro-level entanglement between the space tunnels, themselves entangled, and the artifacts? Isn't that what your current work is about?"

"How do you know what my current work is about?"

"I read what I could follow. On the Net," Kaufman said. Those long hours aboard the *Sans Merci*, avoiding Marbet and trying to follow the physics papers he was not trained for.

Marbet said, "Tom . . . is Lyle right? Is there a chance that the wave at setting prime thirteen might have an *instantaneous* effect on spacetime?"

"No one knows," Capelo said. "There are even some equations

that hint at a lagged effect, like the lag of the destabilization wave itself, but the equations are inconclusive . . . Damn you, Lyle! All right. I'll give your radiant idiocy a try. But I still think the most probable outcome is that the three of us die without accomplishing anything."

Kaufman said, "We'll die anyway," and immediately regretted it. Truth shouldn't sound so grandiose, so gaudy. He had always liked truth to come in sturdy, utilitarian shapes, small shapes that accreted only gradually into a stable, mundane picture.

Not this time.

"All right," he said, meaninglessly. Then, "Tom, change clothes with me."

Capelo laughed harshly. He was three inches shorter than Kaufman and about forty pounds lighter.

"Not the pants," Kaufman said, trying to keep irritation out of his voice. "But give me that shirt, it's gaping on you anyway. Take this seaman's tunic."

"Just what I never wanted . . . to be in the Solar Alliance Defense Navy. Anchors aweigh, my boys . . ."

Marbet said, "Please, Tom," saving Kaufman the trouble.

In the cramped area between the bulkhead and a piece of huge, humming machinery, Kaufman awkwardly stripped off his tunic and put on Capelo's shirt. It wouldn't close; he left it unfastened over his bodystretch. The seaman's tunic fell almost to Capelo's knees and sloped off his narrow shoulders. Both of them must look ridiculous. Marbet smiled.

Toward the corridor, the door opened.

"Come on," Kaufman said, "fast." He led them on the crawl out of the life-support room.

It was Kendai, not Magdalena, who stood waiting for them. The young bodyguard glared at Kaufman. He wasn't quite as disciplined as Rory; his emotions still showed. Kaufman filed away the information for any possible future use.

They slipped quickly through the deserted corridor to the equally deserted docking bay of the vast warship. How had Magdalena managed to have everybody be somewhere else? She had her methods. And, of course, all the fighter craft had gone streaking after the *Sans Merci*, to bring back the artifact that now would never reach World. The only vehicles in the bay were the landing shuttle and Magdalena's flyer.

She waited inside the flyer along with Rory, fidgeting among the six close-packed seats. "What took you so long?"

It hadn't been long. Kaufman didn't argue, just strapped himself in. "Are we cleared for the tunnel?"

"Yes, of course. For three tunnels on, through Artemis System. Come on, Sensitive, move it. No time now to probe everybody's inner brains."

She was taut as elevator cable, Kaufman saw. Tension rose off her like heat. Magdalena took the pilot's chair. The bay doors opened at her command to the bridge, and the flyer hurled out toward Space Tunnel #438, leading from World into Caligula System.

The tunnel hovered straight ahead, an unfathomable array of panels and cables forming a loose doughnut. The inside was murky, a thick gray . . . something. The flyer flew straight toward the gray. Kaufman looked sideways at Capelo; what did the physicist see? A mass of unfinished equations? The product of an unknowable alien physics? The means to (maybe) enable a wave that should have traveled at c to instead travel instantaneously, the better to reconfigure spacetime? Capelo's thin dark face gave away nothing.

Kaufman twisted in his seat to catch a last glimpse of World, but before he could locate it among the stars, the flyer was through the tunnel and he was looking at entirely different patterns in the sky.

• • •

Caligula Station orbited the tunnel, with patrolling flyers in between. It was actually a tunnel system; for unknown reasons Caligula, with no habitable planets, possessed three tunnels. The creators of the tunnel must have considered Caligula space more important than humans did. The other two tunnels weren't close enough for visual perception, but they showed on Magdalena's scanner.

Only military, not colonists, occupied the system. Caligula Station was essentially a traffic cop for perimeter tunnel travel. It had never seen a battle. Ambitious officers strove hard to be transferred out as soon as possible. Over fifteen years, the ones who stayed were the non-ambitious, the incompetent, and the venal.

"Flyer," said a bored young voice, "identify self."

"Flyer from the *Sans Merci*, civilian, travel permit number 1264A, issued July eleven," Magdalena said crisply. "Four persons aboard."

Kaufman counted the seconds: one, two . . . six, seven . . .

"Flyer from the *Sans Merci*?" said the young voice, no longer bored. "You were cleared for return passage of the original craft, not just a flyer."

"Clearance has been changed. Check the priority dispatch you just received from the military flyer that went through an hour ago. You're the action addressee."

This time the pause was considerably longer than seven seconds. Kaufman knew what the OOD was thinking: What the hell were civilian travel clearances doing in an action-addressee dispatch, and why did a civilian know about it?

"Cleared for Caligula Station, four persons aboard," the OOD finally said. "Proceed, flyer. Docking data follows."

"Thank you," Magdalena said, and cut the link. She vibrated with tension.

Marbet said to Kaufman, very low, "When you're in the station, can you get her to make some arrangement for Essa?"

Essa. Kaufman had not given the alien girl a single thought. Essa had been sent home to World along with the artifact, on the *Sans Merci*. But now the *Sans Merci* was not going to reach World. She was going to be captured by Blauman's fighters and returned to the *Murasaki*. Essa would be aboard a human warship with no one to take charge of her. What would Blauman do with her?

"You haven't thought about Essa until this minute," Marbet said. "And now you're thinking of her with more annoyance than guilt."

"Essa isn't the main concern here."

"I know. But she's our responsibility."

Kaufman didn't see that, hadn't ever seen that. Essa was Magdalena's responsibility, at least in theory. Magdalena had brought the alien into space. He knew better than to say this aloud.

But, of course, it didn't matter whether he said it aloud. Marbet knew.

Caligula Station, a huge misshapen complex pitted with countless small meteor hits, loomed on the viewscreen. Several fighters and one *Thor*-class warship were docked alongside. "All right, kiddies, into the toilet," Magdalena said. "Be good in there, you two."

At a warning glance from Kaufman, Capelo didn't retort. Even Tom knew how much they needed Magdalena. Without her, they would not get through Space Tunnels #437 and #210 to Artemis System. And they needed her after that in order to . . . Kaufman put that action out of his mind. One battle at a time.

Capelo and Marbet unstrapped and both squeezed into the tiny head. Flyers were not meant for comfortable or long-term trips; the head was the only place on the flyer that was not visible when the door was opened. The supply cupboards were all too small for a human body, except for those hung with s-suits, which took up the entire space. Even in the head, two people could not both sit down at the same time. But there wasn't any choice. The head door closed and Kaufman heard the lock click.

He said to Magdalena, "You're sure they won't search a civilian craft?"

"They're supposed to, aren't they? You would know that. But they won't. Caligula Station is full of the laziest, fattest, stupidest, dirtiest sailors I ever saw."

It was what Kaufman had been thinking, in politer terms. He hoped she was right.

Magdalena's flyer, on computer, flew into an open bay. It closed behind them and pressurized. Instantly she was out the door. Kaufman and the two bodyguards followed.

"Passports," said the surly gangway petty officer. His hair was uncombed and above his regulation gunbelt, his uniform was decorated with a decidedly non-regulation holo of a bloody knife. The deck was filthy. Where was the OOD? Kaufman itched to discipline the sailor himself, but instead stayed impassive. He was not supposed to look SADC.

The gangway officer inspected their passports and matched each with a retinal scan. Kaufman was once again using his original faked passport, which showed him as the "Eric James Peltier" he'd been aboard the *Cascade of Stars*.

"Four civilians aboard, cleared," he growled into his comlink. "Where're they supposed to go?"

"To Major Hofsetter's office," the comlink answered.

"Carver, take this four to Major Hofsetter," the gangway officer said to the messenger of the watch.

"Three," Magdalena said. She pointed to the younger of her bodyguards. "Kendai stays with the flyer."

"Three," the gangway chief corrected. "Carver!"

The watch messenger, who had been sitting on a crate and gazing at a handheld, lumbered reluctantly to his feet. Kaufman glimpsed pornography on the handheld. He gritted his teeth. Action or no action, this outpost was a disgrace. No wonder Magdalena had been able to buy tunnel clearances.

Well, that was to Kaufman's advantage now.

She said to Kendai, "No one boards the flyer for any reason whatsoever. Are you convinced of that?"

Kendai nodded. It occurred to Kaufman that he had never actually heard the young bodyguard speak. Maybe he couldn't.

Kaufman followed Carver, Magdalena, and Rory through the maze of corridors and elevators that was Caligula Station. Parts of it, Kaufman was cheered to see, were much closer to regs than the docking bay. Deck and bulkheads were clean, soldiers properly uniformed. The entire station wasn't lax, and the army portion looked much better than the navy portion. The turf wars usual on SADC space facilities, with their necessary mix of services, had clearly been won at Caligula Station by SADA.

Except in the case of Hofsetter. He was a fat, greasy lifer who did not rise when they entered. Kaufman had him pegged at a glance. In the days when Kaufman had commanded combat units, this was exactly the type he'd gotten rid of. Hofsetter would sell a warship if the price were high enough and he thought he wouldn't get caught.

"Hello, Hofsetter," Magdalena said. "I'm here to deal."

"New bodyguard, honey? Doesn't look like he's got Rory's edge. And that's half a SADN uniform he's got on."

"Crewman off the *Sans Merci*, and I don't care what the fuck he wears or where he gets it. I have a big offer for you, Hofsetter. The biggest your slimy little operation is ever going to see, so pay attention."

She sat, uninvited, in a chair beside Hofsetter. Kaufman saw that she wasn't using her spectacular body for feminine advantage. This was a straight bargain. Rory stood alert, watching both Hofsetter and the door, and Kaufman did the same.

"I want you to peel all the SADN Belt-incident records for July third of this year. All of them. There's an incident I want the file on, and I'm willing to pay off the entire navy if I have to. Plus a million credits to you."

A million credits.

Something was wrong. Hofsetter's eyes widened, as well they might. But along with surprise and greed, both expected, Kaufman saw something else: a sly, dirty triumph.

"A million credits," Hofsetter said.

"Yes. By retina-verified chip." Necessary, Kaufman thought. There were no communications, including banking communications, through the tunnels. A retina-verified chip would be good whenever Hofsetter returned to Sol, for as long as Magdalena's extensive financial empire existed.

"Then give it to me. I already know what happened to Laslo Damroscher."

Magdalena laughed, a sound totally without mirth. "Sure you do."

"Yes. I do," and even though Magdalena went on sneering, Kaufman saw that Hofsetter was telling the truth. Oh, God, no . . . *not now*. Everything he had planned depended on Magdalena's believing Kaufman could help her find Laslo. Not now . . .

Her eyes tightened. "Prove it."

"The chip first. Verified."

"In hell, maybe. I'll draw up the chip. Verification after you show me your so-called proof."

"Fine by me," Hofsetter said, and again Kaufman saw the gleam of triumph in his piggy eyes.

How was she going to react? Kaufman couldn't predict. He

needed Marbet. But Marbet was locked in the flyer head with Tom Capelo, and however Magdalena acted, Kaufman was going to have to prevent its losing him this one chance.

Hofsetter punched e-codes into his desk safe and drew out a data cube covered with the usual military warnings. He inserted the cube into his terminal. It was two-d, not holo, a routine recording. The terminal flashed the code for data integrity; if this recording had been tampered with in any way, including the integrity warning, it would self-destruct. There were ways around that, but it took expensive expert work. Still, maybe if Magdalena believed the data were falsified . . . Kaufman looked at her face. She knew the data were the real thing. How?

"I . . . obtained this, let's say . . . after you came through here a few weeks ago," Hofsetter said. And that was how Magdalena knew the data cube was real; until three weeks ago, Hofsetter hadn't known Magdalena had a missing son. Caligula Station was almost as isolated as the World System. The resources to create a falsified integrity cube were tunnels away.

The data began to play. Visual and audio—a cockpit conversation? No, this wasn't a craft but a structure.

Kaufman had heard the other side of the conversation before. As it relentlessly happened again, the blip on the screen grew bigger. Kaufman couldn't see the command displays, but he knew what they showed. Distance, speed, acceleration, thermal signature, weapon readiness of the approaching flyer.

He knew what he was going to see: The complement to Magdalena's recording, the same event as seen from inside the asteroid. Terrible yin to horrifying yang.

"Sir . . . craft on the screen."

"I see it. Distance and ID?"

"Still a half mil clicks out . . . a flyer, sir."

"Military?"

"In a min . . . no, sir, civilian."

"What the fuck . . . wait to see if they approach."

Silence.

"Approaching, sir."

"Give them the warning on all frequencies."

A loud mechanical voice: *"You are approaching a highly restricted area. Leave this area immediately."*

And then, after a time lag and from some stupid mistake of a suddenly open comlink in the other craft, Conner's voice, *"It don't want us. Shoot it!"*

"Wait, maybe . . ."

"You are approaching a highly restricted area. Leave this area immediately."

"Fucking snakes! Shoot it!"

"I . . ."

"Fucking coward!"

"Sir, flyer accelerating."

"One more warning, Mr. Tambwe."

"Yes, sir."

"THIS IS YOUR LAST WARNING! YOU HAVE INVADED A HIGHLY RESTRICTED AND HIGH-DANGER AREA. LEAVE IMMEDIATELY OR YOUR CRAFT WILL BE FIRED ON!"

"Unknown craft . . . SOS . . . Help! I'm—"

"What . . . how the hell is that son-of-a-bitch sending—"

"Being held prisoner here—This—"

"Fire!"

"Is Tom Capelo—"

The flyer on the viewscreen was hit by the invisible proton beam and vaporized. One moment it was growing larger and larger on the viewscreen; the next moment there was only empty space decorated with cold stars.

"Got it, sir. Should I file an incident report?"

"No. Not for this project. Just mark the automatic record."

"Yes, sir."

The terminal went blank.

Magdalena didn't move. She looked unchanged, gazing impersonally at the screen, her lips faintly curved. Hofsetter lumbered uncertainly to his feet. He glanced at Rory, whose face Kaufman couldn't see. A long moment passed.

She suddenly sagged against Hofsetter's desk, a quick collapse as if all her bones had dissolved. It lasted only a second. She straightened, and an animal sound was torn from her throat, a sound Kaufman had never before heard a human being make. She launched herself at Hofsetter, her nails going for his eyes.

He dodged, fat and clumsy, and started yelling. Magdalena's terrible sound went on, drowning out his. Footsteps pounded in the corridor. Rory leaped forward and pulled his boss off of the colonel as the MPs burst into the room. Rory threw Magdalena at Kaufman and went into defense stance, moving so fast that Kaufman, with a small part of his racing mind, wondered what kind of augments Rory had. He'd never seen a soldier move that fast. Magdalena sagged in his arms.

The MPs stopped, confused, awaiting orders. Hofsetter waved them out. "Fuck! She clawed me, the bitch! Get her out of here!"

She had gone limp. Kaufman hoisted her dead weight, but Hofsetter snapped, "Retina-signature first! She promised!"

Kaufman looked at him.

"I delivered!"

Kaufman nodded at Rory, who hesitated, looking for orders from Magdalena. She didn't move. Her lips, so drained of color they looked blue, were rigidly clamped. Kaufman knew this stage wouldn't last. He didn't know the nature of Magdalena's other dealings with Hofsetter. He said to Rory, "Do it."

Rory picked up the credit chip, pried open one of Magdalena's eyes, and flashed the chip against her lens. Hofsetter cried, "It ain't legal unless she can blink!"

Rory leaned over and slapped Magdalena lightly. She wasn't unconscious; she blinked. Rory peeled off the chip and threw it on the floor.

Kaufman carried Magdalena out the door, past the staring MPs. He snapped, "Guide us to our docking bay." The MP bristled, but Hofsetter repeated the order and the MP obeyed.

If she would just stay in shock until they reached the flyer . . .

She didn't. In a narrow corridor on E deck, she jerked in Kaufman's arms and struck him. He dropped her, stepping back. She half fell, then got to her feet, and he had to look away from her face.

"They won't get away with it. I won't let them get away with it. They won't get away with it. I won't let them . . ."

Kaufman reached for her hand. She struck his away and he withdrew instantly. He'd seen what Hofsetter had not: The barb shooting from under her nail when she'd clawed him. Kaufman just hoped it was a slow enough poison to let them escape Caligula System before it put Hofsetter in agony.

"They won't get away with it." Now her voice was flat, more horrible than her raging. She looked as if she wanted to pull down the galaxy, and could.

Kaufman said respectfully but firmly, "We're following this MP to the flyer."

To his relief, she didn't argue. She strode along, and Kaufman dropped a few paces back so he didn't have to look at her face. Now, from the back, she resembled the purposeful, cold empire builder she was.

But she couldn't sustain it. Just short of the docking bay, she turned to Kaufman, and he saw that the horror had reached her brain, no less deadly than the poison she had sent to Hofsetter's. "Laslo . . ." It was a whisper now ". . . Laslo . . ." Again she toppled to the deck, and this time it was a genuine faint. Her body had shut down the horror in the only way it could.

That wouldn't last, either. And now came the first part of Kaufman's plan, which was not supposed to happen like this. Although it might make it easier. If Capelo could do it, that is . . .

This time Kaufman didn't pick up Magdalena. Instead he strode toward the flyer, which meant Rory had to carry his boss. He handled her as if she weighed two pounds. Kaufman walked past the open-mouthed messenger of the watch and his slovenly chief, past the uncertain Kendai, and yanked open the flyer door. He stood aside to let Rory go first with his burden. To the watch he said, "Immediate departure. Check your screen, damn it."

Startled at his tone, the same one he'd used on derelict soldiers all his life, the chief scuttled to his watch cabin. The messenger ran after him, and Kaufman heard the lock hiss as they closed the door preparatory to depressurizing.

Rory climbed into the flyer and dumped Magdalena into a passenger seat, not the pilot's chair. The head door opened. Kaufman didn't move. He knew that Rory, from long training, had only half his mind on Magdalena. The rest kept careful track of Kaufman, the trained soldier, and lesser track of the tiny civilian woman and the wimpy scientist. They only had a second before Rory moved to his habitual position, back to the bulkhead with the entire cabin under surveillance.

Tom Capelo fired from the bathroom. Kaufman slammed and locked the flyer door before Kendai could enter.

The nervewash was intended for a normal soldier, not an augment. Also, Capelo—even at this range!—had not hit Rory square in the nape, as he was supposed to, but in one shoulder. The bodyguard whirled and went for Capelo. But the nervewash, acting instantly, had at least slowed if not paralyzed him. Before he could slam his augmented fist into the physicist, probably killing him, Kaufman had grabbed Rory from behind. Kaufman couldn't have sustained a full, direct blow from Rory either, but Rory's eyes wobbled in their sockets and he stumbled. Kaufman yelled to Capelo, "Fire again!" hoping that a double dose wouldn't kill the augment. Capelo fired, missed, fired a third time, and finally Rory collapsed on top of the unconscious Magdalena.

"Jesus Christ, Tom, Marbet could have done better!"

"Then you should have let her do it!"

Marbet had already squeezed past Capelo to the pilot's seat. She said clearly into the comlink to the watch cabin, "Open vehicle bay door. We're leaving."

Kaufman said, "I've got it now, Marbet."

She slid out of the chair and began to pull Rory off Magdalena and into a seat, and to strap both of them in. "Help me, Tom!"

He did. Kaufman said to the stupefied watch and Kendai, pounding uselessly on the flyer, "Your instructions indicate departure, sailor. Do it. Kendai, get into the watch cabin before depressurization or you'll die."

"Sir—" the watch said, and the title told Kaufman the disgraceful travesty of a soldier was going to obey.

"Do it, sailor! It's in your bridge instructions!"

"Aye, aye, sir." The signal for depressurization sounded, a steady clanging.

Kendai sprinted for the watch cabin. Kaufman, relieved, saw the watch let him in and reseal the door. He hadn't wanted to kill Kendai, although he would have if necessary. He had already ended the gangway petty officer's career in a court martial, which the fool hadn't yet realized. Just as he deserved.

The air hissed out of the bay, the outside door slid open, and Kaufman flew Magdalena's flyer out of Caligula Station and toward the space tunnel leading into Allenby System.

• • •

She was half dead and half alive, and Laslo was dead.

Something was happening around her, but Magdalena didn't care what. She would never care again, about anything. None of it mattered. None of it could.

Laslo was dead.

He couldn't be dead. She could see him too clearly, feel him, smell him, that sweet smell babies have at the back of the neck, where the hair curled, fine as spider silk. He lay in his crib, the pink crease around his plump small wrists like a doll's. She hefted him, that dense damp weight of small children, and she could feel the bones in his strong back. He lifted his arms, "Up, up, up . . ." and she lifted him. He rode beside her in the flyer, proud when she let him touch the codepad, craning his head to see better, that head too big for his body the way all little boys' heads seemed too big for their bodies. He laughed, and it was the most powerful sound in the universe, a sound to work and scheme and cheat for so that he would have everything she had never had, be safe as she had never been safe . . . she would always keep him safe. . . .

And now he was dead.

Help me, Sualeen, help me . . .

She hadn't been able to help Sualeen, either. Sualeen had died without the one thing she'd wanted most, real headstones for her family. The first thing May Damroscher had done with Amerigo Dalton's money had been to travel back to Atlanta and buy carved granite headstones for everyone dead in Sualeen's family. She personally watched them be erected in the cemetery.

The second thing she'd done was hire someone to find the Harris uncle from fourteen months before. When he'd been found, she had him robo-raped. She didn't watch that herself, or even the holo the man brought her in corroboration. It was enough to know that it had been done, and that the uncle knew by whom.

She could kill for Laslo, but she couldn't save him because he was already dead. Dead, and no headstone, Sualeen had the best headstone money could buy but Laslo . . .

"Fire!"

"Got it, sir. Should I file an incident report?"

She hadn't known anything could hurt like this. If she moved, if she took a deep breath, pain shot through her body like fire. Burning pain, penetrating pain . . .

"Got it, sir. Should I file an incident report?"

They would pay. She'd make them pay. They'd all pay . . .

She hurt too much to do anything. Oh, God, let it be me, not Laslo, let this end let it end let it end. . . .

Everything was ended.

She was screaming, and no one could hear her, and the pain of losing him would go on forever and ever.

Laslo—

TWENTY-FIVE

THARSIS, MARS

When Amanda returned from accompanying Konstantin and Demetria to church, the apartment was empty. Aunt Kristen and Uncle Martin had left a note: AMANDA—HAD TO GO OUT, BACK BY DINNER.

"That's strange," Amanda said.

"Excuse?"

She showed him the note. "Aunt Kristen and Uncle Martin went somewhere, but they didn't say where."

Konstantin laboriously read the note, and his face brightened. "Demetria to cook splendid dinner at they!" He turned and rattled away to Demetria in rapid Greek. Amanda fought her unease.

Where had they gone? And why did they leave her alone with Konstantin? Of course, Demetria was here. She was answering Konstantin and laughing, her teeth white against red lips and golden skin. They were both so beautiful. Genemod? Maybe. Amanda suddenly felt too pale, too wispy. Too all-one-color. There was a word for that, they'd had it in the vocabulary software, but she couldn't remember it.

Church had been nice and scary and sad, all at once. It turned out that Konstantin wanted something called a "Greek Orthodox church," which Lowell City didn't have. He settled for Our Lady of the Angels. But even though it was Catholic, Amanda could hardly see any way it resembled Ares Abbey. The only singing was by all the church customers, and it was pretty terrible. Amanda, thinking of Brother Meissel and the Holy Office, felt her throat close. Konstantin had noticed her distress and reached for her hand, and that was the scary part. He'd held her hand through all the rest of church. Amanda felt herself go hot, then cold, but she hadn't pulled her hand away. It was so thrilling. She wished she could tell Yaeko or Juliana or Thekla about it.

But not Daddy. Amanda had a feeling he wouldn't have liked Konstantin to hold her hand. That made her feel disloyal, which was silly, but she couldn't help it. Her worry about her father was always there, a vacuum waiting to swallow her.

She'd felt better on the walk back from church. Konstantin had taken her and Demetria to a cafe for breakfast. He seemed to have inexhaustible credit. The three of them had ignored the soldiers with green bars on their caps and eaten greedily, talking in English (Amanda and Konstantin) and Greek (Konstantin and Demetria), laughing at nothing. It had been fun.

Now Demetria bustled into the kitchen and Amanda heard her opening cupboards and taking out dishes. Amanda made up her mind to ask Konstantin something she'd been wondering about, even if the question was nosy.

"Konstantin . . . your family is rich, aren't they?"

"Rich, yes. Much of money. Splendid. I to buy you anything, Ah-man-dah!"

She blushed. That hadn't been what she meant! "Then why does Demetria know how to cook? Don't you have a cook? Or at least kitchen 'bots?"

"Yes, of course. Many cooks. Also 'bots. Demetria to cook because she is good Greek woman. At to marry Greek man."

This made no sense to Amanda. "Then . . . when you marry someday, your wife will have to know how to cook, too."

"Oh, no! I to marry not Greek. Greek womans not too pretty. You are too pretty, Amanda."

"Demetria is beautiful!"

He shrugged. "Nikos to think yes. My father to comlink since morning. He to want Demetria by home. He to want I to take Demetria."

"To Greece? You're going back to Earth?"

"No." He smiled. "I say at my father, I not to go. I to stay by Mars. My father to . . ." he fumbled for the word ". . . another woman to go for Demetria."

"He's sending a woman to take Demetria home?"

"Tonight. She is very good. Friend since many years. She is by Mars now, by Lowell City."

"Oh," Amanda said. "Does Demetria want to go?"

"Yes. Nikos to go Greece again. My father is not know."

Apparently they both defied their father regularly. Amanda couldn't imagine it. Demetria came out of the kitchen, spoke quickly to Konstantin, smiled at Amanda, and vanished into the spare bedroom, firmly closing the door.

"She to go . . ." Konstantin mimicked packing ". . . and to sleep. Before tonight. She to need much of time."

Amanda couldn't imagine what Demetria had to pack that would take much time, or why she'd need a nap. Demetria had always seemed to have endless energy.

"Come to sit by me, Ah-man-dah. Now we to can to talk."

He led her to the sofa in the living room. Amanda had always liked Aunt Kristen's living room. Simple furniture, and not too much of it. Actual books, a sculpture of a soaring bird, flowers even before

Konstantin had emptied Lowell City's florists. ("They're expensive here," Aunt Kristen always said, "but I'd rather have fresh flowers than fashionable clothes. My prime indulgence.") The view out the third-story window and through the dome: The rocky red plain of Mars, austere and beautiful in the changing light. In Amanda's father's house in Massachusetts the living room was dark and frumpy, cluttered endlessly with Sudie's toys and Carol's tennis rackets and physics data cubes and everybody's jackets and shoes and handhelds.

Konstantin said, "I want to say at you something very important, Ah-man-dah. Two somethings."

Her breath came faster, she didn't know why. "What?"

"One, I to do anything to help your father, Dr. Capelo. Anything. You to ask, is my father very rich? Yes. Very very rich. I have . . ." a Greek word Amanda didn't understand ". . . at his money. He good by me. I can to get much of money always, not questions. You to need money to get your father, to ask me. Always. Not question. You to understand?"

"Yes. Thank you." Really, he was so sweet. She didn't see how money would help rescue her father, but he was so sweet to offer.

"Also, my father to know Admiral Pierce. Big buddies. I to ask my father, my father to ask Admiral Pierce, you want somethings to help."

"Be careful, honey. Don't ever criticize Pierce to your new friends," Aunt Kristen had said. Was Konstantin just trying to get her to say something she shouldn't about Admiral Pierce? He didn't seem like that. But, still . . .

She was quiet so long that he said, "Ah-man-dah? You to believe me? I to ask my father anythings to help you?"

"I believe you, Konstantin."

"Splendid. Not money only, also. My father have many flyers, everywhere by Solar System. I know to call by them. All codes. My father to tell me, if I to need transportation quick."

That *was* impressive. Amanda wished she'd had flyers at her command everywhere in the Solar System during the last months. Konstantin was really important. How come he liked her so much?

"Thank you."

"Really, yes. I to send flyers everywhere by you say. Two, I to ask you important question. Is okay?"

"Yes, go ahead." What now? Amanda and Yaeko and Juliana and Thekla had had a lot of discussions about boys and things and, well, sex. They'd all agreed that if a boy ever asked them for sex, they'd say no. It was dangerous and they were too young and it was easier to think about saying no if they all stuck together. Girls needed their friends' support to combat personal pressure, her school said so. She braced herself, not looking at Konstantin.

He said, "How old you are?"

Was that all! But . . . if she told him her age, he might not like her anymore. Suddenly Amanda didn't want that to happen. She didn't want to have sex with him (or anyone), but she didn't want him to stop liking her, either. He was too wonderful.

She said, "I'm not seventeen yet." Well, that was true. She wasn't sixteen yet, either, or fifteen, but she didn't mention that. She knew she looked older than she was.

"I to think you are more old," Konstantin said, and Amanda felt pleased.

"Everybody says I'm very mature for my age."

"Splendid. Your father to let you to visit me by Greece, maybe? He, too, and your family. You have brothers, sisters, mother?"

"I have a stepmother and a little sister. I'd love to visit you in Greece." She was doubtful her father would take well to this expedition, but after all, she wasn't a baby anymore and he should take her more grown-up places. Anyway, Carol would take her. Carol was a sweetheart, and let Amanda do a lot more than her father did.

What really felt good was Konstantin's assumption that her father was going to be around to decide about visiting. Konstantin believed Tom Capelo was coming home.

"Splendid!" Konstantin said. His dark eyes shone. He was sitting very close to her on the sofa, and Amanda felt her chest tighten. "Ah-man-dah . . . I can to kiss you?"

He'd asked before, and she'd said no. Also, Amanda and her friends had all heard that when boys wanted you to get you to have sex, they started by kissing you. From there, everything got complicated. It wasn't worth it, they'd all agreed.

But suddenly she very much wanted to kiss Konstantin Ouranis.

"If . . . if it's just a little kiss, I guess it would be okay."

He didn't say "Splendid," as she expected. Instead he leaned over and gently pressed his lips against hers, his right arm going around her body and holding her as if she were the most precious thing in the entire galaxy. She kissed him back, and such a powerful wave swept over her from head to chest that she actually felt dizzy. She was sorry when he pulled his mouth away.

"I love you, Ah-man-dah."

The wave ebbed. She was still Tom Capelo's daughter. "Konstantin, you don't know me well enough to love me. We just barely met. That's silly."

He only laughed. Maybe he didn't know the word "silly." But he leaned over again for another gentle kiss, and Amanda found herself leaning into him, and again the wave raced over her and she gave herself up to it.

The door to the apartment opened and Amanda leapt up. She and Konstantin had been lying full-length on the sofa with their arms around each other. She felt the blood rush to her face as Aunt Kristen and Uncle Martin came into the living room. Konstantin got to his feet more slowly.

"Oh my God," Aunt Kristen said, which was so unfair! Amanda and Konstantin hadn't been doing anything bad. They had only kissed. What was wrong with kissing? She wasn't a baby anymore, and they shouldn't treat her like one!

Uncle Martin put a hand on Aunt Kristen's arm. He said calmly, "Hello, Amanda, Konstantin."

"Hello, sir," Konstantin said cheerfully. "Hello, Mrs. Blumberg."

"Amanda, could I see you for a moment in the kitchen?"

She followed Aunt Kristen into the kitchen. "What?"

Aunt Kristen looked stern. "Don't you think you're a little young for this sort of thing, Amanda?"

"I'm fourteen!"

"Precisely. Honey, your father would be very upset at this."

"He thinks I'm a baby. Well, I'm not. And anyway, we weren't doing anything."

"I know you weren't. You're basically a sensible girl, I know that, and you aren't even contracepted yet. But you're so young and he's such a very attractive young man."

So Aunt Kristen did understand! Amanda smiled at her. "Yes. But he only kissed me." She decided not to say how many times he'd kissed her.

"And where's Demetria?"

"Taking a nap. Her father is sending someone tonight to take her back to Earth. A chaperone."

"To take Demetria home but not Konstantin?"

Amanda said, not without pride, "Konstantin is old enough to go where he wants."

"Which means he's too old for you, honey."

Sudden, totally unexpected impatience came over Amanda. She said, surprising herself, "Aunt Kristen, in the last few months three people have tried to kill me. I've been in a kidnapping and an illegal ship and a . . . a revolution. I'm old enough to decide if I can kiss a boy." And she turned and walked back to the living room, head high and legs trembling, leaving Aunt Kristen staring astonished after her.

She heard them whispering in bed, after they thought she was asleep. A stern-looking woman had come to collect Demetria, thanking the Blumbergs in flawless English for their "hospitality to my employer's daughter." Uncle Martin had set up a fold-away cot in the master bedroom for Amanda, the same cot she'd slept on during previous visits, although then it had been set up in the living room. No one mentioned the change.

"She's growing up," Uncle Martin whispered. "You have to accept that, Kris."

"She's only fourteen!"

"She's been through a lot to age her."

Well, that was certainly true. Amanda had always liked Uncle Martin best, even though it was Aunt Kristen who was her blood relative. Aunt Kristen was a lot like Daddy, quick-tempered and sometimes even sarcastic.

"I love her so much," Aunt Kristen whispered brokenly, and immediately Amanda felt bad for preferring Uncle Martin. "If Tom never returns . . ."

"Sssshhh, dear heart."

"I just don't trust that boy. He's too rich and too self-assured and too presumptuous."

"He's been raised with all the money in the world, and apparently Ouranis treats him like an adult. He was explaining to me after dinner the decisions involved in their mining operations. I asked him about Pierce."

The bedclothes stirred. "You didn't!"

"Yes. Carefully and casually, of course. Konstantin isn't stupid. He sees Pierce's excesses. But he's loyal to his father and anyway he disliked what Stefanak was doing, especially the kidnapping of Tom. He seems to worship leading physicists."

"Which accounts for his exaggerated attraction to Amanda."

"Amanda has plenty of attractions of her own," Uncle Martin said, and a good warm feeling spread through her. At least Uncle Martin understood.

"She's becoming beautiful, isn't she?" Aunt Kristen said. "Like Karen. I only want her to be careful."

"We'll be careful for her."

"But Dr. Ewing this afternoon . . . identifying the body . . . all frozen and stiff like that . . ."

"Don't think about it."

"It was Pierce's men who did it, no matter what the police said. Why? Because of Tom's work?"

"I don't know," Uncle Martin said. "We may never know," and both of them fell silent.

Later, when she could hear them snoring, Amanda lay awake. Her mind wouldn't stop racing. Dr. Ewing's body, they meant. He must have been found, maybe out on the Martian plain. And he'd been killed by Admiral Pierce's men. Maybe he'd had an allergic reaction to a Pandya Dose, like Aunt Kristen said could sometimes happen. Or maybe they'd murdered him because of something he'd been working on. What if it was the same something her father had been working on? Amanda shivered. And all this was mixed up in her mind with Konstantin's kisses and lying next to him on the sofa and his offer to help find her father in any way he could, with any money he could. Money, and physics, and kisses, and soldiers, and fathers. . . .

Her aunt and uncle still snored. Amanda pulled the pillow over her head but it didn't help, she still couldn't sleep. For hours and hours, she couldn't sleep.

Where was her father?

TWENTY-SIX

ARTEMIS SYSTEM

The flyer approached Space Tunnel #437 leading from Caligula System to Allenby System. The computer was in control, but in a few moments Kaufman was going to have to take the helm and use Magdalena's clearances for the tunnel. The package she'd negotiated on the *Murasaki* had included clearances for the Caligula–Allenby and Allenby–Artemis Tunnels, bringing them to the populous and crucial Artemis System. Military flyers would have already beamed the data ahead, and Kaufman anticipated no difficulty with tunnel guards. Not yet. The current difficulties were all within the flyer.

Rory was still out, cuffed securely to his chair. Capelo sat in the pilot's chair, frowning at Marbet's handheld, oblivious to everything except whatever was going on in his head. Magdalena slumped in her seat at the back of the craft, but Kaufman thought she could probably hear. She wasn't unconscious, wasn't catatonic. She was somewhere deep in an abyss of despair he couldn't imagine and didn't know how to handle. Magdalena angry, Magdalena calculating, Magdalena vengeful, even Magdalena self-deluded because her delusion kept alive hope . . . all those Kaufman could have coped with. They went with negotiating. But this profound despair was outside his own emotional range, and he knew it.

"You never had a child," Marbet said softly, watching him. "Poor Lyle."

Poor *Lyle*? Surely it was the person with a child who was in trouble here. Added to which, Marbet had never had one either. Pushing down his dislike of her assumed superiority, he whispered, "Will you bring her out of this? We need her, Marbet."

"I can't. She would never respond to me. It has to be you, Lyle." She got up, went into the head, and closed the door decisively, leaving him effectively alone with Magdalena. Capelo didn't count; he was oblivious.

Kaufman took the seat next to her and put a hand on her arm. "Magdalena. It's Lyle Kaufman."

To his astonishment, she twisted violently and put her arms around him, hanging on as if she were drowning.

Oh, shit.

He did his best. He held her, patting her back, offering the comfort of another human touch. She murmured something. He didn't hear it and leaned his ear closer to her mouth.

"Sualeen . . ."

The name meant nothing to him. Helplessly he held her tighter, not knowing what else to do, and she lifted her head and kissed him hard.

It was the last thing he'd expected. After the initial shock, he understood: This was the only response Magdalena had to men, other than various types of challenge. Combat or copulation. Pity flooded him, along with impatience. It was the first time since he'd set eyes on Magdalena that he felt no desire whatsoever. Not the place, not the time, and Marbet . . . He kissed Magdalena back, thinking, *Oh God*.

A moment later, however, she pulled away and bit him on the neck, hard. Before he could even react, she sat up straight. "Don't ever do that again, Kaufman. You understand?"

She had kissed *him*. And she didn't even realize it. But somehow his embrace had jolted her into her old combative responses . . . or something.

Kaufman tried to keep his tone level. "What's in your saliva, Magdalena? Am I going to die the same death as Hofsetter?"

"Nothing's in my saliva." Her startlingly blue eyes gleamed at him, and Kaufman realized she wasn't back to her habitual responses after all. Or, rather, she was, but only as habit, role, a part she was trapped into playing. The core of her was elsewhere, and what Kaufman saw in her eyes was not sane. He put his hand to his neck. Blood flowed freely.

She said, "They're going to pay, Lyle. All of them. They're going to pay."

It was what he'd wanted from her, what he'd needed, what he had been going to bring about himself, if Hofsetter hadn't, out of necessity. But not with this sharp hard shine of madness. Her voice came out too high, and when she got up, her usually graceful movements were jerky, as if something else controlled her. Kaufman, who had never been religious in any way, thought suddenly of demon possession.

She squeezed between the seats and plucked Tom Capelo from the pilot's chair as if he'd been so much superfluous padding. Capelo, incredibly, went on scowling at his handheld, and Kaufman saw that her pushing him aside hadn't even registered. Capelo had heard nothing of Kaufman's exchanges with Magdalena, had no realization of the volcano roaring within the cabin. The physicist was absorbed in his physics, and the rest of the world ceased to exist even if it was about to erupt and obliterate him.

They were both nuts.

Magdalena sat in the pilot's chair. Kaufman hurried forward and moved Capelo as unceremoniously as Magdalena had. Capelo took the chair behind them.

Kaufman didn't have much time. He couldn't be sure what she would do next. "Magdalena. You need to go through the next two tunnels according to Hofsetter's clearances. Then in Artemis System—"

"I'm going to blast Artemis System to hell," she said, so casually that he was stopped for a moment. She meant it. Kaufman had investigated the totally illegal firepower aboard the flyer. She could take out at least Artemis Station and a few warships before they got her.

"There's a better way," he said. "You can—"

"There's no better way." Utter, casual certainty. She knew destruction was her response in the way Kaufman knew he needed oxygen to breathe.

His job just got a lot more difficult.

Marbet came out of the head just as Magdalena pushed the flyer into maximum acceleration. Marbet was thrown back against the bulkhead, slid to the deck, and lay there. At least three gees pushed Kaufman against the back of his chair; he couldn't help her. A sudden panic gripped him. Marbet . . .

"I'm . . . all right," she called.

"Stay where you are." As if she had a choice. Kaufman couldn't lift a hand. "Magdalena!"

She ignored him, but she also couldn't keep it up. The autocourse was set for the Caligula–Allenby Tunnel, and the flyer decelerated as it approached. They went through. Kaufman heard Marbet pull herself into a chair. He realized that Magdalena had not remarked on Kendai's absence or Rory's bonds. Perhaps she hadn't even noticed them.

"Flyer," said a voice from the single warship at the tunnel, "Identify self."

"Flyer from the *Sans Merci*, civilian, travel permit number 1264A, issued July eleven," Magdalena said in her strange, high voice. "Four persons aboard, citizen IDs in data packet."

"Flyer from the *Sans Merci* cleared for Space Tunnel Number Four-three-seven, four persons aboard, no docking clearance," the voice said. "Proceed through the tunnel."

In another moment they were in the Allenby System, one hundred fifty light-years away. All three gas giants were visible, almost in conjunction. The flyer was cleared at the other side of the tunnel and again Magdalena accelerated wildly, flying toward Tunnel #210 and Artemis System.

Kaufman had two choices. He could allow her to clear the tunnel and then overpower her before she started firing at anything in Artemis System, or he could take the controls away from her now. He didn't know what other personal weapons she carried besides the poisonous talon. If she'd had weapons installed at one of the chop shops in the Belt—and she probably had—they could be really nasty. Best to do it as soon as she slowed this lunatic acceleration. His chest hurt; every breath was a torture. "M-Mag—"

She took no notice of him. Kaufman fought to stay conscious. Most likely Capelo and Marbet had already blacked out; they were unused to this. Kaufman had been once, but no longer. Why wasn't Magdalena out? Then he understood: She had augmented breathing capacity.

After what seemed infinity, the flyer decelerated. Kaufman gathered his strength. He had never strapped himself in; neither had she. Her first acceleration had left no time for such niceties. He stood.

She said, "If you try to interfere with me, Kaufman, I'll kill you." Casual, matter-of-fact, deadly. "And I can. Before you can do anything at all to me."

He sat down again. "Magdalena, don't just go into Artemis System shooting. We'll all die, and—"

"Too bad."

"The fabric of spacetime itself is at risk. Pierce is going to bring the artifact into the Faller System and set it off. They'll set off theirs and space will tear to—"

"Good," she said, and in her voice Kaufman finally heard that the greater the ruin, the greater her revenge. Destroying all of spacetime itself would not be compensation enough for Laslo's death.

He had no way to deal with her. No way to dissuade her. No way to stop her.

He was preparing to try anyway, to die trying in hopes that Capelo and Marbet alone could carry out his plan, when Capelo spoke behind him. "Magdalena. I've got kids, too."

She ignored him.

Capelo's voice was harsh and flat. "Two daughters. Sudie is seven. Amanda is fourteen. She looks like her mother, who is dead. My wife was killed in a Faller raid five years ago. My kids are all I've got left and I don't want them to die."

"Tough. Mine did."

"I know. I won't say I'm sorry because I know how much I hated hearing that when my wife was killed. Nobody can be sorry enough. Where do they get off, saying they're sorry when in the next half hour they're going to go back to their lives, enjoying their friends and doing their work and eating their fucking dinners like nothing happened? They don't know what sorry is. The universe should have been sorry she was dead. The stars should have gone out, and the Big Crunch retracted the entire misbegotten universe. I would have done it myself if I could have."

"Then you know why I will."

"No, you won't. You'll destroy maybe two or three ships before they get you. That's nothing."

"It's enough."

"No, it's not. I know better. That's why you want to take out all of spacetime, if you can. But listen to this before you do: They won't suffer."

She was silent.

"I'm the physicist who figured this all out, remember? The tear in spacetime from simultaneous setting prime thirteen travels at light speed. Even if tunnel macro-entanglement makes it faster . . . Forget all that. What matters is that the wave will hit at three hundred thousand kilometers per second, as fast as light, so that no one knows it's coming. There's no way to send information ahead. And no one knows when it hits them because they just go out like a candle. The fundamental particles of their body are transformed instantly. They never knew what hit them. So they won't suffer."

Silence. The tunnel came into visual perception.

"You got that? *They won't suffer.* That's not what I wanted when Karen died. I wanted the bastards who killed her to be as torn apart and still breathing, as I was. You want that, too. I know."

Kaufman thought he had never heard a silence as profound as that in the flyer. Magdalena's profile, intent on her displays, told him nothing.

Capelo continued in the same rough, flat voice. "You can make them suffer. Stefanak is dead, but those soldiers who vaporized your son, who gave the order to do that, are still alive. They can be made to suffer the way you do, and I did, which is through people they love. That can only happen if you don't destroy spacetime. Keep spacetime intact before you start getting even. Keep spacetime intact just so the people you choose to kill can be missed, and mourned, and wept over, and the ones you punish will want to die because of what you do to them."

Cold crept down Kaufman's spine. This was reasoning that never would have occurred to him, reasoning that should never occur to anybody. This poison was inside Capelo, inside Magdalena . . .

"Keep spacetime intact, Magdalena. Help us do that. You for

your reasons, we for ours. The end is the same. The means are the same. We can aid each other to get there. For Laslo."

At her son's name Magdalena's body jerked, as if an electric wire had been held to her skin. Kaufman thought, *Tom went too far*. But then Magdalena turned, and he could see her face instead of just her profile.

"Tell me how," she said, at the same moment that the warship on this side of the Allenby–Artemis Tunnel said, "Flyer, identify self," and Kaufman realized how close to destruction, once more, they had run.

They were cleared without incident on both sides of the tunnel, although they had to wait in queue. The flyer drifted, idle. Finally the tunnel guard cleared them, adding, "Artemis System welcomes you," proof that the guard unit dealt as often with civilians as with military. Nobody else had welcomed them anywhere.

Artemis System had five planets, two gas giants, and three rock-balls. Colonies flourished on one planet, two large moons, and in a variety of orbitals. Only five tunnels away from the Solar System and boasting five tunnels of its own, Artemis had been a popular expansion star. It had also been the first human settlement the Fallers attacked when they started their inexplicable war. They had come roaring out of one of the Artemis tunnels twenty-eight years ago, thirty years after humans had first discovered the tunnels. Apparently it had been human tunnel exploration in their home system that had alerted the Fallers to the existence of their own tunnels. No human had ever reached the Faller home system again.

For a decade, emigration to Artemis had halted, and many colonists went home. The military moved in, fortifying Tunnel #218, the Fallers' arrival route, until it no longer was worth Faller losses to attack humanity by that route. Eventually the colonists returned. The system's habitable planet, Baraquio, was as lush and rich as World was, as Terra had once been. Baraquio had no sentient life to be disturbed by humanity's raucous presence. The colonists began to feel as safe as they did anywhere else.

The system's five tunnels were clustered fairly close together. The tunnel on the route to Sol, Tunnel #212, lay the farthest from Magdalena's flyer, fifty thousand clicks. In the same direction lay three more tunnels. In the opposite direction, seven thousand clicks away, floated their next goal. All space tunnels stayed stationary and exerted no gravity on each other; no one knew why either fact was so. If the five tunnels hadn't been clustered so closely together in a predictable pattern, Kaufman's plan would have had no chance at all of succeeding. Now, he thought grimly, it had perhaps one chance in five. Maybe.

The flyer's next—and last—clearance from Hofsetter was to refuel at Artemis Station. This was an enormous commercial station drifting five hundred clicks away, in the direction of the permanent, heavy fortifications walling off Space Tunnel #218—the tunnel to Q space, and from there to the Fallers' star. Artemis Station was a popular leave destination for the sailors stuck on the fortification ships.

Magdalena had the conn. Kaufman didn't know how long he'd been flying; time between tunnels seemed to have passed with weird rapidity. The flyer drifted, in free fall. Strapped into the pilot seat, she leaned so close over the displays that she occasionally interfered with his view. He didn't reprimand her. She was as taut and carefully balanced as a space-elevator cable, and just as dangerous if she snapped.

"How close can we get to Tunnel Two-one-eight?" she asked.

"Nobody will stop us while we're still heading toward Artemis Station," Kaufman answered, although of course she already knew that. She was talking solely to avoid silence. He didn't want to imagine what images filled her silence.

"Yes. And after that . . . it depends on Capelo, doesn't it? Maybe he can do it. He did a good enough job with me." She laughed, a sound so unexpected and harsh that Kaufman glanced at her in concern.

"Don't stare at me, Kaufman. I'm going to get you there, aren't I? Get yourself ready. All of you. You, too, Sensitive. This thing rides on you, God fuck us all."

Kaufman let her give the orders. He unstrapped, floated to the storage closets, and pulled out a military, state-of-the-art EVA s-suit that Magdalena should not have had. The flyer carried four such suits, taking up nearly all available storage space. To get out the third one, Kaufman had to float it over Rory's still unconscious body.

Kaufman was adept at military suiting in free fall. Marbet and Capelo, however, had never done it. He got them dressed, Capelo cursing creatively, and then ran checks on his suit and each of theirs. When he finished with Marbet's, she pushed awkwardly into him and kissed him on the lips. "For luck," she whispered. He smiled at her and then forgot her, as he was trained to do, in concentration on the task ahead.

Magdalena said, "Ready? Here we go." She accelerated at a sedate one-gee. Gravity returned and Kaufman carefully positioned Marbet, Capelo, and himself, Capelo where he could be heard clearly by the comlink. Their helmets went on. Awkward, but later on they wouldn't be able to do it. All the helmet comlinks were open.

"Open the flyer link to all unencrypted military frequencies," Kaufman told Magdalena. She did. Now no one could say anything except what they'd planned.

Artemis Station loomed on the viewscreen. As always, a lot of traffic came and went at the station and Magdalena's flyer attracted no particular notice. It was registering, of course, on dozens of displays, but no one hailed them.

They flew past Artemis Station at one-gee.

From where he stood, Kaufman could see the flyer displays. Space Tunnel #218 appeared as a red spot: "Highly Restricted." Six-thousand, five-hundred-eighty clicks away. The flyer was moving at 3.132 clicks per second.

Magdalena slammed the flyer into three-gee acceleration. Kaufman was pressed against the bulkhead, the familiar weight pushing on his chest. Instantly the comlink said, "Flyer number 1264A, you have entered a restricted zone. Return immediately to Artemis Station."

No one answered.

"Flyer number 1264A, you have entered a restricted zone! Return immediately to Artemis Station!"

The flyer sped on. Six-thousand, one-hundred clicks to the tunnel.

"Flyer number 1264A, if you do not immediately leave this restricted zone and return to Artemis Station, you will be fired upon. Turn back."

Let Capelo remember what to do . . .

"This is Dr. Thomas Capelo," he gasped through the crushing gravity. "Don't shoot! I've escaped from Stefanak's troops!"

Brief silence. So one or more OOD's *had* recognized Tom's name. One hurdle successfully jumped.

"Dr. Capelo, return instantly to Artemis Station!"

"I can't. I don't know how to pilot the ship. I just killed . . ." Capelo deliberately gasped and trailed off, then added, "Help me!"

Now other frequencies came in on Magdalena's highly illegal military scanner, a jumble of voices on fleet frequencies.

"Shoot, damn it! Regs say—"

"If it's really him—"

"—in trouble—"

"—don't care who the fuck it is just—"

And one shrill, young voice, *"Wake up the old man!"*

Four-thousand, one-hundred clicks to the tunnel.

An older, more decisive voice. "Dr. Capelo, or whoever is aboard Flyer number 1264A, you must return to Artemis Station. Decelerate and turn."

"The autopilot won't let me override," Tom gasped. "Please don't shoot, I have the equations . . . that Admiral Pierce wanted . . . don't . . ."

"What does he mean, 'won't let him override'? What the fuck—"

"—no proof it's him—"

"If I shoot down Thomas Capelo—"

"—Protector Artifact—"

A still more decisive voice: "Dr. Capelo, this is your last warning. You are approaching highly restricted space. Decelerate and return to Artemis Station immediately or you will be vaporized."

"I can't!" Tom screamed, rising to heights of insane fury despite the gravity like boulders. "If you . . . shoot me . . . first tell Admiral Pierce . . . listen, record this now! F squared times the cube of gamma sigma minus . . . Are you bastards recording this?"

Despite everything, Kaufman grinned. Throw enough scientific gibberish at non-scientists and they always faltered. Bewildered worshippers at the veiled shrine.

"It's what will win the fucking war!" Capelo bellowed. "Record it before you bastards shoot me!"

And somewhere in the fleet, on a link to a few buddies, not knowing he was overhead, some intelligent science admirer said, "You know . . . it *sounds* like Capelo."

Two thousand clicks to the tunnel.

Marbet, jammed beside him in the airlock already open on the inside, groped with her heavy hand at his suit. She couldn't connect, but he saw the futile movement. There was no way to tell her, *Not yet.*

He wondered if anyone was in fact writing any of Tom's equations down. Of course, they were being recorded everywhere. But sometimes, faced with a raving genius, people forgot that. Capelo, hoarse, yelled about setting prime eleven and macro-entanglement and splitting Faller ships like melons from ranges too distant to be detected.

A thousand clicks to the tunnel.

The silence stretched on. Somewhere, on encrypted frequencies not accessible to the flyer, rapid and desperate conferences went on.

"Prepare to fire at my command . . ."

The flyer went into spectacular evasive maneuvers. That would do it, Kaufman knew. No civilian craft with a malfunctioning computer could do that. "Commence firing!" came over the comlink.

Not close enough!

But Magdalena's software was also state-of-the-art. She bought them another ten seconds through maneuvering. It couldn't last, but ten seconds helped . . .

The airlock door opened. Kaufman, Capelo, and Marbet were ejected into space.

They could no longer hear communications from the warships of the fleet.

She scarcely noticed they had gone. She was one with the computer, dodging and turning, every atom of her tuned to a single vibrating frequency. She was one with the ship, appearing with all the others on the display screen. Most of all, she was one with the proton beam, wide and full strength. It was she who hurled, silent and at light speed, across the void at the enemy.

Again: a miss. Dodge, move. Again: miss.

Time had slowed down. There was all the time in the world as she/they (the computer, the ship, the beam) executed each evasion, each attack. She/they moved with sureness and unfailing rightness through the endless time.

But she/they weren't alone. Two others were there beside her, the only two she had ever loved, completing the world. As it should be. Sualeen smiled at her.

Sualeen . . .

A warship exploded silently, brilliantly, and disappeared from her display.

And on her other side, his hand on her arm, filling the endless time with happiness, sat Laslo.

Laslo . . .

A second ship disappeared from the display.

Now Laslo smiled at her. Magdalena turned to smile back, and everything was whole again, everything justified, as the flyer was hit and vaporized and Magdalena joined her beloved son.

TWENTY-SEVEN

IN Q SPACE

Just before ejection Kaufman had caught one last glimpse at the displays: Seven hundred clicks to the tunnel. He, Capelo, and Marbet were moving at eighteen clicks per second, the flyer's speed. Space Tunnel #218, leading to the enigmatic Q space, was seven hundred clicks away. They would reach it in thirty-eight seconds, unless they were shot down or off-course.

He and Capelo, Kaufman saw with a sudden rush of shit to the heart, were off-course. Marbet was aimed right at the tunnel, an on-target human projectile. Kaufman pushed all thoughts of Magdalena from his mind and used his jets to correct his course.

He had hastily told Capelo how to do this. Capelo was a civilian and had never EVA'd before. Capelo had also completed his part of the job, delaying their being shot down just long enough to be ejected close to the tunnel. Capelo was expendable, just as Magdalena had been expendable. Kaufman calculated this swiftly, one human part of his mind hating the calculations, one military part knowing them necessary and right.

Twenty-three seconds.

Kaufman's theory had been that the tunnel fleet's sensors were set to ignore anything heading for the tunnel—but not, of course, coming out of it—if the intruder had a small mass. Otherwise, the warships would be constantly firing proton beams at meteors, increasing their chances of hitting each other or patrolling flyers. Twenty years ago, when Kaufman had seen combat, this had been not theory but fact, and the cut-off mass had been ninety kilos. Capelo and Marbet, small people, didn't mass that even in their suits. Kaufman was close, but just under the limit.

The limit had grown steadily smaller over the last twenty years, and Kaufman wasn't sure exactly how small it was now. The navy might vaporize Kaufman, or all three of them, in the next twenty-three seconds. If not, the Fallers might do it on the other side.

Kaufman stared steadily ahead at the space tunnel, growing larger by the second, and waited to die. From the corner of his eye he saw Capelo's course lurch abruptly. God, a correction like that at three-gees could crack a rib, or worse. If Capelo succeeded in reaching the tunnel, he might go through it already dead.

Fifteen seconds.

Apparently the navy sensors still ignored anything under ninety kilos heading into a space tunnel.

Capelo's speeding body jerked again. He appeared to be on course. Beginner's luck? Not if he'd fatally injured himself doing it.

Marbet was the one who mattered the most. She was the only human being who had ever talked . . . no, you couldn't call it talking. Who had ever communicated with a Faller. It had taken her months to learn how, and the communication had at best been partial and grudging and inconclusive, but she had done it. Let her have the chance to do it again!

Ten seconds.

Going through a space tunnel in a ship felt like nothing at all. What did it feel like in an s-suit? Kaufman might never have the chance to register whatever his senses picked up from the trip, because the Fallers might very well blow into ions everything that came through to Q space, on their side of the tunnel. No matter how small the intruder's mass. A very small mass could be a nuclear bomb.

Kaufman was counting on exactly that fact. A bomb that detonated the second it came through could take out guard ships. That's why you didn't station your fleet too close to the tunnel. There was space between, enough space to protect the ships, enough space to allow identification of whatever came through the tunnel before you vaporized it. Enough time, perhaps, to see that it was three unarmed human beings, or three human beings anyway. Time to decide, as those three humans continued to speed across Q space, if you wanted to destroy them—or if you wanted to risk one flyer to pick them up and find out why they had tumbled out of a star system hundreds of light-years away into your star system despite the war.

How much curiosity did Fallers have about their enemy? Enough to monitor human broadcasts, which was more than humans had been able to do with theirs.

Five seconds.

The gray "fog" inside the tunnel wasn't misty, like fog on Earth. It looked solid as stone. Yet Kaufman saw Marbet Grant rush through it as if through vacuum. A fraction of a second later Kaufman followed her. He tried to keep his eyes open, but the blink reaction, at hitting what looked like a solid wall, was too strong. Kaufman blinked.

And sailed through the tunnel into Q space, expecting to die, literally before he knew it.

He didn't die. The Faller ships didn't fire.

Kaufman couldn't see them. He saw Marbet and Capelo ahead of him. Marbet was slowing; she had used her jets, as he was now doing. Capelo was not. That probably meant he was too injured to do so. Helpless, Kaufman watched Thomas Capelo dwindle and disappear into the blackness of space.

The Faller ships still hadn't fired.

They'd had time to do so. Possibly that meant the Faller craft were conferring, deciding what to do. They didn't take prisoners, and may or may not have known that one of theirs had been taken prisoner two years ago. Would that change their policy? They had never before been offered humans like this: alive, naked of all spacecraft, in a Faller-controlled area like Q space. In their own empty front yard.

Somewhere in that yard, if the best military minds in SADC were right, floated the Faller's artifact.

At least the Fallers could see that Kaufman, Capelo, and Marbet hadn't brought the human artifact with them. It was too big to miss. The three humans might very well be armed with everything up to nuclears, but they didn't carry the other artifact.

The longer he was left alive, Kaufman reasoned, the better the chances of staying that way. Still, there was a self-imposed limit. The s-suits carried only so much air. The Fallers might prefer to let the humans die and merely harvest their dead bodies for examination.

But they'd harvested dead bodies before. This was a chance for them to acquire living ones, at no cost except a robotic spaceship. If they had such things.

More time passed. Kaufman could no longer see Marbet, nor the tunnel behind him. He saw stars, and one of the system's distant, lifeless gas giants, and his own thoughts.

Magdalena. Dead.

Tom Capelo. Possibly dead.

Marbet Grant, whom he had loved. Possibly dead.

Admiral Pierce. Possibly sending a force right now to Q space, to set off the human artifact at prime thirteen and thus, from greed and arrogance and stupidity, possibly destroy spacetime itself.

The entire Solar System, wiped free of life as spacetime reconfigured into new fundamental particles.

He checked the wrist display on his suit. Ten minutes of air left.

Kaufman closed his eyes and drifted in mind, sped on in body. There were worse ways to die. He had done what he could. It wasn't enough. There were also better ways to die.

When he opened his eyes again, it was to see a ship, peculiarly shaped and brightly colored, silently flying alongside him. It matched his speed and trajectory. As he watched, incredulous, a door on the ship slid open and a net emerged, made of thin filaments, and it too matched his speed and trajectory, slightly in front of him. Then the net slowed, and he was caught like a salmon stopped in its wild plunge upstream toward what the poor fish hadn't the wit or memory to visualize at all.

He came to all at once, with no transition, like a holo snapping on. He sat up, a quick movement that made his vision darken from light-headedness. The gravity was half a gee or slightly less. His head cleared and he looked wildly around.

Kaufman sat naked in a small, featureless room. Naked . . . but he was breathing all right, so the Fallers had analyzed and duplicated the air in his tank. Marbet lay unconscious beside him and, against the wall, Tom Capelo watched him.

"Hello . . . Lyle," Capelo said, and a sudden wave of gladness swept over Kaufman. Capelo was alive, although he spoke like a man in considerable pain.

Kaufman moved toward Capelo. The physicist tried to grin, failed. "We . . . made it. Sort of. I think we're aboard a Faller ship, or station, or whatever."

"What are your injuries, Tom?"

"Broken arm, for sure. I think cracked ribs—it hurts when I

breathe. But nothing's bleeding, unless it's doing it inside where I don't know about it."

There was nothing in the room to even make a splint for Capelo's arm, which hung at an unnatural angle. The Fallers were taking no chances with their captives. Kaufman wondered what sort of body searches they'd performed while he'd been unconscious, and was glad he didn't know.

Marbet stirred. Capelo said, "Go. She's . . . the reason for this . . . lunacy, right? Get her . . . going."

Kaufman moved back toward Marbet. She opened her eyes, saw him, and clutched his arm. "Lyle. . . ." In her voice he heard the depth of her feeling for him, and instinctively embarrassment took over.

"Tom's here, too," he said brusquely, "but injured. Are you able to work, Marbet? We don't know how long before human troops show up with the other artifact."

"Yes." As always, she read more from his body than his words, and understood his brusqueness and her task. "Where is the surveillance stuff?"

"Not visible."

She sat up too abruptly for the lighter gravity, corrected herself, and carefully studied the room, coming to some decision Kaufman didn't follow. "Go sit by Tom, in that corner. Both of you stay still and quiet. Don't provide any distraction from me."

He did as she told him. Marbet stood up and faced an adjacent corner. She gathered herself for a moment, her head down, her small, perfect, naked body alert but not tense. Kaufman heard her take a deep breath.

Then she became somebody else.

He had seen this before, but it amazed him nonetheless. Amazed him, disturbed him, disgusted him. Marbet half crouched, holding her torso and limbs at peculiar, distorted angles. Her facial muscles contorted. Her eyes assumed a different look (*how?*). She began to sway off rhythm, her hands flailing in small, inexplicable gestures. In a few moments she went from a beautiful human woman to something alien and distasteful.

Kaufman knew, but only because she'd told him, that in addition to communicating Faller gestures, Marbet was doing her level best to communicate Faller femaleness. Three years ago, she had tailored her responses to the enemy prisoner in order to provoke lust displays, as she understood them. She mimed submission, pleading, total lack of threat. It was the only way the Faller, xenophobic to a degree unknown even among the most parochial humans, had been able to "listen" to her. This had worked two years ago; Marbet and Kaufman and Capelo were gambling on it working again.

Beside Kaufman, Capelo moaned softly. His eyes had closed. He grimaced in pain.

Was the enemy artifact aboard this ship? Was it a ship they were on, or some sort of station? How much time had passed, time more precious than the enemy could know, since the three humans had been plucked from space?

No answers. And no response to anything Marbet was doing.

She started doing it with more intensity. Her head wobbled, and her feet moved in tiny, trembling patterns. Kaufman had no idea how much of what she was "saying" concerned a simple desire for response, and how much concerned their actual dilemma. How did you communicate that an enemy was in great danger? And why would they believe you?

Still, the Fallers had to be amazed that a human could imitate their body language at all. That had to at least make them take notice.

Marbet had been working for at least thirty minutes. She was visibly tiring. He had almost given up hope when a mesh wall began to descend from the ceiling. It came down swiftly, neatly dividing him and Capelo from Marbet. He forced himself not to react. Then a door on Marbet's side of the mesh opened and what could only be a robot came through. It held her own helmet and air tank, presumably refilled. Marbet put on the helmet, and Kaufman had a bad moment as he saw it seal itself around her delicate throat. The robot kept the air tank. It encircled Marbet with a mesh gate and led her out the door.

She had succeeded in communicating something. But what, and to whom? And what would the Fallers do about it?

Perhaps another fifteen minutes dragged by. Capelo seemed to be asleep, which was undoubtedly a good thing. Sleep muted pain. But when Faller robots finally appeared, it was Capelo they wanted.

They stood on the other side of the room, two alien robots, as the mesh wall ascended into the ceiling. One robot moved toward Kaufman and Capelo. It handed a helmet and air tank to Capelo, who tried to reach for them but fell back onto the floor with a cry of pain. The robot halted.

Kaufman said, careful to make no sudden or aggressive movement, "He's hurt." Kaufman mimed a straight arm and then a bent, dangling one; easy breathing and then labored rasps while he clutched his chest.

The robots froze. Receiving electromagnetic instructions? Probably, because after ten seconds one robot left, returning a few moments later with a second helmet and air tank and a mesh container of what looked like junk. He handed everything to the first robot, who handed it to Kaufman. The junk, he saw, included cloth, metal rods, small circular pillows, shell-shaped objects he couldn't imagine a use for, and a sharp, oddly curved knife. The robot waited stolidly.

"This is going to hurt, Tom. Try not to faint. It's you they want, and that has to be a good sign. Either they know who you are or Marbet succeeded in telling them. Now hold still."

"All right," Capelo said, and scowled fiercely. Kaufman saw what

302 • NANCY KRESS

it cost the physicist to appear weak and dependent. Kaufman could respect Capelo's pride.

He used the knife to cut the cloth, which was amazingly resistant, into strips. The arm first. Capelo cried out when Kaufman probed it, then forcibly aligned the broken bone and bound it to a metal rod. Fortunately the fracture wasn't compound. Kaufman bound Capelo's ribs. Capelo was fading in and out of consciousness.

"Stay with me, Tom."

"Y-yes."

"You'd have made a good soldier."

"N-n-never."

Kaufman finished. God, for just a single pain patch! "Now I'm going to put on your helmet and lift you."

"I . . . can stand."

"No, you can't. Commencing operation." Kaufman fitted the helmet on Capelo, then put on his own. Airflow started automatically. He grasped Capelo around the waist and hauled him to his feet. The physicist was small-boned, not heavy. He leaned against Kaufman.

"Steady, Tom. You can do it. Here we go."

Half carrying, half leading Capelo, Kaufman followed the robots out of the featureless room and into the heart of the Faller station.

TWENTY-EIGHT

ABOARD A FALLER STATION

Something soft and purple underfoot, with tendrils growing up rough walls. No clear distinction between corridor and rooms, just spaces flowing into each other in crazy shapes. Holes halfway up some walls and not others. And everywhere, small flying insects, or insect analogues, landing on his naked skin and hovering in front of his helmet and making a low persistent buzz.

Insects? Something else? If only Ann could see this!

Kaufman saw no Fallers, but the walk was a short one. They stopped in a large space with something huge in the corner. As Kaufman watched, the something heaved slightly, then settled down again. It was an amorphous mass the size of a bus. It didn't look like cytoplasm, or plant life, or hardware, or anything else Kaufman had ever seen or imagined. Maybe it was a computer. Or a food supply. Or a pet. Or a living bedroll. Impossible to tell, impossible not to feel amazed.

Two actual Fallers walked into the room. They ignored the mass, which continued to heave silently every few minutes, shifting against the rough wall.

Maybe it was scratching itself.

Kaufman had seen a Faller up close before, on the *Alan B. Shepard*. He recognized the cylindrical bipedal bodies, the powerful kangaroo-like tail for balance, the tentacled hands and alien faces. These two, in bright-colored clothes (uniforms?), stood on the far side of what Kaufman at first thought was a table. On the near side, Marbet waited, still naked except for her helmet.

It wasn't a table. It was a horizontal screen, a flat triangular surface on a slim pedestal. Marbet and one alien held curved rods that had to be styluses of some sort.

"Tom," Marbet said rapidly, "they showed me these things but I don't know what they're trying to tell me or what I should draw to tell them about Pierce bringing our artifact into Q System. I don't think I connected. Can you hold this thing?"

Capelo's voice sounded stronger than Kaufman had heard it yet. "What the hell are these bugs flying around for?"

Marbet smiled behind the clear plastic of her helmet. "I think they might be intelligent symbiotes. Part of the Fallers' biology."

"Intelligent? Am I drawing for the bugs or the bastards?"

"It doesn't matter," Kaufman said. "Just draw!"

Marbet closed the fingers of Capelo's good hand around the stylus. Everything drawn on the tabletop vanished. Kaufman hauled Capelo over to the table, and now Kaufman noticed something he'd missed before. Neither Faller wore a helmet, since this was of course their air, but both had what looked like plugs stuck in what Kaufman had thought was their breathing holes.

We smell horrible to them.

Or maybe not. Marbet had speculated that the Fallers might be more sensitive to pheromones than even humans. Maybe the Fallers were blocking the smell of humans to damp down their own instinctive, overwhelming aggressive responses to human odor. The nose plugs might be a sign of cooperation.

Capelo leaned forward, staggered, and almost fell on top of the table. Kaufman steadied him at an angle so his good hand could draw. Ceaselessly the "insects" buzzed and circled and alit and hovered.

"All right," Capelo said, evidently for his own benefit, "this is Tunnel Number Two-one-eight, you bastards. See the doughnut floating in space? How the fuck do I know what you see? Here, five planets on the Artemis side of the tunnel. Now over here is Tunnel Number Three-zero-one leading right to your home system. See the little teeny Faller I drew on your side of it? Ah, that got you, look at you look at each other. I'd like to laser you right where you stand."

Kaufman said to Marbet, "Is there any chance these two understand English?"

"No. I tried it with them."

Capelo said, "Here's your artifact, right here in Q space in your big front yard." He drew a sphere with the familiar seven protuberances on it.

One of the aliens made a loud screech. Kaufman saw Marbet jump and he felt himself tense, but Capelo barreled on as if he hadn't even heard. He was a fantastic sight: A skinny naked man in a clear bulbous helmet, dangled precariously over a table, one crudely splinted arm flopping at his side and the other sketching frantically to save several worlds.

"Your artifact is set at prime two, isn't it, you fuckers." He scribbled hard on the setting with two tiny dots beside it. "All ready to detect our artifact if we're stupid enough to bring it into Q space. Which Pierce is, but you don't know that yet. But you're ready anyway. So . . . watch!"

Now Capelo began to draw even faster. Where was he getting the energy? Pure adrenaline, Kaufman guessed, released by tension, by fear, by hatred. Capelo's endocrine system might even be pumping out enough endorphins to deaden pain. But it couldn't last, Capelo couldn't keep it up much longer. The maddening insects buzzed and circled.

"See, this is our artifact coming through the tunnel from Artemis System . . . that got your attention, didn't it? We set it off at prime thirteen—" scribble, scribble "—and you see—watch!"

Capelo abruptly drove the stylus at the tabletop, again and again, making thick black marks all over Q space, except on the artifacts themselves. "Kaboom!"

Marbet said, "Don't make loud noises, Tom. It's an aggression trigger."

"Tough," Capelo said. "Now, look, you assholes come in from your system—" delicately he trailed the stylus through the tunnel from the Faller world to Q space, "and you get to pick up both artifacts. See? Now, Marbet, blank the screen."

"I don't know how," she said helplessly.

"Then we're fried," Capelo said. Kaufman slowly . . . very slowly, don't trigger aggression . . . swept his hand over the tabletop, looking at what he had decided was the higher-ranking Faller. The alien did something and the table blanked.

"Good show, Lyle," Capelo said. Quickly he redrew the two space tunnels, but this time he drew the alien artifact in the Faller home system, blackening in setting prime eleven. His hand trembled. He was tiring.

"Steady, Tom," Marbet said, her voice full of encouragement. Capelo ignored her.

"Scenario number two. Are you listening, slimebutts? Your artifact is quietly doing its little job, protecting home sweet home. We come through with ours . . . see? We pass right by you in Q space because we're on setting two, a nice shield . . . now, we're inside your territory, we set off at thirteen . . . and nothing happens. See? Stalemate. So we go home." The stylus trailed back through two tunnels to Artemis System. "Marbet, how the hell do I know if anything is getting through to these pricks?"

"It's getting through," she said.

"Fine, hate to waste a good tutorial . . . hate to . . ."

"I've got you, Tom," Kaufman said. "You won't fall. Keep going."

"One more. Here are both . . . both . . ." Capelo slipped sideways against Kaufman's body. The stylus fell to the floor.

"Take him, Marbet," Kaufman said, and picked up the stylus. Would they let him continue in Capelo's place? If Marbet was right, their aggression responses, so strong as to be barely controllable, were activated by men like Kaufman: big, used to command. They can tell, Marbet had said, and Kaufman waited for the unknown weapon to hit him.

It didn't. But he didn't have to be a Sensitive to notice the shifts in Faller muscles, the rise of neck ruffs. More unsettling, the clouds of insects buzzing at his face suddenly grew larger and louder.

"Crouch, Lyle!" Marbet said. "Don't look at anybody and start drawing quickly!"

Kaufman bent over, dropping his eyes to the table, hating both actions. Human instinctive responses. He tried to copy Capelo's style, drawing both artifacts inside Q space, blackening both settings prime thirteen. How did you show the tearing of spacetime? He settled for wavy lines obliterating everything, and this time he extended the lines on both sides of both tunnels, wiping out not just Q space but Artemis System and the Faller homeworld. Everything.

"Don't look up, Lyle," Marbet said. "I'll tell them to clear the slate." Carefully she swept her arm over the table. Again a Faller did something and Kaufman was looking at a blank screen.

This was the crucial part.

Capelo and he had shown the Fallers three scenarios: two Faller victories and a stalemate, and the enemy had seemed to agree. Or at least hadn't done anything that Kaufman interpreted as disagreement, such as shooting him. Now he was going to show them a fourth scenario, and it had better be convincing because it was all lies.

He resketched Space Tunnels #218 and #301, with Q space between them and the Faller artifact floating in Q space. He put in the five planets of the Artemis System on the far side of Tunnel #218 and the teeny Faller figure on the far side of Tunnel #301. And then he drew in another tunnel floating in the Faller System, and coming through it he drew a human ship with the human artifact inside. He blackened setting prime thirteen.

We know another way in. We can destroy your home system while you're off protecting your perimeter.

Another screech, loud and piercing. Kaufman determined not to look up, but something so extraordinary was happening that he was forced to. All the insects in the room were diving straight into the mass of the heaving object in the corner. It, in turn, started humming at such a high frequency that Kaufman's ears went into excruciating pain and he dropped the stylus. Then everything disappeared.

"Lyle. Wake up. Lyle!"

Marbet. Kaufman tried to open his eyes, failed.

"Come on, Lyle. You're the only one that can fly this thing!"

Fly? The word was so unexpected, so incongruous that Kaufman thought he was dreaming. Then he realized he wasn't and with a Herculean effort opened his eyes. Marbet, still naked but without her helmet, leaned over him. And he lay . . .

Not possible.

"Get up, Lyle!" she said, and slowly he got up.

Around him were the cramped bulkheads, deck, instrumentation, seats, terminal—everything!—of a human military flyer, series

XXPell3. A simulation? Holo or stage set? No. It was real.

Marbet was tugging him toward the pilot seat. On the view-screen, a curved wall was sliding upward and disappearing, leaving stars. A shuttle bay.

"Ladybug, ladybug," Capelo said from the seat where he was strapped in, several patches on his naked neck and chest. The patches were standard military-issue blue. Marbet had found the fighter flyer's medkit.

"Where are we?" Kaufman asked. "What—"

"They had this flyer stored here," Marbet said, still shoving him toward the pilot seat. "God knows where they got it. They want us to go through to Artemis and tell the humans there that the Faller artifact is being moved to the Faller home world. But you just wouldn't come to, Lyle. I think they misjudged whatever they did to us, hit you too much harder than Tom and me because you're bigger or carry more authority or something. Anyway, Tom and I can't fly this thing and you've got to!"

"Strap in, Marbet," Kaufman ordered. His hands felt for the terminal. It wasn't coded for him, but he knew the overrides, and how to reconfigure them. It had been ten years since he'd flown an XXPell3, but this craft was at least ten years old, too. The Fallers must have captured it somehow, somewhere. Kaufman didn't want to think about what might have happened to the craft's three-man crew.

His displays came on-line. They registered two space tunnels and absolutely nothing else. Q space must have been swept to destroy every stray rock in it large enough to clog up a display screen.

Kaufman pulled out of the bay, and now the display registered two items: the XXPell3 and the Faller station. No, three. As he watched, another craft left the station, moving toward Space Tunnel #301. The Fallers were taking their artifact home.

"They believed us," he said aloud. "The sons-of-bitches believed us."

"And let us go," Capelo said, "but why did they bother? The second we go back through Tunnel Number Two-one-eight to Artemis, our own military is going to vaporize us."

"No," Kaufman said. "Not in this craft. They'll at least listen for a second, and we can ID." He hoped he was right. But at least it was a chance.

"Oh, good," Capelo said. "They'll wait to hear what we told the Fallers before they kill us. Pierce is just going to love that we spoiled his great military coup."

Marbet said, "Shut up, Tom."

"Now she's enlisted, too. General Grant. Where do *I* sign up?"

"Shut up, Tom! Let Lyle fly!"

Lyle flew, heading for Space Tunnel #218. But something didn't make sense. The Fallers wanted him and Marbet and Capelo to tell their fellow humans that the Faller artifact was back in the Faller home system, protecting it. That's what they'd told Marbet. But *why* did they want that message delivered? Why not just let Pierce's troops bring the human artifact through, try to fry the Faller System, and find it impossible? If there was going to be a stalemate . . . blessed stalemate. The three of them had at least brought that much about. The two artifacts would not both be set off at prime thirteen in the same system. Spacetime would not tear, heal itself by a universe-wide flop transition, and so destroy spacetime as life now knew it. But if there was going to be a stalemate, why send Kaufman and Capelo and Marbet to announce it in advance?

So that no more humans would enter Q space. The Fallers were that xenophobic about their front yard.

A third blip appeared on the display screen.

Kaufman stared. No, it was what he'd thought. He'd really seen it, hadn't misjudged it, couldn't will it away. A third blip had entered Q space, coming through Tunnel #218 from Artemis. A fourth blip, a fifth, a sixth. Pierce's forces were here.

And the Faller craft carrying their artifact home was too far from Tunnel #301 to reach it in time. Both artifacts were now in Q space, one of them controlled by a madman.

Kaufman was too late. Everything was over.

TWENTY-NINE

Q SPACE

hat is it?" Marbet said. She'd been watching Kaufman, and her Sensitive eyes had seen. Kaufman didn't try to hide the truth.

"The navy is here."

"With the artifact?" Capelo said quickly.

On Kaufman's display, the Faller space station fired. The SADN ship continued on at top speed, unaffected.

"With the artifact. Set at prime two," Kaufman answered.

"Can they reach the tunnel to the Faller homeworld before Pierce's fleet—"

"No," Kaufman said. "Prepare for acceleration and evasive maneuvers, if necessary."

He flew the ancient craft toward the tunnel from which the navy ships had just emerged. No ID registered on his display for the ships; the small flyer's records were too old to contain these navy models. Kaufman opened the comlink on all frequencies.

"Solar Alliance Defense Navy ship, this is Colonel Lyle Kaufman in a retired XXPell3. Request permission to fly alongside you."

In the transmission lag Capelo said, "God, yes. If they set off both artifacts at prime thirteen there should be a safety zone around the . . . what am I saying? If spacetime goes into flop transition . . . Lyle, try to get permission to go through the tunnel! Fast! We still don't know if the flop transition travels only at c or can go through the tunnels itself!"

"Who the hell are you?" came over the comlink. "Q space is restricted, Colonel!"

"I know. It's a long story. Request permission to use Space Tunnel Number Two-one-eight. I'll tell the story to Artemis System—it looks like you men don't need me in the way."

Another lag. Kaufman increased acceleration as much as he dared. Capelo's ribs were only bound with Kaufman's inept first aid. Finally the answer came:

"Get the fuck through the tunnel, Colonel. Pass code 'San Juan Hill.' We'll give you five minutes!"

Kaufman didn't ask 'five minutes until what.' He knew. The Faller station raced toward Space Tunnel #301, to take the Faller artifact through and protect the home system. It wasn't going to make it. The station couldn't destroy the navy warship, nor the warship destroy the station, not if both were set at prime two. But surely the Faller station would switch to prime eleven, thereby protecting the entire Q System from a prime thirteen attack. Surely it would . . .

He accelerated at five-gees toward Tunnel #218.

Surely the Fallers would switch to prime eleven . . .

Something happened on his displays. Both the warship and the Faller station exploded.

"They did it!" Kaufman screamed, despite the pain in his lungs, despite the uselessness of the cry. They had done it, must have. No zone of safety at prime thirteen, apparently. Syree Johnson's artifact had exploded when it fried the entire World System except World, and she'd thought it had been from taking too great a mass through the tunnel but it hadn't been—

Pierce and the Fallers did it. Two artifacts set off, prime thirteen, same system . . .

The wave had a lag effect, or this flyer would already be gone— They did it, the Goddamn fucking assholes—

Kaufman accelerated madly toward the tunnel. How great a lag effect? He was losing consciousness, couldn't do that, the navy on the other side of the tunnel would fry him if he couldn't account for himself . . . stay conscious . . . 'San Juan Hill' . . . they did it . . .

The flyer dove through the tunnel. Three seconds later, the wave effect of an artifact set at prime thirteen reached Space Tunnel #218. And the inevitable happened.

Darkness.

"San . . . Juan . . ."

Crushing weight.

"Hill . . ."

Darkness again, lifting slowly.

"San . . ."

Kaufman didn't know how long he'd been gasping the words, which were meaningless to his struggling mind. Blackness swept over him, receded, returned. The comlink was babbling . . . something . . . meaningless . . .

He was on the Artemis System side of the tunnel. Still alive.

"Cut . . . acceleration . . ."

The crushing weight abruptly ceased. The flyer hurled on.

"Slow, damn it!" the comlink ordered. With every ounce of

strength he had left, Kaufman gave the command to the flyer computer.

Marbet. Tom.

He turned in his seat. They both slumped in theirs. Kaufman's heart and lungs worked too hard to go to them. His brain seemed to bulge larger than his skull. He had only his voice, and he forced himself to use it.

"Our warship . . . gone . . . also Faller station . . . both artifacts . . . thirteen . . ."

"How do you know that? Colonel, what happened over there?"

"Don't go . . . through. . . ."

But they would. It was inevitable. And on his displays, Kaufman saw the blips detach from the Artemis fleet and race toward Tunnel #218.

"Don't . . . not . . . yet . . ."

"Unknown flyer, deactivate all weapons and wait for boarding," said the comlink. Back to correct navy procedure. Fools.

But they were still alive. So the wave traveled at c, not through the tunnels. The flop transition would spread out from Q System at c, tearing spacetime and then mending it through radical reconfiguration, and it would be hundreds of years until the Solar System was destroyed.

Cold comfort.

"Ready to . . . accept boarding," Kaufman said, and tried to get out of his chair to go to Marbet. The effort was too great. He fell back down, and so was facing the displays when it happened.

He saw it happen, live.

It couldn't happen, but he saw it.

Three SADN ships flew toward Space Tunnel #218. Toward it, and into it. Not through it, into it. Two ships, a half minute apart, hit an invisible solid wall within the floating doughnut, and exploded. The third ship swerved just in time and bypassed the tunnel.

Which was somehow not a tunnel.

Kaufman threw himself out of his seat. Reserve energy he didn't know he had galvanized him. He grabbed Capelo and shook him, heedless of the physicist's injuries. Capelo's thin body flopped back and forth. But he was breathing. Kaufman dropped him and reached for a taser.

Alarms shrieked over the comlink. Fleet alarms. Attack alarms.

But there was no attack, except by Kaufman. He tasered Capelo and the physicist shrieked awake. "What . . . ooooooooeeeee . . ." It was a cry of pure pain.

Kaufman ignored it. "Tom, listen . . . listen, Goddamn it! The tunnels are closing!"

"What—"

"Space tunnel to Q System is closed! It's a solid wall. Both sides set off the artifacts in Q System at prime thirteen and *the tunnel closed*. I need to know if they're all closed, or just the ones to Q System!"

Capelo stared at him, no longer moaning. Then he said, "How the fuck should I know?"

Kaufman dropped him and jumped back into his seat. No help from theory. Only action left. He restarted the XXPell3 and accelerated in the opposite direction, toward Space Tunnel #212. The next tunnel on the route to Sol.

No one fired, no one ordered him to stop. Kaufman wasn't surprised. The fleet had just lost two ships in an *accident that couldn't have happened*. No one with authority was thinking of Kaufman. They would, in a few minutes, but by that time he'd be through Tunnel #212 and inside the star system it led to, Han System.

If it let him through.

He started to decelerate halfway, which wasn't very far; the tunnels orbited close together. Approaching #212, he said on the comlink to the tunnel ships, "XXPell3, designated test flyer for Tunnel Number Two-one-two into Han System, coming through. Code San Juan Hill. Wish me luck, boys!"

Silence: part lag, part confusion. Then a young, scared voice: "I don't have . . . proceed, flyer, and good luck!"

Seconds later: "That's not . . ." but it was already too late. Kaufman's communication had traveled faster than the one from the fleet at the fortified entrance to Q space. Kaufman had reached the floating gray doughnut made of nothing.

Slowly, to minimize impact, he flew into the tunnel.

There was no impact. He was through.

Behind him, Tom Capelo said, "Jesus Newton God."

"What?"

Capelo didn't answer. The tunnel ships on the Han System side said, "Identify self, flyer."

"Flyer XXPell3, Colonel Lyle Kaufman. Emergency information from Artemis System, priority one, Special Compartmented Information."

"Dock at will, Colonel. But your ship—"

Capelo said, "Go through the next tunnel, Lyle! Now! They're all going to close, and I don't know how long we've got! Do you hear me—*they're all going to close!*"

"What was that, Colonel?" said the other ship, sharply.

"Nothing," Kaufman said. There came into his mind, unbidden, a map of the space tunnels between him and Sol. Curiously, the image was not the conventionally formal military rendering but instead the same kind of rough sketch he'd made on Marbet's handheld. Kaufman could see this new sketch, in all its crudeness, as clearly as if it floated in the air in front of him:

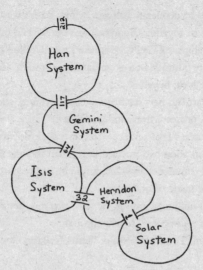

Four more tunnels to the Solar System, and home. Kaufman said to the comlink, "Change of orders, sealed until this locus, priority one, Special Compartmented Information. Request permission to proceed through Tunnel Number One-one-seven into Gemini System."

"I haven't got any authorization to—"

"Then find someone who does! I said I have Special Compartmented Information, proceeding through Tunnel Number One-one-seven!" Kaufman said loudly, firmly, impatiently. The tunnel orbited only twenty seconds away.

"I don't have any . . . can you . . . halt!"

Too late. Kaufman was through. He emerged into Gemini System. Three more tunnels to go.

"Tom, they'll come after us," Kaufman said quickly. "If you can't talk fast to them, they'll shoot us down."

"Evade them, or something! I don't know how rapidly the— Goddamn it how did I ever miss *that* variable . . ."

Kaufman instructed the computer to proceed to Tunnel #64, leading from Gemini to Isis System, and to take all possible evasive action, keep all comlinks open. Then he turned in his seat. Capelo sat covered in blue pain patches, which was how he was working on the handheld. God, so *many* patches, the chemicals he was absorbing to keep himself pumped . . . the physicist coded furiously on the handheld. Kaufman glanced at Marbet and saw she still breathed. Gladness blew wildly through him.

Why? They were all going to be shot down anyway.

"XXPell3, halt instantly or I will commence firing."

"This is Dr. Thomas Capelo!" Tom screamed. "Don't fire! Listen to me, the tunnels are closing, they're *closing*! I know why! Don't shoot or I can't tell you!"

"XXPell3, halt instantly or I will commence firing. This is your last warning."

The Gemini–Isis Tunnel was too far away to reach before a proton beam got them.

Kaufman's chest clutched. He could fire on the tunnel ships, on both of them, there were only two. Taking evasive action he'd probably get them both—

He couldn't do it. He couldn't shoot down two SADN ships on active duty, not to save his life and Marbet's, not even to let Capelo tell the galaxy what was happening to it. They'd know soon enough anyway.

"Halting in compliance," he said, and ignored Capelo's shout behind him.

A ship blew up on his viewscreen, filling it with light.

The data display showed it had been a civilian cargo ship, cleared to go through a different one of Gemini System's three tunnels. The ship had tried to sail through at one-gee acceleration and had hit solid matter. Another tunnel had closed.

"The tunnels are closing," Kaufman said, restarting his ship, "just as Dr. Capelo said! Proceeding through Tunnel Number Sixty-four to Isis System, Priority One, Special Compartmented Information—"

No one even replied. Probably they were all stunned by what had just happened to the cargo ship. Shattered into smithereens by what should have been empty space. How many hands had been aboard?

Kaufman didn't slow down. Twenty-two seconds, eighteen, twelve . . . they were through.

"Flyer XXPell3, identify self," said a puzzled female voice on the Isis side of the tunnel. "No clearances on record."

Capelo said, "You've got more time here. I think. The equations . . . how could I have *missed* it, my God. . . ."

Kaufman's adrenaline rush was dissipating. Unlike Capelo, he wasn't covered with blue patches. Capelo was far too jacked for the patches to be simple painkillers; probably they were systemic accelerators, peen or gull.

Two more tunnels between him and Sol.

"This is Flyer XXPell3, no current clearances. Request permission to proceed through Space Tunnel Number Thirty-two into Herndon System."

"Why is there no record of you, Flyer XXPell3? I'm showing your craft as obsolete and retired military."

"That is correct. I am—" Kaufman said. He cut the link momentarily and said to Capelo, "How much time? When do the rest of the tunnels close? Do you know what the fuck you're doing?"

"No! I've only had ten minutes here with a major breakthrough in physics!"

Kaufman reopened the comlink. "—get the rest of that. Repeat transmission, XXPell3."

"Repeating transmission," Kaufman said wearily. For the first time in what seemed hours—it was actually less than twenty minutes total—he realized that he, Capelo, and Marbet were all still naked. "I said I am on a special military mission, Priority One, Special Compartmented Information."

"Pass code for SCI missions?"

Kaufman didn't know the code, of course. This was the end of their mad dash to Sol. The only thing left was truth.

"Listen, Gemini System. I have Dr. Thomas Capelo, the missing physicist sought by Admiral Pierce, aboard my craft. He has just discovered that the space tunnels are closing, one by one, and the scientific basis for that. It is vital that we convey this information with all possible speed to Admiral Pierce on Mars. He doesn't yet know this phenomenon is happening, so we have no SCI pass code. But the entire galaxy is at stake."

"Dr. Thomas Capelo?" the voice said incredulously. "That's quite a story, XXPell3. Deactivate weapons and prepare for boarding."

"I tell you there's no time for that," Kaufman said. "The space tunnels are closing."

On his display, he saw a ship sail peacefully through the tunnel. It didn't explode.

"XXPell3, deactivate weapons and prepare for immediate boarding."

"In compliance," Kaufman said. "Deactivating weapons and preparing for boarding. This is Colonel Lyle Kaufman, USDC, retired. Will you at least do one other thing? Will you send—"

"Lyle?" came another female voice. "Lyle Kaufman? This is Marjorie Barella."

Kaufman closed his eyes. He had served with her in combat, fifteen years ago. By pure chance then, by pure chance now. "Marjorie? It is Lyle Kaufman. Run a voice-scan match . . . got it?"

"Yes."

"Listen, Colonel Barella . . ."

"General Barella."

Better yet. "General, this is an unprecedented situation. I have Dr. Thomas Capelo aboard. We have just returned from Artemis System." He didn't mention Q System; she wasn't SADC and so wouldn't even know about it, rank of general or no. "This is a long story, but the major outcome is that the space tunnels are closing, one by one, at an undetermined varying rate. I know how fantastic that sounds. All I'm asking is that you send a flyer through to Gemini System to verify that the space tunnels are becoming nonoperative. Meanwhile, I will deactivate weapons and prepare for boarding, if you wish, although I conceive my primary mission to be to convey this intelligence to Sol."

Marjorie Barella said, "You must deactivate and prepare for immediate boarding, Lyle. But you were . . . I'll dispatch a recon flyer."

"Thank you, Marjorie." By pure chance then, by pure chance now. Unfair.

But he'd always known that was true of the universe.

He cut the outgoing comlink and said to Capelo, "How long? And what's going on?"

"I don't know how long. All I have is the data for three closed tunnels, for Chrissake, it's too small a sample . . . I only know why it's happening."

Only. Kaufman was too weary to comment on Capelo's extraordinary word choice. Hauling himself out of his chair, he fumbled for an adrenaline patch for Marbet, still unconscious in her seat.

Capelo, higher than the moon, babbled on. "I don't know how we missed it . . . once you know where to look . . . do you remember all those people who said no, two prime thirteens won't tear all of spacetime, the original makers would have built in safeguards to make sure that didn't happen . . . Do you remember all those hopeful, proofless, optimistic slobs? They were *right*! Or half right, anyway, spacetime does tear, it does mend itself with a radical flop-transition to convert the energy, I wasn't wrong on that . . . but *the flop-*

transition only proceeds so far. It travels through the tunnels and closes them instead, and that absorbs the transition energy, God the amount of energy generated and absorbed . . . and it has the double effect of preserving spacetime configuration and removing such dangerous toys as the artifacts from those who were patently misusing them! Oh, it's beautiful, the math is beautiful, how did I miss this before, this equation that—"

Kaufman stopped listening. He put a patch on Marbet's neck. Instantly she stirred and clutched her chest. "Ooohh . . ."

"Don't move, Marbet. Broken ribs, I think. Tom, too, but . . . just don't move. Help is coming."

"Where *are* we?" In pain, she was nonetheless fully alert.

"Isis System. We're going to be boarded by tunnel administration in a few minutes. Don't move or—"

"Lyle!" Marjorie Barella's voice on the comlink. "Lyle, you were right! My God!"

"Open outgoing frequency!" Kaufman snapped at the computer. "Marjorie, what—"

"The recon flyer found Gemini fleet in a panic. The Gemini–Han Tunnel is a *solid wall.* How—never mind. Proceed to Sol and tell the SADC. No point in sending clearances, you can go as fast as a flyer through the tunnels. If—" She didn't finish the thought. "The pass code for SCI is beaming aboard to you now. It'll get you through any tunnel. Go!"

"Going now," Kaufman said. He was already back in the pilot seat, starting the ship, reactivating the weapons. The encrypted SCI pass code arrived in his secure data bank and he accelerated, dashing toward Space Tunnel #32 while there was still time, if there was still time.

After #32, only Space Tunnel #1 stood between him and Sol.

THIRTY

THARSIS, MARS

manda Capelo and Konstantin Ouranis sat watching the news-cast in the Blumbergs' living room. Uncle Martin sat at his terminal in his study, which was really just a corner of his bed-room, preparing his lectures for the university. The fourth quarter started tomorrow. Aunt Kristen had come home from work early and now rattled around the tiny kitchen, preparing dinner. Uncle Martin was actually the better cook, but it was Aunt Kristen's turn tonight. The newscast was turned up loud so she could hear it from the kitchen.

"Look!" Konstantin said suddenly. "My father!"

Amanda hadn't been paying attention to the news. She'd been stealing looks at Konstantin's profile, so beautiful, and worrying about tomorrow.

The problem was Uncle Martin. No, the real problem was Amanda's lie.

She should never have let Konstantin think she was almost seventeen. It made him . . . expect things. He'd been at the Blumbergs' for two weeks now, and it seemed to Amanda that he expected more things all the time. And tomorrow the university started up again and Uncle Martin would be gone all day, teaching, and of course Aunt Kristen would be at her four-day-a-week job at the farm outside Tharsis, where they grew intensive-yield genemod food crops under low domes built like greenhouses. Until now, both her aunt and uncle hadn't been out of the apartment at the same time, unless Amanda and Konstantin had gone with them. Mostly this was because they wanted someone to be here if there was a comlink about Amanda's father. However, Amanda suspected that it was also because they didn't want to leave her alone with Konstantin.

And now she didn't want that, either.

But he was so sweet! He never argued with her, never pressured her, never did any of the things that Amanda and Yaeko and Juliana and Thekla had told each other boys did when they were trying to talk you into things. Konstantin wasn't like that. He was always kind, always gentle, always concerned about her. She had told him endless stories about her father, and he'd listened attentively and held her if she cried and told her that Dr. Capelo was sure to come home. Konstantin was never pushy. And yet . . . and yet . . .

Somehow each day Amanda found herself going a little farther with him. First light kisses, then deeper kisses, then French kissing, then he had lightly stroked her sides only somehow his hands got closer to her breasts . . .

A year ago she hadn't even had breasts.

Over and over she practiced in her mind telling him the truth. *"Konstantin, I'm only fourteen."* But each time she tried to say it aloud, she somehow couldn't. First, she'd have to admit she lied. Second, he might not like her anymore. Third . . . third was hard to admit even to herself. But she did. *Facts*, her father always said. And this was a fact.

She sort of didn't want him to stop.

But she sort of did! And tomorrow, when Uncle Martin and Aunt Kristen weren't home . . .

"Ah-man-dah? You to hear me? That is my father!"

"Really?" She looked at the screen. Stavros Ouranis surprised her. He was a short, big-bellied man with bristly, funny-looking black hair. Definitely not where Konstantin and Demetria got their beauty. Mr. Ouranis said something in Greek, and an English translator supplied, "I wish Admiral Pierce all possible success in stopping the alien threat at Space Tunnel number one. My own people stand ready to help him any way he wishes."

"Your father really is important," Amanda said, because she had to say something. Aunt Kristen had come out from the kitchen and stood drying her hands on a dish towel, expressionlessly watching the newscast.

"Very very important," Konstantin said, but it didn't sound like bragging, just like facts. "Often he to tell Admiral Pierce things and Admiral Pierce to listen at my father and to do things."

"Oh," Amanda said.

Konstantin twisted in his chair. "After dinner, I and Amanda to walk, Mrs. Blumberg? Is okay?"

"If Amanda wants to," Aunt Kristen said neutrally and vanished into the kitchen.

"You to want to walk by me, Ah-man-dah?"

"Yes. But now I have to help Aunt Kristen in the kitchen."

"Splendid," Konstantin said, and turned back to the news.

She was a little irritated. Konstantin never offered to help around the apartment, as Amanda had been taught a guest should do. On the other hand, he always asked Aunt Kristen's permission to take Amanda anywhere in Tharsis, even to the ice cream shop in the next building, just as if Amanda was Sudie's age. He was selfish, and superpolite, and amazingly generous, and sexist, and respectful, and scary, and wonderful. He confused her all the time.

After dinner he said, "We go to walk, Ah-man-dah?" and smiled at her, and suddenly she wanted to walk with him more than anything in the entire world. Slow color mounted in her face. Aunt Kristen watched her bleakly.

They strolled to the tiny park at the edge of the Tharsis dome. The trees and flowers, genemod for Martian light, made a canopy above them. But the park was crowded tonight, with adults on all the benches and children in the red-sand sandbox and the paths between flower beds clogged with walkers. Amanda saw several soldiers with the green bars on their caps. The dust outside the dome was at a very low level and the sky was remarkably clear, glittering with stars. People had come out to enjoy the evening.

"Ah-man-dah," Konstantin said, "we to walk outside, okay?"

"Outside?"

"Yes, splendid, why not."

"But . . . we don't have suits! Or passes!"

He laughed and winked at her. Taking her hand, he led her quickly out of the park and through the crowded streets.

"Konstantin, where are we going?"

"You to know soon! Surprise!"

She followed him half willingly, half resentfully. He never let her make any decisions! But the pressure of his warm fingers on hers was delicious, and anyway going outside would really be interesting. If they didn't go far, of course.

He stopped in front of a building with no sign, at the edge of the dome. It was built on one side like a ziggurat, with stepped floors to accommodate the curve of the dome; the other side was straight. Konstantin led her up the one step to the raised security platform. He fitted himself in front of the retinal scanner. It said something in

Greek. Konstantin answered at length, and then moved away.

"Now you, Ah-man-dah."

"But where are we? What is this building?"

"Ouranis Enterprises. Now you. I to tell it to let you go in. Come."

She stepped up to the scanner, impressed by the power he had over his father's business. The scanner said something in Greek. Again Konstantin answered, and the door swung open.

Inside, a system spoke to Konstantin in Greek. He answered and a moment later a trolley 'bot brought out two s-suits and helmets. Konstantin grinned at her, and she laughed, suddenly infected with the adventure.

They pulled on the suits. Before he put on his, he pulled a data cube from the pocket of his tunic. Lovingly Konstantin checked her seals and controls and then his own. "See, here is private channel to talk. You and me."

"Okay," Amanda said. "What's that thing?" He had picked up a large, heavy-looking box by its metal handle and had attached its cables to the neck of his helmet.

"Is nothing."

"No, really, Konstantin, what is it?"

He scowled. "My father to say I must to carry outside. Very powerful transmitter. Encrypted. Will receive anything. He to want to reach me always. And to send at me messages for business."

"Well, that's reasonable," Amanda said, and he stopped scowling. She felt suddenly older. He had been ashamed to have to carry the transmitter because he thought it was babyish, and she'd reassured him! She, Amanda! She smiled at him so radiantly that just before he put on her helmet, he kissed her lightly on the mouth.

Konstantin slipped the data cube into the transmitter. They walked through the entire building, seeing no one. Well, it was evening; probably the workers had gone home. The building had its own gate out of the dome. Konstantin gave the codes, and the airlock opened.

Outside, it was beautiful. This was the opposite side of the dome from the walkways to the farm, the train gateway, and the gate where the shuttle picked up and dropped passengers for the spaceport. Amanda saw a few other people walking outside, but no one very close to them.

Konstantin led her, hand-in-hand, away from the dome. The ground was all drawn over with vehicle tracks and footprints. Close to the dome there were few rocks because they had all been picked up by 'bots or tourists. But a hundred meters out, the natural rocks of Mars reappeared, rocks of every size, red and black and brown and yellow. The rocks were mostly rounded and pitted. Dust lay over them all, and to Amanda even the dust looked beautiful.

"Konstantin," she said experimentally over the private channel, "this was all a big volcano once."

"Yes? Splendid!"

"It made the Tharsis bulge. That's why we have such a great view. My father told me."

As always when her father was mentioned, Konstantin turned toward her with respectful concern in his dark eyes. He squeezed her hand. "He to come back soon, Ah-man-dah. I sure."

"Yes," she said, but she wasn't sure she believed it anymore. For a moment the wonderful alien landscape dimmed.

"Soon," Konstantin said. "Look! Up, up!"

A meteor streaked across the black sky. Amanda said, "Quick! Make a wish! Before it hits . . . oh, too late."

"I to wish, yes," Konstantin said, and squeezed her hand.

They kept walking. When the dome began sinking below the horizon, Amanda said firmly, "This is far enough, Konstantin."

Obediently he stopped. He found a big rock and sat down on it, pulling her beside him. The rock felt cold under her bottom; they couldn't stay here very long. But Konstantin put his arm around her and they nestled as close as possible with their helmets.

Amanda giggled. It was so silly! She'd been worried about being alone with Konstantin, and here they were as alone as it was possible to be, and it was with s-suits, intense cold, and bulky helmets that prevented him from so much as kissing her. Of course there was still tomorrow to worry about, but right now she was as protected as those vestal virgins they'd learned about in history class.

"Ah-man-dah," Konstantin said, "I to wish to tell at you my to wish."

It took her a minute to sort this out. "You want to tell me what wish you made on that meteor."

"Yes. Before now, two weeks since, I to tell you I love you. Remember?"

"I remember," Amanda said. She pulled a little away from him.

"Okay. Now I say . . . damn!"

She looked at him in astonishment. But the damn hadn't been for her. Konstantin frowned at the transmitter he'd set down on the rocky ground at their feet. As she watched, his frown changed. Konstantin's black eyes widened, and as he turned to face her, wonder and joy spread across his face.

"Ah-man-dah, a comlink by you! Program I to write have it!"

"What . . . I don't understand . . ." Was Aunt Kristen summoning Amanda back? Was she angry?

"I to write program! To get message addresses by you or by anybody in address parameters! Even encrypted because transmitter have powerful unencryption program, why is big! Comlink at you!"

"But—"

He took her by the shoulders and almost shook her with his intensity. "Ah-man-dah! Is comlink at Blumberg home system! Is from your father!"

THIRTY-ONE

SPACE TUNNEL #1

apelo was crashing from the systemic-accelerator spike he'd given himself.

Kaufman couldn't spare much attention for the physicist. He concentrated on his displays, on pushing the XXPell3 as much as he dared without further damaging her three passengers, on planning ahead. Armed with Marjorie Barella's precious SCI code, Kaufman could get through the final tunnel to Sol. Probably. But then what? Was he really going to tell Admiral Pierce's military forces on the other side of Space Tunnel #1 that the tunnel was going to close? If he did, he would have to tell the entire story, including that Admiral Pierce had hidden Tom Capelo and the Protector Artifact—which had supposedly been protecting the Solar System—on the *Murasaki*, in World System. And that Pierce had then taken the Protector Artifact to Q System and set off the closing of the tunnels by risking the fabric of spacetime itself.

Kaufman might as well sign death warrants for himself, Capelo, and Marbet as tell those particular truths.

But if he didn't tell the military his improbable saga, how did he explain the SCI code in the hands of a retired army colonel? Or the tunnels' closing? How much to explain and to whom?

And then he realized what of course he should have known all along, and would have known if he hadn't been so exhausted: None of those decisions would be his to make.

"Tom, you said the tunnels are closing at a variable rate. Can you plot it yet? How long before Tunnel number one is affected? Do you know?"

"Yes. I . . . think. Ten hours. I think."

Ten hours. It would only take them maybe one hour to reach the Solar System. Plenty of time. But then what?

Something fell to the floor behind him. He glanced briefly backward: Capelo's handheld.

Capelo looked terrible. The drug crash combined with his injuries combined with tension and effort and fear. His face was actually gray, the first time Kaufman had truly witnessed that trite description. Capelo's head and arms trembled, and so did his voice.

"Marbet . . . another . . . patch . . ."

"No," she said.

"Yes! Must . . . work . . ."

"It'll kill you, Tom. No, you can't have it."

"Bitch . . . no, I don't mean . . . let me record message. My daughters. Please!"

Kaufman knew she wouldn't refuse. He piloted the flyer toward Space Tunnel #1, sending ahead his SCI code and request to proceed. *Tunnel #1.* Almost home.

"Can't . . . without . . . a patch . . ."

Marbet said, "You don't have any choice, Tom. I'm not giving you another one. Record it, and as soon as we're through Lyle will send it encrypted to Mars. Do it, damn it."

Kaufman heard anger strengthen Capelo's voice as he began to record. Sensitives were accomplished manipulators . . . Tom hadn't had a chance against Marbet. Then Kaufman forgot them both. The returning message from Tunnel # 1 reached the flyer.

"Flyer XXPell3, SCI code received. Proceed at once through Space Tunnel number one."

Space Tunnel #1 was formidably guarded, an entire fleet on action alert. But the SCI code sent Kaufman past the fleet, straight to the head of the queue and through the tunnel. It was so easy, when everything up to this point had been so hard.

They were back in the Solar System, with nine hours—if Tom was right—until the tunnel closed for good. And once again nothing was going to be easy.

"Identify self, flyer," said the tunnel guard on the comlink. Blips appeared all over Kaufman's displays. This side of the gateway to Sol was also fortified with a tunnel fleet. This was the homeworld. If he made a wrong move, they'd vaporize him, with or without SCI clearance. Even for Stefanak that had been SOP, and Pierce was three times as showy in "guarding the cradle of humanity."

"Flyer XXPell3, Colonel Lyle Kaufman. Emergency information from Artemis and Han Systems, priority one, Special Compartmented Information. Sending SCI code now."

Behind him Marbet said softly, "Send this data, too, Lyle. It's Tom's message to Amanda and Sudie, encrypted. I uploaded it."

"I can't without explaining that—"

"I think Tom's dying, Lyle."

"Oh, hell." He sent the message; the computer beamed it according to the address. It couldn't matter now. With truth drugs, none of them were going to be able to hide anything that had happened. Why hadn't he realized that before?

A different voice came over the comlink. "Flyer XXPell3, SCI code received. Your flyer is unregistered, and your personal identification number does not match military records. Deactivate weapons and prepare for immediate boarding."

"In compliance," Kaufman said. "Please arrange debriefing· by fleet commander in secure area. I have SCI information about the war for his ears only. Also, we have a man here in need of immediate medical attention. He's Dr. Thomas Capelo."

No reaction. "Prepare for immediate boarding," was all the answer Kaufman got, which meant it would be a while before he was let anywhere near fleet commander. If ever. He would be checked for every conceivable sort of weapon, including biological, on a secure medcraft that could be sacrificed, with all hands if necessary, if he were found to be carrying anything dangerous. Probably he'd get a Pandya Dose concurrently with that. SCI clearance was one thing, but Kaufman's appearing in an obsolete flyer that hadn't existed for a decade, from a part of the galaxy with no record of him, carrying information he shouldn't have, and beaming an unauthorized encrypted message toward Mars . . . those were quite other things. The SADC would take no chances with him. There was a war on.

He turned to Marbet and Capelo. With cutting off the engine, the flyer had returned to weightlessness. She had found the storage area and pulled out three old-fashioned s-suits, but couldn't put hers on.

"Marbet?" Kaufman said. For the first time, he noticed that she had put a pain patch on her own neck.

She managed to smile at him. "I can't bend enough to get my suit on. A rib, I think. And for Tom it's hopeless."

Ignoring his own painful rib, Kaufman unstrapped, floated over to Capelo and pulled up his eyelids. The pupils were neither fixed nor dilated. "Tom's still with us. Look in the compartment below . . . no, not that one, the one below it—are there any blankets?"

"Yes," Marbet said gratefully. She pulled out three of the thin thermal blankets. She and Kaufman wrapped them on, covering up their nakedness, and Kaufman managed to get one enough under Capelo's seat harness to at least cover the injured man's genitals.

Marbet said quietly, "What are they going to do, Lyle?"

He looked at her admiringly. She was always brave, always able to face the situation. "Truth drugs. After that, I don't know."

She nodded. "I love you, Lyle."

It was the last thing on his military mind, but he said it back to her, very low, just before he felt the slight bump that meant the medcraft had drawn the XXPell3 alongside for boarding. Doctors, soldiers, weapons specialists, intelligence personnel, to invade every crevice of Kaufman's ship, body, and mind.

Welcome home.

Suited soldiers took Kaufman, Marbet, and Capelo off the flyer. No one asked him anything, which didn't surprise Kaufman. Correct procedure. Nor did Kaufman volunteer any information. By the time they were done with him, he figured, the news would have come from the far systems that the tunnels were closing. After all, Sol had nine hours yet (maybe). That would lend truth to Kaufman's story. So the only thing Kaufman said to the boarding crew was addressed to the doctor bending over Tom Capelo. "Will he make it, Captain?"

"Yes," she said, surprising him. Not even an ass-covering qualifier. He looked at her with respect.

They separated him from Marbet and Capelo, strapped him onto a roboguerney, and put him out. Kaufman felt the light patch touch his neck. His last thought was to wonder whether he would wake up in time for the closing of Space Tunnel #1, humanity's portal to the stars.

A long, blank, featureless time, conscious and yet not. He knew what he was saying, what was being done to him, what questions he was answering, but he knew these things as in a dream, when everything happens both to you and to another self who is not exactly you. Kaufman floated in that white, dreamlike country, and talked, and knew that he was talking, and could not stop. He knew the machines were nibbling at him, sampling blood and tissue and even sperm for biologicals, but they nibbled at someone else. Who was nonetheless him. He felt his broken rib being bound and treated, but it was only partially his rib and he felt only partly proprietary about it. Partial ownership, partial bodily violation, partial outrage. Only compliance was complete.

When they were done, they knew everything that had happened to him since he left Mars. They also knew that it was the truth.

It was out of his hands now. Or, maybe, it had always been out of his hands, although that was no way for a soldier to think.

Lyle Kaufman came out of the truth-drug trance eventually. He lay strapped down, in a blank room on some ship. No one was with him. No one had further need of him; he had been emptied of everything useful. The hollow vessel itself was now unimportant, until someone somewhere had to make a decision about what to do with him.

He was pretty sure what that decision would have to be. For everyone who knew the true story.

Kaufman was suddenly glad he'd sent Capelo's message. Pierce's encrypters would crack it, of course, eventually. But by that time Capelo would have said good-bye to his daughters.

THIRTY-TWO

THARSIS PLAIN, MARS

Amanda stared through her faceplate at Konstantin. Was he joking? No, he wasn't cruel, and anyway it wasn't funny . . . *her father* . . .

Konstantin was manually coding his transmitter. "I to make message to come by your receiver, Ah-man-dah . . . is very long! No, is *two* data sections at different encryptions . . . I don't understand . . ."

Amanda certainly didn't understand, but if she had, all understanding would have fled. Her father's voice sounded in her ears.

"Amanda and Sudie and Carol, this is Tom. Daddy. I'm home, sweeties, I'm back in the Solar System."

"Daddy!" Amanda cried aloud, and didn't even know she'd spoken. But there was something wrong with his voice, it was weak and hesitant, like he was sick.

"I don't know if I can get to Mars or Earth to see you. Admiral Pierce is not going to like what I've been doing, and I don't know what will happen to me. He tried to set off both artifacts at prime thirteen near the Faller home world, and as a result the space tunnels are all closing up. About five hours after you get this, Tunnel Number One will be gone forever. I'm on the Sol side of the tunnel, but I'm injured pretty bad and anyway Pierce isn't going to let . . . but listen to me, that's not what I want you to remember. Instead remember that I love all three of you, and always will, forever and ever."

His voice had faded to a whisper.

"Carol or Kristen, destroy the hardware you receive this message on, and never tell anyone you received it. I don't want you in danger, too. Do you understand? *Never*. Good-bye for now . . ."

"No!" Amanda cried. "No!"

Konstantin said, "Dr. Capelo to think he will to die—why? Makes not sense."

"Because Admiral Pierce will kill him!" Amanda cried hysterically. "Admiral Pierce isn't the good guy you think! He'll kill Daddy!"

Konstantin tried to grab Amanda. She batted him away and started to run wildly, not knowing where, not caring. Admiral Pierce would kill her father . . . It became a certainty to her, a horrifying fact . . . oh please dear God no, *Dei volente* . . .

Konstantin caught her, held her tight against him. "Not to run, Ah-man-dah! Since you to fall, your suit will to tear!"

"I don't care! I want to die, too! Let me go, oh let me go no no no Daddy. . . ."

He held her firmly, her struggles barely seeming to register on him. At last he said, "Two messages. Listen to other message, Ah-man-dah!"

"Kristen, Martin, this is Marbet Grant," came over Amanda's receiver, and she stopped struggling and held still. "I'm with Tom. Attached is an encrypted file of everything that has happened out here, including Admiral Pierce's heroic actions. I'm sending this the minute we get through Tunnel number one. Or rather, I'm making Lyle send it without knowing he is. He's got a lot to contend with right now . . ." Marbet's voice faltered, caught itself.

"It's vitally important you retransmit this message immediately, to every major news media on Mars and Earth. You probably don't have more than an hour. Maybe less. Retransmit my words and *only my words* from this message. People should know that Admiral Pierce stopped the Fallers from destroying the fabric of space. He's a great hero. *Multiply transmit this right now.* There may be additional messages to Mars from the tunnel to follow this one, and they won't be the truth. I doubt those will be more than a half hour behind this. Retransmit now!"

Konstantin said, "Admiral Pierce . . . *she* say he is hero! But Dr. Capelo say Pierce will to kill your father!"

"Yes!"

"Not to make sense, this!"

"Yes, it does!" Amanda cried. "Marbet is saying that because . . . I don't know why! But Daddy's telling the truth! Admiral Pierce is going to kill him!"

"Admiral is not by Solar System. Remember?"

And suddenly Amanda did. Aunt Kristen drying her hands on the kitchen towel and then going back to the kitchen to prepare dinner, just a few hours ago. Amanda following Aunt Kristen in, irritated that Konstantin never offered to help in the kitchen. He sat listening to the news, and Amanda half listened as she set the table, heated some vegetable oil, washed a head of genemod lettuce. A news avatar had said that Admiral Pierce had made . . . what? *"An unprecedented visit outside the Solar System, due to the current military emergency. It is speculated that the admiral will lead a secret campaign with military fleets on the other side of Space Tunnel Number One, and perhaps beyond other tunnels as well . . ."*

Amanda suddenly felt dizzy.

She couldn't do it. Could she?

"Konstantin, how long did this message take to . . . what are you doing?"

"I to take message of your father from transmitter at copy. To leave it here, under rocks of Mars, you to get back later. Message of Marbet Grant, I to transmit. She say to retransmit. But we to save message of your father for you to keep always!"

He pulled a data cube from the transmitter, grabbed her hand, and dragged her after him in no particular direction that Amanda could see. Stooping, he shoved the data cube under a pile of reddish and black rocks and began pulling her back toward the transmitter.

"Now I to retransmit message of Marbet Grant. Soldiers, they to track message, yes? To take my transmitter. Yes, for sure. Not very much of time!"

Take the transmitter! His words hardened Amanda's idea. An insane idea, but . . . she needed that transmitter!

"Konstantin," she said, as fast as she thought his English could follow, "how much time is left before Tunnel number one closes? My father said five hours, but if you sent a message now, I mean, if you sent a message to the tunnel, would it get there before it closes? Would it?"

He stared at her. "Yes. Transmission time is . . . I to think hard . . . to think where tunnel is from Mars orbit . . . maybe four hours ten minutes. But, Ah-man-dah, if your father is injury—"

"He's not injured! At least . . . I don't know! I do know Admiral Pierce is going to kill him!"

"But . . . if Admiral Pierce to kill Dr. Capelo, your father will not to have receiver on your message!"

"I know. I know that." Her hands moved by themselves on his arms; she couldn't seem to hold them still, and suddenly she remembered how Admiral Pierce's long-fingered hands had twitched in Lowell City. Horrible, terrible man . . . "I don't want to send the message to my father."

"Then who . . . look, land rover. It will to look by us."

"Get down!" She pulled him onto the ground. It felt freezing through her suit. They could find her and Konstantin by heat signature, of course, even Amanda knew that. She didn't have much time. Konstantin picked up a heavy rock and drew his arm back to smash it down on the transmitter. Amanda grabbed him. "Don't do that!"

"But your father say to destroy—"

"I know what he said. But wait just a minute, Konstantin. Konstantin . . . do you love me?"

He peered at her in astonishment. "Yes!"

"Then will you do anything I ask? To save my father?"

"Yes!" Then, more cautiously, "What I to do?"

"Admiral Pierce is on the other side of Space Tunnel Number One. It's going to close in less than five hours. You told me, keep telling me, said to me . . ." She couldn't get her thoughts straight, couldn't make them march in straight neat lines. Her hands plucked ceaselessly at his arms. The land rover appeared above the dark horizon, a moving shadow against the sky.

". . . said to me that your father has flyers everywhere. And you have the codes to send them places. Send an Ouranis Enterprise flyer through the tunnel to tell Admiral Pierce your father said the admiral should stay on that side of the tunnel for a few hours more!"

Through his faceplate, with its faint internal light, Konstantin's dark eyes bored into Amanda's. He looked different. Not the boy who held her hand, who kissed her, who talked funny sweet English at her . . . He wasn't going to do it. It had been a stupid idea anyway, an insane idea . . .

He said, "Admiral Pierce to kill your father. Dr. Capelo say, I to believe. No persons never should to kill great scientist. Scientists very great, more great from admirals. My father not to think this. I think this."

She didn't know what to say, afraid to interrupt him.

Konstantin sat up and fiddled with the slightly bashed transmitter. He coded manually, and then began to talk in Greek. Amanda, listening on the connected private channel, was amazed at his voice. It sounded all different. Deeper, harsher . . . *older*.

She had no idea what he was actually saying.

The rover suddenly turned and began to move purposively toward them. It had picked up their heat signature.

Konstantin talked faster. At the end he snapped something very loud and cut the transmission. Amanda drew away from him, suddenly frightened. But a second later he was young Konstantin again, pulling her to her feet, his arm gently around her.

"I say is . . ." a Greek word. She looked at him blankly. He tried again. "I say is many persons to hurt the admiral. He must to go not at Solar System until my father say yes. For his safe."

"You told Admiral Pierce there was a conspiracy," Amanda said. "A . . . a revolution like the one where he killed Stefanak. Only this time against him, and your father is warning him to wait to come back. Is that right?"

"Yes. Splendid," Konstantin said, and Amanda felt dizzy all over again. Would Admiral Pierce really listen to Mr. Ouranis and stay on the other side of the tunnel until it closed? Only if he didn't know it was going to close. Did he know? Would he listen to Mr. Ouranis?

Who was really Konstantin.

Who was really her, telling an admiral what to do.

"Say nothing, Ah-man-dah," Konstantin whispered fiercely. The rover was almost upon them. "Message of your father is by transmitter since. And they will to trace message anyway, but not too soon enough, I think. Maybe. Flyers of my father will to go fast."

"But—"

"Say nothing at peoples by this rover!" Konstantin said, and smiled at the suited figures rushing toward him, his hand raised in greeting.

· · ·

Soldiers. Again. This time they didn't take her to Lowell City. They brought her and Konstantin back to Aunt Kristen's house, and crowded the four of them—Amanda, Konstantin, Uncle Martin, Aunt Kristen—into the storage closet. The only room in the apartment without terminal connections. The soldiers were very polite. Was that because of Konstantin? He had told them his name. But they'd been polite to Amanda before, too. It was creepy.

She said to Uncle Martin, wedged in beside her, "Did you get Marbet's message?"

He put a finger to his lips: *Don't say anything*. Surveillance? In a closet? Still, she nodded.

Aunt Kristen was pushing boxes on top of each other, shoving things onto already overloaded shelves. "If we didn't own so much damn junk . . . Martin, I told you last year we should dump these old books . . . There. Now I think at least there's room for everybody to sit down."

There was, just barely. Amanda was jammed close to Konstantin. She didn't mind.

He had really done it. Sent the message to his father's flyers. For her.

Aunt Kristen was bent over. Amanda couldn't see what her aunt was doing until Aunt Kristen unobtrusively passed her a tiny piece of paper, torn from one of the old books. On it Aunt Kristen had written WE GOT THE MESSAGE AND SENT IT ON TO NEWS STATION.

Amanda nodded and passed the bit of paper to Konstantin. He frowned at it, and she remembered that he couldn't read English. Pretending to stroke Amanda's hair, Aunt Kristen plucked the message from Konstantin and, the next moment, ate it.

Amanda giggled.

Aunt Kristen looked at her severely, but not more severely than Amanda reprimanded herself. What was she thinking . . . giggling! When they were imprisoned here and might die and Daddy might be killed, too . . .

But Aunt Kristen had gotten the story to the news people. Whatever the story *was*. Whatever Marbet had said. So that might protect them. And Konstantin had told his father's flyers to keep Admiral Pierce on the other side of the space tunnel . . .

How could a space tunnel close? Amanda had no idea. But her father said they were. Oh, close fast, close with the horrible Admiral Pierce on the other side!

"What time is it?" she asked aloud. Surely that sounded innocent enough. The soldiers had taken all their watches, comlinks, jewelry.

"At ten-thirty, I think," Konstantin said. He shot Amanda a glance.

Ten-thirty. What time had Konstantin sent the message? Amanda didn't know. Four hours and ten minutes, he'd said, for the message to reach Mars. She remembered from school that c was three hundred thousand kilometers per second. She tried to do the math to see how far away her father was, but failed. It was too hard to concentrate.

How long were they going to be kept in this stupid closet?

The night wore on. Uncle Martin was talking, reciting some old poem, probably from his English classes. Amanda wasn't listening. Drowsiness kept sneaking up on her, although how could anybody sleep at a time like *this*? She was a cretin! But she was so tired . . .

" 'Here, where the world is quiet;
Here where all trouble seems
Dead winds' and spent waves' riot
In doubtful dream of dreams,' "

Uncle Martin's voice said, and then, later, " 'And everything but sleep.' "

Only once did Amanda wake completely. She lay against Konstantin, her head and shoulders almost collapsed in his lap. The closet light had burned out, or been put out. She felt his hand caress her breast. Instantly Amanda was wide awake.

Without thinking, she bolted upright. There was no room to get away. But she could feel his ear, right there beside her head, and she leaned as close to it as she could get, feeling the blood rush into her face as she whispered desperately.

"Konstantin, no, please . . . I'm only fourteen!"

And Amanda Capelo burst into tears.

THIRTY-THREE

SPACE TUNNEL #1

For hours, Kaufman lay strapped naked on the medical table in the bare room. Expecting to be killed at any moment, he minded that less than he minded his own thoughts. He had botched it. Regret gnawed at him like rats.

The Solar System would never know that Admiral Pierce had recklessly risked the very fabric of spacetime in his megalomaniac grab for power. Undoubtedly a story would be concocted to blame the closing of the space tunnels on the Fallers. The war would be over. Lyle Kaufman and Marbet Grant and Thomas Capelo, the three who knew the truth, would quietly disappear. Most of the people who knew Tom and Marbet and Kaufman even still existed would be closed off on the other side of Space Tunnel #1, light-years distant. The few who knew on this side of the tunnel would be silenced with promotions or death.

Of course, Tom's message would reach Carol and Sudie and Amanda (if Amanda was still alive). What would Pierce do about that? Probably threaten Carol into silence. Carol had Sudie to protect; it wouldn't be hard to keep her quiet.

Kaufman should have prepared a full statement, beamed it out the second he passed through Space Tunnel #1, notified the entire Solar System of what Pierce had done. Well, he had been too busy staying alive to think of that.

No excuse. If he had succeeded in telling the media what had happened, Pierce would have had him killed. But that was going to happen anyway, to all three of them. Unless Pierce decided to keep Capelo alive in secret, as Stefanak had done, Capelo's brain held hostage to his family's welfare.

Kaufman's fault. He had not planned, had not seen far enough ahead. Failure of vision was a sin the universe did not forgive. As a result, Admiral Nikolai Pierce was going to be a hero of sorts, Pyrrhic victor in the war with the Fallers, that diabolical enemy who had closed the stars to mankind. And Marbet would die, Capelo might die, Kaufman would certainly die. Magdalena was already dead. And Laslo, and perhaps Amanda. His fault.

The door opened and an officer entered. This was it, then. Kaufman would have liked to see Marbet one more time.

"Colonel Kaufman, put these on, please, sir." The young man carried a full dress uniform.

Kaufman said dryly, "Full uniform is necessary for this?"

"Yes, sir." He unstrapped Kaufman and left the room.

Kaufman put on the uniform he hadn't worn for two years. It was better than dying naked. The ceremonial sword was missing; Kaufman wasn't surprised.

However, the next events astonished him. The officer returned, saluted smartly, and said, "This way, please, sir. The others are already assembled and the admiral is on his way."

Others? Admiral Pierce? No, Pierce would be back on Mars. More debriefing wasn't necessary, not with truth drugs. So what was happening?

Kaufman didn't ask. He observed everything he could as the officer led him down a long corridor. Bulkheads and deck shone; sailors looked like recruiting holos; the air completely lacked the odors and staleness of intensive recycling. They were on a big structure, a station or a flagship.

"In here, sir," the officer said, opening the door and stepping respectfully aside to let Kaufman pass.

"Hello, Colonel Kaufman," said a tall thin man in the SADA uniform of a three-star general. Kaufman didn't recognize him, but there was no mistaking the air of authority. This was the fleet commander.

"Sir," he said neutrally, not saluting. Technically, he was retired. Five other soldiers stood slightly behind the commander, two two-star generals and three bird colonels.

The door opened again and a lieutenant escorted in Marbet Grant. Gladness swept through Kaufman. Marbet wore a sailor's tunic and pants; probably no other clothing had been available aboard ship. They were too big for her. Whatever injury she'd sustained to her rib had been repaired, or at least rendered temporarily insignificant by casts and drugs. Her bright green eyes smiled at him, and then studied everyone in the room, one by one. She didn't look uncertain. Did that mean she knew what was going on?

"Ms. Grant," the commander said, without warmth. Kaufman recognized the familiar antipathy toward a Sensitive. The commander added to the lieutenant, "Where is Dr. Capelo?"

"He's being brought from Medical, sir. They're on their way."

"Colonel Kaufman, Ms. Grant, sit down, please. I'm General Rickman Dvorovenko, Commander, Space Tunnel Number One Defense Fleet. I've brought—"

"Lyle! I thought you were dead," Tom Capelo said from the doorway. "In fact, I thought I was dead, too. This is your doing, isn't it, Marbet? Clever, sneaky lady. I'd take my metaphorical hat off to you if I could move my non-metaphorical arm."

"Dr. Capelo, an honor," General Dvorovenko said.

"Not from my side," Capelo said flatly. "I'm not too enamored of the army that has kept me locked up for six months."

"That was General Stefanak's army," Dvorovenko said. "The situation has changed. However, I would appreciate the chance to talk uninterrupted, Dr. Capelo."

Capelo shrugged. He was propped in a chair, which had been wheeled in by a doctor. He looked terrible, his broken arm and ribs in medcasts and his face sagging, but not as terrible as when Kaufman had seen him last. How many hours ago? No way to tell.

"My first duty," Dvorovenko said, "is to tell you that Admiral Pierce is on his way to congratulate you personally. He's still on the Herndon System side of Space Tunnel Number One, but is proceeding with all possible speed to the tunnel and will pass through well in advance of the closing time your equations indicate, Dr. Capelo. He will be present for the press conference, of course."

Marbet shot Capelo a warning glance. He caught it and shrugged again. Kaufman realized that the two had already been brought together and had had a chance to confer.

"Of course," Dvorovenko continued sourly, "we would have preferred to break the news ourselves to the media about the admiral's heroism and the tragic closing of the tunnels. But since Ms. Grant has seen fit to do so, it's important that everyone understand how much information can be released publicly without compromising military security."

And then Kaufman understood.

Marbet had added a broadcast to Tom's farewell message to his family. While he had been out-racing the closing tunnels and the SADC military, she had quietly recorded the broadcast Kaufman had neglected to make. But unlike Kaufman, she hadn't stuck to the truth. She'd told a version glorifying Pierce, a total lie, and then released it piggy-backing on Capelo's message so Kaufman would have no chance to question its content. She'd tailored that content pragmatically, to save their lives. The transmission represented bargaining, not truth.

And Kaufman thought he was the negotiator on this team.

"I think, General Dvorovenko," Marbet said, "that we all understand the situation. Dr. Capelo and Colonel Kaufman and I will say as little as possible. When asked questions, we will tell the truth, the same truth I explained on my transmission. That Solar Alliance Defense Council forces raced out to meet an overwhelmingly large invasion of Fallers before they could reach Space Tunnel Number One. That a major battle was fought in Gemini System, and when it became evident that the Fallers would win and invade the Solar System, our brave soldiers did the only thing possible, under Admiral Pierce's orders.

"Admiral Pierce knew from the brilliant work of Dr. Capelo, who had been working in secret for the good of the war effort, that if both artifacts were set off at prime thirteen that would not, as previously thought, destroy spacetime. Instead, it would cause the closing of the tunnels. Faced with that terrible alternative, Admiral Pierce ordered the artifact brought through Tunnel Number One. He brought all remaining human troops out and detonated the artifact by remote. And Tunnel Number One closed, saving the Solar System from destruction."

The entire table looked at Marbet: Dvorovenko with the dislike of a person forced to depend on someone he did not trust. Capelo with sardonic irony; he hated having to lie about what had happened, but would do it for the sake of his family. Kaufman with . . . what? With admiration for how fast she'd thought, and for the tidy aptness of her lies. And with sadness that she'd lied at all. Death, accompanied by truth, would have been more honorable.

"Then we are all agreed on the facts," Dvorovenko said, with the same sour tone in his voice. "The next step is to listen again to Ms.

Grant's recording. Then as soon as Admiral Pierce arrives, we can open the comlinks to the press."

"As soon as Admiral Pierce arrives." This time Kaufman heard Dvorovenko's voice, really heard it. That sour note was not because Marbet had released her transmission first. In fact, that probably added to Pierce's credibility; the story of his heroism was being told by an impartial civilian. No, Dvorovenko's sourness was because Marbet had glorified Pierce at all. Dvorovenko would have preferred Pierce to be vilified, because vilification would have led to counterrevolution. Dvorovenko supported Pierce in name only.

Did Pierce know? No, or Dvorovenko would not be commanding the tunnel fleet. There must be many generals like this, supporting the supreme commander because the alternative was death, but also biding their time, waiting for their chance. The old, old story . . . conspirators and the crown.

Kaufman looked at Marbet, shifted his eyes very slightly toward Dvorovenko. She gave a tiny nod. She had heard it, too. Or, more likely, she had known the situation from her first glimpse of Dvorovenko.

There was no way for either of them to use the information. The deal had already been struck. Kaufman prepared himself to publicly praise Admiral Pierce, the man who had murdered Sullivan Stefanak, Laslo Damroscher, Magdalena, Ethan McChesney, Prabir Chand . . .

"Colonel Brady, are the recorders ready?" Dvorovenko asked.

"Yes, sir."

"Then in a few minutes . . . what's that noise?"

Shouting in the corridor. Running footsteps. A captain burst through the door. "Sorry, sir, you're needed on the bridge, a priority-one SCI transmission and we're the action addressee."

"Is that reason for such a disturbance?" Dvorovenko said testily. "Get those men quiet!"

"Yes, sir. It's the newscasts, sir."

Dvorovenko hurried out of the room. The two lesser generals glanced at each other, then followed him. The three colonels remained.

Capelo said, "Put on the newscast, somebody. I don't believe this sumptuous conference room doesn't have newscast capability."

No one moved.

"Oh, Jesus Newton God, I'll do it myself!"

But Capelo couldn't get his powerchair to move without help. He tried to climb out of the chair and fell back, wincing. Kaufman got up and coded the wall screen for outside newscasts; it was standard military issue. He expected the officers to stop him, but they didn't. Probably they were curious, too.

The screen displayed the "MQ&A News" logo. MQ&A was an underground newscast, frequently arrested and shut down by the government and then, phoenix from the ashes, resuming its voice elsewhere. They managed to put robocams or even live reporters in the most unlikely places.

A news avatar who might have been any ethnicity said excitedly, "—still only rumors. However, the conspiracy to erroneously claim the space tunnels are closing is causing widespread panic among the corporations of the Solar System. The target of the conspiracy was rumored to be Admiral Pierce, expected to return from the other side of Space Tunnel Number One later today. Rumors say the admiral might have walked into a death trap. The conspirators, MQ&A has been told, are even now being identified and rounded up by the SADC. Again, these are unsubstantiated reports that have been released to MBC from an unnamed source. However—"

The screen blanked.

"Those irresponsible bastards . . ." one of the colonels growled. She rose and left the room.

Again Kaufman glanced at Marbet. She shook her head. Whatever was happening now, it didn't originate from her wildcat broadcast.

More shouting in the corridor, abruptly cut off. A second colonel left the room. The third one strode to the door and shouted, "Lieutenant?"

"Sir?" She materialized instantly.

"What the hell is happening out there?"

"I'm not sure, sir, but they say . . . someone said . . ."

"Said *what*?"

"That the tunnel closed, sir. That we lost a ship, it just rammed into it and disappeared. And . . . and Admiral Pierce hasn't come through yet."

The colonel glared at the hapless lieutenant. Finally he snapped, "Guard these people!" and left.

"Yes, sir." The lieutenant took up a position half in and half out the door, ears clearly attuned for more news from the rest of the ship.

Capelo laughed. "Pierce on the other side of the closed tunnel!"

"You don't know that's it's true," Kaufman said. He felt dazed. Too much was happening too fast.

"Are you warning *me* to respect facts, Lyle?"

Marbet said, "Do you think MQ&A was right? That there was a conspiracy . . . No, wait a minute. The news avatar said there was a conspiracy to convince Pierce the tunnel closings were true although they're really lies! But they *are* true!"

Capelo laughed again. "And if Pierce is really trapped on the other side, the conspiracy's against him, all right."

Kaufman saw the lieutenant was listening avidly. Kaufman said, "The conspiracy . . . if there is a conspiracy . . . was someone trying to get Pierce to believe the tunnels were *not* closing, and that saying the opposite was only an attempt to lure him into ambush. If that's so, it implicates you, Tom. Your work."

"So what?" Capelo said. "My work *is* real. The tunnel closed, just about . . . let me see . . . ten minutes ago. And if that's the way it happened, Pierce is trapped on the other side of the tunnel. Forever. Man missed the last lifeboat on the *Titanic*, the last ship out of Atlantis."

Slowly the lieutenant turned to face the three civilians in the room. Kaufman was suddenly glad he was wearing an army uniform; it might make the young man answer. "Lieutenant, if Admiral Pierce is trapped on the other side of the tunnel, who's in charge here?"

"General Dvorovenko, sir."

Would Dvorovenko have engineered this? No, Kaufman decided. Dvorovenko had been reluctant for the entire press conference to go forward. So who?

Marbet said to Kaufman, very low, "Not Dvorovenko. Not any military. The reactions of the officers are wrong for that."

Capelo heard them. Unlike the others, he didn't bother to keep his voice down. Maimed and battered, covered with foamcasts and med patches, too skinny and too stressed, the physicist looked like a chewed-upon rat. He said loudly, "Not military? But who else would Pierce listen to? What bloody civilian genius would have had the sheer balls, not to mention the sheer influence, to convince Pierce that scientific truth wasn't actually truth but just a political conspiracy directed at him personally? Somebody played on Pierce's weakest point, his paranoia."

General Dvorovenko came back into the room, trailed by his officers. Kaufman didn't have to be a Sensitive to read the shock and excitement in their bearings.

"Gentlemen, madam," Dvorovenko said, "we have a change of plan. The press conference will go forward, but not with you. The situation has changed. You will be conducted to your quarters to await further briefing."

"Wait, please, General," Marbet said sweetly. All at once she looked younger, very vulnerable, a defenseless woman appealing to a knowledgeable source of power. "Could you tell us what happened? I mean, we'd hear it on the news, I know, but . . . could you tell us?"

"Certainly, Ms. Grant. Admiral Pierce has been tragically trapped behind the closing tunnel while fighting off a last sudden attack by Fallers. He cannot return. The effective government he left behind will guarantee a smooth transition to his second-in-command on Mars, Acting Supreme Commander General Yang Lee."

Capelo gave a hilarious snort.

Kaufman knew nothing of Yang Lee; the general must have risen in power while Kaufman was on World. He said to Dvorovenko, "General, is General Lee in a position to keep in check the unrest that will inevitably occur with such huge changes to the . . . the Solar System as a whole?" No war. No space tunnels. No commerce with colonies. Half the navy gone forever behind the tunnels.

"I'm sure he will be able to do that," Dvorovenko said. "You three will be escorted now to your quarters."

"Thank you," Marbet said.

They followed the young lieutenant from the room. In the corridor Marbet said to Kaufman, "I'm staying with you, Lyle."

"Me, too," Capelo said. The lieutenant, eager to return to the conference room, made no objection.

In a stateroom Kaufman had never seen before ("your quarters"), he and Marbet and Tom looked at each other. Marbet said, "Another revolution? More fighting?"

"Can't tell," Kaufman said. "Everything's different."

"And Pierce is gone," she said.

Capelo said, "When do you think they'll take us home?"

"Oh, soon," Marbet said. "We're public figures now. Of course, Tom, you were before."

"Fuck that," Capelo said, "I just want to see my family again."

Kaufman said, "We still have to stick to the story Marbet concocted."

She faced him. "You resent me for that, Lyle, don't you."

He didn't answer.

Capelo said, "She saved all our lives, Lyle."

"I know."

Capelo said, with sudden force, "And if you'd have thought of it, you'd have done the same thing, Lyle. Look at all the lies you told to get us as far as Tunnel Number One. Don't resent it now because this time you're not the one who masterminded the brilliant deception. Give her the Goddamn credit and stop trying to be the only one who can run the show."

Anger flooded Kaufman. Before he could react, Capelo had headed his powerchair toward the door. "I'm going to sleep while I can. But I know one thing . . . I'd really like to meet whoever set up Pierce to stay behind that tunnel long enough for it to close. *There's* the brilliant deceiver that makes both you and Marbet look like snake-oil salesmen.

"I wonder who the hell it was."

THIRTY-FOUR

THERA STATION, MARS ORBIT

During the weeks traveling from Space Tunnel #1, Kaufman divided his time between the observation deck and the confused, contradictory, delayed broadcasts from Mars.

He and Capelo and Marbet traveled first class, aboard a luxury liner with the silly name *Golden Diamond*. The ship had been carrying businesspeople, diplomats, and tourists to Artemis System. Now, having no tunnel to Artemis, it had turned around and sailed for home with its bewildered load of passengers. Most of the tunnel fleet was likewise being detached and sent back to Mars. At this end of the Solar System there was nothing left to defend, and no one to defend it against.

General Yang Lee's provisional military government fell within a week. Kaufman gathered from the broadcasts that Lee, although firmly in command of the navy, had neither the army support nor a sufficient political base to hold onto power. Mars had controlled the Solar System because she controlled the space tunnels. Without the tunnels, Earth's enormously greater population asserted its force. That force, however, was two months away from Mars. Fighting broke out in Lowell City, in Tharsis, in Arcadia, in N'sanga, in Pomeroy, in Kepler City, in Shangsitsu. A triumvirate was formed and struggled to organize a popular election on two planets, two moons, space stations that were declaring themselves separate political entities, and the Belt. The effort failed.

Businesses declared bankruptcy. Others were suddenly privatized, sometimes with opposition and sometimes without. Out of the chaos the Martian utilities emerged as popular heroes. Against great odds, and pretty much without choice, they kept operational the domes, the farms, the transportation infrastructure. Would-be dictators began to cultivate ties with leading civil servants, who had accomplished practical miracles far exceeding their authority. Since no one could define that authority anyway, the people of Mars began to pledge support for engineers and transport czars.

In this confused time, communications were disrupted, restored, disrupted again. The data packets that Kaufman viewed sometimes contradicted each other. Trying to sort through them all, Kaufman began to sense something else underlying the political hysteria, the military maneuvering, even the endless tearful interviews with people whose families had been cut off forever by the closings of the space tunnels.

"The Lost," the broadcasts were calling those souls. But it was more than individuals, Kaufman saw, that had been lost. More than colonies or warships or business empires. Humanity as a whole had lost something large in its conception of itself.

Sol System's expansive optimism had come from the space tunnels, even in wartime. We travel to the stars! We are in conflict with aliens! The galaxy is at stake! We have potential control of spacetime itself!

No more. Gone, all of it, severed like some healthy limb amputated by mistake: an arm, a leg. Even though the Solar System believed it was the Fallers who had closed the tunnels despite Admiral

Pierce's heroic fight to stop them, the tunnels were still amputated. Humanity was in systemic shock. It was also diminished.

Mankind had lost the stars.

No one believed that current human technology could build ships to span the huge distances between star systems. No one had needed to even begin to develop such technology; there were the tunnels, handed to humans by gods so long gone that no one felt the human godship threatened. Now that Space Tunnel #1 was a floating solid invisible wall, all that was left was the Solar System. Once it had seemed a huge unknowable ocean of space. But in contrast to what had been lost, it was a puddle.

From the observation deck Kaufman traced the familiar constellations in the black sky. In the direction of Draco lay Artemis System. Han System was not far from Betelgeuse, in Orion. Virgo "held" Gemini System. Inhabited, all three of them. Visible but unreachable from Sol. Nor could their human colonies reach the mother world. It was a shared loss among systems that would never share anything else again.

Kaufman tried to express some of this to Tom Capelo. The physicist was unsympathetic.

"Lyle, the alternative was to put spacetime through a flop transition. Compared to that, this isn't such a bad outcome."

"I know. But what we've lost—"

"Look at what we gained," Capelo said impatiently. "The new equations—not that I'm boasting, of course—shed tremendous light on the physics of large-scale flop transitions. Plus losing Hell-Bent-On-Destruction Pierce. Not that this new string of would-be rulers looks any better."

"They might be."

"No evidence of it so far," Capelo said, and moved gingerly away to check his messages again. With the superb medical care on the *Golden Diamond*, he was healing rapidly. But he still moved carefully, and his stress over his family was not helping. Carol and Sudie were safe on Earth. It had been a great joy to Capelo to learn that Amanda was with his sister Kristen and her husband. But since this message had come through, from a third party on an official channel (another unexplained mystery), Capelo had heard nothing of their whereabouts. The broadcasts reported fighting in Tharsis.

To Kaufman's surprise, Marbet didn't share his sense of loss over the space tunnels any more than Capelo had. "We should never have been trusted with those tunnels in the first place," she said.

" 'Should'? 'Been trusted with'? Those are moral judgments, Marbet. History isn't morality."

"I know that," she said, her chin hardening as she looked at him. Things hadn't been easy between her and Kaufman since Marbet had concocted the elaborate public lie about Pierce's heroism and their own passive role as observers. The lie had, as Capelo acidly pointed out, saved their lives. But it had also bound them, including Kaufman, to live the lie for the rest of their lives. Kaufman didn't like it.

"History might not be moral," Marbet continued, "but whatever beings made the tunnels and artifacts were intensely moral. They set it up so that any species who didn't respect the limits of the artifacts and tunnels didn't get to use them anymore."

"You make it sound as if we're naughty children who have been sent to their room."

"We are. We were never ready for the space tunnels. Think of Essa."

Kaufman never thought of Essa. He said, "To you, she's some sort of symbol, isn't she?"

"Yes. Reckless, adventurous, totally undisciplined. Like humanity. Even though she wasn't human, she came from the same DNA seed. And where is Essa now? If she's lucky, she's been confined again to World. If she wasn't lucky, she's dead. We were lucky, Lyle. We got home. Ann and Dieter were lucky, too—they got confined to where they wanted to be anyway. The unlucky ones are trapped in systems that can't support them without supplies from Sol. We caused that—the bigger we, humanity—with our recklessness and undiscipline. Until we can do better, we should stay in our own star system."

He looked at her bleakly. So beautiful, so perceptive, so tender. And he had never before realized how far apart their thinking was.

She read him accurately, of course. Marbet said quietly, "You don't agree, I know. You're thinking we two really don't belong together, aren't you?"

"I don't know."

She looked away from him, out at the stars. "That's your decision, of course."

"And yours."

"No," she said. "It takes two people to make a human tie. But only one to break it."

To that there was no answer. He moved away, but Marbet caught his arm. "Lyle . . . don't . . ." But what he wasn't supposed to do took her a while to get out.

Finally she said, "Listen, dear heart. It's a hard truth, but truth nonetheless. Let me borrow an image from Tom. From his physics."

She stopped again, and Kaufman saw in the working of the smooth brown skin at her throat how much this mattered to her.

"In Tom's quantum universe, as I understand it, everything is probable. *Everything*, even the existence of matter. Things like mass and energy can change form but can't ever get lost. Time can flow forward or backward. Nothing is completely irreversible. But that's just not true in the human universe we live in. Some actions—some choices!—are irreversible. The tunnels closed. Ann and Dieter chose World. Tom's first wife died. At the human scale, many things happen forever, and all we can do is live with the consequences."

He said stiffly, "I don't understand the significance of your trite little homily."

"Yes, you do," she said, dropping his arm. "I told a lie you didn't like. It can't be undone. I don't even want to undo it, although it wouldn't have been your choice for yourself. You either accept that it happened and we go on together, or we don't. But not this polite, half-together-half-not stance you've taken. I don't accept that. So choose, Lyle, and accept the irreversible consequences."

He said nothing. Marbet said, "I won't wait forever." Still Kaufman didn't reply. A ripple ran through the crowd of passengers at the other end of the observation deck, and Kaufman turned to see what had happened. It was Tom Capelo, barreling heedlessly toward them, elbowing people aside. "Lyle! Marbet!"

"Tom," she said, "don't crack your cast against—"

Too late. Capelo winced. The elderly woman rubbed her own arm and glared at Capelo, who remained oblivious. "I heard from Kristen!"

"Wonderful. Where are—"

"On Thera Station, in orbit around Mars. I don't know what they're doing there, the message was short, but she and Martin have Amanda with them and they're all safe!" Capelo's thin dark face glowed. His hair needed cutting; it gave him the wild look of a happy drunk.

"I'm so glad," Marbet said warmly.

"Come with me to convince our paranoid captain that the ship can make a brief docking at Thera Station without being vaporized into quantum particles."

Marbet and Capelo left. Kaufman keyed data into his handheld, which connected him to ship's library. Thera Station was owned by Ouranis Enterprises, a huge business complex with heavy military contracts, extensive presence throughout the Solar System, and a reputation for maneuvering somewhat outside interstellar law. A large Ouranis facility might be a player in the political chaos on Mars; the station would certainly be heavily defended against any bellicose results of that chaos. But Kaufman couldn't see how Tom's sister would have ended up at Thera Station.

As the *Golden Diamond* approached Mars, the disturbing view of lost stars was partly blocked by the dark curve of the planet's night side. Kaufman watched the curve grow larger and larger. It looked solid, eternal.

The newscasts had introduced a new name into the political struggle going on below: General Tolliver Gordon, SADC. Gordon was the person who had sponsored Kaufman's initial trip to World, to dig up the Protector Artifact. Without his deft, visionary, practical maneuvering, that expedition would not have happened, nor anything that had followed. Gordon was trying to forge a workable alliance among the military factions and commercial transnationals that contended for control of Mars.

"Tom is everywhere at once," Marbet said to Kaufman, practically the first words she had spoken to him in days. They stood with Capelo in the shielded reception area of the *Golden Diamond's* vehicle bay. The ship's captain hadn't agreed to dock at Thera Station; he had too many passengers urgently clamoring to get home. But he had agreed to allow a shuttle from the station to pick up the famous Dr. Thomas Capelo. Capelo's wife and his younger daughter remained on Earth, where Capelo was headed to resume his professorship at Harvard, but in a few minutes Kristen, Martin, and Amanda would be aboard the *Golden Diamond*.

Capelo couldn't stay still. The reception area, which didn't depressurize when the vehicle bay did, was no more than ten meters long and three wide: a miniature observation deck of clear tough plastic. Capelo paced it rapidly, bumping into people, his every movement jerky as an armament recoil. *For every action*, Kaufman thought wryly, *is an opposite and equal reaction*. Capelo hadn't seen his beloved daughter in months. His gleeful impatience infected them all. Even the ship's tech smiled.

The captain of the *Golden Diamond*, a genemod-handsome man with sharp blue eyes, watched Capelo warily. Kaufman recognized the look. It was how he himself had once regarded Capelo: as an alien to be carefully kept track of before he did something too bizarre to control.

The vehicle bay door slid open. The shuttle, marked with the Ouranis logo, edged inside. Kaufman saw the reception display chart the repressurization. The second the plastic door unlocked, Capelo hurtled through it.

"Amanda!"

The shuttle airlock opened, and Amanda Capelo threw herself into her father's arms.

Kaufman blinked. He hadn't seen Tom Capelo's daughter in—what? Two years? Three? He remembered her as a polite, tall, skinny young girl with straight fair hair. Hugging Capelo now was a young woman with a spectacular figure and short, fashionably-sheared blonde hair drawn back to show wickedly expensive diamond earrings. He said to Marbet, "How old is Amanda?"

"Older than Tom thinks."

They followed the captain of the *Golden Diamond* into the vehicle area. Three more people emerged from the shuttle airlock. The short thin woman who looked like Tom was undoubtedly his sister. Her husband hung back, smiling quietly, in sharp contrast to a handsome boy who thrust his hand at Capelo the moment he released Amanda.

"Dr. Capelo, I so happy to meet at you! Splendid! Great honor by me!"

Capelo looked at him questioningly. Amanda said, "Daddy, this is Konstantin Ouranis, my . . . my friend." And blushed a mottled maroon.

"Oh oh," Marbet whispered beside Kaufman's ear.

Capelo shook the boy's hand, not really seeing him, and turned to embrace his sister. Amanda waited until they had babbled and hugged a few minutes. She then said firmly, "Daddy, Konstantin saved my life. And we're on Thera Station because of him. He's coming with us back to Earth."

Capelo turned slowly toward his daughter.

"I have a lot to tell you," she said, "and some of it is really incredible!"

Martin Blumberg said quickly, "Tom, we are indeed Konstantin's guests, and it's one of his father's ships that's going to take us to Earth. Today, if you want. Kristen and I are going with you, at least for now. Mars isn't the most tranquil environment right now."

A man with a gift for understatement.

Capelo may or may not have heard him. He had an almost comic expression on his face: surprise and suspicion and joy in unholy mixture. His gaze swept up and down Amanda's body, dressed in blue shorts and close-fitting tunic. Kaufman had already noticed the girl's beautiful long legs. Under her father's scrutiny Amanda suddenly groped for Konstantin's hand, and Capelo's expression contorted his features so much more that Kaufman had to suppress a grin.

Kristen said hastily, "I heard from Carol just this morning, Tom, she and Sudie can't wait to see you! Our ship is one of those fast new G-four's, we can make Earth orbit in less than three months, Konstantin says . . ." She faltered.

"Hello, Amanda," Marbet said loudly.

"Marbet!" And then Amanda was hugging Marbet tightly, towering over the Sensitive. Kaufman shook hands with Kristen, with Martin, with Konstantin. The captain was introduced and began a flowery speech. Capelo eyed his daughter as if she had sprouted wings. Or horns. His hand caught at her free one, and his face gathered into bewildered wrath.

"Colonel Kaufman, Miss Grant," Konstantin said, "is space at you two by my ship. To go to Earth. Very welcome!"

"Thank you," Kaufman said.

"Come with me, everyone," the captain said. "There's a little party for you in my quarters."

"Amanda," Capelo said, "I want to speak with you alone."

"Of course. But we have tons of time. Oh, God, I was so scared you were dead, Daddy! And so many things happened that you don't know about yet!" She kept hold of Konstantin Ouranis's hand.

"Now. I want to talk to you now."

"Later, Daddy," she said in her high clear voice, and led her father forward with the others.

Kaufman hung back. He said to Marbet, "An irreversible action if there ever was one. She grew up. And Tom will just have to adjust to that, won't he?"

She stopped dead. He turned to look at her, knowing that she had heard more in his voice than the words themselves, had read more in his body language than words—his words, anyway—could hold.

"Lyle?"

"I'm not going on to Earth with them, Marbet. There's nothing for me there. But Mars is going to need every impartial negotiator she can get, and General Tolliver Gordon is moving into a favorable position. I know him well. He's a good man."

She waited.

"I need to do something useful. This is it, I think. And one other thing. Magdalena told me, before she died . . . I'm going to have a tombstone made for her on Mars. She told me about a woman named Sualeen Harris . . . but all that can wait. Marbet, will you stay with me on Mars?"

Still she waited.

"There's work for you here, too. God, yes. As a Sensitive, as a symbol—I suppose we're both that, after the press announcements at the tunnel. As . . . as someone I need with me."

"Yes, Lyle. I'll stay."

He took her hand. Capelo and Amanda had already started to argue. Kaufman could hear them even though they were trying to keep their voices down, Amanda with one hand clutching her father's and the other holding the fingers of Konstantin Ouranis, who went on smiling, a strong young figure with the inevitability of the gravity on the conflicted planet below.

Kaufman and Marbet followed the others out of the docking bay and into Thera Station.